*Sanity returned in a rush,
battling the wild need.*

She wasn't his. Even if he could win her from
Maxim, he had nothing to offer her but a dangerous male with an uncertain future. And misery. For
Maxim would never willingly let her go. Not to
him. If she were to leave Maxim for him, the war
between them would never end. And Faith would
forever be caught in the middle.

As Hawke strode into the hallway, he knew it
would be better if he set her down and walked away.

But his grip on her only tightened. Neither man
nor beast wanted to let her go.

Praise for the
FERAL WARRIORS

"Palmer's dark and intense Feral Warriors series delivers
plenty of sexy passion and high-testosterone drama."
Chicago Tribune

"Thrilling."
New York Times bestselling author Anya Bast

"Fans of out-of-the-ordinary paranormal romances
are going to add Pamela Palmer's
Feral Warriors series to their keeper list!"
New York Times bestselling author
Maggie Shayne

By Pamela Palmer

ECSTASY UNTAMED
HUNGER UNTAMED
RAPTURE UNTAMED
PASSION UNTAMED
OBSESSION UNTAMED
DESIRE UNTAMED

PAMELA PALMER

ECSTASY UNTAMED
A FERAL·WARRIORS NOVEL

AVON

An Imprint of HarperCollinsPublishers

AVON BOOKS
An Imprint of HarperCollins*Publishers*
10 East 53rd Street
New York, New York 10022-5299

Copyright © 2011 by Pamela Palmer
ISBN 978-0-06-179473-5
www.avonromance.com

First Avon Books mass market printing: November 2011

Avon Trademark Reg. U.S. Pat. Off. and in Other Countries, Marca Registrada, Hecho en U.S.A.
HarperCollins® is a registered trademark of HarperCollins Publishers.

Printed in the U.S.A.

10 9 8 7 6 5 4 3 2 1

This one's for Keith, my real-life hero

Acknowledgments

Many, many thanks to Laurin Wittig, Ann Shaw Moran, May Chen, Robin Rue, Pamela Spengler-Jaffee, Jessie Edwards, Sara Schwager, Kim Castillo, and all the wonderful people at Avon Books who've had a hand in getting my books on the shelves and into the hands of readers. I love working with you all!

Thanks, too, to Tara Zullo for sharing her Sahara experience with me.

To my readers, my deepest gratitude for your enthusiasm for my stories and for falling in love with the Feral Warriors as much as I have. You make the hours in front of the keyboard an absolute labor of love.

Chapter One

White-hot rage glowed, burning away his mind until only banked coals remained, coals ready to erupt into flame at the slightest stir of thought, of consciousness. His own yell rang out, silent and horrible in this suffocating dark, pounding at the insides of the skull he'd long since ceased to feel.

A perfect blackness had become his only reality, devoid of sound, touch, taste, smell. Devoid of life. His only awareness, the screaming rage, the endless fury.

From far away, a voice whispered, an echo of another time, another place, tormenting him with memories of what he'd lost. Memories of life, of light, of freedom. Of the Feral brothers he longed to rejoin and knew he'd never see again. His friends. Shape-shifters. Immortals. Though that was a lie, wasn't it? Immortal meant "unable to die," and he was certainly not that. None of them were. Quick to heal, incapable of aging, yes. But unable to die? No creature was that.

And his own death stalked him now.

The moment he'd realized he'd fallen into a Daemon spirit trap, he'd known all was lost. The animal spirit that had long ago marked him to be one of the Feral Warriors, one of the last nine shape-shifters that remained in the world, was being torn from him. And a Feral, once marked, couldn't live without his animal. Within days, he himself would be dead. Worse . . . much worse . . . the animal spirit, too, would be destroyed. Or trapped for eternity where it was as good as dead, unable to mark another.

The nine would become eight. No, not eight. He and Tighe had fallen into this trap together.

Seven. Seven Feral Warriors to stop the Daemons from once more rising and destroying the world.

The voice sounded closer now, no longer quite a whisper, yet indistinct, melding with others. As if they'd come to say good-bye. Or perhaps not good-bye. Perhaps the spirits of the seventeen Feral Warriors who'd been lost in this trap centuries ago had come to welcome him into their brotherhood. The brotherhood of the dead.

His soul shriveled at the prospect of spending eternity in this ceaseless dark.

Behind his thoughts, the animal within him screeched his fury, blending with the rising insistence of the voices. For a time, he'd thought the hawk spirit had left him, but he was back, raging with anger.

"Hawke." A voice broke through, his name slicing through the banshees in his mind. *Kougar's voice.* If he were able to feel his pulse, it would be racing. The blood would be pounding in his ears.

Was he hallucinating, now? Kougar sounded blessedly near.

"Come on, Wings." *Tighe*. "We need you, buddy. Come back to us."

Why would he imagine Tighe's and Kougar's voices in the same place? Unless Kougar, too, had fallen into the spirit trap. Were they all lost to the world? Were the last of the shape-shifters gone forever?

The rage that had become part of him in this place swelled, a river of fire burning away voices and thought. In his mind, he heard a snarl that sounded like his own, and felt as if his fangs were dropping, as if the claws had erupted from his fingertips in the way they did when he, or any of the warriors, *went feral*, a partial shift enabling them to access their wilder natures, yet fight as equals whether hawk or tiger, wolf or snake.

The growl began to vibrate in his throat, rumbling in his ears. *Real*. It felt . . . *sounded* . . . *real*.

Was his mind going, too?

The fury drove him to strike out, and he felt his arm move, felt his claws snag in flesh. Warm blood slid down his fingers onto his palm.

His heart pounded against his ribs, the thudding pulsing in his ears as he fought to break free of the darkness, driven by a meld of fury and desperate hope. Strong hands clamped down on his arms. He fought the restraint with all the wildness of the storm that possessed him, thrashing against his captors.

"Hawke." Kougar's voice rang with a strange note. A warmth he'd never heard in it before.

"Hawke, cease!" Lyon's voice ripped through the chaos, commanding as always.

As he'd done all his life, whenever the Chief of the Ferals commanded, he obeyed. Hawke fought to stop thrashing, his breathing fast and hard as the rage slowly receded. Sensation rushed at him from every direction—the sound of his friends' voices, the smells of Feral House—male sweat, the sweeter fragrances of the women, the warm, aged mustiness of a centuries-old house, and the rich, aromatic scents of roasting meats and fresh bread.

And finest of all, the feel of hands holding him down. Strong, but never cruel. The hands of his brothers.

Goddess, let this be real.

"Hawke, you're safe," Kougar's voice assured him.

As the last of the fight left him, the red haze receding from his mind, he blinked, his eyelids heavy, as if he'd been asleep for weeks. Slowly, his vision focused on the three men hovering over him, holding him down. Lyon. Kougar. Tighe.

"You're real." His voice cracked with disuse.

Tighe smiled, flashing a dimple. "We're real."

"Welcome back," Lyon said, his voice thick.

Hawke's gaze swung slowly to Kougar and found the usually emotionless cougar shifter with a smile in his eyes that Hawke had never seen. Kougar extended his hand, and when Hawke lifted his own, Kougar slapped forearms with him in the traditional greeting of the Ferals and pulled Hawke up.

The room shifted, and he found himself sitting on a pallet on the floor, a temporary dizziness swinging through his head, then abating as he eyed the blessedly familiar floral wallpaper and the chandelier hanging above the massive table.

He lifted a single brow. "I've been sleeping in the dining room?"

Lyon clapped him warmly on the back. "The Shaman recommended we keep you within the heart of the house and activity. We'd hoped our voices would eventually pull you back."

His gaze shifted to the wall of windows beyond the long table and the woods behind the house. The trees had leaves, but the leaves were thin and still the bright green of spring. "How long?"

"It's been two weeks since you fell into that trap," Lyon told him. "A week since we got you out."

Hawke's gaze swung to Kougar. "How? No one escapes a spirit trap." Somehow he knew his escape was Kougar's doing.

"Long story."

Hawke's gaze shifted to Tighe. "Did I imagine you went down with me?"

The haunted look that entered his friend's eyes was answer enough. "Delaney kept me tethered as best she could, but it was close, Wings. It was close." The shadows evaporated, a look of pure joy taking their place. "We're going to have a son."

Hawke blinked. "You're going to be a father?"

"Again." Tighe's gaze momentarily unfocused as if he were pulled by a distant memory. "Finally." Tighe shook his head with a grin, clasping Kougar on the shoulder. "I'll let Kougar share his own news. Oh, and the new fox shifter should be here by the end of the week. He's flying in from Poland."

Hawke laughed, the sound little more than a rough burst of air. "I'm beginning to feel like Rip Van Winkle." The man of human legend had supposedly fallen asleep for a hundred years and awoken to find that the world had passed him by. "We're going to be nine once more? No one's . . . been lost?"

"No one's been lost." Lyon rose to his feet but continued to watch him with a small smile and eyes filled with deep relief. "We'll be nine again soon. And it's a good thing. We've detected some strange activity in the Daemon layer of the earth's energy. We don't know what it means yet, but it can't bode well. The Mage are clearly trying yet another way to free the Daemons."

The anger, so temporarily banked inside him, sparked, then flared. *The damned Mage.* Daemons would rampage and torture, terrorize and kill, destroying life by the thousands—humans and immortals alike.

His fangs dropped, his claws erupting. He snarled. "*Those fucking idiots.*"

"Hawke, easy buddy."

But Tighe's entreaty sank beneath the rising roar in his head as his frustration exploded into fury, erupting into a firestorm of rage. Pulling him under.

Drowning him, once more, in darkness.

"Hawke!" Lyon tried to hold his friend, but it was too late. Reason had fled Hawke's eyes, replaced with a snarling, spitting anger. "Hold him down!" he ordered even as Hawke lashed out with his claws.

But as the three men tried to contain the thrashing, violent warrior, Hawke shifted into his animal in a spray of colored lights. As one, they pulled back. "Kkkeeeeer." The red-tailed hawk took off on a wild flight through the dining room, flying at the windows, crashing through the glass.

Kougar ran for the window. Lyon followed, certain the bird had shredded his wings. But if Hawke had done himself any damage, Lyon couldn't tell. The hawk soared above the treetops and disappeared. When the Ferals shifted, they retained their human minds, able to control the animal bodies as they did the human.

Hawke wouldn't have taken off like that if he'd been in control. Lyon feared his friend was lost to the wildness inside him.

"I thought he'd be okay once he came to." Tighe took a step toward the window, glass crunching beneath his boot.

Lyon shook his head, his expression grave. "He's damaged." The question was, just how damaged? He prayed the answer wasn't *beyond repair*.

"Faith, look! A rainbow."

Maria's cry of pleasure had Faith pushing herself off the sagging mattress to join the teen at the cracked window of Faith's small apartment.

"Lame," Paulina muttered from the bed where she sat, bent low, drawing on her palm.

Sure enough, a rainbow glistened above the tenements across the street in one of the worst sections of Warsaw, Poland, a neighborhood virtually untouched in more than a century—beautiful old buildings derelict and crumbling, their art nouveau façades nearly hidden beneath decades of grime, wrought-iron window rails rusting and bent as if they, along with the city's people, had suffered the Nazis' bludgeoning and the communists' iron fist.

Shoulder to shoulder with Maria, Faith smiled. "It's a beautiful rainbow."

"You're both lame."

Faith turned to the dark-haired girl on the bed with a shrug. "I like rainbows."

"You like everything."

"Not everything. Just things that make me happy."

"Like me?" Maria piped up.

Faith laughed. "Especially you."

Maria turned back to the window with a wistful sigh. "I wish I could follow the rainbow to its end, to see where it goes."

"Maybe we should do that." Faith hadn't known either girl long, but she'd quickly become fond of them. They'd become her latest projects, or more accurately, getting them off the streets had become her latest in a lifetime of such missions.

"I couldn't leave Stanislov," Maria said mournfully. "He needs me."

Faith bit down on a sound of frustration and the words she longed to voice—that Stanislov wasn't Maria's lover, he was her pimp. That he only needed her for the money she brought him. But Maria didn't see it that way. A year ago, at just thirteen, Maria had been orphaned by an alcoholic mother and left to fend for herself. Stanislov had taken her under his wing, fed her, and made her feel loved. That he pimped her out was a small price to pay in the young teen's mind, Faith knew that. She also knew it was only a matter of time before Maria wound up on drugs or too dead inside to be rescued.

As Maria returned to the bed, running her fingers over the cover of the worn Second World War history book sitting on the crate that served as a bedside table, Faith pulled three small containers of orange juice from her rusted refrigerator and joined them, sitting cross-legged. Maria tore into the drink as if she'd been given the greatest of treats, but Paulina merely laid hers on the bed beside her and resumed her drawing. Even if she'd been as anxious to taste the sweet fruit juice as

Maria, she'd never show it. That she came to the apartment at all told Faith just how desperate she was for company—safe, female company.

At sixteen, Paulina had already been on the streets two years. A couple of weeks ago, in an unusually open mood, she'd confided to Faith that her stepfather had raped her, and her mother had accused her of seducing him and thrown her out of the house. The girl was smart and tough, with a significant artistic talent. But she was also a bitter girl, hard beyond her years. So far she'd managed to avoid both drugs and alcohol, which gave Faith hope she'd eventually find her way to a better life. With a little help. If she'd take it.

To anyone else, Paulina and Maria were just a pair of young Polish hookers. But when Faith had arrived in Warsaw a few months ago, she'd recognized in these two the cleverness and character it took to escape this life. After years of helping street kids, she knew how to get past the barriers so many of them threw up. They didn't trust easily, especially not adults. Fortunately, Faith didn't look much older than the girls. She could pass all too easily as one of them—another runaway, or throwaway. With her blue-tipped hair and the silver studs circling one ear, Faith worked hard to foster that illusion. Whenever she moved to a new country, a new city, a new neighborhood, she told the girls she met that she was eighteen, that she'd been abandoned by her family at fifteen.

The last part was true, at least. She had been abandoned at fifteen. But not three years ago. The last time she saw her own mother had been the summer of 1914.

Faith was immortal. A Therian.

Once upon a time, thousands of years ago, all Therians had been shape-shifters. Not any longer, not unless they were marked by one of the nine remaining animals. Not unless they became one of the legendary and revered Feral Warriors.

But that wasn't her world anymore and hadn't been since she was a girl. This was her world. The rough city streets, whether in her native Belgium, here in Poland, or any of the two dozen European cities where she'd lived in between.

Leaning forward, she studied the small intricate sketch of a child's face Paulina was drawing on her palm with a ballpoint pen. Beautiful. "Did you know him?" she asked the girl.

"He's my brother." Paulina's misery was all the more pronounced by the terrible lack of emotion in her words.

Faith knew the girl couldn't have seen him since she was thrown out two years ago. Her heart broke for Paulina, her determination to help her find a better life hardening inside her. "I waited on a lady at the diner last night," Faith said casually. "She works at the art academy."

Paulina's pen stilled.

"I showed her the sketch you gave me, of the kids in the park." Faith opened her orange juice and took a sip, letting her words sink in. "She wants to meet you."

Paulina's head snapped up, angry blue eyes shadowed with raw vulnerability pinned her. "Meet me? To do what? I'm a whore!"

Dammit. Her own temper flared. "It's not like you chose this life!" She hated that these girls were victimized, then reviled for it. It was so unfair. "That's not all you are, Paulina. You're a girl, too. And according to that lady, a talented artist."

Paulina's expression didn't soften. "You had no right to show her my picture!" She grabbed her orange juice, leaped from the bed, and stomped out the door, slamming it behind her.

Faith sighed. Getting past Paulina's defenses was going to be a challenge. Not that she hadn't run into girls like her before. They were the ones she most often targeted. Unfortunately, she failed with them as often as she succeeded. Bitterness that thick often made it impossible for them to ever see themselves as anything more than the prostitutes that circumstances had made them.

Maria turned to Faith with wide eyes too old for her face. "She wants it too much, you know. To be an artist. It's better not to want anything."

Faith turned and leaned back against the stained wall. "That's what I used to think, too."

Maria scooted over to sit beside her, dropping her head against Faith's shoulder. "What do you want, Faith?"

What did she want? To help these girls. And then others in another city. And others after that. That was all she'd ever wanted.

But was it really? In a strange way she envied Maria because Maria believed she was loved, even if it was only by her pimp. And Faith couldn't say the same.

It's better not to want anything.

She'd long ago learned it was true.

Faith pulled her sweater closed against the evening's dampness as she walked home from work. It had rained earlier, driving a lot of street traffic into the diner, and she'd wound up having a lucrative, if busy night. The tips from tonight alone should be enough to buy food for another week, all of which she'd share with Paulina and Maria. Assuming Paulina came back.

On the street in front of her building, she passed several of the girls she'd had no luck in befriending. As she neared the tenement's half-broken door, she spotted a familiar form standing against a brick wall scarred by wartime bullets. Her head down, shoulders bent, her pimp at her side, was Maria.

Faith started to pass them, unwilling to do anything that might alienate her from this girl, too. Until Maria lifted her head and the streetlight illuminated her swollen and bleeding lip and the tears streaking her face.

Faith stopped, hands fisting at her sides. She might not have the power of her shifter ancestors, but her immortal blood made her as strong as many human males.

As if hearing the silent threat, Stanislov looked up, meeting her gaze. "I'll find him. And I'll kill him."

Faith saw the truth in his dark eyes and knew he wasn't the one who'd hurt Maria. Not with his fists, at least. In his own warped way, the man cared for the girl. Maybe even loved her.

Maria buried her head against the young pimp's chest, and he led her away, leaving Faith standing on the sidewalk feeling sick and angry. And, as so often happened, confused. There were so few clear rights and wrongs on the street. Stanislov was a pimp who'd taken advantage of a young girl's utter vulnerability. A villain of the worst sort. And yet, tonight, he was absolutely Maria's champion. And Faith was glad for it. Tonight. Even as she knew Stanislov's protectiveness would only make it that much harder for Faith to get Maria to leave him.

Faith sighed and was about to turn back toward her

building when a man caught her eye. Walking down the sidewalk toward her, he looked like he belonged on the pages of a fashion magazine, not these streets. In his expensive-looking sport coat and white turtleneck, he looked wholly out of place. Beneath the flickering light of a streetlamp, he appeared quite tall, his shoulders broad, his hair overly long and slicked back. With a small jaw and a weak chin, his face was forgettable. But as the streetlamp illuminated his profile, the hungry, predatory look in his eyes as his gaze combed the girls on the street corner had her inner alarm bells going off.

He stopped suddenly, freezing for a harsh moment before whipping something from his inner jacket pockets. Steel flashed in the streetlight.

Knives.

Faith's breath caught on the fear that he was going after one of the girls. But his stance turned suddenly defensive, his knees bending as if he prepared for an attack. His gaze had veered away from the girls and closer to Faith until he was staring at something just over her head.

Faith pivoted, prepared to protect herself from whatever danger approached, but she saw nothing out of the ordinary. Nothing to warrant such a blatantly defensive stance. Then a flash of movement caught her eye, and she saw them. Two draden, each about the size of a large man's fist. Flying right toward her!

She tensed for the attack, strangling a cry. The humans couldn't see them and wouldn't be bothered by them, but the creatures she'd always thought looked like jellyfish with scary faces were the most deadly things in her world. They fed off Therian life energy and could kill her within minutes if she didn't manage to kill them first. Fortunately, few existed so far from the Therian enclaves. She hadn't been attacked in years.

Unfortunately, they'd found her tonight. Without weapons, her only means of defense was to reach into their bodies, through mouths lined with sharp, wicked teeth, and tear out their hearts.

Her skin turned cold. Her heart began to pound.

As the first attacked, she lifted her hand to ward him off and felt the dozens of sharp little teeth tear into her wrist, latching on. Before she could react, the stranger was beside her, stabbing one draden with his knife, then the other. As quickly as they'd appeared, the creatures were gone, reduced to puffs of smoke.

Gripping her throbbing wrist, dazed from the attack, she slowly turned and stared at the man. "You're Therian."

He gave a shallow bow, little more than a deep nod. "I am. As are you." His gaze skimmed her, head to toe, his expression telling her he wasn't much impressed.

Her pride rose, her chin lifting. She was dressed for work, not a night on the town. But as they eyed one another, something happened. A strange feeling began to bubble up inside her, a feeling of recognition. *Connection.* As if she belonged to him somehow.

The startled expression on his face told her he felt it, too. "*Who are you?*"

"I'm Faith."

"I've never seen you. I did not know there was a Therian enclave nearby."

"I've only lived here a few months. And I have no enclave."

He studied her, his eyes taking on a speculative light. "You're mine."

"Yes." Why had she said that? But it was true. She felt it deep inside. She *knew* it. Goddess, this wasn't right. She shook her head. "I mean, no. I don't even know you."

"Destiny clearly has plans for us, Faith. It is said, one always recognizes one's mate."

The word stopped her cold. "But I'm not . . . you're not . . ." Her pulse began to thrum. *Her mate?* Her trouble radar had started beeping at the first sign of him, and if not for the draden attack, she'd have given him a wide berth. Or watched him like a hawk until she was certain he was no threat to her girls.

Had she misjudged him? He wasn't human, after all, but Therian.

Her mate.

Was it possible? The thought tantalized. As a child, she'd heard stories of the rare and wonderful mates that few Therians could hope to find. The mate of one's heart, one's soul. What if she'd found hers? A man who would love her without question, who would understand her as no one else ever had or ever would. The idea bloomed inside her, a burst of warm excitement and longing.

"I leave for America tomorrow. You'll accompany me." His tone was certain. Arrogant.

Faith's jaw dropped. "America? *Tomorrow?* No. I can't possibly . . ."

But he continued as if she hadn't spoken. "I've been marked to be the next Feral Warrior."

She stared at him, surprise turning to awe. A real honest-to-goodness *shape-shifter.* Goose bumps lifted on her arms.

"Feral House is in America, now, near Washington,

D.C. The Ferals await me. We'll travel together and be mated there."

She continued to stare at him, thoughts and emotions careening into one another, catching and tangling. It was too soon, too fast. *Her mate.* She didn't know him. *A Feral Warrior.* She wasn't even sure she liked him. *The animal only ever marked the best, the finest.* And the certainty remained that she belonged to him.

What if he was the one? The *one*? Soul mates came along so rarely and only ever once. If she let him walk away now, she might never see him again. She might never know . . .

"Where do you live?" he demanded. "I'll bring a car around for you tomorrow morning."

With a shake of her head, she stared at him helplessly. "I have . . . people . . . here." Paulina and Maria. Girls she wanted to help, but she could hardly call them her people. It was all too likely she'd fail with both of them. Paulina might already be lost to her.

This is your chance, a small voice inside her whispered. *You've spent your whole life seeking a better life for the girls you meet. Now it's your turn.*

Feral House. The home of the Feral Warriors. *Her mate.* Every girl's dream.

The man's jaw—*she didn't even know his name*—tightened in frustration, then slowly relaxed, his tone turning almost cajoling.

"Come with me, Faith. We'll not seal the mating bond until we're both certain. But how will we know if we are meant for one another if we remain apart? And I cannot delay my flight. The Feral Warriors need me."

The longer she remained in his company, the stronger the tug inside her grew—waves of emotions that lacked all logic, a need to please him. Loyalty. Devotion. The utter certainty that she belonged at his side.

"Yes, of course I'll come with you." The words were out of her mouth before her mind even made a decision. *She didn't know the man!* Then again, she never would unless she went with him. And she'd wind up spending thousands, perhaps tens of thousands of nights alone, wondering if she'd lost her one chance at love. "But I have to come back, at least for a little while." She refused to disappear from Maria's and Paulina's lives without one more concerted effort to get them off the streets and into a safe environment.

He frowned. For a minute, she feared he'd refuse her, forcing her to choose between him and the girls. Instead, he gave a curt nod and glanced at the building behind her with ill-concealed distaste.

"Is this where you live?"

"Yes."

"I'll meet you here at eight tomorrow morning." Without a backward glance, he turned and started walking.

"Wait!" she called. "What's your name?"

"Maxim." He didn't even bother to turn around.

"Who's Maxim?" Paulina asked at her elbow, surprising her. Thank heavens she'd come back.

"I'm not sure," Faith answered truthfully. *My future husband?*

"I don't like him."

Faith looked at the girl. "Do you know him?"

"No. I've never seen him before." Paulina scowled, but her expression lacked its usual belligerence. And when she spoke, her voice was low. "There's something wrong about him."

Faith turned and stared after the man until he disappeared from sight. Wrong, yes, but not in the way Paulina thought. Maxim wasn't human. He was immortal and soon to be a shape-shifter. A Feral Warrior. One of the finest men the race had to offer. No matter his arrogance, she knew he must be a good man deep inside.

And the fates, the goddess, had chosen her for his mate. How could she possibly turn her back on that?

Faith took Paulina's hand, relieved when the teen didn't pull away. "I'm leaving for a little while, Paulina. I'm . . . going with him. To America."

Paulina jerked her hand out of Faith's hold, her mouth dropping open. "When?"

"Tomorrow."

The look of betrayal in the girl's eyes was there and gone so fast, Faith nearly missed it, but it cut her to the quick.

"I'll be back, Paulina. In a few weeks, at the latest. At least for a little while."

The girl whirled away. "Don't bother!" She took off at a run.

As she stared after the girl's retreating form, Faith's shoulders sagged beneath the weight of guilt and the certain knowledge that she'd made a lot more progress with Paulina than she'd realized. And had now almost certainly destroyed it.

She should stay here. Find her. Try to make it right. Try to rebuild that trust and finish the job she'd begun.

But deep in her mind, a soft voice urged her to do otherwise. *You belong to Maxim.* Anticipation stirred within her at the prospect of accompanying him to Feral House, of meeting the Feral Warriors. But it was the thought of having someone who cared about her, who loved her, that made her eyes sting with tears and her heart ache with longing. *You belong to Maxim.* Already, the mating bond was forming, growing. There was no denying it. No fighting it.

And, goddess help her, she didn't want to.

Chapter Two

Hawke lifted a bare forearm and swiped away a fat bead of sweat rolling down his temple as he picked up his pace on the treadmill in the basement of Feral House. He'd been down here all night, lifting weights, running, working every muscle in his body over and over again while his brothers prowled the rocky banks of the nearby Potomac River, fighting the draden that swarmed near Feral House. Exercise was the only outlet that remained for the pent-up frustration, the anger that had come to haunt his every waking moment.

Five days ago, he'd regained consciousness, escaping the darkness of the spirit trap. An escape that had been incomplete. The rage that had nearly consumed him inside the spirit trap remained, a seething anger that sprang to life at the slightest provocation. An anger that wasn't his own, but the hawk spirit's, as if the animal blamed him for getting them stuck down there and nearly wrenched apart.

The fury waited, ready to pounce at the slightest

provocation, the faintest hint of annoyance or frustration. Then the red haze would rise, clouding his vision, and, though he'd struggle to control it, he lost more often than not. Things got broken, flesh got torn if anyone was close enough to feel the rip of his claws. And he usually ended up shifting involuntarily into his hawk. Ferals shifted at will, with ease, retaining their human minds while in their animal bodies. But that was no longer the case for him. When he shifted now, on purpose or accidentally, he tumbled back into that dark fury for hours at a time.

It was as if the hawk spirit took over, leaving him behind, unconscious, until the hawk decided to return control. Hawke came back to awareness sitting on top of a barn or high in a tree every damn time he shifted. So he was left with nothing to do but spend his days and nights working to control the rage. He was useless. Worse than useless. He was a danger to everyone around him.

Hawke turned off the treadmill and grabbed a couple of free weights, pumping iron until he cooled down.

Out of nowhere, pain ripped across his brain, slamming into the insides of his skull and crawling, like jagged fingers of lightning. *Kkkeeeeer.* The hawk screeched as if it, too, felt that god-awful pain. But even as the first blast faded, a second began, like talons raking at his brain, as if the hawk inside him retaliated, punishing him.

"I'm not doing it on purpose!" he growled at the damned bird spirit.

Slowly, the talons released their hold on his mind, the pain sliding away. The connection between him and his animal had been damaged, without a doubt, but he and his bird had never had an easy relationship. The animal spirit had always demanded a freedom Hawke had never been willing to give him. His father, the previous hawk shifter, used to say that his animal wasn't like the cats. It needed to take the reins at times, or it got cranky. And his father had done just that, given the hawk his head, disappearing sometimes for hours, even days, on a wild flight.

For years after Hawke was marked, the hawk had demanded that kind of freedom from him, too, but Hawke had always refused. He wasn't giving in to that kind of wildness again. Not after what happened to Aren.

The hawk spirit had never entirely forgiven him. But they'd always worked together well enough. Until the spirit trap. Now Hawke was beginning to think they'd become rivals. Perhaps even enemies.

Goddess help them both.

He set down the weights and retreated to the gym shower, where a spray of cold water cooled down his body though doing little to ease the frustration that had become his constant companion. As he dried off, the sound of footsteps on the stairs reached him—a Feral's tread accompanied by a lighter, more feminine step. Kara's, no doubt. She searched him out at least twice every day.

Moving quickly, he pulled on a clean pair of sweatpants before she reached him. Not that he really needed to. Half the Ferals couldn't keep their clothes on when they shifted, and all were naturally comfortable in the nude. Any woman living at Feral House saw naked males. It was unavoidable. But Kara's cheeks still flushed occasionally at the sight, telling Hawke her human upbringing was still too firmly rooted. The last thing he wanted was to cause her, or any of his brothers' mates, discomfort.

He met them as they entered the gym—Kara with Lyon close behind. Hawke had made his brothers promise that none of the women would come near him without an escort. And none of the Ferals had been inclined to object.

Kara, dressed in pink flannel pants and a camisole that looked like sleepwear, strode to him on bare feet, her blond ponytail swaying softly behind her, blue eyes warm with affection and concern. Sweet and courageous, she was their Radiant, the one woman in all the world who could pull from the Earth the energies the Ferals needed in order to access the power of their animals.

As Kara wrapped an arm around his bare waist, he pulled her tight against his side, relishing the feel of her warm body against his, feeding the need for touch all Therians possessed.

Lyon greeted him with a Feral handshake. "Feeling any better?"

"I am now."

Lyon's mouth twitched. "Don't get too comfortable."

Hawke smiled. "As if she'd let me." He adored Kara. They all did. But the love between her and Lyon, their chief, was a powerful force that both awed and lifted. He dreamed of loving a woman like that someday. Or he had. Before he'd become a danger to anyone within striking distance of his claws.

"How are you really?" Kara pulled back, her gaze soft and worried. Though she worked her magic on him twice a day, giving him radiance, she'd yet to heal him.

He shrugged. "I haven't spontaneously shifted in nearly twenty-four hours."

Lyon nodded, twisting Kara's ponytail around his hand in an absent gesture that spoke of deep and easy affection.

Kara studied Hawke. "Has anything set you off?"

"Frustration, but I've managed to rein it in before it got out of control. I'm getting better at controlling it."

"Good. It's a start." She clasped her hands in front of her. "How about some radiance? The stronger you are, the better you'll be able to control it. I hope."

Hawke nodded. "Is it dawn already?"

"Almost," Lyon told him. "The hunting party just got back."

"Isn't this the day the new fox arrives?"

"It is." Lyon's voice echoed with relief. "He'll be here this afternoon."

The last fox shifter had died only a month ago, the victim of a Mage plot to infiltrate Feral House and destroy the nine Feral Warriors. When one shifter died, the animal spirit flew to the strongest Therian with that animal's shifter DNA and marked him to be the next Feral Warrior. The Therian would find a set of what looked like long-healed claw marks somewhere on his body and he'd begin to need radiance, instinct driving him to seek Feral House and the Radiant, no matter where in the world he lived. If he failed to reach the Radiant within a couple of years, he'd die, and another would be marked.

"Ready?" Without waiting for his reply, Kara closed her eyes and lifted her arms gracefully. Almost at once, her flesh erupted in a brilliant, sun-bright glow that made the light from the overhead fluorescents pale in contrast. Outside, she'd been known to turn the backyard from night to day. Never had a Radiant been able to pull the Earth's energies through solid structures as Kara could.

She opened her eyes and arms, reaching for Hawke with one hand and Lyon with the other. Though she strengthened them and empowered them simply by living in proximity to them, this direct line to the energies provided a jolt of power none of them ever refused.

Hawke slid his hand into Kara's glowing one. At once, a warm flow rushed into him, a pure strength straight from the Earth itself. Inside, he felt the hawk calm and settle as if lifting its face to the sun.

For long minutes, they remained like that, soaking up the power. Finally, Kara's light went out, and she released him, a small smile on her face.

Hawke leaned forward and kissed her temple. "Thank you."

Her eyes met his, warm with affection. "I'll give you radiance anytime, you know that. Whatever you need."

Lyon's hand landed softly on the top of Kara's head, but his gaze met Hawke's. "You've been down here all night." It wasn't a question. "You need food and sleep."

Hawke's mouth kicked up. "Everyone thinks he's a doctor, now."

No answering smile lifted Lyon's mouth. "We need you healed."

"I know," Hawke replied quietly. The Ferals were too few against an enemy that was growing too strong. The Daemons the Mage were trying to free would prey upon humans and immortals alike, feeding on pain and fear until there was no place on Earth to escape the screams. The Ferals had to stop them.

The sound of new footsteps reached his ears a moment before Tighe and Delaney walked in.

Hawke froze at the sight of the tiger shifter and his mate.

"There you are." Tighe's half-naked flesh gleamed with the sweatiness of a long night of draden fighting. His short blond hair was spiked and damp, as it often was when he'd been shifting back and forth. His hand rested on the shoulder of the tall, attractive ex–FBI agent who'd become his wife. A woman who'd only recently become immortal. And pregnant with Tighe's son.

A woman who shouldn't be anywhere near a Feral with limited control. Delaney might be immortal, now, but she hadn't always been, and that babe inside her could be mortal. He could kill the infant with a single rip of his claws. The horror of that thought set off the anger inside him, igniting the red coals of his rage. The red haze began to rise around the edges of his vision.

"*Get her out of here.*" He hardly recognized the low, snarling voice as his own. The tips of his fingers began to tingle with the impending thrust of claws. Fangs erupted from his gums.

Pain tightened Delaney's features even as Tighe shoved her behind him. Tighe and Lyon captured Hawke's arms in iron grips.

"Delaney, I'm sorry," he growled through fangs that were more suited to a large cat or wolf but were the hallmark of all shifters. "I don't want to hurt the babe. I *can't* hurt the babe."

"Hawke, I know," she assured him. "I know you'd never hurt us."

"*Intentionally.*" He swung to face Tighe. "Don't let me near her."

"Hawke . . ." Tighe's voice was low, leaden with

misery. "Buddy. You're not going to hurt them. I'm not going to let you, and neither are you."

"When I'm in control, no. *Never.* But I lose it, Stripes. You've seen it happen. I'm fighting as hard as I can to control the fury, but I keep losing. You can't let me hurt them." He wouldn't be able to live with himself. He'd barely been able to live with what he'd done to Aren.

"I won't, buddy. I won't." Tighe got in his face, his gaze like a lifeline, snaring him in the fierce love they all felt for one another. "You're going to get past this. You'll see. You're getting better."

But it was a lie, and they both knew it. Two weeks had passed, and he not only wasn't any better, he was pretty sure he was getting worse. Though he was learning ways to hold on to control, when he lost it he was gone for longer and longer periods of time, until he feared that one day soon, he'd shift into his hawk and never come back.

What use was a shifter who couldn't shift?

None. None at all.

Though no one would say the words out loud, they were all thinking the same thought. If he didn't get any better, if he couldn't shift, sooner or later, they were going to have to clear the way for a hawk Feral who could.

The Feral, Vhyper, turned the huge yellow vehicle—a Hummer, Faith thought it was called—into the long drive. There were trees everywhere, but the trees weren't densely spaced, and she could see large homes dotting the woods in the distance on either side. By far the largest of the homes, a true mansion, stood at the end of the drive, three imposing brick stories adorned with dormers and black shutters. An awe-inspiring sight with the late-afternoon sunshine filtering down through the surrounding hardwoods, making the randomly planted azalea bushes gleam like rubies.

Pleasure stirred, and the desire to share the pretty sight with Maria pinched inside her. She hadn't even been able to tell Maria good-bye. Often, life's chapters refused to wrap themselves up in neat little packages. She knew that from long, bitter experience. But her sojourn in Warsaw had ended on a particularly ragged tear. Fate had thrown a wrench into the works when Maxim walked into her life. She glanced at him now as he sat in the front seat beside Vhyper, eyeing the mansion with a look that told her he was unimpressed.

Vhyper, who'd picked them up at Dulles International Airport outside Washington, D.C., pulled up in front of the house, parking the Hummer among the variety of other vehicles already there. He tugged on the snake earring that hung from one ear. "Welcome to Feral House. Home of the wildest animals in Fairfax County."

Faith looked at him in the rearview mirror, uncertain whether he was being wry or self-important. Wry, she decided at the hint of humor lurking in his eyes. Definitely wry.

"Then I will civilize them." Maxim's tone made it clear he was serious. Painfully serious.

That hint of humor in Vhyper's eyes fled, his expression turning cool even as a smile lifted his mouth. "Good luck with that."

Faith didn't need a formal education to recognize a rough road ahead when she saw one. She'd known Maxim only a matter of hours, but it had become increasingly clear the man was utterly without a sense of humor. Which was too bad since she had one. But Maxim was educated and cultured. A good man, or the animal would never have marked him.

Vhyper turned off the ignition and swung his long frame out of the car, a bright beam of sunlight slicing through the trees to illuminate his bald head. Faith reached for her door handle, uncertain if Maxim would insist on opening the door for her. His attention to her since he'd picked her up that morning had been erratic. One moment, he treated her like a queen with formal, old-world manners. The next, she wondered if he remembered she existed.

As she hesitated, he swung out of the car, shut his own door, and started up the brick walk to the wide front stoop alone. With a sigh, Faith let herself out of the car, glancing at Maxim's retreating back with a stab of uncertainty. Was he just preoccupied? Certainly that would be understandable under the circumstances. Or was he embarrassed by her? Heaven knew she wasn't of his class. Not even close.

As her gaze tracked farther, she caught sight of a man standing in the open doorway, a man as tall or taller than Maxim though perhaps not quite as broad through the chest and shoulders. Sunlight struck short brown hair that curled just a little at the edges, weaving into it fine threads of gold that set off a handsome face with sharply arched brows over dark eyes.

As Maxim reached the steps to the front porch, the man stepped forward and thrust out his hand—too far, nearly to Maxim's jacket button.

"I'm Hawke. Welcome to Feral House."

Another Feral Warrior. But she'd suspected as much.

Maxim looked down his nose at the proffered hand, making no move to take it.

"Do you speak English?" The Feral's tone remained even though it had lost that layer of warmth.

"I do."

"Grasp my forearm, then, just below my elbow. It's the way we greet one another."

Maxim hesitated, then did as the Feral directed, looking somehow awkward as he did so. As they grasped one another's forearms, Maxim lifted his chin. "I wish to confer with the Chief of the Feral Warriors."

Hawke gazed at him calmly, his expression cooling more, just as Vhyper's had.

Faith's heart sank at Maxim's attitude. He was acting like a prince forced to consort with peasants. She wanted to like and respect this man whom fate seemed to have chosen for her. But she was finding it increasingly hard to do so.

Hawke lifted one arched brow. "Lyon is in the foyer." As Maxim brushed past him, Hawke shook his head, then descended the steps and started toward the vehicle. His gaze swept over her, moving to where Vhyper pulled Maxim's suitcases out of the Hummer, then back to her again. The friendliness returned to his expression, along with a hint of curiosity. Her blue-tipped hair tended to bring that out in people.

She smiled at him as Maxim had not.

The appealing man returned the smile slowly. His eyes lit first, crinkling at the edges before his mouth spread. It was a small smile, a close-mouthed smile, but its effect on her was devastating. A fluttering arose in her stomach like a whirl of dove's wings. As he drew nearer, her face . . . her entire body . . . began to flush with a heat that had her wishing she could peel off her sweater. With a face that was perhaps a bit too long and a nose that was a tad too pronounced, he wasn't movie-star handsome. But his eyes, a beautiful brown shot through with flecks of gold, were kind, his mouth beautifully sculpted. And the overall effect was breathtaking.

Dismay seized her heart, a deep disappointment that she felt no such physical attraction to the man fate had chosen for her. But physical attraction wasn't everything. Deep inside, that pull remained as strong as before—the certain knowledge that she belonged to Maxim.

Hawke stared at the smiling girl, his mind at once racing and blank, his pulse thrumming a fast, erratic beat. She was a little odd-looking, with dark hair painted bright blue at the ends and one ear entirely enclosed in earrings, yet she was . . . extraordinary. That smile . . . Goddess, that smile could slay an army, knocking them all to their knees. Though of average height, her features were small and pert, giving her beauty a pixieish charm. *Beautiful.* And clearly too young.

He told himself to keep his gaze on her face, but his eyes had a mind of their own. He couldn't help noticing that her thin sweater, the same blue as the ends of her hair, clung to small, sweet curves, and that the sleeves half covered her hands. On slender legs she wore holey jeans. On her feet, badly worn sneakers.

Slowly, he forced his gaze back to her face, to the smile that sent his pulse into a wild flight all over again, then up to eyes that held an odd mixture of awareness, laughter, and shadows. And a wisdom that had him reassessing her age. Perhaps she wasn't as young as she looked.

Relief had his smile widening. "Hi."

"Hello." Her eyes began to sparkle, her voice light and musical with a slight European lilt, as enchanting as her smile.

He passed close to her as he tore his gaze away and went to help Vhyper with the luggage, close enough to catch a whiff of soft female and raspberry sweetness.

She followed. "I'm sorry," she said as Hawke reached in and pulled out a huge suitcase. Vhyper already had four of them sitting on the pavement. "I think he's used to servants."

"We'll break him of that quickly enough," Vhyper muttered darkly.

Hawke grunted. Maxim was a fool if he thought they'd put up with that kind of attitude. Perhaps it was a defense mechanism that would ease once he felt like he was one of them. They could only hope.

Vhyper grabbed three of the huge pieces of luggage and started toward the house. The woman watched him go, her smile gone, her brows dipped in worry.

Hawke felt the need to ease her mind. "Don't worry about Vhyper. Or Maxim, for that matter. Newly marked Ferals are rarely at their best. While their bodies come to terms with the animal spirit, they tend to be unpredictable, aggressive, quick-tempered, you name it."

The woman turned to him, wrinkling her nose.

Adorable.

"For how long?"

"The worst of it will pass when he's brought into his animal—his first shift. But for some, it takes several years."

She sighed. "Wonderful."

He grinned at her. "I'm Hawke."

Her expression shifted with delightful speed, awe lacing her gaze and her words. "You're the hawk shifter."

"I am. And who might you be?"

"I'm Faith. I'm with Maxim, though I'm not sure that's something I want to admit at the moment."

With Maxim. He didn't like the sound of that. "His daughter?" he asked hopefully.

She laughed. "I was born in 1899. I just try to look like a teenager."

Not too young at all. Which would be beside the point if she was truly *with Maxim*. Ferals never, ever poached another Feral's female.

He held out his hand. "It's nice to meet you, Faith."

Her eyes sparkled as she slid her slender hand into his on a rush of soft pleasure. "It's nice to meet you, too."

Hawke found himself suddenly torn between modern manners, which dictated he simply shake her hand, and a surprising desire to raise her knuckles to his lips in the old way. The desire to inhale the scent of her skin, to feel her flesh beneath his lips, was dismayingly powerful. But until he knew which way the wind blew between her and Maxim, he'd be wise to err on the side of caution.

With a twinge of regret, he shook her delicate hand, then released her and turned to pull out another of the suitcases. "Is there a reason you enjoy looking like a teen?" He glanced back to find her brown eyes sparkling like dark gems.

"It's either piercings or tats, or I'd look like a poser." She shrugged a delicate shoulder. "The tats are permanent. The piercings aren't." Immortal flesh healed any wound, even those inflicted intentionally.

And piercings she had, at least on the one ear. "A poser to whom?" Genuinely curious, he set the suitcase on the pavement.

Her smile grew, one corner quivering with suppressed laughter, drawing his gaze to that lovely, kissable mouth. "To the street kids."

"What street kids?"

Her expression sobered, the pixie disappearing as if she'd never been. "The lost ones. Mostly girls."

And he realized this was no game to her. In the dark depths of her eyes, a crusader's passion gleamed. And suddenly he understood. "You enter their world. You earn their trust in order to help them."

The look she gave him was a mix of surprise and approval. "They need help, and I have a lot of experience with gaining their trust and finding them that help. Setting them on the right paths."

He nodded, unaccountably moved by the emotion he saw in her face, the deep well of compassion and fire. Many Therians worked among the humans to earn a living. But how many, he wondered, threw the whole of themselves into bettering the short lives of a few mortals? And he felt certain that's exactly what Faith did.

"Humans," he murmured.

She lifted her chin. "Human kids." A note of defensiveness crept into her voice, a small warrior standing before him now. "The most defenseless creatures of all."

"I'm not criticizing you for it, Faith. I'm impressed. Not many Therians would bother."

Dark, intelligent eyes studied him as if searching for

the truth of his words. But he'd meant what he'd said, and the smile that slowly began to spread across her face told him she'd figured it out. Her smile burrowed inside him like a small ball of heat deep in his chest.

He reached for another of the suitcases as she bent forward to grab a small, worn duffel that looked incongruous beside the large, expensive luggage. Their arms brushed. Her sweet scent flowed over him, sending a thrill through his system.

She turned to him as she pulled out the duffel, slinging the strap over one shoulder. "In my experience, Therians don't often care what happens to humans."

He wanted to argue that point, but in all honesty couldn't. The Ferals and Therians of his acquaintance were careful with humans, protecting human life wherever possible. But dedicating their lives to the betterment of a few individuals? No.

She tilted her head at him, her eyes curious. "Do you have a human mom or dad?"

"My father was a Feral Warrior." He leaned in to pull out the two remaining suitcases. "He was the previous hawk shifter and my mother the Radiant."

Her jaw dropped a little before snapping shut. "You're Therian royalty."

He started, then laughed. "I've never heard it put like that."

"So why the affinity for humans? Are you really as nice a guy as you seem?"

A nice guy. He'd always been that, or tried to be. He liked people, humans and Therians alike, more than many of his brothers. He liked kids, in particular. But nice guys didn't erupt in fits of rage, endangering anyone and everyone around them. And that was something he definitely did these days. Goddess, she shouldn't be out here with him alone. For a few enjoyable minutes he'd forgotten the rage that simmered inside him.

He blinked. The rage was barely noticeable. When had that happened?

The moment Faith smiled at him.

He set the last two suitcases on the pavement. "I'm not entirely sure what I am anymore." As soon as the words were out, he wished he hadn't answered quite so truthfully. It wasn't something he wanted to talk about. "So how did you come to accompany Maxim to Feral House?"

Her eyes lost their sparkle. "I think I'm going to be his mate."

His mate? Hawke tried to mask his dismay but knew he'd failed when she shrugged.

"We're not exactly a matched pair."

Hawke tried to laugh, but the sound was forced. "Not exactly."

His *mate*? He'd feared they might be lovers. By the way Maxim had walked off and left her in the car, he'd hoped she was just his servant. Disapproval curled in his gut. Newly marked or not, the man was lacking basic manners if he could treat the woman he'd chosen to spend his immortal life with so carelessly. That Feral didn't deserve this jewel of a woman.

But it didn't matter, did it? They'd clearly chosen one another. Maxim had brought her with him all the way from Poland. Soon, Faith would be just another of his brothers' mates, living at Feral House permanently. Just one more happily ever after to watch from afar. Except . . . he hadn't been attracted to the others. This one he was.

"You've been with Maxim a long time?" he asked as casually as he could manage.

"Not exactly." The sheepish twist of her smile had him lifting a brow. "I met him yesterday."

Hawke frowned. He didn't try to hide his surprise and wasn't sure he could have even if he had. She'd chosen to come all the way to America with the man, to bind herself to him *for eternity . . . the first time she saw him?*

"Don't judge." Her words were soft, her expression serious. "The moment we met, we knew we were meant to be together. Sometimes, it happens that way."

"Does it?" He shook his head. She was talking about binding herself to a stranger for *eternity*. Once the mating bond was formed, there was no severing it except by death. And the death of one mate often left the other living a half life. But it wasn't his business. In the current state he was in—his animal hijacking him at every possible juncture—he didn't need to be worrying about anyone but himself.

As Hawke picked up one of the suitcases, Faith reached for another. Hawke shook his head. "I'll get it."

"I can take one of his. I have two empty hands."

Hawke eyed the small duffel on her shoulder, then snorted. "That's all that's yours?"

Faith shrugged, that pixie grin lifting her intriguing mouth. "I travel light."

He reached for the duffel. "Let me have it."

All he earned himself was a good-natured scowl. "I'm not going to walk in empty-handed while you carry all this. I'm not helpless."

Maybe not helpless, but she was as slender and pretty

as a lily, and he wasn't having her schlepping luggage. "Once you move in, you can carry your own weight. Today, you're a guest." He motioned her to hand it over, pretty certain her soon-to-be mate wouldn't appreciate her carrying her own duffel even if it was microscopic. Which might serve him right. But Hawke wanted to carry her bag. For some reason, it was important to him. "You'll bruise my masculine ego."

She laughed, the sound making the air sparkle between them. "It's a duffel."

He felt those sparkles inside him. Goddess, when was the last time he'd felt so . . . *free*? "Give me the bag, Smiley."

"Smiley?" Though her smile remained, something about it changed.

His own dimmed. "I shouldn't have called you that."

"No, it's okay. I just . . . haven't heard that name since I was a child. One of my human friend's dads used to call me that."

He'd hit a memory, if not a nerve. He was sorry for that. "Give me the duffel, and I won't do it again."

As he'd hoped, her grin returned full force, even as she rolled her eyes. "You're relentless."

"You're stubborn."

"Always." With a sigh of mock resignation, she pulled the duffel off her shoulder and handed it to him. "I'll give you the duffel, but . . ."

Slinging the small bag over his own shoulder, he waited, watching her intently, not sure he was going to be able to pull his gaze away when he had to. "But what?"

Her teeth tugged at her lower lip in a move that was at once shy and charming. "But you don't have to stop calling me Smiley. I like it."

Warm pleasure burst inside him. "Good," he said quietly, as their gazes locked in a way they hadn't . . . quite . . . before now. He felt himself sinking, felt the ground turning soft and unsteady beneath his feet as he stared into those twinkling brown depths. His pulse accelerated with the strange feeling that he was losing his balance even as he knew his boots were planted firmly on the pavement.

She was the first to look away, confusion clouding her eyes.

What was he doing? She was about to become the new fox shifter's mate. And even if he thought that was insane, he had nothing better to offer her. With a shake of his head, he grabbed three suitcases and started forward, Faith falling into step beside him as they started up the brick walk.

"Did you have a good flight?" he asked, trying to find his footing again.

"It was wonderful." The smile she tossed him was nothing short of brilliant.

The ground beneath his feet tilted precariously. "As good as that?"

"I've never flown before."

He looked at her with surprise. "Never?"

"No. I loved it, rising through the clouds, seeing them floating below." She looked at him with wonder. "I can't imagine what it must be like for you to fly as a bird, the wind in your face, soaring under your own power."

His gut tightened. "It's incredible." And he'd lost the ability. Not since he'd left that spirit trap had he been able to fly and retain his awareness of it. And he missed it bitterly. But that wasn't something he needed to share with her, not now. Not when she was smiling. "I wish

I could take you up there with me. If I could upsize like some of the animals can, I'd grow to horse size and carry you on my back." A fanciful thought for a man facing disaster, but she made him feel . . . light as air.

An impish gleam leaped into her eyes. "Or shrink me to bird size. Blue-haired Barbie."

He threw back his head and laughed so loud, he startled the birds out of the nearby trees. Tighe stepped through the front door, meeting his gaze with a curious smile and a speculative glance at Faith.

As they started up the steps, Tighe grabbed one of Hawke's suitcases, glancing at Faith. "I'm Tighe."

"The tiger shifter?"

Tighe sketched a quick bow, flashing his dimples. "One and the same."

"I'm Faith. Maxim's soon-to-be mate."

Tighe lifted his chin, as if to nod, but the downward tilt came slowly, his gaze cutting to Hawke, his smile disappearing. "After you, Faith." Tighe motioned Hawke to follow her, but as he drew beside him, Tighe threw him a look of sympathy and frustration. A look that said, *You can't catch a break, can you, buddy?*

Hawke shrugged. It didn't matter. Even if Faith were as free as the wind, he wasn't. His connection with his animal spirit was a screwed-up mess, and he was a danger to anyone in his vicinity.

He followed Faith into the foyer, where Maxim stood with Lyon and Paenther. In his white silk turtleneck and black suit jacket, his hair slicked back with some kind of styling cream, Maxim stood with his chest puffed out and chin lifted as if he thought himself too good for the lot of them. The new Feral met Hawke's eye, his mouth tight, his gaze hard as he held out his hand to

Faith. She went to him without a backward glance or a moment's hesitation.

Jealousy slid like a blade between Hawke's ribs.

But even as Maxim pulled Faith tight against his side, his gaze remained locked on Hawke, sharp with warning.

Hawke's jaw hardened, anger sparking inside him, ignited by a jealousy he had no right to feel.

Tighe nudged him from behind. "Upstairs. This suitcase is heavy."

Which was a lie, but Hawke took the hint and moved toward the stairs, tearing his gaze from the couple. But even as he climbed, he remained intensely aware of the woman below him, every sense tuned to Faith.

He'd never believed in love at first sight, but infatuation was another matter. And he was suddenly, inescapably, drowning in it.

In the space of a handful of minutes, he'd fallen for the woman destined to become another Feral's mate.

Chapter Three

Excitement trilled inside Faith as she joined Maxim in the foyer of Feral House. *Feral House*. It was every bit as grand as she'd imagined from the stories she'd heard of it as a child. The spacious foyer, lit by a huge chandelier, soared a full three stories, hung with lovely wallpaper. Along two curved walls, twin stairs rose. And on one of those stairs two warriors climbed. Hawke preceded Tighe, both men laden with Maxim's luggage, yet their muscles barely flexed. A small smile tugged at her mouth as she watched Hawke's sure, light stride, grace and power in every step.

Maxim's grip on her waist tightened, and she tore her gaze away from the stairs and back to the men to whom Maxim had been talking. Two more Feral Warriors. Her pulse raced with excitement. Sweet goddess, she was really here, standing among the rock stars of the immortal world.

One of the men, a broad-shouldered blond with a look of authority eyed her with curiosity, his gaze dropping to her shoulders and the blue-dyed ends of her hair.

"Hello." She gave him a cheery smile, wrenching her right arm out from between hers and Maxim's bodies and thrusting it out to him. "I'm Faith."

She'd always had a way with people, men and women alike, and expected them to like her. But it wasn't until her hand was thrust forward that she really looked into the man's eyes and saw the coolness there. For a moment, she wondered if she'd made an error. But as she watched, his eyes warmed, a small, if genuine, smile lifting his mouth.

"It's nice to meet you, Faith. I'm Lyon, Chief of the Ferals."

"The *Chief*?" The words were out before she could stop them. She wrinkled her nose. "Sorry, I'm afraid I'm a little starstruck. I wish I had an autograph book."

Lyon's smile widened.

"You will be living here," Maxim said coolly beside her. "She is to be my mate."

When Lyon released her hand, she turned to the other man, extending her hand again. He turned an assessing gaze on her, his expression revealing nothing of his thoughts. He was at once darkly attractive and dangerous-looking, his hair long and black, his skin and features those of a Native American. Across one eye ran scars, like the claw marks of a large animal.

She gaped at him. "Are those *feral marks*?" Belatedly, it occurred to her that Maxim must have the marks somewhere on his body. All the Ferals did. "That is so cool."

Amusement lit the black-haired Feral's eyes, and he nodded. "I'm Paenther." He released her hand and straightened, his amusement fleeing as his expression took on a hard edge. His gaze flicked to Maxim. "I should warn you both, my mate is Mage."

Faith's eyes widened as she felt Maxim's hand flex. "I've never met a Mage." Like the Therians, the Mage were virtually immortal, but while the Therians had once all been shape-shifters, the Mage were the magic ones. Both races had lost the bulk of their power millennia ago in a joint and desperate effort to overcome the Daemons. But the truce hadn't lasted. The Mage were the enemies of the Therians. Yet a Feral Warrior had married one.

As if reading her thoughts, Paenther met her gaze. "Skye is as pure of spirit as anyone you'll ever meet. She'll be a good friend to you."

"Skye is a powerful ally and asset." Lyon's sharp gaze landed on Maxim and stuck. "You'll find we are a diverse group. All will be treated with the utmost respect, from the cook and her helper to *your chief*."

The hard edge on the last two words made Faith wonder what she'd interrupted when she'd walked into the foyer. And what Maxim had said that had the Chief warning him instead of welcoming him.

Faith caught Paenther's eye and smiled. "I look forward to meeting Skye."

The lift of Paenther's mouth told her he believed her. "You'll meet her soon enough. She and the other wives are preparing a welcome reception."

A cute blonde joined them, sliding her arm around Lyon's waist as if he belonged to her. By the soft look in the Chief of the Ferals' eyes when he glanced down, sliding his own arm around her shoulders, Faith suspected he did. "I'm Kara." The woman's smile was warm and genuine, a crooked eyetooth lending her smile charm.

She thrust out her hand to Maxim. "I'm your power plug."

"My what?" Maxim asked.

Lyon reached up and gave Kara's ponytail a gentle tug. "She's your Radiant."

Faith stared at her in wonder. The Radiant was the one woman in all the world with the ability to pull the Earth's energies that empowered the Ferals. Just as there was only ever one of each of the nine shape-shifters, there was only ever one Radiant. When one died, another was marked to take her place. Faith had always imagined the Radiant to be a queen among immortals, reserved, royal. Kara stood in bare feet, a pair of jeans, and a T-shirt that read TEAM JACOB across the profile of a howling wolf. And called herself a power plug.

Faith grinned. Everything about Kara appeared open and genuine and friendly, and Faith liked her at once.

Kara returned her grin. "I like your hair."

Faith dipped her head, still smiling. "Thank you."

"Would you like me to show you to your room so you can freshen up before the reception?"

"Faith will share my room." Maxim's autocratic tone had her stiffening. His words had her pulling away. She barely knew the man. Coming to America with him was bad enough. But sharing a room? *A bed?*

Kara seemed to read her thoughts. "You could borrow my room for a while." She glanced up at Lyon, a smile lighting her eyes. "I never use it."

I belong to Maxim. The thought hit her again, accompanied by a sudden, odd need to stay near him. *Should* she share his room? That connection pulled so strongly, she almost said yes. But . . . *no.* She needed to shower and change, and the thought of doing those in front of him, let alone anything else, didn't appeal. Not . . . yet.

Faith nodded. "Thank you, Kara. I'd appreciate the use of your room." She felt Maxim's disapproval and turned to meet his hard gaze. "For now. Until we know one another a little better."

Maxim didn't argue, but his expression turned glacial, and she knew she'd embarrassed him by rebuffing him in front of the other men. A small frisson of unease slid over her flesh. Unhappiness twisted her gut. This wasn't the right way for things to be starting between them. The thought of sharing a room with him should excite her, shouldn't it? If Hawke had asked her to share his room . . .

The thought sent a sudden and startling flush of heat spiraling through her body. Her cheeks grew warm with dismay.

"Ready?" Kara asked, then turned and led them up one flight of stairs and down the hall to the biggest bedchamber Faith had ever seen. A huge bed took up a fraction of the room, dark red velvet curtains hanging from the rails across the top and tied at each of the four bedposts. The bedspread was gold silk, the walls papered in deep greens, reds, and golds. Even the ceiling had been decorated—a full mural of cherubs—making her heart pinch with the thought of how Paulina would love such artwork.

"It's beautiful," Faith murmured.

"It's a bit much." Kara shrugged. "But it's been the Radiant's room since Feral House was built."

"I assume the Chief's is larger," Maxim said stiffly.

Kara gave him a bemused look. "No. Actually, mine is the largest. The Feral Warriors want their Radiant to be happy here. They shower her with luxuries." She gave Faith a wry smile. "If she wants them. My tastes are much simpler than the previous Radiant's." She glanced at Maxim. "Your room is on the third floor. We thought we'd give you an hour to freshen up before the reception. Is that enough?"

"That is adequate." Maxim turned to Faith. "Wait for me to collect you."

Faith nodded, then suddenly remembered . . . "My duffel. It's with your luggage."

"Just a duffel?" Kara smiled. "I'll bring it to you on my way back down."

A few minutes later, Kara returned, Faith's duffel hanging from her shoulder. "Here you go. Do you need anything else?"

Faith hesitated. It wouldn't take her more than twenty minutes to shower and dress for the reception and dinner. Sitting in here by herself for an hour was the last thing she wanted to do when Feral House was just waiting to be explored.

"Is there a kitchen where I could find something to drink? Perhaps fruit juice or a Coca-Cola?"

Kara's smile bloomed. "Come on."

Faith followed Kara down the stairs, through the now-empty foyer, and down the hall to a large dining room as beautifully decorated as the rest of the house. As she entered the room, she spied Hawke sitting at the huge dining table talking with Vhyper.

Hawke saw her and smiled, sending her pulse into a flutter. Vhyper acknowledged her with a nod that was neither friendly nor unfriendly.

"Faith's thirsty," Kara announced cheerily as she led Faith through the room, toward a door at the far end.

Out of the corner of her eye, Faith watched Hawke rise and start after them. The excited pleasure the realization triggered had her feeling a moment's guilt. Then again, what woman wouldn't get a thrill from having a Feral Warrior smile at her? Hawke was just being friendly. And she was just a little starstruck. That was all.

Kara pushed through the swinging door. Faith followed, feeling Hawke's presence at her back, watching as one muscular arm reached over her head to hold the door open for her. Warmth spread through her body, the desire to grin nearly overwhelming her. Voices carried from deeper in the kitchen, a youthful male's and a high-pitched but pleasant female's.

Kara stopped so suddenly that Faith nearly ran into her, and turned a worried gaze to Hawke. "I should have warned her."

"She'll do fine," he said quietly. As Faith looked up at him questioningly, he met her gaze with a warmth that curled her toes. He spoke quickly, his voice barely above a whisper. "Pink is half-flamingo and very self-conscious. I'll explain more later."

Faith nodded, her attention split between his intriguing words and the delight that danced inside her at his attention. At his nearness. She felt . . . quivery. Unsettled. Like a kid with her first crush.

Good grief. That was exactly what she felt like. Which was ridiculous, of course. She'd just met the man. And she was marrying another.

Whom she'd also just met.

It was crazy. She'd gone decades without a single male turning her head in any but the most cursory way. Then again, never before had she met a Feral Warrior. Perhaps it wasn't such a surprise that two had caught her eye. She should probably be grateful that she wasn't having heart palpitations for more of them.

"Pink, Xavier," Kara called. "I have someone I'd like you to meet."

The voices went silent. A moment later, from around the corner walked the oddest pair. The woman, just as Hawke had warned her, looked kind of like a flamingo. Bright pink feathers covered her human-looking face and arms—human-looking except for the unblinking bird eyes that watched her warily. At the bird-woman's side stood a young man, several inches taller, his eyes shifting unnaturally, clearly unseeing. His arm was slung casually across Pink's shoulders, his expression open, curious, and radiating a friendliness Faith couldn't help but respond to.

"This is Faith," Kara said. "Soon to be the mate of the new fox shifter."

"I'm very pleased to meet you both," Faith said sincerely.

Xavier grinned. "I'd like to shake your hand, but I don't want to knock anything over."

Faith slipped out of Kara's hold and stepped forward, within his reach. "I'm here, Xavier. I'd like to shake your hand, too." She glanced at Pink. "Both of yours, if that's okay."

The bird-woman said nothing. Xavier reached for Faith, and she intercepted his hand. When he released her, Faith smiled at Pink, letting her know she wasn't at all offended if Pink chose not to reach out to her. But to her surprise, Pink lifted her own hand, mimicking Xavier.

Faith felt a strong stab of empathy for this woman who must feel so out of place in any company. Gently, she took her hand and squeezed ever so slightly, marveling at the soft feel of feathers. "It's a pleasure to meet you both. I'm so honored to be here."

"Xavier and I made oatmeal cookies," Pink said quietly. "Would you care for some?"

"Yes, very much. Thank you."

As Pink turned toward the back counter, Faith felt a large, warm hand curl around her shoulder from behind, squeezing lightly. "Well, done," Hawke said quietly.

She glanced up at him, turning, her temple brushing his jaw before he'd pulled fully back. Their gazes met, warmth and embarrassed laughter arcing between them at the small collision.

Hawke stepped away. "Lemonade?" he asked as he strode to the refrigerator.

"Pink makes the best lemonade," Xavier enthused. "She only uses real lemons, and she rolls them first to make them warm and soft so they give up all their juice."

Faith glanced at Kara to find the other woman watching her curiously. But a moment later, Kara stepped over to her and slipped her arm through Faith's. Together, they turned to watch Hawke pour several glasses as Xavier revealed all of Pink's lemonade secrets.

"X? Pink?" Hawke asked. "Lemonade?"

"Sure!" Xavier replied.

"No thank you, Hawke." Pink ambled toward them carrying a large tin and set it on the black granite countertop. As Pink lifted the lid, the smell of freshly baked oatmeal cookies filled the kitchen.

Kara reached for one and motioned Faith to join her. Hawke slid the glasses toward them, then took one to Xavier.

"Thanks, Dude!"

A moment later, Faith felt Hawke once more at her back, brushing her shoulder as he reached for a cookie.

Kara looked at him with amusement. "Since when did you acquire a sweet tooth?" She glanced at Faith. "When I first got here, all they ate was meat."

Hawke turned sideways, leaning against the island only a few inches from Faith's elbow. He was crowding her, just a little, in a way she suspected was common to shape-shifters since she knew them to be particularly physical creatures. In a way that shot her awareness of him sky-high. She could almost feel the heat from his body.

"It's hard not to crave a little sweetness when there's so much in the room," Hawke said quietly, a twinkle in his eye.

Kara laughed.

Though the words were blatant flattery, Faith sensed sincerity in them. Faith turned to find him watching her with a look in his eyes that made her chest feel suddenly tight, turning her breathing rapid. And shallow.

She supposed it was a good thing all the Ferals didn't affect her like this, or she'd never take a full breath again.

She forced herself to nibble the soft, delicious cookie as she struggled to ignore her body's inappropriate reaction to the male at her side.

As Xavier regaled them, in detail, about the food they'd prepared for the reception, they each had several cookies. Finally, Kara glanced at the clock. "I'd better get moving. Are you ready to head back upstairs, Faith?"

"If you want another cookie first, I'll show you the way," Hawke offered.

Faith looked at him with surprise, and their gazes caught. He wanted her to stay, she'd heard it in his voice and could see it in his eyes. Was he feeling this . . . weirdness . . . between them, too? Not weirdness. *Attraction*. Those dark eyes watched her in a way that set butterflies to flight in her stomach. And she knew this was a mistake. She could feel the electricity arcing in the air between them.

She needed to stop this, to leave with Kara and end it now. But staying a few more minutes, enjoying the decadent pleasure of a rare and harmless flirtation, was such a temptation.

"That works," Kara said, a smile in her voice. "I'll see you both soon."

Faith pulled her gaze from Hawke's just as Kara disappeared through the swinging door. Pink and Xavier, too, had wandered away at some point, leaving her alone in the kitchen with Hawke. Maxim would not be happy. And the way her pulse was tripping, she couldn't really blame him.

She stepped away, casually circling the island until the wide counter separated her from Hawke, then reached for another cookie. Just one more, then she'd go. "You really don't eat sweets?"

As soon as the words were out of her mouth, she remembered the way he'd alluded to her and Kara as "sweets." Her gaze snapped up to his, heat rising in her cheeks at the weak double entendre. He wouldn't have caught it, surely.

The mix of laughter and heat in his eyes told her he had. Most definitely. But to her relief, he acted the gentleman, answering the question she'd intended to ask, not the far more carnal one.

"None of the current Ferals has much of a sweet tooth, nor have the past couple of Radiants. Kara's the exception. Skye, too, loves sweets, so Pink bakes on a regular basis for the first time in years." His eyes smiled at her. "What about you?"

Faith returned his smile. "I enjoy a sweet treat when I have a little extra money." She felt herself falling into his eyes. Jerking her gaze away, she looked around— the dark cherry cabinets, the gleaming appliances . . . anywhere but the man. "This kitchen is beautiful. How long have you lived here?"

"We redid the kitchen about ten years ago. But we built the house centuries ago."

"*You* built it?" She looked at him with surprise.

"Not me personally. I haven't been alive that long. Lyon, Tighe, Kougar, and Wulfe have, though. They came to America from Europe in 1540. Initially they lived in a series of small houses while they sought a place with a strong conduit to the Earth's energies. They finally found it here, among the rocks that make up the cliff face overlooking the Potomac. We call it the goddess rock."

"Where did the Ferals live before America? I know they were in Scotland at some point. One of the men in my childhood enclave had lived near them then."

Hawke nodded. "They came to America from Spain. But before that, they'd lived in Ireland, Scotland, what's now Germany, France."

Faith watched him, fascinated as much by his words as by the play of light on his rugged face. "If I asked, could you tell me the dates and the reason for each move?"

As she spoke, the door swung open, and Tighe strode

in. "Hawke can tell you anything you want to know about any subject, trust me." He glanced at them curiously. "Just the two of you?"

Hawke's expression tightened slightly. "Kara and Faith snuck down to raid the kitchen. Kara just left to get ready for the reception."

Tighe nodded. "Maxim?"

Faith tensed. "I think he's still in his room. Have you seen him?"

"No." The contemplative look in Tighe's eyes only deepened. "Delaney was trying to hold out for the reception, but she's too hungry." A smile broke over his face. "She's always hungry."

As Tighe began piling cookies on a small plate, Faith turned back to Hawke. "So how do you know so much? You must have gone to school."

Tighe snorted. "Twenty-four degrees. Or is it twenty-five?"

Hawke's smile had a charmingly self-deprecating quality to it. "Twenty-seven, though most are obsolete. They were earned a long, long time ago."

She watched him with wonder. Twenty-seven degrees. "What are your favorite subjects?"

"She's as curious as you are," Tighe muttered as he turned and went back through the door, cookie plate in hand.

Hawke shrugged. "I've studied everything from philosophy to engineering, but I've always been most fascinated by people."

"Humans?"

"All people. At heart, we're basically the same regardless of race—human, Therian. Even Mage."

"I love to study people, too. I envy you getting to go

to school. Everything I know I've gotten out of books. Or living."

"You never had a tutor?"

"No."

"I used to be one. Before I was marked. I can be one again." A gentle smile spread over his mouth. "For you."

Her own smile ignited until she felt herself beaming. "I'd like that." And she meant it. How she would enjoy sitting by this man's side hour after hour, listening to his rich voice as he opened the secrets of the universe to her curious mind.

As they smiled at one another, something began to change. His eyes began to gleam and darken as if opening to fathomless depths. The already-charged air between them thickened and danced, caressing her skin, sensitizing her flesh until even the touch of her clothing became too intense.

Slowly, his smile died, his eyes glowing with an intensity that set her pulse to hammering, calling to her until it was all she could do not to step forward, close the distance between them, and slide into his arms.

With dismay, she wrenched her gaze from his. This wasn't right. She shouldn't be feeling this. She shouldn't be with him at all, not alone.

Swallowing hard, struggling to corral her unruly pulse, she glanced at the clock and groaned. Maxim would be at her bedroom door to pick her up in fifteen minutes.

"I have to go." She spun toward the swinging door.

"Can you find your way back to your room?"

"Yes." What had she been thinking, staying with Hawke so long? She'd given in to a temptation she should never have indulged in, fanning an attraction that had to die a quick death.

Maxim was the man she was intended for, not Hawke. She knew it deep in her heart and had since the moment she'd met him. Which meant she was going to have to stay away from Hawke until his attention turned elsewhere. And hers turned where it needed to stay.

On Maxim. Her soon-to-be mate.

Fifteen minutes later, an imperious rap sounded at her door. Maxim. And she wasn't quite ready.

"I'll be out in a minute," she called. She'd taken a quick shower, careful to keep her hair dry since she'd washed it that morning, then pulled on a black dress with capped sleeves and a modest v-neck. The dress was made of a lightweight knit with a full skirt that fell to her knees. Hopefully, it would be appropriate.

She slipped on her only pair of heels—well-worn black pumps—then brushed out her hair. She was swiping on a little mascara when the knock sounded again, quick and impatient.

"I'm almost ready, Maxim." A quick brush of lip gloss on her lips, and she hurried to the open door. And stared with dismay.

Maxim stood on the other side, impeccably dressed in a full tuxedo, his hair slicked back from his face. She was hopelessly underdressed. As his gaze skimmed her attire, his expression soured. "Have you nothing better to wear?"

Embarrassment stained her cheeks. "It's my only dress, Maxim."

Without reply, he turned and started down the hall as if expecting her to follow. Or not.

Part of her wanted to stay in the room and skip the reception altogether, but what if they dressed up for dinner, too? For every dinner? She couldn't hide in her room forever.

Unhappily, Faith started after him, her stomach cramping. She'd been afraid of this—that she was out of her league with Maxim. Especially with the Feral Warriors. Would they all look at her with dismay? Kara? Hawke?

The thought of it made her want to sink into the floor. She'd never pretended to be any kind of royalty. She'd never pretended to be anything more than what she was—a sometimes waitress who tried to help street kids. And now . . . Maxim's soon-to-be mate. A role she was beginning to fear would never fit.

At the bottom of the stairs, Maxim came to a stop, apparently waiting for her, though his face remained turned away. When she caught up with him, he offered her his arm and she took it, feeling gauche and miserable beside his tuxedoed splendor. But there wasn't anything she could do but lift her chin and paste a smile on her face.

Together, they followed the voices to a large, formal room furnished in black and white with splashes of deep red. A number of the Ferals and their women were already there, some of whom she'd already met—Lyon, Paenther, Vhyper, and Kara. They were pouring drinks or grabbing beers, but the easy conversation died as all eyes swiveled toward Maxim and her.

It took a moment before she realized that her mortification over being underdressed was unfounded. To her relief, the only one who had dressed formally was Maxim. The other men were in pants and collared shirts of one kind or another, with one—a giant with a badly scarred face—in a plain black T-shirt.

Kara wore a brightly colored green-and-yellow sundress with a matching green sweater. And flip-flops. *Flip-flops.* Faith realized she was staring at the other woman's feet. But when she forced her gaze upward, Kara's shrug and grin sent the rest of Faith's tension tumbling away.

One by one, each Feral stepped forward and introduced himself and his wife, if he had one. Jag and Olivia, Kougar, who promised they'd meet his wife later, and Wulfe, the giant with the scars who didn't appear to have a mate.

She wondered suddenly if Hawke was mated. Was she to meet his wife tonight, too? Surely he wouldn't have been smiling at her the way he had if he'd had a mate. Just as she shouldn't have been smiling at him.

Paenther stepped forward, his arm tight around the shoulders of a woman in a violet dress not too different from Faith's own. A woman with the strangest eyes—copper rings around the irises. *Mage eyes.* With her short cap of dark hair, Skye possessed an ethereal quality that wasn't at all what Faith had expected of one of the race that had long been enemy to the Therians and their Feral guardians.

Skye's smile was cautious as she glanced from Maxim to Faith and back again. "Welcome to Feral House."

Faith waited for Maxim to say something, or at least nod, but he remained stonily silent. She wanted to elbow him but didn't.

"Thank you," Faith said pointedly, flashing Skye a friendly smile.

But her response wasn't the one that mattered. Paenther's mouth took on a hard line as he stared at Maxim, his expression suddenly granite, his protectiveness a living shield around the woman.

"If you ever hurt her *in any way,* I will kill you."

Still Maxim didn't speak. If only he'd *try* to be nice. But men had always been something of a mystery to her. Was this merely male posturing? Once they took one another's measure, would Maxim settle down and become friends with these men? She could only hope.

Paenther steered Skye away from them, angling his body in such a way that his gaze never quite left Maxim. As if he half expected an attack.

Skye threw Faith an apologetic look, which Faith quickly returned. *Men.*

Out of the corner of her eye, she saw two more of the big men step into the room along with a woman. Her heart gave a small, excited leap. *Hawke.* Tighe had his arm around the shoulders of a brunette dressed, interestingly enough, in a pair of black pants and a red silk blouse, a gun hanging from the belt at her waist. A gun?

Together, the three started toward them.

Faith's pulse began to thrum as she shifted her gaze to Hawke and found him watching her, a small smile playing at the corners of his mouth. Her breath quickened, butterfly wings brushing the insides of her ribs even as she looked away. Even as she tried to ignore him. But, just as it had in the kitchen, the air began to thicken and dance around her. Why did he have to affect her like this? Why didn't Maxim?

Maybe Maxim isn't the one meant for me. But even as the thought formed in her head, another blasted it down. *You belong to Maxim.* The voice pulsed within her mind, burrowing deeply. Disturbingly.

As the three neared, she hazarded another glance at Hawke. He'd turned to Maxim, his eyes losing all warmth. A shiver skittered down Faith's spine as she glimpsed the warrior behind those kind eyes, the Feral capable of handing out death with a few quick blows. Tighe's expression wasn't much warmer. Maxim had done a bang-up job of alienating the entire household, it appeared.

The woman beside Tighe thrust out her hand toward Faith as if she felt the tension between the males and thought it best to leave them to their glaring. "I'm Delaney. Tighe's wife."

Faith shook her hand gladly. "I'm pleased to meet you." Her curious gaze dropped to the gun.

Delaney's gaze followed. She smiled ruefully. "Ex-FBI. I feel naked without it. We're always glad to have another Feral wife around here. We're slowly evening out the numbers."

"I'm not a wife. Yet."

"You will be." Maxim's voice was as cold as the other males' expressions. "But first you will need a wardrobe fit for my mate."

Faith flinched. Delaney's eyebrows shot up.

Hawke's jaw tightened as he looked at her, his eyes at once hard and as warm as the summer sun. "You look lovely, Faith."

The ring of truth in his words had her blushing. Maxim hauled her against his side, a low growl rumbling from his throat.

Tighe clasped Hawke's shoulder. "I need a beer. So do you."

Jaw clenching, his gaze spearing Maxim, Hawke allowed his friend to steer him away.

Delaney threw Faith a curious look before taking the hand Tighe held out to her and following the men to the bar at the other side of the room.

Maxim's grip on Faith eased, but his arm remained around her shoulders as he started forward, leading her toward Lyon and Kara. Lyon watched their approach, his expression stony. They all watched. The room had gone silent, the atmosphere wary, as all pairs of Feral eyes followed them across the room.

"My accommodations are inadequate," Maxim informed Lyon. "I require larger quarters."

A scattershot of grunts and scoffs erupted around the room, but Lyon merely stared at his newest Feral with cold eyes. "Every room is the same size."

"The Radiant's room is far larger. More suited to my needs."

The sounds of disbelief grew louder. Faith wished she could sink into the floor and disappear.

"He's got to be kidding," one deep male voice rumbled.

"Who does he think he is?" another replied.

"I'm all for giving him lots of space," Vhyper muttered. "The whole backyard. I'll stake him myself, and we can see how well he enjoys the nightly draden visit."

A thinly veiled threat, for the draden would quickly kill any Therian who couldn't shift into an animal. But Maxim ignored them all.

Lyon's voice rose above the others. "You're a rank-and-file soldier, Maxim, and you're currently low man on the Feral totem pole. Until you're brought into your animal, you're not even that."

Maxim's hand spasmed on her shoulder. "And when will that ritual occur?" he demanded.

"Daybreak tomorrow." Lyon turned away. But when he would have steered Kara away with him, she shook her head.

"Give me a minute," Kara said quietly, and her mate obeyed her wishes, giving her shoulder a gentle squeeze before joining Paenther and Skye. Kara's eyes were full of sympathy as she met Faith's gaze. "Do you like champagne? We always initiate new wives into the Feral sisterhood with champagne."

Faith smiled, grateful for Kara's attention, for the open declaration that the enmity against Maxim did not extend to her. "I've never had any, but I'm sure I'll love it."

"Never?" Kara asked incredulously, then gave a quick, self-deprecating shrug. "Then again, the only times I'd ever had it before I came here were at a couple of wedding receptions in my home town. I'm certainly no connoisseur." She grinned. "But I do enjoy a good bottle of champagne, and the guys never buy anything but *good* champagne."

"What animal am I to become?" Maxim asked in that imperious tone of his.

Faith looked up, wondering who he was talking to. No one and everyone, she realized. The way his head turned, he was well aware that all had chosen to keep their distance. Instead, he spoke to them like a commander addressing his troops.

"The fox," Kara told him.

Maxim's mouth twisted with ill-concealed disgust. "A fox is quite small."

"The previous fox could enlarge his animal until he was as big as Wulfe," she assured him. "He was huge."

"The fox shifter has always been a fierce and effective warrior," Tighe added, though his tone said he was withholding opinion on this newest fox.

Faith's gaze, drawn by Tighe's words, slid all too easily to Hawke, standing beside him, taking in the casual way he stood, his beer bottle dangling at his side, and the long, muscular lines of his body. Unable to resist, she glanced up, meeting his gaze, watching with fascination as the frost in his eyes melted instantly.

"A fierce and effective warrior," Maxim repeated with a nod. "That will do." He gave a short, humorless laugh, and said with a thickly disparaging tone, "Unlike the hawk, which is a useless animal, completely unsuited for battle."

As growls of outrage peppered the room, Faith's gaze snapped to her soon-to-be mate. The heat of shame rose into her cheeks, and she could no longer hold her tongue. "*Maxim*."

The grip on her shoulder tightened in retaliation, Maxim's strong fingers digging into the joint until she cried out. Faith tried to pull away, but though Maxim shifted his fingers and no longer hurt her, she remained tight against him, held by his visclike grip.

The low growl of a vicious animal had her head turning. Hawke. Her jaw dropped, her blood going cold. *My God*. His eyes now glowed a golden orange, the pupils engulfing the whites. *Animal eyes*. Fangs had erupted in his mouth, claws springing from his fingertips.

Faith stared at his terrifying visage with a mix of horror and fascination even as she recognized the in-between stage between man and animal. *Going feral*, she'd heard it called. Deadly, terrifying. And utterly . . . *thrilling*.

Hawke took a step toward them, but Tighe grabbed

him. Kougar leaped to his other side. "Easy, buddy."

Hawke stilled, his gaze fixed on Maxim. "*Let her go.*"

But Maxim's hold on her only tightened.

All of a sudden, Lyon was in front of them, his own face looking much like Hawke's, with the fangs and the animal eyes. His hand whipped up to encircle Maxim's throat, his claws biting deep into Maxim's neck.

"*Release her.*"

The hand at her shoulder slowly disappeared, as did the man at her side. Lyon picked him up by the neck and slammed him back against the nearest wall making the paintings rattle. "You *will* show respect for your Feral brothers and every person in this house. And you will *never* harm one of the women. *Ever*. Not even your own. Is that understood?"

"Of course." Maxim's words gurgled with the blood in his throat as his white tuxedo shirt slowly turned red.

For a dozen seconds, Lyon held him like that. Finally, he released Maxim and stepped back, his claws and fangs receding. "You'll retire to your room, now, and remain there until dinner at seven."

Maxim pushed away from the wall, straightening his bloodstained clothes, his expression as haughty as ever. Raising his chin, he speared her with his gaze. "Come, Faith."

Lyon turned to her. "You're welcome to remain here."

She was trembling, shaken from the violence and from seeing two Ferals in their half-animal forms. Hazarding a glance at Hawke, she found that, like Lyon, he was back to normal, having retracted fangs and claws, and watching her now with enigmatic eyes.

They all watched her, waiting to see what she'd do.

If she stayed, denying Maxim's request to stand beside him against the others, she might as well pack her duffel and go home. No man would forgive that, especially one as prideful as Maxim.

You belong to Maxim. Go with Maxim.

"Thank you, Lyon, but Maxim is my soon-to-be-mate." Resisting another glance at Hawke, she turned and fell into step beside Maxim as he strode from the room.

She accompanied him up two flights of stairs, confused and frustrated by how right it felt to walk beside him. And at the same time, how wrong as she became increasingly frustrated with him. He was arrogant and rude. And he'd intentionally hurt her!

Although he'd been nice enough on the plane. Before they'd arrived at Feral House.

Was she being unfair to him? There was so much more to any man than the way he reacted when faced with such a difficult and unique situation—turning into a shape-shifter, leaving his home for good, becoming one of a group of men who had known one another for decades, if not centuries. Becoming a soldier when he was clearly used to being a prince.

To pass final judgment on him in the midst of such chaos was unfair. She had to give him and the mating connection time.

Maxim pushed open the door to reveal a well-furnished, if unadorned, bedchamber six times larger and a thousand times nicer than anywhere she'd lived in the past sixty or seventy years even if it was half the size of Kara's.

Maxim closed the door behind him, threw the dead bolt, then walked across the room to the window.

"Hawke wants you." The words were emotionless, a simple statement of fact.

"He was just being friendly." But she knew better, she knew that the attraction between them was real. She felt it every time he came near her. And his eyes told her he felt it, too.

"He's not getting you. You're mine."

Faith stared at the back of his head, wanting to argue that it was her decision, not his. Not Hawke's. But the pull of the slowly knitting mating bond between her and Maxim said otherwise.

Maxim sighed and turned around, regret in his eyes. "I behaved badly, I'm afraid. The way he was looking at you . . ." He shook his head. "I wanted to hurt him. I hurt you instead." He shrugged. "It was a foolish way to act. You're a beautiful woman. They will look." When he smiled, his expression turned almost charming. "Forgive me? I am not myself. Once I come into my animal, I will be the mate you deserve, Faith. I vow it."

Faith watched him, her instincts jumbled and confused. "I've spent a lifetime rescuing girls from men who would use them and abuse them. I won't be one of them."

His mouth thinned, then relaxed. Slowly he nodded. "Fair enough." But there was something about the rigidness of his shoulders and the way his right hand clenched and unclenched that told her this argument was far from over.

She was perplexed at fate's having chosen her for this man. They were so different. He was an aristocrat, and she hung with the street kids. If she were a gambler, she'd wager they'd never make it as a couple, regardless what fate decreed. She'd wager that in six weeks, she'd be back in Warsaw trying to coax Paulina into trusting her again. Back to living alone, sleeping alone, with Feral House and her warriors nothing but a bittersweet memory.

"Wondered where you were."

Hawke looked up from his plate as Wulfe sauntered into the dining room, then returned to the thick, savory slices of roast beef Pink had brought out to him a short while before.

Wulfe sat down beside him and poured himself a glass of ice water from the pitcher on the table. "You missed a fun time at dinner." He leaned back in his chair. "It's like he thinks he's the new general sent to lead the troops. He's pissing me off."

"Join the club." At least his brothers felt the same. This would be so much worse if Maxim were genuinely a nice guy whom everyone else liked.

Hawke glanced at Wulfe. "Faith?"

Wulfe looked at him for a long moment, sympathy slowly deepening his gaze. "You're smitten with her," he said quietly. "I saw the way you were watching her during the reception."

Hawke turned away, digging his fork into another bite of meat. "No one uses the word *smitten* anymore."

"Doesn't change the fact."

Hell. "I don't know what I am. Yeah, actually I do. I'm a fucked-up mess."

Wulfe's dinner-plate-sized hand landed lightly on Hawke's shoulder. "I'm sorry, Wings. You're too good a guy to be dealing with so much shit. If I could take some of it off your shoulders, I would."

Hawke met his friend's gaze and nodded. "I know."

Lyon and Kara walked into the room a moment later. "There you are," Kara said quietly.

Hawke grunted. "The moment I don't show up, everyone assumes I've flown the coop."

"I had a feeling you'd decided to avoid another confrontation." Lyon held out a chair for Kara, then seated himself. "That was a wise move."

Hawke nodded and took another bite. Hell, wisdom had nothing to do with it. He still couldn't shake the sight of that stunned look on Faith's face when he'd gone feral. Or the crazed jealousy that nearly flattened him every time he saw Maxim's arm around her. He'd *wisely* stayed away from dinner because his control had been razor-thin, and he'd feared he'd lose it completely and rip the bastard's head off. None of the Ferals would have minded, he was sure. But Faith would have really looked at him in horror, and he couldn't bear that.

Lightning bolted across his skull, fiery fingers crawling across the inside of his head, setting off the hawk's angry cry.

Dammit. Enough! I'm not hurting you intentionally!

"You okay?" Lyon asked, watching him worriedly.

As the talons released him, Hawke nodded. "Fine."

Lyon pinned him with his gaze for several seconds, apparently deciding not to press the issue. "I think it's best if you stay out of Maxim's path until we bring him into his animal. Hopefully, he'll be more agreeable afterward."

Wulfe grunted. "Do you really think that's going to happen?"

"Goddess, I hope so."

"Where is he now?" Hawke asked, then wished he hadn't. The last thing he wanted to hear was that he'd taken Faith up to bed. He had no business feeling that way! She'd come with Maxim. She belonged to Maxim. But the wildness inside him vehemently disagreed. *Mine.*

"The media room," Wulfe said. "Lyon managed to elude Maxim after dinner, so he cornered Paenther."

"Poor Faith," Kara murmured. "She's so embarrassed by the way he's acting."

"We'll bring him into his animal in the morning." Lyon sighed. "At least then I can put him on nightly draden-hunting duty. Maybe the draden will wear down that outsized ego of his. Before we have to beat it out of him."

Hawke smiled dangerously. "If the draden fail, I'm first in line."

But he wouldn't be, of course. The moment he started fighting, the damn hawk took over. He was of no goddamn use anymore.

A movement in the doorway caught his eye. "Faith." In the dress she'd worn during the reception—a soft, clingy, black number at once modest and sexy as hell— she eyed them with dismay and embarrassment, and a look that told him she was about to turn and bolt. After watching Lyon and him go feral earlier, he could hardly blame her.

"Hi, Faith," Kara said, having followed his gaze. "Come join us."

To Hawke's relief, Faith nodded and started forward, slowly at first, then with less hesitation. He felt sorry for her, certain that her partner's disfavor had her wondering if she was even welcome anymore. When she reached the table, she dropped wearily into the chair beside Kara.

"Is everything okay?" Kara asked gently.

Faith ran a slender hand through her hair, scattering the blue-tipped ends over her shoulders. She opened her mouth, then closed it, as if loyalty to her future mate kept her from voicing her frustration. "I'm sorry," she said at last. "I don't understand him."

Kara's hand covered Faith's. "No one's judging you by his actions."

Lyon grunted. "New Ferals are often a pain in the ass."

Faith's gaze slid to Hawke for the first time since she walked into the room, then away again, as if she couldn't quite bring herself to look at him. Out of loyalty to Maxim? Or because he'd scared the shit out of her by going feral? He ached at the thought that it might be the latter.

"I'm surprised he let you out of his sight," Wulfe muttered.

Faith's expression turned rueful. "Maxim's attention is . . . erratic."

In other words, as long as Hawke wasn't in the room, he ignored her. The prick. She didn't belong with him. But Maxim would never willingly let her go. Certainly not to him. War would erupt, and Faith would forever be caught in the middle.

No, if she left Maxim, she'd leave Feral House. And neither of them would see her again. Which was the worst outcome of all.

She stood, and he was afraid she already meant to leave. "I actually came to find another glass of lemonade."

"I'll get it," Kara offered, starting to rise, but Faith waved her back.

Hawke rose and caught up with Faith just as she

reached the swinging door. She glanced up at him with shadowed eyes but no fear. If he'd seen fear, he'd have backed away.

"I'm sorry, Faith," he said quietly, as they entered the empty kitchen together. He could hear the sound of a television coming from Pink's apartments on the far side of the kitchen, accompanied by Xavier's voice and the soft ring of Pink's laughter.

Faith glanced at him uncertainly. "Sorry for what?" She reached for the refrigerator, turning her slender back to him.

His fingers itched to reach for her, to pull her back against him, to feel her in his arms. Instead, he leaned back against the island, crossing his arms over his chest.

"I'm sorry for provoking him."

She pulled the glass pitcher out of the fridge and set it on the counter, her brows drawn as if to argue, but he lifted his hand. "I did." His voice softened. "I told you how pretty you looked, right in front of him. His comment about your wardrobe made me angry. But I shouldn't have said anything. I knew how he'd react. I wanted him on the defensive with you. Unfortunately, I didn't foresee the chain of events that had him retaliating with the dig about my animal and you paying for it. He hurt you, and it was my fault."

She turned away from him, found a glass, and poured herself some lemonade. "Do you want any?" she asked, without glancing at him.

"No, thank you."

Without replying, she put the pitcher away, then took a sip of her drink, not letting him off the hook. Not accepting his apology. He couldn't read her at all right now, and it bothered him. He still worried . . . "Did I scare you when I went feral?"

Black lashes swept up as she met his gaze. For several seconds, she said nothing before finally answering. "A little. I can't imagine anyone not feeling a thrill of fear the first time they watch a man grow fangs and his eyes turn to those of an animal. Though I was surprised you didn't have bird eyes and talons. You looked like you might shift into a jungle cat."

"All shape-shifters look the same in that in-between state. Except the vipers. Once upon a time, the non-predatory animals would have been at a serious disadvantage otherwise."

She took another sip of the lemonade, her expression pensive. Smiley was nowhere in evidence.

"Tell me what you're thinking, Faith," he said softly.

Her surprised gaze snapped back up to meet his, and again, she took her time to answer, taking a long drink of the lemonade before setting the half-empty glass on the counter. "I don't want to be responsible for you and Maxim never getting along. I don't want to be the bone of contention between you."

Her words shamed him. "I don't want that either."

"He's going to be my mate, Hawke."

"I know." And he did, as much as it ate at him to admit it. Goddess, how had he screwed this up so badly? He'd never before overstepped with any of his brother's mates. Then again, he'd never felt anything more than affection or protectiveness for any of them. Only this one. And it was probably no coincidence that he was at his lowest right now. "Neither Maxim nor I are completely ourselves at the moment, Smiley. Once everything settles down, we'll be fine. All of us. I'll make sure of it."

Her mouth compressed, then slowly softened with a small, grateful smile that filled him with a pleasure far greater than such a small smile warranted. "Thank you, Hawke."

He returned her smile, his own no bigger than hers despite feeling the urge to grin. "You're welcome."

"I better get back to him before he comes looking for me."

With a rueful nod, he had to agree. Without another word, Faith turned and left.

Slowly, Hawke followed her back into the dining room, watching as she disappeared into the hallway before returning to the table and his friends. The food on his plate was cold, but he ate it anyway, promising himself he'd steer clear of Faith . . . of both her and Maxim. He had nothing to offer her but the anger of her soon-to-be-mate. And that was no gift at all.

Faith sat on the edge of the big leather sofa, staring at her fingernails as Maxim stood a few feet away, drilling Paenther with more questions. As she'd expected, he hadn't even noticed she'd slipped away for a few minutes.

"Why would you allow humans to live so close to Feral House?"

"We possess nearly fifteen acres of prime real estate," Paenther replied evenly.

"And force so many men and their mates to occupy a single tiny dwelling." After the reception, Maxim had changed out of his bloodstained tux and back into a white turtleneck and blazer.

Paenther growled low in his throat. "Feral House is not tiny."

Heavens, it had been like this all through dinner, too.

The questions, the condescension. It was as if he thought himself too good for these people, and he wanted them to know it. All he was doing was alienating them. Every last one of them. And she was so tired of it.

Maxim crossed his arms. "It's an easy solution to buy up the surrounding properties. The homes could be used for Ferals and their wives and a proper castle erected in place of this hovel."

Paenther snorted. "And if the humans aren't interested in selling, we simply cloud their minds and tell them to move? Or would you have us kill them and dispose of the bodies?"

Maxim smiled. "Either." Had he really not heard the acid in Paenther's tone?

Paenther rolled his eyes and looked away. "We don't work that way."

Maxim sneered. "It's no wonder the Mage are about to free the Daemons. The Chief of the Ferals has no backbone."

Faith winced.

Paenther growled, a sound that sent chills skittering down her spine. "*You go too far.*" As if in slow motion, his arms uncrossed, dropping to his sides, his muscles flexed as if preparing for attack, claws sprouted from his fingertips.

Her pulse began to pound as she watched fangs erupt from his gums and his eyes change to those of a jungle cat just as Hawke's and Lyon's had in the living room. She would never get used to this.

But this time Maxim mirrored the move. She watched in stunned fascination as he, too, went feral, the savagery of the look so at odds with his nice clothes and his painfully sophisticated demeanor.

Maxim snarled as he slipped off his blazer and tossed it aside. His stance shifted, his arms flaring out, his knees bending as if he prepared to attack an opponent.

They were just posturing. Surely they wouldn't . . .

Paenther launched himself at Maxim, missing her by inches, tearing a cry from her lungs. She scooted back onto the sofa, pulling her legs up and away from the tangle of limbs and claws at her feet as they went at one another like animals, tearing and slashing both clothes and flesh, sending blood flying everywhere.

Her pulse pounded, bile threatening to rise in her throat as she stared at the viciousness with horror.

She'd always imagined Feral House to be a fairy-tale castle. Now she knew better.

It was a madhouse.

Hawke had just dug his fork into another bite of meat when he heard the thud of bodies. And Faith's scream. He shot out of his seat and ran for the hallway.

"Hawke, wait!"

But Hawke ignored Lyon's order as he did his own promise to stay away from Faith. She was in trouble, and that trumped everything. With Lyon and Wulfe following close behind him, Hawke reached the media room to find a feral battle in full swing. Maxim and Paenther.

On the sofa, watching in horror, was Faith. Too close. An errant swipe of a clawed hand, and she'd be bleeding, too. As Lyon and Wulfe waded in to break up the fight, Hawke reached for Faith. One hand beneath her knees, the other at her back, he swept her off the sofa and into his arms and was slammed with such a feeling of rightness, such a furious, primitive possessiveness, he feared he might crush her in his savage need to hold her close. As he strode from the room, his hawk screeched in triumph, the wildness inside him urging him to keep going, to take her to his bedroom, bolt the door, and keep her for himself. Take her. Claim her.

Mine.

Her sweet scent enveloped him, the weight of her in his arms so perfect, so natural, it was as if he'd always known the feel of her and had been waiting his entire life for this moment. The need to bury his face in her blue-tipped hair, to nuzzle the curve of her neck, was almost beyond bearing. Would she taste as perfect as she felt? As she smelled? He shook with the need to know. With the need to touch her skin, to kiss her. His body throbbed with the desire to make them one, watching her eyes darken with rising passion as he drove into her.

Would she rise for him? Would she even want him?

Sanity returned in a rush, battling the wild need.

She wasn't his.

As he strode into the hallway, he knew it would be better if he set her down and walked away. If they remained casual friends and nothing more.

But his grip on her only tightened. Neither man nor beast wanted to let her go.

Chapter Four

Faith held on to Hawke's neck as he carried her from the room, the sound of breaking furniture, tearing fabric, and fierce growls following them. Her heart thudded in her ears, her body trembled. Yet her senses exploded at Hawke's closeness, at the feel of being in his arms. He smelled of soap and warm male, and something more, like a sunlit forest on a crisp autumn day, at once welcoming, calming, and thoroughly exhilarating. Heat flushed her skin, sinking into her blood with a startling arousal.

Her head spun with conflicting thoughts and warring emotions. Her arm tightened even as she fought off the sudden and overwhelming desire to tuck her face against his corded neck. To taste the skin there.

Heavens, Maxim would come after them both if he heard her thoughts.

In the hallway, Hawke stopped and turned his head, their faces so close she could feel his breath on her cheek. "Are you hurt?" His gaze captured hers, his eyes dark with concern yet utterly electric.

"Cease!" Lyon's voice boomed from the open entryway, directed at the combatants.

"No. Just . . . shaken." Soon Maxim would come looking for her. If he saw them like this . . . "You need to put me down, Hawke."

A low growl rumbled from Hawke's throat, and she started, half-afraid he was going feral again. But the look on his face had a savageness of an entirely different kind. He stared at her as if he wanted to devour her.

Her breath caught. Heat bloomed low inside her, pooling at her core.

"Hawke."

"I'm trying." His words surprised her even as his arms began to shake. The desire in his eyes flushed her skin and sent her pulse leaping.

She lifted her hand, needing to touch him, then clenched her fingers into a fist and pressed them against her thigh, knowing she'd only fan the flames of this inappropriate relationship if she did.

"Hawke, please put me down. Please don't let him find us like this."

He closed his eyes, the struggle clear in the hard set of his jaw as he leaned forward, burying his nose in her hair, inhaling long and deep. With a violent shudder, he let her legs slide to the floor, then released her, putting a small cushion of air between them even as he remained too close, crowding her between the wall and his long, hard body. He pressed his hands to the wall on either side of her, his head tipped forward, enclosing her in a cage of rioting sensation. Her heart pounded, her body liquefying, as she met his whitehot gaze.

"Your heart is thundering." He watched her carefully,

the softness of his words in direct counterpoint to the piercing intensity of his eyes. "Are you afraid of me?"

"No. I'm afraid of Maxim catching us like this. He's so jealous."

Hawke's face hardened, his mouth thinning. "Promise me something, Faith. If he *ever* hurts you, or threatens you, you'll come to me. Or to any of the other Ferals."

She stared at him, at the fierceness in his eyes. A chill went up her spine, but she shook her head. "He's not going to hurt me." He'd just squeezed her shoulder too tight was all.

"You don't know that. I don't trust him, Faith. And you barely know him." His gaze never left her face. Slowly, his expression softened even as his gaze gripped hers in a satin vise. "I don't want you to get hurt, Smiley," he said gently. "Not by him. Not by me."

The lump that formed in her throat at his words was sudden and unexpected. The peculiar sweetness of believing someone cared. As the seconds ticked by, as the sounds of fighting continued, their gazes held, deepening. Awareness flushed her body, rising to stain her cheeks.

The sound of falling bodies and wood splintering broke the spell. If Maxim saw them staring at one another like this . . .

Pressing her hand to her forehead, she slid out from between Hawke and the wall, putting a little distance between them before she turned back. "Does this happen a lot?"

"The jealousy?"

"The going feral. The fighting."

Hawke's mouth turned rueful. "All the time. You'll get used to it." He shrugged. "We're animals."

She stared at him. There was no judgment in that statement. No irony. "You really are, aren't you?"

"We put on a civilized front. But once we're marked, once the animal spirit claims us, the animal nature that used to be part of all Therians is triggered. We are not civilized men."

Lyon's voice barreled out of the room, thick with anger. "Training. In the basement. *Now*."

A moment later, Maxim strode out of the room, his fine clothes torn, that slicked-back hair sticking up at odd angles around his bloodied face. But whatever wounds he'd suffered had already healed, and in his eyes shone a hard light, a light that burst into a furious flame as his gaze caught sight of her with Hawke. It didn't matter that they stood three feet apart. She'd known it wouldn't.

Hawke straightened. Maxim growled, his face taking on that terrifying, fanged animal mask again. As he started toward them, Hawke stepped forward, angling himself so that she was behind him, then drew his own fangs and claws.

"Maxim, stop this!" she cried, but he ignored her.

Lyon, Wulfe, and Paenther erupted from the room. Wulfe started to go after Maxim, but Lyon stopped him with a single word. "Hold."

Maxim lunged, taking a swipe at Hawke, turning his cheek into bloody ribbons.

Faith gasped.

All hell broke loose for a second time as the two Ferals crashed together, but this time was so much worse. Because this time she knew she was the cause. This time Hawke was involved.

She pressed herself back against the wall, then scooted

past them to where Lyon and the others stood. *Doing nothing.* "Aren't you going to stop them?"

"No." Lyon watched the battling pair with keen interest.

She turned back to the horrific battle where the two Ferals tore at one another like wild animals, clawing, slashing, biting, snarling. Blood soaked their faces and what was left of their clothes as they crashed into the long, narrow hall table, breaking it in two. A large vase fell to the floor, shattering.

"He hasn't been able to fight like this without shifting since he got out of the spirit trap," Paenther murmured.

"Maybe he's finally coming out of it." Lyon's voice sounded equally surprised.

"Lyon . . ." Faith pleaded.

"Faith, it's better if you go upstairs. Kara?"

Kara stepped out from behind the men, giving her a sympathetic look. Faith hadn't even realized she was there. "Come on," Kara said, with a tilt of her head.

Faith hesitated, then joined Kara, deciding Lyon was probably right. If she left, Maxim might decide to come after her and leave Hawke alone. But as they started down the hall to the foyer together, the sounds of animal battle made her shiver, compelling her to turn and watch.

Kara didn't try to stop her.

"This is my fault," Faith muttered. She'd come with Maxim to help make this transition easier for him. Not harder.

"You're not at fault, Faith," Kara said, standing at her elbow. "You're just an excuse. They're always fighting, whether out of anger, frustration, or just for the fun of it. This is normal for shifters. As long as the Ferals remain in human form or this in-between place, they fight as equals and never really hurt one another. Not permanently. You'll get used to it."

Perhaps she'd get used to the fighting in general, but she would never get used to Maxim's attacking Hawke, or any of the men, out of jealousy over her. Maybe the best thing to do was leave, return to Warsaw for a time. At least until after Maxim was brought into his animal and had had a chance to settle in. And settle down. Then, perhaps, she'd come back to Feral House for a visit, to see if the man had truly changed. To discover whether they still had a chance together. Because it was becoming increasingly clear that this Maxim was not a man she wanted to be with, let alone spend an eternity with, connection or not.

She forced herself to watch the fight, traitorously proud that Hawke was tearing "her" man to shreds. Hawke was by far the better fighter. But she refused to remain the cause of such animosity. Her remaining at Feral House helped no one.

Resolutely, she turned away, meeting Kara's sympathetic gaze. "Okay, let's go."

Maxim might have started the fight, but Hawke was damn sure going to finish it. The rage was egging him on, the red haze floating at the edges of his vision, but for the first time since he'd escaped the spirit trap, he was holding it at bay. Furious, yes. Fighting, absolutely. But not out of control.

Hallelujah.

And he needed this fight. He needed to tear this asshole to shreds and had since the moment he'd heard Faith's cry of pain in the living room. He almost wished he weren't in control because in his true berserker form, he might just kill the prick. And he wanted to. Goddess, he wanted to.

"Cease!" Lyon's order rang through the hallway. He'd let them fight, but was now calling a stop to it.

Hawke started to pull back, but the wicked gleam in Maxim's eyes preceded a vicious swipe of claws across Hawke's chest, and the battle was on again.

"Maxim, stand down!" Lyon roared.

The newest Feral completely ignored his chief's command. The prick wasn't going to quit fighting until someone made him. And Hawke was more than happy to be that someone. He'd already assessed the man's weaknesses. Maxim was fairly strong though not as strong as Hawke. And he wasn't particularly quick. What's more, he was a dirty fighter. Two could play at that game.

Less than a minute later, Hawke found the opening he was looking for, swept Maxim's feet out from under him and body-slammed him to the ground, face-first, digging his knee into the small of the prick's back and his claws deep into his neck.

Maxim continued to growl and snarl, trying to buck Hawke off him, to no avail.

"Get back in your skin, Maxim!" Lyon ordered. "Retract your claws!"

Still, Maxim refused to bow to his chief's authority. Hawke leaned forward, and, in a vicious move he'd never before pulled on a brother, he shoved his claws deep into Maxim's side. The shifter roared with pain, trying to slash behind him with his own claws, and missing.

"How about I yank out your liver? Maybe that will

teach you some respect." Inside, he felt the control that had been holding back the red haze begin to slip away.

"Go, Wings." Wulfe's quiet cheer penetrated the bloodlust, reminding him he had an audience. An audience that included Faith. *Hell*. But when he looked up, he couldn't see her.

"Hawke."

At Lyon's prompt, he realized that Maxim's claws had finally retracted. He was losing it, and if he didn't move fast, he was going to do precisely what he'd threatened—yank out the bastard's liver, then rip his heart out so that he never touched Faith again. Killing the man she cared about.

He couldn't do that to her. He pushed off Maxim, backing away, but there was no retracting his fangs and claws. The red haze had begun to rush in, and he was losing control. As Maxim rose, Wulfe crossed to Hawke, gripping his shoulders, tethering him. After the sensory deprivation of the spirit trap, touch was often the one thing that calmed him.

"Ease down, Wings," Wulfe said. "Easy. Deep breaths."

"You were doing so well," Tighe muttered, suddenly beside him, too. Hawke hadn't seen him come up.

Beyond them, he watched as Lyon grabbed Maxim by the neck, slamming him against the wall. "I don't know who you were in your former life, and I don't care. Here you are one of my men. Nothing more. You will do as I order, *when* I order, or I will personally clear the way for your replacement. Is that understood?"

"Go, Roar," Wulfe said quietly.

For long seconds, Maxim just glared at his chief.

Lyon's grip tightened, his claws erupting and sinking deep until blood ran in streams down the bastard's neck, soaking his chest and the remnants of his shirt. *"Is that understood?"*

"Yes," Maxim spit, his tone and body language proclaiming otherwise.

Lyon growled low in his throat, a sound of warning Maxim would do well to heed. "It better be." Lyon released him and stepped back. "To the basement for training."

Maxim brushed past him. "My mate . . ."

Lyon grabbed him and slammed him once more against the wall. *"Now.* Paenther, Wulfe, Vhyper, you will accompany him. We'll bring him into his animal before sunrise. I don't want him out of the basement until it's time to walk out the door."

Maxim snarled. Paenther and Vhyper grabbed his arms and propelled him toward the basement door.

Maxim's humiliation helped calm the red haze. Slowly, Hawke pulled himself back from the brink. Wulfe gave his shoulder an encouraging squeeze, then left to join the others.

Lyon came over to Hawke. "You fought and didn't shift. You're getting better."

"I was. For a while."

"I'll send Kara to you tonight for more radiance. I don't want that forgotten in all the commotion." Their chief shook his head. "I don't know what I'm going to do with Maxim. I haven't gotten through to him. Not at all."

Tighe joined them. "Do we really want to bring him into his animal?"

Lyon sighed. "I've got to believe he'll get better. Half of you started out nearly as bad."

Hawke growled low in his throat. "If he hurts Faith again, I'll solve your problem for you."

"I can't imagine what she sees in him," Tighe said.

"She barely knows him." Hawke dragged a hand through his hair. "They only met yesterday. She says there was an instant connection. She knew he was the one."

"It happens," Lyon said.

"It does." Tighe shrugged. "I saw Delaney for the first time through the eyes of that clone. I thought she was already dead, and I *mourned*. I hadn't even met the woman, but on some level I knew she was meant to be mine."

The bird gave a cry of frustration deep in Hawke's mind, a frustration the man shared because for the first time in his life, he knew what they were talking about. He got it. Trouble was, the woman wasn't his.

Lyon gripped his shoulder, his gaze at once hard and sympathetic. "For your sake . . . for all our sakes . . . you need to give Maxim a wide berth for a while. And Faith. Especially Faith."

The hawk cried out in anger. Hawke bit down hard on the need to knock Lyon's hand away and tell him to go to hell. Because Lyon was right, dammit. He was right. Maxim wasn't going anywhere, and neither was Faith. They were about to become a constant and permanent part of his life. And one another's.

Faith was never going to be his.

And he had no choice but to live with it.

As Faith and Kara reached the foyer, they met Delaney and Olivia coming down the stairs.

"What's happening?" Olivia asked. The petite redhead frowned. "Did Hawke lose it again?"

"Surprisingly, no. This one was all Maxim." Kara winced, meeting Faith's gaze. "Sorry."

Faith smiled at her. "Don't be." She wasn't about to blame Kara for speaking the truth. "Maxim's been a first-class jerk since the moment we arrived at Feral House. I don't think he likes not being the one in charge."

Delaney grunted. "You can say that again."

Kara took Faith's hand. "Come on. We'll continue this discussion upstairs. Any objection to our using your room, Faith? The Radiant's room has become our unofficial hangout."

"No, not at all."

Kara looked at Delaney. "Where's Skye?"

"With the menagerie. I'll get her."

"Is Ariana around?"

Olivia grunted. "Does anyone ever know? Ariana," she called, as if the woman might be hiding nearby. "If you're here, we'd love for you to join us."

Faith frowned.

Olivia shot her a rueful smile. "Have you ever heard of the Ilinas?"

"No."

"We'll explain later. You have enough to deal with right now."

Faith wasn't about to argue.

Five minutes later, Faith was seated on the huge bed in the room Kara had loaned her. How different this bed was than the sagging, decrepit one in the little apartment in which she'd sat with Paulina and Maria just a few short days ago. She wondered how the girls were doing. Hopefully, Stanislov had kept his word and kept Maria away from the man who'd beaten her. If only she had some way to check on them.

Kara hopped onto the bed and motioned the others to follow. Skye slipped into the room, a small kitten curled in one arm.

"Where's the rest of the brood?" Delaney asked with a smile.

"Sleeping." Skye looked at Faith. "I like animals."

"An understatement," Delaney muttered.

"For wedding gifts, several of the Ferals gave me pets—a puppy, a kitten, a cockatiel." Skye's sweet smile told Faith precisely what their thoughtfulness had meant to her.

"Hawke gave you the cockatiel." Faith didn't even have to ask. She knew.

"Yes."

"What's the matter with Hawke?" Faith asked cautiously. "The way everyone's acting, I'm guessing he doesn't simply suffer from a hair-trigger temper."

"He doesn't," Kara assured her. "He's the kindest, most even-tempered one of the bunch. Or he was." Skye joined them on the bed, and they all settled into a cross-legged circle. "How much do you know about the Feral Warriors?"

"A lot less than I thought I did. Stories of brave heroes who fight in their animals."

"They are that," Kara assured her. "But they're more than that, too. They're men."

Olivia chuckled. "Goddess help us all."

Faith grinned. "I'd never seen a Feral Warrior until I met Maxim. I haven't lived around Therians since I was fifteen, since World War I scattered my enclave to the winds."

"World War I," Delaney murmured, giving her head a little shake. "Sorry, I'm human. Or I was. I'm still not used to this immortality stuff. Were you in Poland, then?"

Faith shook her head. "Belgium."

Delaney cocked her head at Faith. "Have you always lived in Europe?"

"Always."

"Amazing. Your English is flawless, with only the slightest trace of an accent. You even use American slang."

"I have a gift for languages." Faith shrugged. "It's as if I was born knowing them all."

"Wow. I'd love that as one of my superpowers."

"It's made moving around easy. Perhaps too easy." She looked at Kara, silently encouraging her to continue.

"Anyway, a couple of weeks ago, Hawke was caught in a spirit trap." Kara sighed, pressing her hands against her jeans-clad knees. "Let me start at the beginning. If you haven't been around Therians since you were fifteen, I don't know how much history you know."

Faith shook her head. Neither did she.

"Do you know why there are only nine shapeshifters?"

"Yes. Five thousand years ago, the Therians gave up their power to shift in order to defeat the Daemons, locking them in an enchanted blade. Only one of each animal retained the power of his animal."

"Right. Only there were a lot more than nine, originally. As recently as six hundred years ago, there were twenty-six Feral Warriors until seventeen were trapped in a spirit trap, which we now know to be of Daemon origin. The men were killed, and their animals never marked another."

Delaney took over the tale. "A few decades ago, a powerful Mage by the name of Inir was infected by dark spirit, wisps of Daemon consciousness left when the Daemons were ripped from this world. We think he was infected with the consciousness of the High Daemon, Satanan, himself—the most evil creature who has ever walked the Earth. Inir quickly rose to become leader of the Mage, and his sole purpose, now, is to free the Daemons from the blade. His problem is, only the Feral Warriors can do that, and the decision to free them has to be unanimous."

Faith frowned. "But that would never happen."

Kara's mouth grew hard. "No, it wouldn't, which has forced the Mage to get creative. They've tried stripping the souls of the warriors, they've tried creating clones. A few weeks ago, they created a wormhole into the spirit trap, hoping to end the existence of as many of the warriors as possible. Two fell in—Tighe and Hawke."

Faith's stomach fisted. "But they got out."

"Yes. Thanks to Kougar's mate, Ariana. But it was close. And they suffered."

"Hawke suffered worse than Tighe." Olivia's hand reached for Delaney's shoulder. "Delaney's bond with Tighe's animal is strong. Through her love for them both, she kept them tethered to her and to one another. Tighe is fine. Hawke wasn't so lucky."

Faith's fingers twined together in her lap. "What's the matter with him?"

Olivia's mouth tightened. "The spirit trap is designed

to separate man from animal. In Hawke's case, it nearly succeeded. Though still joined, man and animal are acting as two separate entities. Whenever Hawke shifts, the bird takes over completely, body and mind. He's also suffering bouts of uncontrollable rage. When he loses control, he shifts."

"He didn't tonight," Kara told them excitedly. "He fought Maxim just now. A full feral fight, and he didn't shift."

All their eyes widened.

"Excellent," Delaney breathed. Her gaze cut to Faith. "What happened?"

Faith grimaced. "Maxim had been fighting with some of the others in the television room. When he came out, he saw Hawke. With me."

Olivia frowned. "I thought you were with Maxim."

"I am. Hawke and I were just talking. When the other fight started, Hawke got me out of the way."

"Sounds like a Hawke thing to do." Delaney eyed her shrewdly. "But it's not that simple, is it? Hawke likes you. More than he should."

Four sets of curious gazes swiveled toward Faith.

"He's been . . . very nice to me."

Delaney grunted. "Hawke's nice to everyone. But I've never seen his eyes follow anyone like they follow you."

"Delaney," Kara admonished quietly.

"Sorry. I just call them like I see them."

"How long have you and Maxim been promised to one another?" Olivia asked.

Faith grimaced. This was the question she'd been dreading. "I just met him. Yesterday."

"*What?*"

"*Yesterday?*"

Faith groaned, burying her face in her hands. "It's all so weird!"

She felt a hand on her right knee, another on her left shoulder. "Tell us," Kara said softly.

Faith looked up, her gaze moving from one face to the next. If she'd seen only more curiosity, she might have held back, but in their faces she saw sympathy, too. And concern.

"The moment I met Maxim, I felt this powerful certainty that we belonged together. We both felt it."

Olivia sighed. "I know that feeling. I knew Jag and I were destined to mean something to one another the first time we met. Of course, I thought that something was *enemies*."

Skye nodded. "I fell for Paenther the first time I saw him." A pink hue rose in her cheeks. "Or maybe I just wanted him."

Delaney snorted. "God, Tighe was hot. He scared the crap out of me, but I couldn't stop wanting him. Still can't."

"You're talking about lust," Faith objected. "I'm talking about . . . a knowing. I can't even explain it. But not lust. I don't think of Maxim like that."

"You're kidding."

"Seriously?"

"Now that's just wrong."

Their voices pelted her with disbelief, all talking at once.

"Do you love him?" Kara asked softly. "Was it love at first sight?"

No, she realized. She didn't love him. It wasn't love at first sight, not at all. Just that strange conviction that they belonged together. But she couldn't tell the women that. Not when she and Maxim might still someday be mated. It wouldn't be fair to either of them. So she hedged. "I don't know, Kara. I don't know what I feel right now."

"What about Hawke?" Skye asked quietly.

And that was the real problem, wasn't it? "I like Hawke," she hedged, wanting to say more; but admitting the way Hawke made her feel was so unfair to Maxim. Still, she felt comfortable with these women as she hadn't with anyone in a long time. When was the last time she'd had real friends besides the girls she tried to help? "There's something about him."

"He has the kindest eyes, doesn't he?" Kara asked.

Delaney nodded. "And a great smile. It doesn't break often, but when it does, it makes your whole day."

"He's incredibly protective," Olivia added. "Of all of us."

Skye smiled. "If I weren't in love with Paenther, I think I'd be in love with Hawke."

"Me, too," Delaney and Olivia chimed in unison.

Kara smiled sympathetically. "It'll all work out."

Faith sighed. "It's going to work out better without me here for a while. I think I'm going home."

Kara made a sound of dismay. "You just got here."

"I know. But it was monumentally foolish to follow a man I'd just met halfway around the world, pull or no pull."

Kara took her hand. "But if he's really meant to be your mate . . ."

"Then he'll wait for me. When I first met him, I felt this kick of recognition. But maybe that's all it was. Maybe I recognized him from somewhere and mistook it for something more. And what I feel for Hawke is just

. . . well . . . he's a very attractive man. You all know how rare it is to find a true mate."

Olivia sighed. "I'm afraid you're probably right, Faith, as much as I hate to admit it. Half the women on the planet would lust for our Feral Warriors if they got anywhere near them. The other half are too young, too old, or into other women."

"Will Maxim let you go?" Delaney asked.

"No, not happily."

"We don't want you to go." A hard light entered Delaney's eyes. "But he won't keep you here against your will. We won't let him."

Faith felt tears prick her eyes as she looked at the fierce, protective faces that surrounded her. She'd been watching over others for so long, yet she could barely remember the last time anyone had watched over her.

"Thank you."

Olivia gripped her knee. "Faith, don't be too quick to move on this. Give both of them a little more time, please? They all say that newly marked Ferals can be a pain in the ass. Once Maxim shifts, he might surprise you. And you said yourself, you've only known him a day. Have you even been . . . this is none of my business . . . intimate?"

Faith's cheeks heated. "No. Not even a kiss."

"There you have it." She patted Faith's knee and straightened. "You don't know what's between you, yet. He's probably too screwed up with the raging testosterone new Ferals are known for to be thinking straight. Give him a little time." She shrugged, a small, knowing smile lifting her mouth. "Speaking as the mate of a former asshole, sometimes they're worth all the trouble."

"There's another consideration," Delaney said. "Hawke's seen something in you that he responds to. Maybe it's just sexual attraction, maybe it's more than that. But you made him smile and laugh for the first time since he got out of that trap. Tighe commented on it. Taking that away from him right now might do him more harm than good."

Faith shook her head, her heart contracting. "I can't be what Hawke wants me to be."

"You don't have to be anything to him," Delaney assured her. "But having you around has been good for him. It's gotten his juices flowing again."

Olivia snorted. "His *juices*?"

Skye and Kara giggled. Faith laughed.

Delaney hooted. "God, you have a gutter mind, Olivia. I didn't mean literally." Still grinning, Delaney turned back to Faith. "All I was *trying* to say is, don't take all this too seriously, or too personally. If there is one thing shape-shifters love to do, it's draw claws and fight. They'll take any excuse, and a woman is the most obvious of all. Males have been fighting over females since the dawn of time."

"It'll work out, Faith," Kara said earnestly. "You'll see."

"And if for some reason it doesn't," Delaney added, "you've got us. We'll help you in any way we can."

Faith's eyes burned, her chest swelling with a sharp longing to stay, to be a part of this rare friendship. "Thank you," she said softly.

"How about some wine?" Kara asked, hopping off the bed. "I've got a new red I'm dying to try. Sorry, Delaney."

"No problem. I brought fudge. Enough to share."

Delaney grinned at Faith. "I'm pregnant. No one thinks a little wine can hurt a Therian baby, but I'm not taking any chances. I'd rather have the fudge anyway."

When the glasses were filled, and a plate of fudge sat on the bed in the middle of the circle, Skye lifted her glass. "To friendship."

"To sisterhood," Kara added.

Delaney lifted her water bottle. "To the best friends I've ever had."

Olivia nodded. "Me, too. And to Faith. May she find happiness, as we have." Her gaze met Faith's. "Selfishly, I hope you find that happiness in Feral House. You fit in nicely." Her smile was warm and genuine and bloomed inside Faith.

As she sipped her wine, as the discussion turned to the celebration feast being planned for after Maxim's first shift, the longing to stay sharpened until it was an ache inside her. But Hawke's face rose in her mind, the way he'd looked at her in the hallway, the fierce need in his eyes. The tenderness. And she feared there was no good solution but one. She had to leave. For all three of their sakes.

Maybe after he'd settled down, Maxim would seek her out again. Maybe they'd have another chance. By then, Hawke might have found a mate of his own. The rivalry would be over. Perhaps then she could return and be part of this sisterhood once more.

And perhaps some things were simply never meant to be.

Chapter Five

An hour before sunrise, Hawke stood in the foyer among his brothers. Like the others, he'd stripped to the waist and left his boots in his room. To a man, each wore nothing but a pair of pants·or jeans and the golden armband adorned with the head of his animal.

This morning, Maxim would get his own armband during the ritual—*the Renascence*—that would bring him into his animal. The band would appear during his first shift, allowing him to channel the Earth's energies, to become a full-fledged Feral Warrior.

Bully for Maxim, Hawke thought sourly.

The only good news was that the Ferals would once more be nine.

They milled about, waiting for Tighe.

"Tighe! Get your ass down here," Jag shouted, ever the diplomat.

Kara, the only one of the women who would accompany them, stood beside Lyon in a flowing blue ritual gown and a pink hoodie zipped against the morning chill. The other women sat on the stairs, looking sleepy. Olivia and Skye.

And Faith.

Hawke tried to ignore her, knowing any attention he paid her was a mistake. But he was helpless to keep his eyes turned away. Dressed much as she had been yesterday, in a pair of jeans white from wear, a hole in one knee the size of his fist, and a sweater with sleeves that fell past her fingertips, she looked young. There was a strength about her, a resiliency he'd sensed from the start. But also a vulnerability that tugged at him. A hint of sadness that even her quicksilver smiles couldn't entirely hide.

Olivia said something he didn't catch, and Faith grinned, igniting that warm, tight place in his chest that he hadn't known existed until she came along.

Lyon stepped into his line of sight, blocking her from him. But when Hawke would have moved, Lyon caught his gaze, his own pointed.

"Right," Hawke muttered. *Quit staring.*

He glanced toward the door where Maxim stood boring a hole in Hawke's chest with his glare, his mouth set in a hard, angry line. Obviously, Lyon wasn't the only one who'd noticed the direction of Hawke's gaze. Retribution gleamed in Maxim's eyes, and Hawke welcomed the battle. He only hoped he could keep from shifting long enough to beat Maxim's ass a second time.

But there would be no fight in the foyer. Paenther and Wulfe had been glued to Maxim's side since they came upstairs a few minutes ago, all three dripping with sweat from training in the basement all night. But the fight was coming, Hawke had no doubt. He wouldn't put it past Maxim to attack him in his fox even though attacking one another in their full animal forms was strictly forbidden. Hell, if any one of them tried to strike at him when he was a bird, he was a dead shifter. But Maxim had proved over and over again he couldn't be trusted, and Hawke was ready for anything. In his pockets, he carried switchblades. Strapped to his calves, he wore a pair of hunting knives. Fighting might not be his hawk's strength, but in his human body he was very, *very* good with his fists. And his knives.

Without warning, jagged bolts of lightning ripped apart his skull. He forced himself to breathe through the miserable pain, counting the seconds . . . three, four . . . six, seven. The pain was getting worse. Damn bird. He couldn't decide which was a bigger pain in his ass, the one in his head or the one who was about to shift into a fox.

Finally, Tighe appeared at the top of the opposite stair from where the women sat and quickly made his way down.

"Sorry. Delaney wanted to come down to see us off, but she was asleep on her feet. I put her back in bed."

Jag snorted. "And joined her?"

Tighe smiled, but there was nothing carnal about it. Nothing in his expression but deep, abiding love for his mate. "She falls asleep more easily in my arms." After the hell Tighe had suffered in the spirit trap, and the equal hell Delaney must have suffered thinking she was about to lose him, there wasn't a man among them who begrudged the pair the few extra minutes. Except, perhaps, Maxim.

Lyon clapped his hands together. "Let's go."

Olivia rose and descended the dozen steps as Jag met her at the base of the stairs and gave her a quick, thorough kiss. From her perch beside Faith, Skye blew Paenther a kiss. He returned it with a look that promised far more when he returned. Then he grabbed Maxim's shoulder and turned him to the now-open door.

Hawke glanced back at Faith and found her gaze locked on him. But no smile winged its way down to him. The look in her eyes was one of regret. Then she looked away, dismissing him. Stabbing him through the heart.

"Hawke."

At Lyon's prodding, he nodded and turned away with a sigh.

"Olivia's in charge until we return," Lyon said to no one in particular. The women, except for Kara, would remain at Feral House. They couldn't be part of the ritual, nor could they get close enough to watch since it needed to be performed beneath the curtain of a mystic circle where no human could see or hear what went on. Besides, the women were needed to guard Feral House in the Ferals' absence. Delaney might need sleep, but she was ex-FBI. If they came under attack, she'd be in the front of the fighting, he had no doubt. Olivia was a warrior by trade, a leader of the Therian guard, and even Skye had proved herself capable of pulling strong attack energies, when needed. And if it came to it, if they could communicate their need, Ariana commanded an entire army of Ilina mist warriors. Left to the women, Feral House was in excellent hands.

Lyon and Kara stepped through the open front door. Hawke followed, closing it behind him, then joined the others, who waited in the drive. An hour before sunrise, they were now safe from the nocturnal draden, who always disappeared about this time. Shoulder to shoulder the nine and Kara strode across the lawn and into the woods beyond, the breeze blowing damp fingers through Hawke's short hair. This would be only his second Renascence—third if he counted his own. The last had been for the young, now-deceased, Foxx four years ago. Once again it was a fox shifter he would watch come into his animal for the first time.

They crossed a couple of residential streets, moving silently between mansions tucked into the thick woods, finally reaching the rocks high above the Potomac River. One by one, the nine shifters climbed down to the wide, flat goddess stone, Lyon holding tight to Kara's hand.

Golden armbands gleaming in the light of a half-moon, Lyon and Kougar raised the mystic circle that would enclose them, both in sight and sound, from the outside world and any human who might wander by. Magic in place, Lyon called for the warriors to take their spots as he led Kara to the center of the stone and gave her a brief, gentle kiss on her mouth. Kougar led them as they raised their voices in chant, repeating the ancient words, bringing back memories of Hawke's own Renascence.

What a hellacious time that had been for him. He'd had to watch a Radiant who wasn't his mother call the radiance for him to be brought into his father's animal. The honor and satisfaction of becoming one of the men he'd admired from the time he was old enough to understand that all men weren't Feral Warriors had slammed up against the bitter grief of his parents' recent deaths. It was a night he'd never forget, and one he'd never want to go through again.

Kougar slashed the ritual knife across his bare chest, slapped his palm against the bleeding cut, and curled his fingers into a fist around the blood. Then he handed the knife to Lyon. One after another, each warrior followed, slashing his own chest, fisting his hand around his blood. When it was his turn, Hawke carved a thin line into his flesh, clamping his jaw against the searing pain, breathing through his nose as he slapped his free hand to the warm stickiness before the wound could heal. By the time he handed the knife to Vhyper, the pain had fled.

When Vhyper was done, he handed the blade to Maxim. "Your turn."

Maxim met Hawke's gaze, a gleam in his eye that had Hawke wondering if the new Feral meant to throw the knife at him. Instead, he cut himself, as he was supposed to, without hesitation.

Kougar shoved his fist into the air, and the others followed.

"Kara," Lyon said softly.

Kara unzipped the hoodie and tossed it aside, then lifted her arms to the sky, drawing the Radiance from the Earth, and began to glow with the light of the sun.

Lyon turned to Maxim. "Remain where you are. If you touch her without an armband, the radiance will kill you."

Maxim dipped his head but continued to stare at Kara, clearly intrigued by the glowing woman. Hawke supposed such a sight would fascinate anyone who hadn't grown up with it.

The eight stepped forward, closing around Kara. As Hawke's fingers curled around one slender wrist, power surged into him, a rush of blessed energy. Around him, the others gripped one of Kara's hands, her other wrist, or knelt to grasp one of her ankles. Lyon stood behind her, stroking her slender throat before pressing his palm tenderly against the side of her neck.

Kougar released Kara first and turned to Maxim. One by one, the others followed, Hawke bringing up the rear. Kougar pressed his bloodied palm on top of Maxim's fist. Lyon pressed his atop Kougar's, Paenther's atop Lyon's. One by one they added their blood until only Hawke remained. As he pressed his palm to the top of the pile, his gaze met Maxim's. Hatred arced between them, a live wire of threat shooting both ways. Deep inside, his hawk gave a cry of anger, a cry not directed at him. The bird didn't like the new feral any better than the man did. For once, they were in complete agreement.

Kougar began to chant, switching to English as the others joined in. "Spirits rise and join. Empower the beasts beneath this moon. Goddess, reveal your warrior!"

Thunder rumbled in the cloudless sky, the sound of powerful magic. Beneath Hawke's feet, the rock trembled as if in anticipation of this first shifting of the newest fox.

Maxim threw his head back, a look of bliss racing over his features as he disappeared in a flash of colorful, sparkling lights, shifting into his animal.

Hawke froze, blinking with shock. The huge, strange creature standing within their circle was no fox.

"Holy shit," Jag breathed.

Hawke's jaw dropped as he stared at the cat in their midst. His pulse began to hammer. The animal was nearly the size of an African lion, though far thicker, probably weighing close to twice what Lyon would in his animal form. Its legs were stocky and muscular, its tail bobbed. And from its mouth hung huge twin fangs like seven-inch blades.

The men exchanged shocked glances, uncertain what had just happened.

"A saber-toothed cat," Hawke said out loud, his voice rough with awe and confusion.

"One of *the seventeen*." Kougar's voice was triumphant. "Ariana must have accidentally freed the animal spirit when she pulled us out."

Understanding arced across the group like a jolt of electricity. Raw excitement filled the mystic circle as the full import crashed over the warriors.

The great cat, its natural cousin long extinct, swung his massive head around until he was staring straight into Hawke's face, threat in his eyes. Hawke pulled his knives. The red haze began to lick at the edges of his vision and rise, showing no sign of stopping. Whatever force sometimes seemed to help him keep it at bay was absent.

Lyon stepped between them, his voice deadly calm. "Shift back, Maxim."

For once, Maxim did as he was told. As Hawke fought back the anger, the cat began to shimmer. Once more, Maxim stood, fully clothed, a look of pure triumph on his arrogant face as he turned to the others.

"Not a fox," he said simply, then threw back his head and laughed.

"Praise the goddess," Jag said. "Maybe this is just the beginning. Maybe they all escaped that trap."

Kougar shook his head. "It's too soon to know." But his eyes gleamed like diamonds.

Around the circle, his brothers' faces shone with joy, relief, wreathed in grin after grin. Hawke got it—this was the break they'd needed, the miracle they'd been waiting for—but it still annoyed the hell out of him that Maxim was the center . . . the *cause* . . . of such rejoicing.

Beside him, Tighe laughed out loud. "This almost makes it worth being caught in that hell." His gaze met Hawke's, apology, then concern, tightening his features. He reached for him, his hand going to Hawke's shoulder. "You okay?"

The physical contact helped Hawke pull it together. "Yes."

Tighe nodded, but he kept his hand on Hawke's shoulder, his smile gone.

Hawke wondered if they shared the same thought, that the most physically powerful animal belonged to the one among them they couldn't trust.

Kougar's voice rang out. "Henceforth, you will be known among us as Catt."

"How about Tooth?" Jag asked.

Jubilation had shot the ritualistic atmosphere to hell, and no one seemed to care.

Wulfe grinned. "Fang."

Vhyper snorted. "Bob."

Jag shot the snake a comically disbelieving look. *"Bob?"*

"For his bobbed tail."

Jag groaned, then snorted. "Glad to have you back, Snake Man, oddball sense of humor and all."

"You're one to talk." But even Vhyper's tone held laughter.

Lyon eyed Vhyper with a nod of satisfaction, then pulled Kara back against him as the circle dissolved into backslaps and handshakes, euphoric roars echoing over the rocks. They were nine again, and once the new fox showed up, ten. Maybe more. Maybe, ultimately, twenty-six.

It was a day for celebration. And wary caution. His rival had just gained a strength Hawke could never hope to match.

The men and Kara returned to Feral House to the smell of roasting meat and baking bread, and glasses brimming with bubbly champagne or whiskey. Paenther had called Feral House the moment the ceremony was over to share the news, and they'd returned to a full-fledged celebration.

Still in the foyer, Tighe thrust his glass into the air. "To the full return of the seventeen. May we be twenty-six once more!"

A loud cheer erupted as the Ferals and their mates all joined in.

Maxim stood at the center, thrusting his glass into the air. "To the sabertooth!" With his free hand, he pulled Faith against his side, nuzzling her neck, making her squirm. His gaze cut to Hawke, a malicious gleam in his eye.

"Ignore him," Tighe said quietly beside him.

Hawke forced himself to look away, throwing back half his whiskey. He couldn't let Maxim get to him. He had too much to lose.

"Bringing him into his animal doesn't seem to have improved his manners," Delaney said under her breath. "If anything, he's even more obnoxious."

The thought of spending a lifetime with this prick, watching him paw Faith . . . Dammit, this was his own fault. If he'd hidden his interest in her, as he should have, Maxim wouldn't be trying to provoke him.

Delaney moved away to grab the stack of T-shirts on the hall table, all black, all XXL. As she handed them out, the men set down their glasses and pulled them over their heads. They might be half animals, but they ate their meals with shirts on. And the celebration feast would soon be served.

"Why are Feral celebrations so . . . *tame?*" Maxim demanded, taking the T-shirt Delaney offered with a look of distaste. "We need music, revelry!"

Hawke forced himself to look elsewhere because if he looked at Maxim, he'd just see Faith.

"In the old days, the celebrations were anything but tame." Kougar's quiet words silenced the group as nothing else would have short of a sharp command by Lyon.

"The old days?" Maxim asked.

Kougar nodded. "Five thousand years ago. Before the Sacrifice. Though I can only speak for the cougar clan." A hush descended as all heads swiveled toward him, every expression intrigued. Only very recently had Kougar begun to talk of the past.

"In those days, when all Therians were shifters, a celebration began with a friendly, if bloody fight, generally in our cats, males and females alike. A fight that quickly turned sexual in nature."

"An orgy?" Jag asked with relish.

A small smile lifted the corner of Kougar's mouth. "Unlike any orgy you've ever imagined. Several dozen cougar shifters copulating in both flesh and fur, shifting back and forth with abandon. The lights and energy from the shifting fueled the sexual excitement, building until we were crazed with lust."

With all eyes focused on Kougar, Hawke risked a glance at Faith. Their gazes collided, his pulse leaping then plummeting at the look of unhappiness in her eyes. Resolutely, she turned back to Kougar. Hawke could feel her discomfort, could see the tense lines of her body and knew she was frustrated by this war that wouldn't end and embarrassed by Maxim's public displays of . . . ownership. Not another woman in the room squirmed away from her mate's touches. Even Jag treated his mate with respect and tenderness. In a room full of celebration, Faith wasn't happy. And he wanted her to be. Fiercely.

"When the majority were sated," Kougar continued, "we'd take off on a wild hunt of real game, killing and feasting in our cats."

If he pretended he no longer had any interest in her, would she turn to her intended mate and find true happiness there, as she'd believed she would? He had to give her that chance. He had to pretend well enough that he started to believe it himself.

"We were much closer to our animal natures back then, almost entirely lacking in human inhibition."

All were silent for several moments, absorbing Kougar's words and the vision he'd painted of a far-more-primitive time.

"It might be time to open a few windows," Vhyper drawled, earning a few chuckles. "They're starting to steam."

"Food's up, Dudes!" Xavier called from the hallway leading back to the kitchen and dining room. The young human had been caught by the Daemons in the same battle that had sent Hawke and Tighe into the spirit trap. Now he'd been snared in a different kind of trap, unable to leave Feral House until or unless they found a way to steal his memories of that night as they had the two women who'd survived along with him. The problem was that Xavier was blind. And memories could only be stolen through the eyes.

Beside him, Wulfe muttered, "Dudes," with a resigned shake of his head. "Always *Dudes*."

"Wulfe?" Xavier called.

Wulfe grimaced guiltily. "Yeah, X-man? I'm right here."

"Any news of Nat?"

"Who's Nat?" Hawke asked.

Wulfe glanced at him, a funny look in his eyes. A hint of soft longing that had Hawke's curiosity spiking. "Natalie. Xavier's sister. She was one of the ones the Mage had staked around the vortex you fell into."

"Shit."

"She's fine. Now. It took us about a week to clear her memories and free her." Wulfe turned to Xavier. "I haven't heard anything in a few days, X. That's good news though. If there were a problem, the reporters would be all over it."

Xavier's face fell drastically. Being blind, he had no concept of hiding his emotions. "Let me know if you hear anything, will you, Dude?"

Wulfe rolled his eyes, meeting Hawke's gaze. "I will, Dude."

They filed into the dining room, gathering around the huge table. Though he usually sat in the middle, Hawke joined Lyon and Kara at the opposite end from where Maxim seated Faith, on the same side, so he wouldn't even be tempted to look at her. Part of him wanted to avoid the meal altogether, but that was the worst thing to do if he wanted to start making everyone believe he didn't care.

As the dishes were served, conversation remained on saber-toothed cats and speculation that others marked by the seventeen lost animal spirits might start coming forward. Maxim's voice plucked at Hawke's nerves all too often. Faith's, he never heard.

The interminable meal was nearly over when Lyon's cell phone rang. He excused himself and took the call in the hallway. A few minutes later, he returned, beaming, or as close to beaming as Hawke had ever seen the Chief of the Ferals. At least, when his gaze wasn't wholly captured by his mate.

"Another new Feral?" Tighe asked, his voice rich with anticipation.

Lyon smiled. "Two."

"Hot damn!" Jag crowed.

"That was Kieran, a Therian Guard stationed near Dublin."

"I know him," Olivia exclaimed. "Oh my god, Kieran a Feral Warrior? The entire female population of the planet is about to get heart palpitations."

"As if they don't already whenever they look at one of our guys," Delaney said.

Olivia lowered her voice to a bare whisper, but Feral hearing being what it was, Hawke heard, as did every male at the table. "You haven't seen Kieran. He's . . . *golden*. Utterly beautiful and an Irish charmer of the first order." She laughed. "He's a doll, but . . ."

"But you only have eyes for me." Jag hooked his arm

around his mate's neck and pulled her close, pressing a kiss to her temple.

The look Olivia turned on her mate started out teasing, then melted into one of such certainty, such devotion, it made Hawke's chest ache a little.

"I will only *ever* have eyes for you." She kissed him back on the mouth, then pulled away slowly. "But Kieran's a good friend, an excellent fighter, and, despite his unnatural beauty, doesn't take himself too seriously. I think he'll fit in well here."

Several pairs of eyes cut toward Maxim as if all shared the same thought . . . *unlike their new sabertooth.*

"Good," Lyon said. "Kieran just realized he'd been marked though he doesn't know when it happened. His feral marks aren't where he could see them. He got into a fight with another guard just now, and they both went feral. Shocked them both and everyone watching."

"Who's the other one?" Olivia asked.

"He didn't say. He wanted to know if such a thing were possible, and I told him to get both their asses on the next flight. I'll have to notify the heads of the Therian councils to spread the word." A satisfied smile lifted his mouth. "It seems that at least some of the seventeen have returned. At long last."

"I can't wait to see these new animals," Kara murmured.

Olivia made a sound of agreement. "I want to know when we're going to see our sabertooth."

"Now." Maxim—Hawke refused to give him the honor of his Feral name—rose from his seat with an exuberant burst that had Hawke's fingers flexing around the handle of his fork.

"In the gym," Lyon ordered, as Maxim stepped back a few feet from the table.

But the newest Feral had yet to learn to follow the dictates of their chief. Tipping his head back, he closed his eyes and began to sparkle with a thousand colored lights. As the large saber-toothed cat materialized, most at the table rose, those closest moving away, those on the other side of the table coming around for a better look until the great sabertooth stood at the center of a large semicircle.

Hawke glanced at Faith. She was staring at the cat with an awe that pricked at his nerves. As if the creature were the most fascinating thing she'd ever seen. And he probably was.

Maxim lifted that massive head and gave a roar unlike any of the other cats—a deep, rumbling staccato, almost like a series of barks. A sound not heard in six hundred years. And not heard in nature in twelve thousand. With his jaw opened fully, he was a sight to behold, those fangs gleaming in the light from the dining-room chandelier.

Vhyper grunted. "Fairfax County Animal Control is going to shit in their collective pants if they ever get an eyeful of this one."

Closing his mouth again, fangs hanging down nearly to his chin, the great cat began to pace in a circle, closer and closer to the other Ferals and their mates, swinging his head from side to side as if he longed to snatch one for dessert.

The mated males all angled themselves between their women and the huge predatory creature. Across the room, Faith backed up against the far wall. Alone.

Everything inside Hawke demanded he go to her, protect her as the other males protected their women. He took a step, then paused as he felt Lyon's hand on his arm.

"Don't," Lyon said quietly.

But every muscle in Hawke's body tensed with the need to protect.

Mine.

No. She wasn't. He forced himself to stand down as that great head swung toward Faith, as the great cat slowly stalked her.

Lyon's grip on his arm tightened. "He won't hurt her." Not the woman he intended to make his mate.

The problem was, deep in his gut, Hawke didn't believe it. His own animal screeched in his head, demanding he act, but he forced himself to remain rooted, watching as the cat bumped his head against Faith's hip playfully, if roughly, making her stumble a couple of steps sideways.

Faith laughed, her hands pressing against the cat's large forehead. But Hawke could sense the primitive fear in her warring with the fascination, and he suspected Maxim could, too. And like any bully, Maxim enjoyed that fear.

The cat swung his head down and around, butting against Faith from the other side. She was prepared this time and barely moved.

"Maxim, enough." The note of pleading in her voice cut at Hawke.

But the cat wasn't through with her. He nestled his nose between her legs, dipping his head and raising it again, forcing her to spread her legs.

Faith's cheeks flamed as she pressed at the great head, unable to dislodge it. "Maxim, stop." Her growing anger only seemed to encourage the cat more.

Hawke's muscles tensed, the anger that sparked inside him for once fully his own. The bastard enjoyed her discomfort. Enjoyed embarrassing her in front of others. Hawke growled, low, a sound his bird would never make. A sound that belonged to the feral male alone.

"Lyon," Kara pleaded softly beside her mate.

"Catt, enough," Lyon barked.

But Maxim ignored him, as he had all along. Instead, he leaped up, his massive paws landing on the wall on either side of Faith's head, his enormous mouth wrenching open. Faith lifted her hands as if to ward off the attack, heart-thundering fear in every line of her body.

"Catt!" Lyon roared. "Enough!"

The anger within Hawke ignited in a wild rage—a rage that demanded he tear that cat's head from his body. His fangs sprouted, his claws erupting. Though he struggled to fight for control, too great a part of him wanted this, wanted to attack the bastard, to protect Faith.

When the red haze engulfed him, for once he dove into the storm.

Chapter Six

Faith pressed back against the wall, heart thundering in her ears, her legs shaking as the hot breath of the terrifying beast bathed her face, his mammoth canines inches from her collarbones. He was scaring her, dammit. Humiliating her in front of the Feral Warriors and their mates. In front of Hawke.

"Maxim, *stop*."

She forced herself to look into those yellow eyes, knowing the man was in there. And what she saw turned her fear to anger. Laughter. He clearly loved his power over her, loved that she couldn't do a thing to stop him.

The last of her doubts disappeared. Maxim was not, and had probably never been, the man she thought he was. And she wasn't staying with him another day.

She grabbed his teeth like the bars of a jail cell. "Get them out of my face before I rip them off!"

"Hawke!" Lyon's voice rang out.

Faith released those saberlike teeth just as the awful

cat was wrenched away from her by a snarling Feral Warrior with fangs dripping from his man's mouth, daggerlike claws sunk deep into Maxim's fur.

Hawke.

Vhyper leaped into the fray, combining his body weight with Hawke's to take down the great beast. Wulfe, shifting into a wolf midleap, landed on the big cat, holding him down and snarling into his face as Hawke lifted a wicked-looking knife and pressed the tip between the cat's eyes.

"Hawke!" Lyon roared.

Without moving the blade, Hawke lifted his head, breathing hard, as if struggling for control. Vhyper, Faith noticed, made no move to take the blade from him.

Hawke looked down into the cat's eyes, snarling, "Shift back or die."

Faith's heart thudded against her ribs, anger burning inside her until unshed tears stung her eyes. *Dammit, Maxim!* Pushing away from the wall, she strode through the dining room and out the door, heading for the stairs.

"Faith, wait!" Kara's soft voice called to her from behind.

Faith stopped and turned.

"I'm sorry," Kara said, catching up, the genuine sympathy in her expression undoing Faith. "He's not a nice man."

"No, he's not. Kara . . ." The tears were beginning to fall, and she swiped at them impatiently. "I'm leaving. This isn't going to work."

Kara's face fell. "I was afraid you were going to say that. As much as I hate for you to go, I'd do the same in your shoes. Exactly the same."

"The trouble is . . ."

"You need money for a flight home. And a way to the airport."

Faith nodded, Kara's kindness and understanding like a tight band around her chest. "I'll pay you back, I promise."

Kara opened her arms, and Faith fell into them, accepting the hug Kara offered. *Needing* it as tears began a steady slide down her cheeks. In so many ways, she wished she'd never met Maxim, wished she'd never agreed to come with him to Feral House. She hadn't known what she was missing. And now she did. Here she'd glimpsed sweet friendship and precious sisterhood. And the promise of laughter and tender passion with a powerful, protective male. Just not the one she'd come with. She'd gotten a taste of what it would be like to have a family again after so many years of being alone.

And she had to walk away from it all.

"Don't worry about the money. Trust me, it's not an issue." Kara pulled back. "Go pack your bag. I'll find a volunteer to drive you to the airport and meet you in the foyer."

Faith nodded. "Thank you." As she turned to the stairs, a coldness swept over her, the promise of loneliness in its bleakest form. Yes, she was anxious to get back to Paulina and Maria, to try to help them find better lives, but six months from now, she'd be moving again. Another city. Another rough street half a world away from the warmth and friendship she'd found at Feral House.

Her future lay before her like the tundra in winter—frozen, colorless. Empty.

*   *   *

Fury rode Hawke. His hand shook from the battle raging inside him—the need to drive the point of his knife deep into the sabertooth's brain warring with the certain knowledge he mustn't. The wildness inside him demanded this creature die, but the man would never kill a brother, no matter how much he hated him. Nor would he hurt Faith like that, stealing the man she believed was meant to be her mate.

The red haze pressed hard around the edges of his vision, fighting to rush in and steal his control, steal him from himself. Out of the corner of his eye, he saw Faith leave the dining room, saw Kara follow her out.

"Catt, shift!" Lyon commanded.

The hawk's anger poured over him, the red haze rushing in.

From a distance, he felt himself lift the knife, gripping the handle with both hands in preparation for plunging it down. Someone knocked him back. Shouting. Fighting. A berserker's rage. The laughter of the one he hated.

Then he knew no more.

"Hawke! Ease down!"

"*Shit.*"

"Where's he going?"

"Someone open the front door!"

As the male voices rang through the house, Faith paused halfway up the stairs and looked back.

"He's shifted," Kara said unhappily and ran the few feet to the massive front door, wrenching it open wide.

A moment later, a bird soared into the foyer, a huge, beautiful, red-tailed hawk. But instead of flying out the door as Faith expected, he made a spiraling turn through the foyer, following the curve of the opposite stair, then around toward where she stood frozen. Mesmerized.

She backed up against the wall, uncertain of his wingspan, but he didn't pass her by. Instead, he landed on the rail a few feet in front of her. Faith swallowed as the great raptor stared at her with unblinking eyes.

"Hawke?" she asked uncertainly. "Are you in there?" In Maxim's eyes, she'd seen the man, but she saw no emotion in this bird's eyes. Certainly no human emotion.

The great bird let out a loud *kkkeeeeer* and took off, soaring down through the foyer and, on a perfect downward sweep of wings, out the front door.

Kara slowly closed the door behind him.

Faith swallowed. "How long will he be gone?"

"I don't know. Each time, he's gone longer."

Several of the Ferals strode into the foyer—Lyon, Tighe. Maxim.

"He's gone?" Lyon asked Kara.

The Radiant nodded, and two of the men sighed.

Maxim showed a modicum of restraint and said nothing. For once. He looked up at her, and she met his gaze. "I'm going back to Warsaw." She wanted them all to hear, in case Maxim tried to stand in her way.

His jaw tensed, his fists drawing closed, then relaxing again as a look of chagrin crossed his face. "My actions are unforgivable." The genuine regret that laced his words surprised her.

"It's happened too many times, Maxim. I told you I won't be treated like that, and I meant it. I'm going home." The others—Lyon, Kara, and Tighe—didn't even pretend they weren't party to the discussion.

"She needs a ride to the airport," Kara told her mate. "And money for a flight."

Lyon met Faith's gaze with a small nod. "Of course."

"I'll take you, Faith," Tighe said.

She gave Tighe a small smile in thanks.

Maxim raked long, straight hair back from his face with a frown that almost turned pleading. "Don't go, Faith. I'm not like this, not usually. Hawke . . . angers me. The way he looks at you."

"I know."

"I become someone I don't know . . . and don't care for . . . when he's around." He lifted his hand, then dropped it at his side. "Please, Faith. Let us at least discuss this in private."

Talking it out would just make it harder. And yet, part of her longed to be convinced that Feral House was where she truly belonged, that she never had to go back to that cold, lonely life. Despite everything she'd seen, everything Maxim had done, she continued to feel that tug, that certainty that she belonged to him. She supposed she could listen to what he had to say.

"All right."

"Let me know what you decide," Tighe said.

"I will. Thank you." She turned to continue up the stairs, Maxim following behind. He caught up to her on the second flight of stairs. At his room, he opened the door and stood back for her to enter, playing the part of the gentleman, at last. When he'd closed the door behind him, they faced one another.

"Don't leave me, Faith." He strode to her slowly, and she took an instinctive step back. "We're meant to be together. You know it. I know it." He lifted his hand, stroked her jaw.

"Actually, I don't know it, Maxim. You've shown me little respect and less kindness. I don't care what your reasons are. There's no excuse. I won't stay with a man who mistreats me."

He gripped her jaw, too hard. His mouth tightened. "You won't leave me. I forbid it."

Her heart began to race with a fear she hated and the sudden certainty that he was one of *those* men. One who would kill her before he'd let her walk away.

"Maxim . . ." She met his gaze fully, searching for the words that would ease his hold, wondering if the other Ferals would hear her if she called for help.

But as she stared into his eyes, her thoughts began to scatter, her mind going slowly numb.

"You're mine, Faith. I love you." Maxim forced his fingers to loosen their death grip on her jaw, forced himself to stroke her fragile cheek gently as he willed her to believe the lie. He hadn't understood why she was important to him, not until the Renascence. Now he knew everything. And she would not leave him. Ever. "Tell me you know I love you."

A strange look came over her eyes, like clouds blotting out the sun's bright rays. "I know you love me." Her words sounded odd. Toneless. Robotic.

He eyed her with annoyance, a flash of anger once more tightening his hold on her until his fingers shook with the effort to keep from breaking the fragile bones. Though he loved the sound of breaking bones, that would not do. Not here. There could be no screams here.

"You will be my mate, Faith."

"I will be your mate." Her reply was as toneless as before.

Beneath his fingers, he felt the tension in her jaw and body melting away, her eyes unfocusing as if he'd . . . *clouded her mind.*

Holy goddess. Such a thing was usually impossible with nonhumans. To his knowledge, no Therian could ensnare the mind of another of their race. Was this one of the legendary powers he'd gained from his animal?

"Put your hands on your head, Faith."

Slowly, she complied, her expression as blank as an imbecile's.

Maxim began to smile as he turned her and pulled her back against him, then covered her mouth with his hand.

"Do not make a sound, Faith." Concentrating, he called to the newfound animal strength within him and drew the claws and fangs without difficulty. Without pain of any kind. No, the pain would be hers. Lifting one finger, he touched the tip of his claw to her cheekbone, then pressed until he punctured the skin, drawing blood. She tried to jerk away, but he held her. "Be still."

She froze. Silent. As he'd commanded.

He grinned. With a quick, downward pull, he raked a bloody furrow in her cheek from cheekbone to jaw. Her body tensed. A glistening tear ran down her cheek, mingling with the blood. But she made no sound, just as he'd commanded. She was his to control.

The smell of her blood, the feel of her pain, even if her screams were necessarily silenced, fed the awful craving inside him. "*Finally.*" Excitement thrummed through his head as he wiped at the blood running down her jaw and neck with his shirtsleeve until the bleeding stopped and her flesh healed. Pulling off his shirt, he cleaned her up, then turned her, staring deeply into her eyes.

"You won't remember I hurt you, Faith. You don't want to go back to Warsaw. You want to stay here and be my mate. You love me. Now wake up, Faith."

The blankness left her expression, and she blinked. "Your shirt . . ."

"It's time to get some sleep."

"I . . ." She shook her head, as if confused.

"I was speaking to you, and you barely seemed to notice. You're asleep on your feet, Faith."

"I must be."

Maxim's pulse was beginning to thrum with excitement. She didn't remember.

"You'll be happy here with me."

Her gaze met his, confusion slowly being pushed aside by certainty. "I know. I love you." The words were monotone, expressionless.

He smiled in silent triumph. "Faith?"

"Yes?"

He took her jaw, staring into her eyes until once more he'd snatched her mind. "Take off your clothes, then go stand in the empty bathtub. You will make no sound, Faith. No matter what I do to you. Afterward, you'll remember none of it. I would never hurt you Faith. I love you. Would I hurt you, Faith?"

"No. You would never hurt me. You love me."

"Now do as I said."

As she slowly stripped and walked toward the bathroom, Maxim watched with distaste. How he hated the feminine form. Unless it was painted with blood. And bowed in pain. Then it was quite beautiful, indeed.

He shifted back into his saber-toothed cat, then padded behind her, speaking to her telepathically. *You'll make no sound, Faith. But you'll feel the pain.*

You'll feel the terror of what I'm about to do to you.
Tremble with fear of me, Faith, for your blood will run.

She stepped into the tub, visibly trembling.

On your hands and knees!

When she'd lowered herself as he'd demanded, he opened his cat's mouth wide and moved forward until his massive canines, his saber teeth, were poised over her lower back.

Make no sound.

He slammed his jaw closed, impaling her. As she arched in silent agony, warm blood flowed into his mouth, drenching his throat, filling him with a fierce, vicious joy. *Hail Catt, soon to be Chief of the Feral Warriors.*

The nine wouldn't even see it coming.

Chapter Seven

Dusk shadowed the sky as Hawke dragged his tired body through the front door of Feral House. He'd come back to himself about ten miles upriver and discovered his cell phone was dead. At any other time, before his plunge into the spirit trap, he'd have simply flown home. But shifting into his bird would have only ripped away his consciousness and his will a second time. So he'd walked.

On the way, he'd been hit with another of those lightning-strike headaches, quickly followed by his hawk's furious retaliation. That ripping torment had lasted longer than ever before, and he'd found himself half-tempted to shift back into his bird simply to escape the agony. Finally, as always, it had faded away.

Lyon saw him come in the door.

"You've been flying all this time?" his chief asked.

"All except the walk home. It's still Thursday?"

Lyon shook his head, his expression grim. "Friday. Thirty-seven hours since you flew off."

Hell. "I thought I was getting better." Clearly not. Each time he shifted, he was lost to the bird for a longer time. An hour, two. Five. Thirty-seven. "I need sleep."

"I want Kara to give you radiance, first." Lyon gripped his arm in the Feral greeting, his other hand clasping Hawke's shoulder as worried eyes embraced him in deep, abiding friendship. "I'm glad to have you back."

"Is everything okay here?" Hawke asked, as Lyon motioned him to follow him. He wanted to ask about Maxim. About Faith. But he remembered too well his decision to back out of their lives. If he'd done it sooner, maybe he wouldn't have just lost thirty-seven hours.

"Well enough. A couple of the new Ferals showed up. Five have made contact so far. It looks like they're going to be a rowdy bunch. You can meet them in the morning."

They found Kara curled up in a chair in the corner of Lyon's office, an open book in her lap. At their entrance, she leaped to her feet, tossed the book carelessly into the chair behind her, and ran to Hawke, throwing her arms around him. "I'm so glad you're back."

Hawke pulled her tight against him, affection for this woman pressing against the walls of his chest.

"He could use some radiance." Lyon's voice was rough, but without a trace of jealousy as his mate embraced his no-longer-missing warrior.

"Of course," Kara said softly, and began to glow.

For the first time since his Renascence, the energy jolting through him brought no pleasure, no feeling of power. Only a dull, tingling ache. He waited for the ache to fade, the power to rush into him, but nothing changed. And when Kara pulled back at last, her light going out, he felt worse than when they'd started.

Hell.

He kissed her forehead. "Thanks, Kara."

Kara smiled sweetly at him as she backed into Lyon's waiting embrace.

Lyon wrapped his arms around her, his worried gaze on Hawke. "Get some sleep, Wings."

Hawke nodded. Minutes later, he pushed through the door to his bedroom, stripped, and collapsed onto his bed. What the hell had just happened in there? It wasn't enough he'd been gone thirty-seven hours . . . *thirty-seven*. Now radiance wasn't helping him? With a stab of fear, he knew. He remembered all too well the way Kara's radiance had sent Paenther crashing into the wall like a man electrocuted when he'd nearly lost the connection with his animal a few weeks back.

His own connection with his hawk was getting worse. More and more they were acting as separate entities. He feared it was only a matter of time before the connection shattered.

Hawke woke a couple of hours before dawn, went down to the kitchen, and fixed himself a plate, eating alone in a room as dark as his mood. The seventeen animals seemed to be returning after a centuries-long absence, but if they were as rowdy as Lyon suggested, their chief was going to need the original Ferals on their game. And Hawke couldn't be any more off his. He couldn't shift, couldn't fight without risking disappearing for days at a time. Maybe, eventually, forever.

With twenty-five others, maybe it wouldn't matter.

He shoved his chair back, running a hand through his

hair. It mattered to him. The only way he could avoid that fate was to keep himself calm. Collected. A near impossibility with Faith and Maxim in the house.

Goddess. If not for his need for radiance, he'd leave and go live at one of the enclaves. Maybe he should consider it anyway.

He wandered into the hall. Television didn't interest him, so he headed for the library, his private sanctuary. The room belonged to everyone, of course, but he was the only one who used it on a regular basis. He loved the smell of books, loved to spend an hour or two every day deeply immersed in the words of another mind and, often, another time. It never failed to settle him, calming his soul. And he needed that calm now. Desperately.

But as he approached the double doors to his sanctuary, he saw light spilling out beneath. He'd found Kara in there a few times, but she was usually asleep this time of night.

He pushed open the door and stopped short. Not Kara.

Faith.

She looked up from where she sat curled in his favorite chair in that holey pair of jeans and a faded blue T-shirt, a huge Civil War tome open on her lap. As their gazes met, he felt like a damned deer caught in the headlights. His rational mind told him to back away. Get the hell out of there. The woman was a danger to his equilibrium, to his sanity, to his very life. If Maxim was in there with her . . . or if he found them together again . . .

Just the thought of that prick had his hands clenching into fists, the anger sparking deep inside him. Yet the ever-present rage dimmed, that calming hand pushing it down. He blinked, understanding washing over him. It was Faith who'd been helping him keep control. Or more accurately, the damned bird's infatuation with her. He could almost hear the hawk's sigh in his head.

But it didn't matter that she calmed him. It didn't change a thing.

Back away, he told himself. *Turn around and go downstairs to the gym. It's safer. Far away from temptation and disaster. Far away from Faith.*

But before he could force his feet to move, she tucked a lock of blue-tipped hair behind her ear and gave him a soft, sweet smile that arrowed straight into his chest. And he knew he was lost. Instead of backing out of the room, his traitorous feet carried him forward, through the double doors.

"You're back," she said quietly, then closed the book and set it on the table beside her chair. With unstudied grace, she swung her legs down and stood up, taking a couple of steps toward him. "Hawke . . . I'm so sorry."

"It wasn't your fault. Where is he?"

"Draden hunting."

The worst of the tension leached out of him. Maxim wouldn't return for at least an hour. "Are you still on European time?"

"No." A small furrow creased the flesh between her brows. "I've been sleeping a lot the past couple of days. I guess I just needed to catch up. I found this room after Maxim left tonight, and I've been here ever since." Her smile reappeared, brighter than before. "I've never seen so many books."

His chest ached at the sight of her, at the soft curve of her jaw, the slender length of her neck, the sweet fullness of her lips. Goddess how he wanted to taste those lips.

"What are you reading?" he forced through his own instead.

"*The Battle of Antietam*."

He lifted a brow. "Trying to find something to put you to sleep?"

She smiled, slaying him. He felt that smile penetrate like a sun shot straight into his heart, bursting into brightness inside him, sending brilliant light and perfect warmth radiating into every corner of his body.

"No, I love reading about history and wars." She shrugged self-consciously. "I wish there were books on the Therian-Mage wars, but I didn't see any."

"Therians rarely write anything down."

"Because the humans might find it? They'd just think it was fiction."

"Oral history has always been our way. If you wish to know something, find a Therian who was alive back then and get a firsthand account."

She frowned even as her eyes began to twinkle. "I prefer books."

"Me, too."

His words earned him one of her small, brilliant grins. Every time she smiled, he felt reborn.

Dammit, he'd promised himself to stay away from her.

No, that wasn't true. He'd promised himself to be nothing more to her than a casual friend. They still had to live in the same house, didn't they? And it was friendly to talk to her when he found her alone in the middle of the night. Right? *Goddess.*

He scrubbed his face with his hands.

"Are you okay?" Faith asked softly.

"Yeah. Just tired." Which was true enough. He was tired deep in his soul.

"Are some of these books yours?" she asked.

He glanced around him, at the wall-to-wall, ceiling-to-floor stacks broken only by the windows, the double doors, and the big, old-fashioned hearth. "They're pretty much all mine."

Her expressive eyes widened, and he couldn't turn away. She fascinated him, pulled at him like a dangerous drug. He knew he should leave. He told himself to go. But if there was one thing he was lacking these days, it was self-control. "You're genuinely interested in the Civil War?"

"Is that so surprising?" A glimmer of laughter lit her expression, but her eyes didn't sparkle the way he remembered. Was that his doing? The thought hurt.

He shrugged. "I don't think I've ever run into a woman, a Therian woman, who cared one way or another about human history."

"Human history is the history of the world. We might not play a direct part in it most of the time, but that doesn't mean it's not relevant."

He smiled, impressed. "Exactly. You sound like a student of more than just the American Civil War."

"I am." She sat down, curling once more into his reading chair, tucking her legs up beside her. He'd never again see that chair, or sit in it, he suspected, that he wouldn't think of her. "Honestly, I'm interested in everything. I adore books and have read anything and everything I can get my hands on, though generally nonfiction. History, philosophy, psychology, the sciences." As she talked, the sparkle briefly reappeared in her eyes. "But I've long been fascinated by the nature of the Civil War. Unlike the European conflicts, it wasn't about conquering another nation. It wasn't about world domination. It was about ideological differences, one side fighting for independence, the other fighting to preserve the whole. It split villages, families."

"I know," he said quietly.

Her mouth dropped open. "You were here. Right in the middle of it."

"The Ferals were. I wasn't."

"You weren't a Feral Warrior, then?"

"No. Not at first. I was in Finland. My father was killed during that conflict, struck by a mortar shell that blew his heart out of his chest. The wrong place at the wrong time."

"Oh, Hawke, I'm sorry."

"It was a long time ago. A few weeks later, I was marked to be the next hawk shifter. By the time I returned, the Civil War was nearly over. But I saw the destruction. I saw the hollow eyes of the humans, eyes that had once glowed with such fervor, such purpose."

Faith nodded. "I saw the same in Europe. The hollow eyes, at least." Her expressive face turned pensive, shadows of old pain crossing her features.

"You were there, during the world wars?"

"Yes. I was very young during the first war, the Great War. My love of history was born of a need to understand why my village had been attacked and so many killed. I wanted to know who'd ordered the destruction. But I found myself fascinated with the workings of power and greed. And by the strategies of battle." She shrugged. "What doesn't kill you makes you obsessed."

"Were the people in your enclave killed, or simply scattered?"

"Neither." Her mouth gave a wry twist. "I was the only one scattered."

He lowered himself to the chair that sat at right angles to hers, arms on his thighs as he leaned toward her. "What do you mean?"

She sat back, pulling her knees against her chest. All softness fled from her face, replaced by old pain. And anger. "A few hours before the village was attacked, we received a warning. My enclave packed up and left. I didn't." He waited for her to say more. Instead, she shrugged, visibly pushing away the memory. "It was a long time ago. So, have you visited all the nearby battlefields—Manassas, Harpers Ferry, Gettysburg?"

He wanted to press her for more, sensing a deep, open wound. But he'd caused her enough pain. "Yes, numerous times, plus a number of smaller ones. The armies traipsed all over this area at one point or another."

"I'd love to see them." Once more, the sparkle briefly returned to her eyes.

"I'd love to show you." Goddess, that was true. He imagined the two of them walking hand in hand through the old battlefields, her quick mind taking it all in as she fired off questions and observations. None of his brothers had ever had any interest. How he would love to share his own passion for history with someone. With Faith. "One of these days, I'll take you." In a move as natural as breathing, he reached for her, covering her soft hand with his.

Her gaze snapped up to his, her eyes softening, then tightening with a plea he didn't understand. A plea laced with desperation. She leaned toward him, and, for one brilliant moment, he thought she meant to throw herself into his arms.

His hawk screeched with triumph.

But as quickly as the look appeared, it vanished. Her

face screwed up with a pain that slew him. She jerked her hand away. "*Don't touch me,*" she whispered, her voice breaking.

He reared back. "Faith."

"I love Maxim!" She leaped from her chair, moving behind it as if to protect herself from him. Her eyes had turned wild, unfocused. The eyes of a stranger.

What the hell? Was everyone going crazy, or was it just him?

"Go." Her face crumpled. Tears began to run down her cheeks. "Just go," she whispered.

Goddess. All he'd done was touch her hand. He stared at her in confusion, every instinct he possessed demanding he go *to* her, not turn away. But she was crying and he'd caused the tears, him and his damned infatuation.

Walking barefoot over broken glass couldn't hurt any more than turning his back on her as tears skated down her cheeks, but he forced himself to do just that, to leave the room and close the doors behind him. Then he leaned back against the nearest wall, dug his fingers into his scalp, and ached. He'd made her cry.

He had to stay away from her. Until he was himself again, until he was certain he could be polite and nothing more, he couldn't go near her. And never could he allow himself to be alone with her again.

He'd made her cry.

It was too much to ask that he might stop caring about her. It was too late for that. In a few short days, she'd become the light shining in his heart. The music. The life.

But no one could ever know. He had to bury his feelings deep, so deep no one ever saw them again. So deep no one ever knew that he'd fallen in love with the woman destined to become his enemy's mate.

The next afternoon, Faith stood beside Maxim in the foyer, the other wives nearby as Olivia greeted Kieran, the latest of the new Ferals to arrive at Feral House.

"Olivia, you weren't kidding," Delaney said. "He *is* beautiful."

Kieran grinned and rolled his eyes.

Tighe hooked his arm around his wife's shoulders, pulling her close. "Excuse me?" But his dimples flashed with his own grin, and Delaney laughed. "Not as pretty as you, my tiger."

Tighe growled, but it was a funny growl, a feral *You know it.*

Kieran *was* beautiful, Faith couldn't deny it, though she found his beauty a bit too . . . flawless. His face perfectly shaped, his jaw perfectly sculpted, his nose perfectly straight, and his eyes a perfect, crystal blue. His hair, a gorgeous, flawless gold, hung in perfect waves to his broad shoulders. Even his mouth, with its full lower lip, was utterly, perfectly sensual. As eye candy, he was a nonpareil. And, as Olivia had promised, he seemed to take it in stride, which made him likable as well. But Kieran's face lacked the character of Hawke's, and while he seemed to be nice enough, his eyes lacked that endless well of patience and kindness that belonged to Hawke alone.

Belatedly, she realized it should be Maxim she compared Kieran to, not Hawke. She hadn't even seen Hawke since he'd walked into the library early yesterday morning. When she'd started crying and ordered him out.

Her scalp tingled with remembered shame. He hadn't deserved that, not at all. She'd been so glad to see him. Her pulse had quickened at the sight of him in a simple black T-shirt and jeans, his golden armband winking beneath the cuff of his shirt, circling one muscular arm. He'd stolen her breath as he'd towered over her, his eyes gleaming with warmth, with friendliness and kindness and an emotion not nearly so gentle. One that had made her flesh heat, her body grow restless, and her heart thud with reckless excitement.

She'd wanted him there. As they'd talked of his books and war, she'd watched the movement of his beautifully shaped lips and fallen deeply into those dark eyes. She'd wanted him to stay there with her, desperately. And then he'd reached for her hand, touched her, and she'd gone a little insane, demanding he leave her, and he had. She hadn't seen him since.

Her gaze flicked to one of the hallways that led off the foyer, then the other, but she saw no sign of him. Where was he?

"Told you he was beautiful," Olivia said with a grin, giving Kieran a big kiss on the cheek. "He's a god, aren't you, Kieran, my love?"

The big blond grinned, his smile as movie-star perfect as the rest of him. "I'm a god." But his expression was deadpan, his voice, lightly dusted with an Irish brogue, ironic, the laughter in his eyes pointed clearly at himself.

"Adonis in the flesh." Olivia moved to his side and introduced him to Lyon first. Once the men had slapped forearms, she took Kieran by the elbow and turned him to Jag, then slipped from his side to Jag's, sliding her arms tight around Jag's waist. "This is my mate."

Faith tensed, certain she was about to witness another explosion of male pride and jealousy, certain the two big men were about to go feral. But Kieran grabbed Jag's hand and shook it hard, his expression close to awe.

"I never thought I'd see the day that Olivia took a mate. A thousand men have tried to win her, and failed. You must be one hell of a man."

Jag snorted. "I might decide I like you, Pretty Boy."

Kieran laughed, the sound as beautiful as the rest of him. "One of these days, you'll have to tell me your secret."

Jag cut his eyes at Olivia, his tone turning soft and loving. "That story's not mine to tell."

Kieran nodded with approval. "I just might decide I like you, too, boyo."

Jag clapped the newest Feral on the shoulder, and the three started for the living room and the third welcome reception in as many days. Three new Ferals in addition to Maxim, and another five on the way. So far.

As everyone started toward the living room, Kara slipped through the crowd to join Faith, eyeing her curiously. "How are you?"

"I'm fine."

Kara's gaze flicked to Maxim and back again. "Good. I'm glad. Jag, Olivia, and I are going shopping later. We need more sheets and towels. Most of the rooms on the third floor have never been used, but if new Ferals keep arriving, we're going to be filling them all. Would you like to come shopping with us?"

Oh, she would! She'd love to see something of America other than the airport and Feral House. Going on a shopping adventure with Kara and Olivia would be wonderful. But before she could open her mouth to say yes, something clicked in her mind. *I belong with Maxim.* She found herself shaking her head. "I'm going to stay with Maxim."

Kara gave her a curious look, then smiled. "Okay. Maybe another time."

As Kara turned away, Maxim took Faith by the arm and steered her toward the stairs. Toward his bedchamber. A stab of fear bolted through her mind, her pulse beginning to race, her skin growing damp. What was wrong with her? They were only going upstairs. Clearly, Maxim didn't feel like suffering through another social gathering.

Her feet dragged, her gaze darting back to the foyer, seeking Hawke. The need to see him welled up so thick and so suddenly that her eyes began to sting. The litany in her mind continued. *I belong to Maxim. I belong to Maxim.*

But her heart cried out for Hawke.

Chapter Eight

Four days later, Hawke stood with Lyon and Kougar in the doorway of the media room, observing—babysitting—six of the newly marked Feral Warriors, who sprawled across the room, cheering on one team or the other, leaping, shouting, and shoving one another. So far, no blood had been spilled, but the soccer match was only twenty minutes old. Since they'd started showing up five days ago, there had been nearly constant fights, constant arguments, the testosterone thick as tar. If the past five days were anything to go by, the blood would start spilling soon enough. They'd already destroyed all the televisions in the media room and two of the sofas. Kara had forced a couple of them to accompany her and Wulfe in hunting down replacements at local yard sales.

"There's no sense in bringing in new ones when they'll only wind up at the dump in a couple of days," she'd said reasonably.

The walls were a mess, holes in the plaster the size of fists, of heads, and occasionally of entire bodies.

"I've seen new Ferals arrive in groups before," Lyon muttered, "but I've never seen it this bad."

"It may be the spirit trap," Hawke said. "I heard the animals in there, their cries of pain. Centuries of that has to be screwing with them. And, in turn, the men they've marked."

Kougar grunted, standing with his arms crossed over his chest. "Every one of you arrived at Feral House raging with testosterone. Paenther nearly dug Lyon's heart out. Jag didn't want to be here. Both Lyon and Wulfe went feral on anyone who looked at them sideways." He glanced at Hawke, his eyes narrowing. "You kept it bottled better than most, but it was there. Raw anger tempered by raging grief." He shook his head. "I was concerned about you, worried you were going to erupt before it was over, but you got it under control."

Hawke nodded. "*Then*." He sure as hell wasn't in control, now.

Kougar leaned closer until their shoulders touched. "You'll do it again. I have no doubt you'll come through this as you did the other, Wings. No doubt at all."

"That makes one of us." Everyone had tried to help him with no success—the healer Esmeria, the Shaman, Skye with her enchantress's gifts, and over and over again, Kara. The second time Kara had given him radiance after his thirty-seven-hour free flight, he'd felt flat-out pain, like he'd touched something electrical that he shouldn't have. It had been all he could do to hang on and not reveal his weakness. But like the last time, it hadn't gotten any better. And he'd declined radiance ever since.

Kougar straightened. "Once they come into their

animals, they'll settle down. Just as all of you did. Eventually."

"It could take years." Lyon grunted. "Jag took centuries."

Hawke hoped to hell they snapped out of it soon. The constant fighting and stupid-ass behavior were wearing his already-fraying control thin as copper wire. They were breaking things with abandon, coming on to whatever woman happened to be within sight, which had brought the original Ferals into the fighting. A dozen times a day, he had to stop himself from diving in for fear he'd lose control. Two dozen times a day, he had to pull himself back from the brink of fury. The good news was he seemed to be getting better at it. Knock on wood, he'd only lost control and pounded the hell out of one of the newly marked twice now, and he hadn't shifted once. Not once. But whatever had been calming the rage had been absent. Faith. It was Faith who'd been absent. No, not absent. He'd been avoiding her.

Goddess, he missed her. At least he knew the bastard wasn't with her now. Maxim was in the middle of the throng of new Ferals, as he so often was, the only one they never fought with.

"What is it about him?" Hawke muttered, watching one of them clap Maxim warmly on the back. "They act like he's the football star or something."

"I've been wondering the same thing." Kougar stroked his beard slowly. "He's become the ringleader."

A shout rang out from the foyer, echoing up all three stories and back, quickly followed by the loud splintering of wood and an earth-shattering thud that rattled the paintings on the walls. As one, the three Ferals ran to find the other two newly markeds going at it with claws and fists amid the splintered ruin of one of the stair railings. Hawke looked up and shook his head. They'd fallen from the second floor. It was a damn good thing they were immortals.

This pair were two of the biggest of the new Ferals—Ewan, a Therian Guard who'd been part of Olivia's squad and stayed on to assist them in their battle to stop the Mage, and the one they'd dubbed Mountain Man, the biggest of any of the Ferals, new or old. An inch or two taller than Wulfe, he was seven-plus feet of pure, angry male. His hair hung halfway between short and long, black as pitch, his face in constant need of a shave. But it was his eyes that had them giving him a wide berth, eyes raging with anger. He was at the middle of at least half the fights, pushing, shoving, refusing to give way.

"Cease!"

Though Lyon's roar of command rang through the foyer, only Ewan attempted to pull back. And got slammed into the nearest wall for his effort. Lyon and Kougar interceded, both grabbing Mountain Man, and still they struggled. Ewan snarled but stayed where he was.

Lyon pushed Mountain Man back. "You need a serious attitude adjustment!"

The big Feral's lip curled. "I didn't fucking ask for this job."

"None of us did!"

Mountain Man threw his hand outward, motioning to the hallway that carried the sound of cheers and thudding fists from the media room. "Half of those fuckers are beside themselves with glee."

"You haven't shifted, yet," Kougar said, his voice even. "Don't knock it until you've tried it."

Mountain Man growled and muscled his way free, then stalked up the stairs. Ewan headed for the media room. Hawke, Lyon, and Kougar watched them go.

"I hope to hell they settle down once they shift," Lyon muttered. "Like Catt has."

Hawke's jaw clenched. He'd been giving the saber-toothed shifter a wide berth for the past few days, but he'd come in contact with him a couple of times, and as much as he hated to admit it, Lyon was right. The prick had turned into a new man. He followed Lyon's orders without question and was civil, if not warm, to the older Ferals. He and Hawke ignored one another now instead of battling. They might even be able to live like this.

Then again, Faith was never there. He wasn't sure what would happen if she started accompanying Maxim again.

Goddess, he hadn't seen her in four days, not since that morning in the library when he'd made her cry. The thought of it still hurt.

Jag and Kieran strolled into the foyer, shoulder to shoulder.

"Shit," Jag muttered. "Look at this mess."

Lyon turned to him. "Feel like a little carpentry work?"

"I'm good with my hands," Kieran said with that light Irish accent. "Do you have tools?"

Jag slapped him on the back. "Do we have tools, Pretty Boy? You should see the tools we have. Come on, I'll show you."

Kieran grinned. "After you, Pretty Girl."

Jag hooted with laughter and headed toward the basement.

Lyon shook his head. "Kieran doesn't seem to be affected at all."

"Everyone reacts differently." Kougar turned to Lyon. "But I do think the sooner we get this lot shifted, the better. Is the Renascence still on for tonight?"

"It is. Just before dawn. Kara's ready." But a glimmer of concern entered his eyes.

"How is she feeling, Roar?" Hawke asked. Maxim's Renascence had taken a lot out of her. Which was why Lyon wasn't bring each new Feral into his animal as he arrived.

"Lyon, what happened?"

At the sound of Kara's voice, all three men looked up. Kara stood before the destroyed railing, a look of disbelief on her face. But it was the woman standing beside her that stole Hawke's attention.

Faith.

His heart soared at the glimpse of her standing in those same holey jeans and overlong sweater. His pulse took off in a fast, excited sprint. But while Kara started down the stairs, Faith remained where she was, a story away. It was all he could do not to go to her. She was so lovely, her dark hair framing her delicate face, the blue tips teasing her shoulders. Through the thudding in his ears, he barely heard Lyon's brief explanation of the railing's demise. He'd starved for sight of her. But as his focus narrowed from her face to her eyes, he frowned. Her eyes were as flat as he'd ever seen them. The sparkle completely gone. Dead.

His hawk cried out, the tone mournful and angry.

As Faith met his gaze, her mouth lifted in a semblance of a smile, a shadow of what he knew her capable of. Had he done this to her when he made her cry? No. No way had touching her hand stolen the life from her eyes. And she was trying to smile at him, wasn't she? There was no anger in her expression.

This was Maxim's doing, dammit. *Dammit.* The red haze began to tease the edges of his vision. Maxim was hurting her. He knew it. He knew it!

Kougar's hand grasped his shoulder none too gently.

"I'm fine," he growled.

"Then what's with the steam coming out of your nose?"

Funny, he thought sarcastically, then jerked his gaze to Kougar. He still wasn't used to Kougar's having a sense of humor. The surprise of Kougar's comment broke the spell long enough for him to get the rising anger back under control.

But when he looked up at Faith, she was turning away, starting up the stairs to the third story.

He tensed to follow. Kougar's grip on him tightened. "Don't."

He watched until she disappeared from sight, then whirled on Kara as she descended the last of the steps. "Why didn't you tell me?"

Kara looked at him with surprise. "Tell you what?"

"That he's been hurting her."

Kara shook her head, looking confused. "That who's been *what*?"

"Maxim's been hurting Faith. Her eyes aren't right."

"What do you mean?" Lyon demanded.

Hawke growled with frustration, turning away, then back again. "I can't explain it. I just . . . *know.* That bastard is hurting her."

Kara frowned. "She's never said anything, but I've hardly seen her since she and Catt worked things out. I hardly see anyone. We've all taken to our rooms to avoid the zoo animals. But she seems to be settling in okay."

"You were with her just now."

"Actually, I saw her coming down the stairs when I came out to investigate all the commotion." Kara looked around. "Did she go back up?"

Hawke nodded.

"I'll check it out," Lyon promised. "But, Hawke. Catt's room is between Wulfe's and mine. Neither of us has ever heard Faith cry out. We'd have investigated if we had, you know that."

Frustration burned in his blood. His instincts told him something was wrong with her, but he had no proof. No one else had noticed. Goddess knew, he hadn't thought straight since the moment he first saw her, but he couldn't be this mistaken, could he?

What if he was?

No, he wasn't. He'd thrilled to the sparkle in Faith's eyes too many times to not notice the lack. Even his hawk agreed, and they didn't agree on much these days. He'd rather risk her anger, even her tears, than realize later that she'd needed him, and he hadn't been there to help her.

Tonight, after her prick of a soon-to-be mate left to go draden hunting, he was paying the lady a visit.

Faith stood in the dark at the window of Maxim's bed-chamber, looking out over the moonlit trees, seeing nothing. She felt . . . nothing. Drained. Empty. Sad in a way she couldn't explain. And scared, a dark terror swimming just below the surface of her thoughts, like a nightmare she couldn't quite remember, but that refused to fade.

She was losing her mind.

She'd moved into Maxim's room after he came into his animal, no longer sure why she hadn't to begin with. Now, every time she left the room, she found herself returning before she got very far. This was the only place she belonged. This room. These bare four walls. She pressed her fist against her breastbone as if she could hold back the misery she didn't understand and couldn't shake.

A soft knock sounded on the door, pulling her out of her dark thoughts. Turning from the window, she padded to the door in bare feet, the denim of her worn jeans brushing uncomfortably against her legs. Her skin was so sensitive these days. Everything hurt.

She pulled open the door, expecting Kara. But she found herself staring into a muscular chest instead. Her gaze slowly rose, her breath catching as she stared into Hawke's face, falling into warm, tender eyes. A fierce longing rushed up inside her, pressing against her lungs and heart, making her tremble with the fierce need to close the distance between them and feel his arms around her as she had, so briefly, when he'd swept her out of harm's way a few days ago.

I can't let him touch me. I belong to Maxim.

Hawke lifted his hands as if he'd heard the longing in her heart, then dropped them slowly to his sides. "We have to talk."

"You shouldn't be here."

Hawke grunted. "Tell me something I don't know." He ran a hand through his hair. "Please, Faith? I won't touch you. I promise. I just want to talk."

No instinct reared up to block her, so she stepped back, letting him in, then closed the door behind him.

"Turn on a light, Faith."

"Do I have to?" She could see him well enough in the moonlight filtering through the trees outside. At least she could see his shadowed form. And she preferred the dark these days. In the dark, she was safe.

"I want to see you."

With a sigh, she flipped the switch, illuminating the bedside lamp, then turned away from the light that blinded, turning her back to Hawke.

"Look at me, Faith." His words were velvety soft, achingly gentle despite the thread of steel that told her he would not take no for an answer.

"I'm blinded," she grumbled.

He chuckled, the sound holding little humor but a wealth of tenderness. "You'll get used to it soon enough."

The ache beneath her breastbone swelled and spread. In some corner of her mind, she knew that Hawke could banish the nightmares if only she remembered them. If only she didn't belong to Maxim.

Slowly, she turned to face him. He stood a few feet away, his hands now shoved into his front jeans pockets, his eyes watching her, probing as if he could look inside her, all the way down to the soles of her feet.

"What's happened, Faith? Where has your light gone?"

She swallowed, caught in the power of his gaze, her pulse hammering, her emotions in turmoil. "I don't know." She wanted to cry, to dive into his arms, to turn and run.

"What's he done to you?"

"Nothing."

"He's hurt you."

"No! He would never hurt me. Maxim loves me."

He shook his head, his face a mask of disbelief. "That's the cry of abused women everywhere! They hide it, even from themselves, justifying their men's behavior."

"I'm not!" She rounded on him. "I've been helping abused girls for decades. I would never . . . *never* . . . allow a man to treat me that way. Never! I'm not justifying." Tears began to threaten, and she dashed at one that escaped her eye. "He. Is. Not. Hurting me."

Pain tightened his features, and he turned away, tipping his head back. For long moments, she watched that rigid back, aching with a need to comfort him, trembling from the battle raging inside her—the longing for one man and the devotion to another.

"I love him, Hawke," she said softly.

Finally, he turned back, his eyes filled with misery. "Then tell me why you're so sad."

Why was she? She didn't even know.

You know, her heart cried. *It's because you need Hawke, but it's Maxim you belong to.*

"I don't know." If only she'd never left Warsaw. If only . . . "I want to go home."

He stared at her for long seconds. "You're homesick?" After a moment, he sighed, a big exhalation, the tension draining from his shoulders. "I guess that might do it." But he didn't sound convinced.

"I miss the girls I've been trying to help, Paulina and Maria." The words started and wouldn't stop because Hawke would understand. "Maria's so young and too old for her age, but she still has this wonder inside her, this belief that life is good. Paulina knows better. She's so bitter, but she has this brilliant artistic talent, and if she ever got her hands on paints and canvas, all that angst would come pouring out and maybe, just maybe, heal her." She caught her breath, then sighed. "I wonder if they're all right."

"Maybe Catt will let you go back to visit them."

"He will." This she knew with utter assurance. "We'll go back in a couple of weeks."

"There you have it." Despite his words, Hawke watched her as if he wanted to continue arguing, as if he still weren't entirely convinced. His gaze dipped to the floor, then back up, giving her a small, sad smile. "You'll be happy here once you get used to it. Once everything settles down."

"I'm sure you're right."

He nodded again, then glanced unenthusiastically toward the door. "I guess I'd better go."

"Yes. Good night, Hawke."

He reached for the door handle, then looked back, meeting her gaze, his eyes at once gentle and sad, and a little bit fierce. "If you ever need me, I'm here for you. You know that."

"Yes, I know."

"Good night, Faith." Then he opened the door and left, closing it behind him.

As she stood there, staring at the closed door where Hawke had been moments before, she began to tremble, then shake. The tears that had threatened moments before began to flow in earnest as the nightmare's shadows flayed her mind, memories that remained just out of reach. Horrible, terrifying memories.

The tears turned to wracking sobs.

Hawke, I need you. I need you.

She slid to the floor, curling into a fetal ball on the rug. *Don't go.*

* * *

"Spirits rise and join," the Ferals chanted upon the goddess rock an hour before dawn. "Empower the beasts beneath this moon. Goddess, reveal your warriors!"

Thunder rumbled in the moon-bright sky. The rocks began to tremble as the eight new Ferals disappeared in a flash of sparkling lights, animals appearing in their places.

Hawke stared at the incredible sight, goose bumps rising on his flesh. An unnaturally large fox now stood where Kieran had a moment ago, which made sense since Kieran didn't seem to be suffering the testosterone overload some of the others had. The fox spirit had never been in the spirit trap. Mountain Man, the one with anger-management issues, had turned into a grizzly. Just what they needed. Ewan was now a polar bear. On either side of him paced two other animals more suited to arctic climes than Washington, D.C. suburbs—a snow leopard and a huge white tiger. The last three were a lynx, a crocodile, and an eagle. Finally, he'd have some company in the skies. If he were ever able to fly again.

One by one, the eight shifted back into men. The snow leopard's short hair, Hawke noticed with interest, had turned snow white.

"Henceforth," Kougar intoned, "you will be known as . . ." His straight arm came down, pointing from one new Feral to the next. "Fox, Grizz, Polaris, Lepard, Whit, Eigle, Lynks, Croc."

The new Ferals leaped together, slapping forearms, congratulating one another with as much fervor as they'd done everything so far, especially fight. Except for Grizz, who stood apart, a grim, don't-mess-with-me expression on his still-angry face.

Kara started toward Lyon, but as she dodged the exuberant bunch, she stumbled, then started to go down. Lyon leaped forward, sweeping her up before she hit the rock. "Kara!"

The new Ferals didn't seem to notice, but the old surged in close.

"Kara?" Tighe asked worriedly.

"What's the matter with her?" Kieran/Fox joined them.

Wulfe growled. "If someone hit her, I'll rip his head off."

Lyon swung her into his arms as if she weighed nothing, but she roused, her arm slipping around Lyon's neck.

"I'm okay. It's just . . . the rituals. It's like they're sucking me dry."

Nine collective breaths released at once.

Lyon tipped his head against Kara's. "You scared me."

With a soft smile, she reached up and pressed her palm to his cheek. "I love you."

He kissed her tenderly. "My heart." Cradling Kara in his arms, he turned to the others. "Let's move this celebration back to Feral House. Keep your voices down, or we'll wake the humans." But the new Ferals acted as if they hadn't heard him.

Lyon muttered under his breath, "I'm going to lock them up, every one."

They started home, Hawke walking between Lyon, who insisted on carrying his mate, and Kougar.

"We're no longer the nine," Tighe said behind them, his voice deep with satisfaction. "We're well on our way to being twenty-six."

"Thank the goddess," Lyon murmured. "For once, things are going our way."

For the Feral Warriors, that was absolutely true. For Hawke personally? Not so much. Not only was his break with his animal getting worse, but he was worried about Faith. Despite her assurances that her sadness was just homesickness, he couldn't shake the feeling that it was more than that, that Maxim was to blame. Then again, that's what he wanted, wasn't it? For his rival to turn out to be a villain? Because the alternative was that Hawke had ridden in on his white steed only to discover the damsel in distress wasn't being abused. She was homesick. And her prick of a beloved had already promised to slay that beast, leaving Hawke with no role. No place in her life.

If only he could stop dreaming about holding her in his arms, kissing her, undressing her. If only he could stop thinking about her for five damn minutes.

Faith rose from the chair by the window as the door opened, and Maxim strode into the bedroom. Dusk had fallen nearly an hour ago. Soon the draden would be out and the hunters out with them. All the new Ferals would fight draden tonight. She'd heard Lyon tell them so at the celebration feast that morning.

Maxim would be going with them. She liked it when he was gone, which was probably a terrible thing to admit about one's soon-to-be mate. But she'd gotten into a routine of sleeping all day and reading or sitting by the window all night while he was out hunting. She rarely saw him, which was fine with her, and probably another terrible thing to admit, even to herself. But they loved one another. A chill slid down her spine. They belonged together.

Maxim had that look he sometimes wore, his eyebrows lowered, his mouth hard. His mean look, though he never actually became mean. "I got tied up playing war games in the basement," he said with disgust. "As if these barbarians have anything to teach me. We're leaving in a few minutes to hunt draden, but I had to see you before I left. I'm hungry."

She looked at him quizzically. "There's no food up here." And she knew he wasn't being suggestive. They didn't have that kind of relationship. He'd never even kissed her. Not except for the few nuzzles he'd given her simply to antagonize Hawke. That should probably upset her, but she knew he loved her. And she didn't want him to kiss her. *She didn't want him to touch . . .*

He loves me. The thought pushed away whatever she'd been thinking, leaving her pulse skittering uncomfortably. Her emotions had been a mess lately.

Maxim came to her and knelt by her chair, his face eye level to hers as he studied her. A frisson of fear crept out of the shadows where her nightmares lurked, running cool fingers over her scalp. "My dear Faith. Somewhere inside, you know what I'm hungry for. You know everything."

She looked at him in confusion, even as her heart began to pound in earnest. "I don't know what you're talking about."

"Of course you don't. I make certain you never remember. But I've told you over and over again how I happened upon that street corner the night we met, how I was trolling for girls, looking for the right ones to send my men to collect."

"Collect?"

His eyes began to gleam, his mouth tilting up in what—on any other man—would be a look of high arousal. "I take them to my castle. And string them up." He licked his lips. "Then I make them bleed."

She stared at him in sick disbelief. "Why are you saying this?"

He reached for her and she flinched. "Because even though I can't enjoy your screams . . ." His thumb slid lightly across her bottom lip. " . . . I so enjoy watching the horror dawn in your eyes night after night as I reveal myself to you." His thumb stroked her cheek, a featherlight touch that might have seemed gentle if not for the cruelty in his eyes. And the terror of his words. His hand moved, his knuckles barely grazing her breast. "Then I hurt you."

"*Why* are you saying this?"

His hand slid between his legs. Her gaze followed, terror slicing through her as she saw the huge bulge in his pants and the way his fingers slid over it.

With his free hand, he gripped her jaw hard, lifting her gaze back to his. His eyes burned with hatred. "Women are the vilest of creatures, incapable of true emotion. They seduce those who trust, then betray them. And in the end they're only good for one thing." His fangs slid out, his eyes changing. His claws erupted, tearing open the flesh of her face where he gripped her in a river of fire. "The way they scream when you cut them."

Faith tried to cry out, but he slammed her jaw closed against the sound. Tears of pain ran down her cheeks. "You're sick," she hissed through clenched teeth.

"So they say. But no one knows that but you. And in a few moments, you won't remember. But there's more, dearest Faith. Much more. Because just today I discovered the greatest irony of all. The new Ferals . . . we aren't destined to be the saviors of the race. We're not destined to keep the Daemons from rising. We're here to free them."

She frowned, her head pounding in concert with the thudding of her heart. This wasn't happening. And yet the shadows leaped, wisps of nightmares escaping, memories of terrible pain. Of screams she couldn't voice.

Trembling, she fought to get up, but his grip held her immobilized. "I don't believe you." Her words escaped between her closed teeth. "The animals only mark the best of the race."

"Usually, yes. With the seventeen, no. These Ferals were never the ones meant to be marked. When the time is right, we'll rise up and slay the nine, then free the Daemons. But first, your Hawke will suffer."

Her Hawke.

"He'll go feral during the uprising, of course, and leap into the fight. But the moment he loses control and shifts, I'll cage him. The great hawk." He smiled with genuine pleasure. "And when he regains his human form, I'll torture him until he loses it again, over and over, until his mind is as wrecked as his body. And then he, too, will die."

No.

Maxim smiled, pure evil glittering in his eyes. "Now look at me, and I'll cloud your mind, shift into my beast, and feed off your pain. Be glad you have no memory of what destruction these saber teeth of mine can wreak on a woman's flesh, Faith. For you've felt it before, and you'll feel it again. Over and over and over."

"No!" She squeezed her eyes closed, refusing to let him steal her memories. She had to warn Hawke!

But a moment later she felt the sharp prick of one claw on her eyelid. With a strangled cry, she fought him. The picture Maxim had painted of what he'd do to Hawke burned in her mind, igniting a pounding, righteous rage that tore through her body, triggering a strange tingling in her mouth and fingertips.

She swung at his face, trying to knock away that clawed hand before it tore her eyelid, and she felt her fingernails rip deep furrows in his flesh.

Maxim reared back, releasing her. Faith wrenched open her eyes and stared in shocked horror at the bright red ribbons of flesh hanging from his cheeks. Her wide-eyed gaze dropped to her hands, to the bloody claws where her fingernails should have been.

Heaven help me.

Her head pounded. Her tongue felt at the foreign shapes touching her lips and darted back, pricked.

Fangs. Claws.

Before Maxim could react, she leaped up, darting for the door.

Maxim began to laugh. "I should have known! The connection I feel to you is much like I feel with the other new Ferals, but your being a woman got in my way."

Feral. She'd been marked to be a Feral Warrior.

One of us. Never the ones meant to be marked.

Wrong.

Wrong.

Wrong.

Chapter Nine

Faith darted across Maxim's bedchamber, the horror of his words pounding in her head—that he was a monster, that he'd been hurting her. That the new Ferals were the wrong ones and meant to kill the real ones, the good ones. *Hawke.*

And she was one of them!

As the blood congealed in her veins, her fangs disappeared as suddenly as they'd appeared, her claws slipping back into her fingertips.

Heaven help me.

Maxim lunged for her, but she was quicker, and closer to the door. She wrenched it open, terror powering her movements. As she dashed into the hall, Maxim close behind, she saw Lyon at the top of the stairs starting toward them.

"What's going on?" he demanded. "I heard a crash." His eyes narrowed on her. "You've been bleeding."

Faith didn't slow. Instead, she picked up speed, running past him as if the hounds of hell were on her heels. Or an evil saber-toothed cat.

Behind her, she heard a grunt and glanced over her shoulder to find Maxim slammed up against the wall, Lyon's hand around his throat. "If you raise a hand or claw against a woman in this house again . . ."

Faith didn't wait to hear the rest. She reached the stairs and started down, taking them as quickly as her feet would move. She found Kara standing by the new railing.

"Faith, what happened? Are you okay?"

"Yes. No." Her hammering heart threatened to pound out of her chest. Her thoughts had scattered, none of them coming clearly. One burst through. *Stay in the room. You belong to Maxim.*

She started to slow and had nearly turned back when, with a blinding burst of clarity, she understood. The voice was Maxim's. The thoughts of belonging to him, of loving him, of not letting Hawke touch her. All Maxim's.

That foul-smelling piece of gutter trash! She didn't love him, she *hated* him. Kidnapping girls, *torturing* them?

She began to shake in her horror, in her fury. "Where's Hawke, Kara?"

Kara frowned. "I don't know. Probably his room." She pointed down the opposite hall. "Last door on the right."

Without a word, Faith took off at a full run. Reaching Hawke's door, she wrenched it open without knocking, then pulled up short. He stood in the middle of the room in a pair of unbuttoned jeans, a towel slung over one bare, muscular shoulder, his hair damp as if he'd just come out of a shower.

In an instant, he flung aside the towel, his body

predator-tense, as he closed the distance between them. At the last moment, he pulled up, his reaching hands jerking back as if he were afraid to touch her. "He hurt you." His words were a rumbling growl in his throat.

Pushing past Maxim's voice in her head, she reached for him, pressing her hands against his bare chest. "It's worse than that . . ."

Hawke gripped her arms, his hands tender vises even as his expression turned fierce. "*I'll kill him.*"

The list of things she needed to tell him exploded in her head. "He and the other new Ferals are going to rise up against you, all of you. They want to free the Daemons."

He stared at her as if she'd spouted a foreign language. His hands tightened on hers. "When? How? *Why?*"

"I don't know. He meant to cloud my mind, Hawke, so I wouldn't remember what he'd told me. He's been . . ." She shuddered. "I escaped before he could take my memories. He knows I know. He knows I'm—"

"I'll take care of it." He brushed a lock of her hair back from her face and pressed a kiss to her forehead. "Stay here."

Moments later, he was gone, and she was standing in the middle of his room, shaking, her heart thundering in her ears. Yet, never had she felt . . . safer. As she touched the spot on her forehead that still tingled with his gentle kiss, adoration welled up inside her.

Hawke would stop Maxim and the new Ferals. Goddess help her. *Of whom she was one.*

Her stomach rolled. Why her? She wasn't a fighter. She wasn't a bad person. Why would anyone think she'd attack the good Ferals? Or have any success if she tried? It was ludicrous. Yet, apparently, she'd been marked anyway.

How had her life gotten so screwed up?

He was going to kill that saber-toothed bastard.

Hawke stormed down the hall, the red haze rising in the corners of his vision with a fury that was all his own. He fought it back, needing to tell Lyon what Faith had told him before he totally lost it and wound up shifting. Lyon needed to know they had a traitor in their midst. Maybe a bunch of them.

He found Lyon and Kara descending the stairs into the foyer.

"Where's Maxim?" he called down, not wanting out of sight of his bedroom door in case Maxim tried to find Faith. *I'm going to kill him.*

"He just left to go draden hunting. I warned him about hurting Faith again."

"He *left*?" Shit. "Where's everyone else?"

"Everyone's out but us."

Hawke started down the steps. "Maxim told Faith that the new Ferals are going to rise up against us, kill us and free the Daemons. He's been clouding her mind and intended to again, but she escaped him." Hawke had never heard of a Therian having the ability to cloud another Therian's mind before, but Ferals often acquired gifts with their animals beyond the norm.

Lyon stared at him. A man who didn't know the Chief of the Ferals well might have thought he hadn't heard, but Hawke had known him all his life. He saw the emotions another might have missed—the disbelief, the struggle for comprehension, the acceptance. The fury.

"Since he wasn't able to silence her . . ."

Hawke finished his thought. "He's going to initiate the attack while he still has the element of surprise."

Lyon yanked out his cell phone and punched a couple of numbers.

"Lyon!" Delaney's shout rang out from deep in the house. She came running into the foyer. "They're under attack, and not by draden. I can feel Tighe's pain."

Lyon and Hawke exchanged grim glances. "Guard Feral House," Lyon ordered. He was going alone. Leaving him behind.

"No." Hawke's fangs sprouted, his claws erupting as the red haze threatened to overwhelm him.

"Hawke." Lyon started toward Hawke when he needed to be helping the others.

Hawke struggled against the rising anger. "I'm okay. Go!"

Lyon hesitated, clearly torn, not wanting to leave him where he could go berserk on the women yet needing to reach the Ferals who were under attack.

"We'll calm him," Kara said.

That was the last thing she should have said to her mate. Lyon wouldn't want her anywhere near him. Goddess, he had to get this under control! He needed Faith.

Olivia ran into the foyer. "Jag's in trouble. I'm going."

Lyon shook his head. "You're staying here. Calm Hawke if you can." He met the fierce gaze of the petite redhead. "But your only job is to guard the Radiant, Olivia."

Hawke saw Olivia's need to reach her mate written all over her face, but she'd been a warrior for too many centuries to object.

"Yes, sir."

"I'm going." Lyon grabbed Kara and gave her a swift kiss. "Lock the doors and let no new Ferals inside for any reason. Hawke can fill you in. Or Faith can."

If he lost it, dammit. "Faith!" Halfway down the stairs, he stayed where he was, knowing, *knowing*, Faith's presence would calm his hawk and help the man keep it together.

The moment Lyon was gone, Kara started up the stairs toward him. "Get back," he growled between fanged teeth. "If I shift, let me out, then lock up again."

Olivia followed Kara, neither of them listening to him. As Kara slid her arm around him on one side, Olivia mirrored her move on the other. He hated them risking themselves, and yet . . . his eyes swept closed as he absorbed the feel of their soft bodies against his sides, their slender hands on his waist and back. But he was still riding the edge of fury. It burned inside him, the anger that was always there melding with hatred for Maxim, terror that the bastard might actually succeed in stealing the lives of some of his friends. And bone-deep frustration that he couldn't be out there fighting that battle, too.

"Easy, Hawke," Kara said softly.

He kept his arms out and away from them so that he didn't accidentally catch them with his claws, but if he lost it, goddess only knew what he'd do to them. He should leave them, not risk it. Just go outside and let the shift happen. They'd be safer without . . .

His hawk cried out a welcome. And all of a sudden the red haze began to lessen. His fangs and claws retracted.

Kara looked up at him in surprise. "What just happened?" Her gaze shifted, gliding up the stairs to where Faith was coming down.

"You called me," Faith said quietly, meeting his gaze.

"It's her," Kara said.

As one, the women released him, and he turned to Faith, watching her descend, needing her in his arms with a fierceness that shook him. He wouldn't push her. The memory of the way he'd made her cry was still too raw.

But she never hesitated, never slowed, her arms sliding around his neck, her scent enveloping him as his arms gathered her tight against him. A shudder went through him at the utter rightness of her in his arms.

"She calms you," Kara said from behind, her voice filled with wonder.

"My hawk is taken with her," Hawke replied, his cheek pressed against the top of Faith's precious head. "Whenever she's around, the animal loses just enough of his fury to allow me to wrench back control."

Kara's laughter was soft and sweet. "The animals always seem to be taken with the one meant to be a Feral's mate."

But Faith wasn't mean to be . . .

Shock barreled through him. Maybe she was.

Faith pulled back, her eyes widening as her gaze locked with his. In the middle of utter disaster, hope burst inside him, flooding him with a joy he could hardly credit. He struggled not to grin like an idiot. But the happiness that had flared in Faith's eyes disappeared suddenly, doused as if it had never been. In its place, he saw devastation.

"What's the matter?" he asked gently.

Faith shook her head, and he suspected she was overwhelmed by all that had just happened. Which was understandable. He was a patient man. He'd never push her. If they were meant to be together . . .

Goddess, no wonder she looked so unhappy. He and his animal were a wreck.

Faith pulled her arms from around his neck and he held out his hand to her. With a soft smile, she took it, and, together, they followed Olivia and Kara down the stairs, to where Delaney waited.

"What did I miss?" Delaney eyed the two of them curiously.

"Apparently Faith is the one who's been keeping Hawke from going off the deep end." Kara whirled to face them from three steps below. "This is huge, Hawke. Have you ever shifted when Faith was close by?"

He thought back and realized Kara was right. "No. She'd always left the room."

Kara nodded wisely. "Keep her close." She smiled. "A hardship, I know."

Hawke met Faith's gaze and clung. *Keep her close.* There was nothing he wanted more. *Mine.* His hand tightened on hers as he prepared to pull her closer.

The sudden pounding at the door had him whirling and tensing for battle.

"Stay back," he told the women as he descended the remaining stairs and strode to the door.

"Olivia! Quick, let us in."

Olivia drew her knives. "It's Ewan . . . Polaris."

"New Feral. Don't open it." He peered out the peephole to see Polaris and the far-less-solid, ruddy-cheeked Lynks, then turned to the women, speaking quietly. "I need to know how many of them are around the house. Try not to be seen."

Three of the women scattered, Delaney and Olivia heading in opposite directions, Kara up the stairs for a bird's-eye view.

But Faith didn't move. She crossed to stand before him, a fierceness in her eyes he hadn't seen before, an anger he understood all too well. Maxim was going to die for what he'd done to her. For what he was doing to Hawke's brothers right now.

"I'm sorry I told you not to touch me earlier," she said softly. "Those weren't my words. I wanted nothing more than to throw myself into your arms." She swallowed. "But he wouldn't let me."

"My arms are always open to you." His words were low, soft, as his gaze caressed her sweet face.

As he watched, a soft smile curved her mouth even as her eyes began to glitter with unshed tears. They reached for one another simultaneously, Faith launching herself at him and he sweeping her up until she was eye level. She wrapped her legs around his waist, her arms around his neck, and pressed her cheek to his.

"I've needed this." Her voice was thick with tears. "I've needed you."

Hawke closed his eyes against the pummeling emotions—the fierce tenderness, the terrible protectiveness. The breath-stealing joy of holding her without guilt, at last.

Her mouth brushed his cheek, a soft kiss that sent heat spiraling through his blood. She kissed his cheekbone, then pulled back until their gazes caught, sparks igniting.

They met halfway, their mouths colliding in a savagely gentle, passionate melding that sent his senses spinning and his body hardening. Her scent intoxicated, her lips tasted like sweet berries. With one hand, he held her to him while the other dove into her soft-as-silk hair, curving around her small, precious head, claiming her. His pulse raced, the kiss grew frantic as he caressed, licked, nipped at her mouth, reveling in the feel of those soft lips, drowning in the passion that rushed over him.

With a sweep of his tongue, he parted her lips, then slid inside, pulling a moan from her throat that only inflamed him more. She tasted like raspberries as their tongues slid against one another in a sensuous dance that had his blood pounding. Never had anything felt as right as holding Faith. As kissing Faith.

He pulled back a fraction, delighting in her low sound of distress until he brushed his lips over her cheek, her eye, her temple, tasting her, drinking in the sweet scent of her. But it was her kiss he needed, her mouth he would die for.

"Olivia!"

The pounding on the door had them breaking apart, pulses races, breaths coming hard and fast. He set Faith down, but held her against him, shaking his head, trying to clear it of the wool. Goddess, the house could have burned, and he wasn't sure he'd have noticed.

"Open up or we're going to break the door down!"

Shit. They were going to let the damned draden in. He grabbed Faith's hand and ran for Lyon's office and the closest stash of full-sized swords. The draden would be drawn to Kara, and while she could go radiant and save herself, Faith would be in terrible danger. Possibly Delaney, too. So far, the draden had had little interest in the ex–FBI agent since she wasn't Therian. But she carried a Therian babe in her womb. He wasn't risking it. Paenther had gotten Skye and her Mage eyes out of there a couple of days ago. Smart man. If only they'd sent the rest of the women with her.

Unless he shifted, he, too, was going to be a sitting duck for those life-sucking fiends. He glanced at Faith, releasing her to grab a pair of short swords. "Can you wield a weapon?"

A half smile, half grimace met him. "No. But I'm pretty good with my fists. Against humans."

"Too bad these aren't humans." He handed her one of the short swords anyway. "I want you out of the way when the fighting starts. But you have a weapon in case you need it."

"You're pretty sure they're going to get in."

"I'm positive they'll get in. This house was never built to defend against Feral Warriors." When they were back in the foyer, he kissed her again, a quick peck this time, and released her at the base of the stairs. "Wait here."

He returned to the peephole just as Polaris put his head down and ran at the door, slamming into it shoulder first. The entire front of the house rattled with the force of the blow. The steel-reinforced door held. For the moment. He needed to get the women in one of the cars, but that meant leaving through the back door. With their superior hearing, the new Ferals would be on them long before they could reach the cars to make a clean getaway.

Polaris made another run at the door, rattling the windows and sending the chandelier into an awkward sway.

Olivia returned from the dining room, pain creasing her features. "Is that Polaris?"

"Yes. Any sign of others?"

"No, none. Why are they here instead of fighting the other Ferals? To kill you?"

"They're not here for me. Certainly not just me." Hawke's jaw clenched. "They're Ferals. There's only one thing they absolutely need to survive."

Olivia grimaced. "Radiance. Kara."

Hawke nodded. "That's not to say they don't also want to kill me and steal Feral House. But, yes. They're going to need Kara. Sooner or later, they're going to break in, and the draden will follow. We've got to get out."

Xavier strode into the hallway. "Dude. Are we under attack or something?"

Hawke nodded before catching himself. The kid couldn't see a nod. "We are. I need you and Pink to hide. She'll know where. *Now,* Xavier. Quickly." The two would be safe from the draden. Pink was, for all practical purposes, always in her animal. And Xavier was human. Neither attracted the draden, and both should be safe enough from the new Ferals. Hawke's jaw clenched. He and Kara were likely the only targets, if for different reasons. Remove Kara from the equation, and even if they overpowered him or sent him shifting and flying away, the attackers wouldn't stay long.

"I don't see anyone," Delaney said, returning.

"Me, either." Kara started down the stairs.

Hawke peered out the peephole just as Polaris disappeared beyond sight of the door. Lynks battled-rammed the door in his place, barely making the door rattle. Polaris was going to be the problem, not the lynx. "Polaris is heading around back." Hawke grabbed the keys to Vhyper's Porsche, pressed them into Olivia's hand, and caught all four women in his gaze. "Stay to the side of the door until I give you the sign." His gaze focused on Olivia. "Then get them out of here."

Olivia shook her head. "We're not leaving you to face them alone."

"Yes you are. Lyon gave you direct orders to protect the Radiant. She's your only concern."

"Hawke . . ." Faith touched his arm. "You need me here."

It was all he could do not to pull her against him again. "You won't survive a draden swarm, Smiley. Go with Olivia."

Her jaw tightened, and while she didn't reply, a stubborn, determined light lit her eyes.

"I mean it, Faith. I can still shift. I won't die from draden bites."

Her mouth thinned, but she nodded and looked away. Good.

The shattering of glass in the dining room ended the discussion. His heart began to thud with the certain knowledge that he had to keep it together, he had to make this work, or goddess only knew what would happen. If he lost it and shifted, leaving the women to fight it out on their own, would Polaris and Lynks kill them? The Ewan they'd known would never have, not in a million years. But something had happened to the new Ferals. Something that reeked of dark magic. And Hawke wasn't about to risk it.

As the four women pressed back against the wall beside the door, he peered out the peephole. Any moment, Polaris would be racing into the hall behind him from the dining room. *Come on, Lynks,* he thought to himself. If his timing was off on this, they were in trouble. But as he'd counted on, Lynks was gearing up for another battle ram. Hawke silently pulled back the well-oiled locks and curled his hand around the latch. As Lynks once again threw his entire weight against the door, Hawke wrenched it open and grabbed the man, using his own momentum against him to throw him against the far wall. By the time Hawke turned around, the women were racing out the door, Delaney taking up the rear, her gun drawn.

Hawke slammed the front door closed behind them and stepped in front of it as the polar bear raced down the hall, a quarter ton of angry, charging beast.

The red haze threatened, creeping around Hawke's vision as if it knew his defense against it was about to leave in Vhyper's Porsche. As if it knew that this time it would win. He drew fangs, gripping his swords in clawed hands. And prayed this wasn't his final battle. Not when the love of his life was finally his to claim.

The moment Delaney closed the front door, Faith stopped. "I'm staying."

Delaney stared at her. "You can't. You must know what the draden will do to you."

"It doesn't matter. Hawke needs me."

Olivia tossed the keys to Delaney. "You drive."

Delaney looked at Faith worriedly. "She's staying."

Olivia nodded. "I know. If he were the man I loved, I'd do the same. No matter the cost. So would you."

With a press of her lips, but understanding in her eyes, Delaney turned and took off at a run for the car.

Olivia pointed to the distance. "The draden will be coming from that direction. If you see them, get yourself into one of the cars ASAP. They're all unlocked and all warded against them. You're no good to Hawke dead." She turned, then swung back. "Don't die, Faith. We need you." Without another word, she raced back to the low-slung sports car. As she reached it, Delaney started the engine. Olivia dove into the front seat, and Delaney took off.

Suddenly alone, Faith pressed her back against the brick, listening to the crashing and growling coming from inside the house. If only she could help Hawke for real. If only she could fight beside him. But as long as she heard the sound of battle, she knew he was okay. And, hopefully, she was helping him. Hopefully, the hawk knew she was here. Regardless, it was worth the risk.

Something caught her eye. A dark cloud blowing in over the trees. No, not a cloud.

Draden.

Hawke shifted his swords, one in each hand. He didn't want to kill Polaris. The new Feral was a friend to Olivia and almost certainly enchanted. But Hawke would do whatever he had to in order to give the women a fighting chance to escape. Lynks rose from the floor slowly, one ruddy cheek streaked with blood, but Hawke focused on the charging polar bear. Waiting . . . waiting . . .

He swung his swords as he dove out of the way at the last minute, slicing one blade deep across the bear's shoulder, the other across his face, catching one of his eyes.

The bear crashed into the door, roaring in pain, blood blooming red on the snow-white fur.

As Hawke rolled to his feet, Lynks lunged at him with his own blades. One tore through Hawke's thigh, sending him into a lurch. But Hawke easily dislodged Lynks's other blade, taking off his hand in a quick, upward stroke. Lynks screamed with pain as his severed hand went flying. The man was clearly no fighter. Polaris was another matter. As Hawke swung back, the polar bear charged again. This time Hawke didn't have time to dodge. As he swept his blade at the bear's throat, a huge claw ripped through the muscle of Hawke's shoulder. For a few precious seconds, he lost control of his hand, and the blade slipped from his fingers to clatter on the tiled floor.

Before Hawke recovered, the polar bear opened his jaws and clamped down on Hawke's thigh as if he meant to take off the leg. Like hell. If Hawke didn't suspect Mage magic behind this attack, if he really thought Polaris his enemy, he'd hack off the animal's head, killing him. Instead, he drove his remaining blade through the bear's snout, feeling the prick of it in his own leg. But the strike had the desired effect. The polar bear released him and reared back with a furious growl.

Through the noise, Hawke heard the sound of the Porsche engine. The women had gotten away. Thank the . . . *no.* His hawk was too calm, too damned pleased. Faith was still nearby, still helping him. The stubborn woman hadn't left with the others as he'd told her to!

Polaris shifted in a spray of sparkling lights, turning back into a naked and bleeding man. Hawke shoved to his feet, gripping his blade. But the Feral didn't attack him as he expected. Instead, Polaris lunged for the front door.

Faith.

Hawke tried to leap after him, but that last attack had torn away too much muscle, muscle that would take time to heal. Fifteen, twenty seconds, at least, which might be fifteen or twenty seconds more than Faith had. He struggled forward, lurching awkwardly on one solid leg and one that didn't want to hold him, willing his body to heal faster. Lynks ran to cut him off, blocking him from the door. Hawke swung, catching the shifter in the shoulder.

Out of the corner of his eye, he saw smoke barreling down the hallway. No, not smoke. *Draden.* And not a few. *Hundreds.* A thick black cloud of living death burrowed through the hallways of Feral House like bees through a tunnel. But as the first one bit him, a second cloud flew in through the front door. The little fiends weren't big, about the size of his fist, their bodies little more than floating gas beneath heads that resembled hideously misshapen human faces. But their teeth were razor-sharp, and they could, and would, drain the life out of a Therian, even a Feral Warrior, given half a chance.

And Faith was out there in the middle of them.

He swung back toward Lynks, prepared to take off the idiot's head if he had to in order to get past him, but Lynks saw the cloud of deadly little beasts and began to shift . . . with his opponent far too close. A mistake no Feral made more than once.

Swinging with a timing born of long experience, Hawke cut off the lynx's two hind legs just as he fully formed. As the cat screeched in pain, Hawke lunged through the open front door, his leg and shoulder nearly healed at last. Pushing into the night, he fought through the deadly, biting cloud, desperate to find Faith.

The draden descended on him, latching on to his bare flesh with their sharp little teeth—his arms, his neck, his scalp, his face—sucking at his life force. At this rate, he'd be dead in five minutes.

He tossed his sword aside and yanked their hearts out with his free hand, but more just took their place. He could hardly see through the mass of them.

He had to reach Faith!

A flash of white caught his eye—big, lumbering white racing into the woods on the other side of the drive. Polaris.

"Faith!"

"Hawke." Her voice was muffled, the pain in it cutting him worse than the ripping, tearing teeth of the draden.

Goddess, they were both going to be dead in minutes if he didn't get them to safety. He dropped his second sword and ripped at the draden blocking his vision, and finally saw her huddled in a ball on the grass. He ran to her, scooped her up along with her blanket of draden, and ran for his Yukon.

Moments later, they were in the big SUV, along with several dozen draden. No more could breach the warded glass, but a single draden could kill given enough time, never mind dozens. While Faith struggled to remove the deadly little fiends from her face, he tore them off her scalp and arms, digging his hands into their gaseous bodies, curling his fingers around their pulsing hearts and ripping them out.

As he pulled them off her, she began to get the hang of it. But instead of removing her own attackers, she reached for his, her small hands moving with a quick grace he could only admire even as he wanted to argue with her to save herself first. But the effort seemed too great. He was already tiring and was glad he was sitting, afraid he might not be able to stand. His hands began to move slower and slower. Faith's movements, too, began to slow.

The draden were winning, sucking their lives away.

"Stay with me, Faith. Stay with me. We're almost there." He had them off her head and neck and hands, but they'd dug in through her clothes and still clung to her back and hips and legs.

He plucked and pulled, yanking the draden off her, turning them to smoke one after another until he could hardly see, until his hands were bleeding and so heavy he could hardly move them. He picked them off her even after she collapsed, unconscious, and his heart began to bleed with fear that she might not awaken again. He tore the draden from her until he could find no more on her anywhere.

Not dead. She couldn't be dead. No. He could still feel her keeping the fury at bay. "Stay with me, Smiley. Stay with me, Faith." Now that the draden were gone, she'd recover. He'd saved her.

But he couldn't say the same for himself. His energy was gone, and he was still covered in the biting, killing beasts. He was out of time.

Chapter Ten

"Hawke. Hawke!" Faith's sweet voice came at him from a distance. Hands pulled at him, the knifelike draden slowly releasing him from their deadly hold. "Hawke, don't you dare die on me. Don't you dare!"

Faith. He smelled her sweet scent, felt the brush of her hair along his cheek.

"Fight, dammit!"

She yanked him forward, plucking at the creatures at his back and hips. "Are you sitting on any? Of course you are." She shoved him toward the window. "Lift up!"

He barely heard her and wasn't certain he was doing anything at all, but he was trying. Goddess, he was trying. The red haze slunk away as blackness came for him.

"Do you feel any more? . . . Hawke!"

Her voice disappeared, then slid back into hearing. He felt her weight in his lap, her hands sliding down his legs, lifting his legs, her fingers burrowing under him, behind him.

"I got them all." Soft fingers stroked his face. "They're gone, Hawke. You'll get better, now. Please get better."

The feel of her hands on his face, warm and caring, would assure it. His head was still too heavy to lift, his eyelids too weighted down to open. But he managed to reach for her and pull her close. She melted against him, her arms curling around his neck, her head pressing against his shoulder.

"You should have gone with Olivia," he said softly, when he could make his mouth function. His body's natural healing abilities were beginning to kick in already. In a minute or two, he'd be himself again. "Do you know how close you came to dying?"

She pulled back, but he kept one arm close around her as he opened one eye, then the other, and glared at her. Her face was covered in small, unhealed bites, making her look like a measles victim. Draden bites always took much longer to heal.

"Helping you was more important." An impish smile lifted her mouth, a shadow of one of her grins, but it was enough to raise his spirits. She pressed her palm to his cheek. "You needed me."

As much as he hated to admit it, she was right. Without her there, he'd almost certainly have shifted. And the way things had gone tonight, he could have easily ended up as polar-bear food.

His hands slid up her back. "I did need you. I still do."

Mine. The word was a fierce growl in his head, echoing through his body, wrapping around his heart like a steel band. He curled his hand around the back of her head and pulled her close, kissing her soft parted lips, branding her, marking her his.

"If I can interrupt . . ." The caustic, feminine voice came from the backseat. "You're needed elsewhere."

Faith jerked back. Hawke swung around to find the Ilina, Melisande, sitting in the back, more ghostly mist than form. He'd met her once, the day he came back to himself after the spirit trap, but he was still astounded by the fact that the Ilina race existed at all. Dressed in the traditional dress of an Ilina mist warrior—brown tunic and tan leggings, a knife strapped at her waist—Melisande reminded him of a female Peter Pan with a long blond braid.

The tension went out of him. Faith scrambled back to her own seat, staring at the woman as if she were a ghost.

"Can you get this bus in gear, Feral?" Melisande snapped. "Kougar's injured. They're all injured, some too badly to mist out. We need corporeal transport."

Melisande's words cleared his head as nothing else could have. His brothers were injured. Badly. He shoved open the car door—the cloud of draden having dispersed the moment he closed them out—and bent to snatch the key out from under the mat, then jumped back in, started the car, and took off down the drive.

"The battle?" he asked.

"Is over. The bad guys ran."

He glanced over his shoulder. "Melisande, I need your maidens to do something for me. There's an injured lynx in the foyer of Feral House. I need him moved to the basement and locked in one of the prison cells. Pink can show you where the prisons are."

Melisande made a sound that made it clear the request put her out terribly. "Anything else? Shall I clean the house while I'm at it?" The woman made no bones about her dislike of all Therians, including Ferals. But her queen, Ariana, had pledged their full support. Melisande had little choice but to work with them. That didn't mean she had to like it, and she made certain they all knew that.

Melisande disappeared as silently as she'd appeared.

"What *was* she?" Faith's eyes were as big as saucers.

"The Ilinas are another immortal race, one we all believed went extinct a thousand years ago. They'd faked their extinction."

"But . . . are they ghosts?"

Hawke smiled. "No. Their natural state is mist—noncorporeal—but they can turn to flesh and blood at will. The entire race is female. Their queen, Ariana, is Kougar's mate."

As Faith settled back, taking all that in, Hawke turned his attention to his driving, to reaching his friends before it was too late. Without taking his eyes off the road, he reached for Faith's hand, twining her cold fingers with his, holding on tight. *Mine.*

His hawk screeched in agreement.

Neither of them was letting her go again.

Faith held tight to the door handle with one hand, clinging to Hawke with her other as he zipped through the tree-lined, hilly roads near Feral House. Her skin stung in a hundred places from the draden bites. But she was alive. They both were.

Never had she imagined so many draden in one place at one time. But as horrific as the draden attack had been, it was something else that preyed on her mind.

"Hawke?"

"Hmm?" His thumb brushed the back of her hand

in a tender caress that stirred the warmth in her chest, squeezing her heart with affection.

"How do you unmark a Feral Warrior?"

He glanced at her, frowning. "You don't."

Her face went cold. "But, what if you hadn't brought them into their animal, yet?"

"It doesn't matter. Once we're marked, we're marked. If we aren't brought into our animals in a couple of years, we die."

Oh.

Hawke squeezed her hand, misunderstanding her dismay. "We'll catch them, Smiley. We'll get to the bottom of this. I feel certain the Mage are involved. They're always involved when things go wrong these days."

And things couldn't have gone much more wrong than the Ferals turning against their own. Except *she* hadn't turned against them. Why? Maybe she wasn't really marked. Maybe she'd just contracted some kind of strange disease. Right. What were the chances?

Minutes later, Hawke pulled the vehicle to a stop on a narrow residential road between a pair of large homes nestled among the trees, parking behind a Porsche.

"Isn't that the one Kara, Olivia, and Delaney took?"

"Yes, it's ours. If we've got badly injured Ferals, they're going to need Kara's radiance. Lyon would have called for her the moment the coast was clear. Wait here." He reached for the door handle.

"You might need me."

He gripped her hand, pinning her with his fierce gaze. "The battle's over, but the draden will still be swarming. I mean it, Faith. I'm just going to help get the injured into the car. *Stay here.* Promise me."

"Okay. I promise."

His fierceness dissolved, and he kissed her, a quick, tender brush of lips. Then he slipped outside, closing the door behind him. In moments, the shadows swallowed him as he ran into the woods.

Faith pressed her palm to her forehead. Part of her wanted to run after him anyway. Even without a battle to fight, he could lose control and shift. But another part of her never wanted to go outside after dark again. Especially not here, where the draden numbered in the thousands. The tens of thousands.

Lights appeared behind her, visible in the outside rearview mirror. As she watched, a vehicle pulled up directly behind Hawke's. Then another behind it. Humans? Her pulse began to race. Or Maxim and the other new Ferals?

The lights went off. She waited, tense and worried, watching out her mirror. But nothing happened. No one opened the car doors in her line of vision. She turned in her seat, looking back. The car behind her appeared empty. How . . . ? But then she remembered Melisande. Ilinas wouldn't have to open the doors and run into the woods, would they. They'd simply appear there.

As the minutes ticked by, she became more and more restless, more agitated. What if Hawke was struggling not to shift? What if he needed her help, and she was too far away?

Finally, she saw him leave the woods, helping Lyon carry some kind of animal. More than a dozen men and women ran for the cars as the draden swarmed, most carrying injured animals of one kind or another. Several climbed into the two cars behind.

Fox opened the back hatch of Hawke's vehicle while

Hawke and Lyon laid what appeared to be a leg-less brown bear into the back. Grizz? They slammed the hatch closed, then ran to the driver's side, where Fox and Lyon attacked the draden covering Hawke. Hawke opened the door and slid inside, slamming the door closed behind him. Two draden flew at Faith and she lifted her arms to ward them off, but Hawke was quicker, stabbing the beasts before they reached her, then turning to kill those still attached to him. As he plucked them off himself, a shimmer of lights on either side of the car had her whirling in time to see Fox shift from an unnaturally huge fox back into a man. He and Lyon dove in opposite doors at the same time, and she realized they must have shifted to release the draden, then shifted back to get in the car.

As Hawke started the ignition and took off, they killed the last of the draden who'd flown in with them.

She looked at Hawke in question. "How bad?"

"Bad, but the only one who's died so far is Eigle."

So far. Eigle was one of the new Ferals though she couldn't place him.

Fox made a sound in his throat like a low growl. "Croc bit Jag through the middle. Tore him in half."

Her jaw dropped as she turned to meet the gaze of the new fox shifter. "But he's still alive?"

"Barely. The blood loss and the organ damage are . . ." His bit off as if unable to find a word that described it. "If he lives, he'll have to regenerate from the waist down."

"Kara's giving him radiance in the car," Lyon added. "She's trying to keep him alive while they race him to the best healer in the area."

Faith felt ill. Poor Olivia. It was so clear she and Jag adored one another. "The others?"

"No one else is in danger except Paenther." Lyon's jaw turned to rock. "His skull was crushed. Several of the others are missing arms or legs, but they'll grow new ones."

Hawke squeezed her hand. "Everyone's meeting at the Georgetown Therian enclave. Their healer, Esmeria, is the finest there is. We'll join them there once we drop Grizz in the prison."

Faith turned toward the front, shaken that the new Ferals had caused so much damage yet infinitely relieved that they'd failed in their quest to actually kill any of the true Ferals. So far. The group remained silent the rest of the short drive back to Feral House, but as they drove into the long circular drive, Lyon spoke.

"We need to be on guard. The new Ferals may have returned here. If so, we leave and come back when our numbers are stronger."

Faith frowned. Wasn't Fox one of the new ones, too? Not that she was about to question Lyon.

Hawke pulled up in front, threw the vehicle into park, then took her hand and pulled it to his mouth, placing a gentle kiss on her knuckles. "Stay here. We won't be long."

"The draden?"

"Probably won't find us before we're done."

"Good." She pulled her hand from his and grabbed the door handle. She was going to be a worthless Feral Warrior. But right now she served a purpose, and not even Hawke was going to take that away from her. "Then I'm coming."

"Faith . . ."

She met his gaze. "There's only one thing I'm needed for, and that's to help you. Let me do it."

He sighed, then nodded. "I'd rather keep you where I can protect you, anyway."

She grinned at him. "See? We both win."

She was rewarded with an endearing Hawke smile that lit her up inside and, for a few precious moments, banished the horror of the past hour.

Lyon raised a brow as he and Hawke lifted the injured and growling grizzly out of the back. "What's this about her helping you?"

"She calms the rage. Not completely, but enough to help me keep it under control."

Lyon nodded, giving her a speculative glance. "That's good."

Fox swung the hatch closed, then ran ahead to open the front door.

She followed the three men and their burden through the foyer and down a long, long stair into the basement.

Deep below the house, they passed into a fully equipped gym and through a door hidden in a floor-to-ceiling mirror on the far side. The door led into another long passage, this one appearing to be cut directly from the stone. As soon as they passed through the mirrored door, the cry of an animal in pain met her ears.

"Lynks," Hawke said. "Limbs are a bitch to regrow."

As the animal's cries grew louder, the passage opened into a small prison, individual cells lining two walls.

"In here." Lyon led the way into the nearest open cell. He and Hawke dropped the injured and snarling grizzly, then backed out, closing the barred door behind them.

Lyon and Hawke exchanged a glance. Hawke looked at her. "Go back to the gym, Faith. I'll meet you there in a moment." The look in his eye told her this command wasn't up for debate. Whatever they needed to discuss didn't involve her.

Her pulse began to sprint. Did they know she'd gone feral? Had Maxim told them during the battle?

She turned and started back down the stone passage, a dull ache forming beneath her breastbone. Halfway down the passage, she heard a shout and the grunting sounds of a scuffle. Faith froze, uncertain whether to go back.

The clang of another prison door clicking shut reached her ears along with Fox's voice. "You feckin' idiots! I fought on *your* side."

"Nothing personal," Lyon replied. "It's just a precaution until we know what we're dealing with. Shift into your animal and stay that way until we return for you. Draden don't bother animals."

"And if those feckers return?"

"Let's hope they don't. I'm doing the best with what I have, Fox. Like I said, it's nothing personal."

Faith sank back against the wall, pressing her fist to her stomach, her heart hammering. Now probably wasn't the time to admit to them that she'd gone feral.

Hawke and Lyon joined her. Hawke slid his arm around her shoulders and pulled her close as they continued down the passage. "It's been a hell of a night," he muttered.

She shivered. He had no idea. "I'll be glad when it's over." But it would never be over, would it? Being marked as a Feral Warrior was a life sentence. She could never leave Feral House and the Radiant, not for any amount of time. Returning to Warsaw, to Paulina and Maria and her rolling-stone life, was out of the question.

Tears burned her eyes, a hopelessness sweeping over her.

The Ferals, the real Ferals, were going to be furious when they found out she'd been marked, that one of the animals had been wasted on her. She'd be useless to them as a fighter.

The only good thing to come out of any of this was that she now had no choice but to stay close to Hawke. For as long as he wanted her. Would he want her, once he learned the truth? Sooner or later, she'd have to tell him.

But for right now, she was keeping her secret to herself.

An hour later, Hawke followed Lyon through the front door of the Georgetown enclave—a long line of town houses that opened into a single mansion inside. He held Faith's hand tight in his, unwilling to let go of her. She'd been silent on the ride over. They all had, lost to their own thoughts and worries. But there was a turmoil in Faith's silence that ate at him. She'd been through hell today between the revelation that the man she thought she loved had been hurting her and the draden attack. He wouldn't have been surprised if she'd needed some time . . . and space. He'd have given them to her . . . anything. But she'd leaped into his arms as if the only place she'd wanted to be was with him.

Goddess, he adored her. Whatever happened, he would make sure she was safe, and that Maxim didn't come after her again.

Kara met them, her face pale, dark shadows under her eyes. "They're stable," she said, calming their fears as she slid into Lyon's embrace. "Paenther's still unconscious, but he's doing better now that Skye's here. Jag's torso is almost completely regrown, so his organs are no longer falling out, but his legs haven't started to re-form, yet. He's in terrible pain. But they're alive. They're going to make it."

Lyon met Hawke's gaze over the top of Kara's head, his eyes revealing the same, soul-deep relief Hawke felt. His chief's sigh was lion-sized. Lyon pulled back to look into his mate's face. "And you?"

"Tired. But fine."

"Good. Take me to them, little one."

As Kara led Lyon toward the stairs, one of the Therian women strode over to Hawke, a woman he knew only casually.

"Hello, Hawke. If we'd known the Feral Warriors were coming, we'd have prepared a proper feast. As it is, we can make you sandwiches if you're hungry."

Hawke glanced at Faith. She shook her head tiredly, the shadows in her eyes tugging at him. "We're fine, thanks, Irina."

Faith pulled her hand from his. "I'd love to use the bathroom."

Irina smiled. "Of course. This way."

The pain hit him out of nowhere, like it always did, jagged bolts radiating along the inside of his skull. Right on cue, the hawk screeched in his head, digging his talons into Hawke's brain until he almost felt as if they were drawing blood. Seven seconds, eight . . . fourteen, fifteen. Finally, the misery began to recede, and he could breathe again.

Faith, led by Irina, had already turned the corner, out of his sight, and it was all he could do not to go after her. She was his. He felt it in every bone in his body.

But the last thing she needed was to get involved with him in his current state. For all that she seemed to have a calming effect on the rage, her presence had done nothing to help when he *had* lost control. Thirty-seven hours he'd been gone.

He didn't even know how she felt about him. He wondered if *she* knew. She was drawn to him, certainly, had kissed him with passionate abandon in the foyer of Feral house. But whether or not her feelings for him were anywhere near as deep as his own were for her was anyone's guess.

He shoved his hands in the front pockets of his jeans. It would be best if she never developed strong feelings for him, not if the break with his animal continued on its current downward spiral.

If he really cared about her, he'd push her away.

But it would be easier to stop breathing.

Chapter Eleven

Faith slipped into the bathroom, closed and locked the door, and began stripping. If she had feral marks, she wanted to see them. And if she didn't? Then something else was at play. With determined hands she yanked her shirt over her head, unfastened her bra and tossed it aside, then stood in front of the mirror, turning her back to peer over her shoulder, lifting her arms, her breasts. *Where are they?*

Kicking off her shoes, she unsnapped her jeans and pulled them off, then studied her legs, front and back. Still no sign of the scars that all Ferals sported somewhere on their bodies. That glimmer of hope grew inside her. Maybe it really was something else that had made her draw claws and fangs.

She closed the toilet lid and used it as a step to the counter until she was standing stark naked in front of the oversized mirror, hunched over so she didn't hit her head on the ceiling. Turning her back to the mirror, she looked over her shoulder, and that was when she saw them, high on her inner thigh—four small claw marks.

Damn.

Reaching between her legs, she felt for them, her fingertips sliding over the shallow indentations she could barely feel and wouldn't have noticed unless she'd been looking for them. That glimmer of hope sputtered and died. After a last, dismayed glance at those treacherous marks, she jumped down, then quickly dressed again. At least no one would accidentally see them. Unless she went feral again, no one would know. She'd have to tell someone eventually, of course. When the time was right.

She swallowed. Not now.

Hawke was waiting for her when she left the bathroom. His brows drew together as if he could read her thoughts. "Are you okay?"

"You keep asking me that."

"I care." His hand slid beneath her hair, cupping her neck, his eyes warm as a summer sun, then dimming as he frowned. "You're shaking."

Who wouldn't be at the prospect of having nine Feral Warriors furious at her? Maybe even ready to toss her in their prison. She shrugged and tried to smile, uncertain how good an effort she'd made. "It's been a rough day."

Hawke's eyes softened, his hands lifting to frame her face, his thumbs stroking her cheeks. "I'm sorry." The truth of those words throbbed in his voice, bringing tears to her eyes. He leaned close and placed a gentle kiss on her forehead, then pulled back, watching her for several long moments before his gaze dipped to her mouth. His nostrils flared as his touch grew more firm, more . . . needy.

She trembled in anticipation as his head bent down to hers. The moment their lips touched, reason fled. With a groan, he hauled her against him, sweeping his tongue into her mouth, stealing her breath, her thoughts. His lips were at once firm and soft, his kiss tender and fierce. She slid her arms around his neck, pulling him tight as their tongues stroked one another, sliding together in a spiraling, sensual ballet, a melding that teased and inflamed, sending a flush over her skin and damp heat pooling between her legs.

She pressed herself against him, needing to be closer, and felt the hard press of his erection against her stomach.

Hawke groaned, then leaned down and swept her into his arms, still kissing her. Vaguely, she was aware that he carried her a short distance, around a corner, into an empty sitting room of some kind. Still kissing her, he released her legs, holding her upper body tight against him until she twisted and wrapped her legs around his waist, pressing swollen, sensitive flesh against his male hardness.

Hawke gripped her buttocks, pulling her tighter, and she gasped at the stroke of sweet fire. He tore his mouth from hers, kissing her cheek, then pulled back just enough to look into her face as he slid himself slowly along her mons, sending rippling shards of pleasure straight up into her core even with them both fully clothed. Her eyes too heavy to fully open, she smiled at him.

"You like that," he murmured, his voice rich with male satisfaction.

"Oh, yeah."

Holding her hips tight, he rubbed himself against her

again and again until she was rocking back, gasping with impending release. The orgasm broke over her, fast and explosive and she cried out, the sound swallowed by Hawke's hard, passionate kiss. He continued to rock against her as the spasms rolled through her, one after another, until finally she floated back down from the ether.

As she calmed, he buried his face against her neck, kissing the curve, kissing her jaw. Beneath his gentleness, she felt the strain of his own unrelieved need in the tension of his back and neck and the fine vibrations in his hands.

Slowly, he pulled back and let her legs slide to the floor. He pressed her against the wall behind her, looking down into her face with heavy, sexy-as-sin eyes. "You are so beautiful. Always. But in the throes of passion . . ." He shook his head, his eyes growing even heavier, burning with a fire that made her shiver with longing all over again. He gripped her waist, his warm hands sliding under her shirt, caressing her heated skin, then rising to cover her breasts.

He leaned forward, kissing her temple as his fingers found her nipples and squeezed, making her gasp and arch into his touch. His hands were shaking, his breaths coming hard and fast as he pulled one hand away, pressed his palm against her abdomen, and slid it down into her pants, inside her panties, and down into her wetness.

His big body shuddered, his cheek pressed against her temple. "You're so hot, so ready for me. I need to be inside you."

She pressed against his seeking fingers, moaning with pleasure as he stroked her sensitive clitoris, then slid inside her heat. "*Yes.*" She wanted him inside her, covering her, under her, beside her. Now. Always.

"I need to find a room with a lock. And a bed."

Where he'd undress her. Part her legs. See her feral marks.

She froze.

Hawke stilled, then slowly pulled his hand from her pants. "When you're ready."

She stared at him, drowning in the gentle concern she saw in his eyes. But this wasn't about Maxim as Hawke believed. They'd never had any kind of physical relationship. A wisp of nightmare seared her mind. *Pain.* Her breath caught on a shudder. Yes, they'd had a physical relationship, just not a loving one. None of her feelings for Maxim had been real.

Hawke cupped her jaw, stroking her cheek with his thumb, as he watched her with a gentle intensity, the fire banked beneath layers of tenderness. "I'll give you all the time you need, Smiley. But you're mine."

Inside, an answering cry sounded from her heart. But would he feel that way when he knew the truth of what she'd become?

"There you are." Tighe stuck his head in the room. "Lyon's called a meeting. The conference room is at the end of the hall." He motioned with his head and was gone.

Hawke turned back to her, still stroking her cheek as he looked deep into her eyes as if he'd find and steal her secrets. As if he'd keep them safe for all eternity. As if he'd keep her safe. He slid his hand over the back of her head, pulling her against his side as he turned for the door.

Minutes later, they were seated side by side at a large

conference table. Kougar took the seat beside Hawke.

"I heard you were injured," Hawke said to his friend.

"Lost an arm and shoulder." Both of which had fully grown back.

Wulfe, Tighe, and Olivia filed in and took seats across from them. Olivia looked pale. Faith understood why as Jag's yell echoed down from high in the house.

Wulfe frowned. "I thought he was doing okay."

Olivia grimaced. "His legs are regrowing. Along with everything in between."

Several of the Ferals blanched.

"There's nothing in this world more painful than regrowing a penis," Kougar said quietly.

"It's taking longer than the legs." Olivia crossed her arms tight as if shielding herself as another of Jag's yells echoed through the house.

"That's part of the reason it's so painful. It takes forever."

"How much longer?" Olivia asked.

"Another hour, maybe."

Every man shuddered this time. Olivia squeezed her eyes closed. "It better come back as good as new, that's all I'm saying."

Vhyper joined them, and Lyon took his place at the front of the room. Over the next ten minutes, they recounted the battle, everything that happened on that battlefield, even before Maxim reached them.

"They attacked all at once." Tighe leaned forward, his hands fisted on the table in front of him. "One well-choreographed move that we never saw coming. One moment they were fighting the draden, the next, us. If we'd been any less skilled, they might have killed us all."

Olivia made a sound of disagreement. "I've known

Polaris for centuries. He's as good a man as any man here, and he would never have turned on you willingly." Her gaze sought Lyon's. "You know that. He had to have been enthralled."

"I have to agree with Olivia." Beside Faith, Hawke leaned forward. "Maxim told Faith that the new Ferals planned to kill us and free the Daemons. The Mage have found yet another way to fill the Feral ranks with those who'll release the Daemons from their magical prison."

Wulfe frowned. "Fox didn't attack us at all. He fought with us. He got a chunk of fur torn out of his hide from one of the seventeen in that initial battle. He fought them, not us."

"Grizz was the one who went after Fox," Vhyper added. "I was too preoccupied with fighting to pay a lot of attention, but I remember thinking it was a lame-ass attack."

Lyon watched him. "How so?"

"He leaped on the fox so fast I thought he was going to tear his head off. I think he could have. Instead, he nipped him in the butt."

Wulfe grunted. "If you call a soccerball-sized chunk of fur a nip."

"My point is he pulled his punch. At the very least, he could have ripped off his hind leg. And he didn't. I shifted and cut off his two back legs far too easily."

"What are you saying, Vhype?" Lyon asked.

"I don't think Grizz wanted to be fighting us. Something was controlling him."

"Which doesn't fit with enthrallment. The enthralled can't fight it." Lyon paced the front of the room. "Is there any possibility their souls were stolen?"

Faith clenched her hands together in her lap. They were looking in the wrong place. Because they didn't have all the facts.

Kougar stroked his goatee. "I didn't see any evidence. Then again, none of us realized our previous fox had lost his soul until it was far too late."

Lyon frowned. "We have to figure out what the Mage have done to them."

Faith reached for Hawke, touching his arm. When he turned to her, she whispered, "I might know something."

All heads swiveled her way, putting her in a spotlight she wasn't entirely ready for. She took a deep breath, then said what she needed to. "Maxim told me that the new Ferals were the wrong ones. They weren't the ones who were supposed to have been marked."

To a man, their gazes narrowed. Faith's pulse began to race.

"How did he know that?" Lyon asked.

"I don't know. He didn't tell me."

"Is there anything else, Faith? Anything else he told you that you haven't mentioned yet?"

Her pulse began to pound. She swallowed. "He told me that the only thing women were good for was the way they screamed when you cut them." Sounds of anger and disgust erupted around the table. "He told me he steals girls off the streets, human girls, and makes them bleed."

"He dies," Wulfe snarled.

Tighe nodded. "Slowly."

Vhyper hissed. "With his cock shoved down his throat."

While the harsh voices ping-ponged across the table,

Faith turned to Hawke. His gaze was fixed on hers, fury in the dark depths of his eyes. And pain.

"He hurt you, didn't he?" he asked quietly.

She nodded. "I don't remember much. He clouded my mind." A shudder tore through her, and she shook her head. "It doesn't matter. This isn't about me."

Hawke's grip on her hand tightened, a silent promise that she'd never endure that kind of pain at Maxim's hands again. She managed a smile for him, then looked toward Lyon and the others. "My point is, Maxim is a monster. He should never have been marked to be a Feral Warrior."

Lyon turned to Kougar. "Have you ever heard of this happening? A marking gone wrong?"

"No." Kougar stroked his beard. His eyes narrowed, clearly focused on something not before him. "What if this is what Hookeye was doing at the Ilina temple? Not trying to set up another wormhole into the spirit trap, as we believed, but this. He was there to access the spirit trap and free the seventeen animal spirits. Free them and make them into weapons."

All were silent, startled and thoughtful, except for Tighe and Hawke, who exchanged a confused glance.

"Hookeye?" Tighe asked. "Something else we missed while we were caught in the spirit trap?"

Kougar nodded. "Hookeye was Mage, the self-professed poison master and the one who attacked the Ilinas a millennium ago and drove them into hiding. We found him a couple of weeks ago in the abandoned Ilina temple in the Himalayas. A temple with access to the spirit trap. He's dead."

"Did you hear the animal cries when we were in that trap?" Hawke asked Tighe.

Tighe nodded. "At first, they were just sounds. Snuffles, low growls, a whinny. But then they turned agitated, clearly in pain. I thought I was imagining it."

"I did, too. I wondered if those cries had been echoing down there for hundreds of years. Now I wonder if we weren't hearing the spirits being torn from that place."

Silence descended for the space of a dozen heartbeats.

"So are we saying the animal spirits were poisoned?" Vhyper asked. "With some kind of dark magic?"

Faith swallowed the sound of distress that dug at her throat. Dark magic?

"Have they turned the new Ferals evil?" Tighe asked the question she couldn't.

But she hadn't turned evil. Surely she'd know if she had. She'd have risen up against the good Ferals along with the others. Right?

"It's possible the animal spirits were just the carriers." Kougar's pale eyes turned hard. "If we're lucky, this was a one-time thing. They passed the infection on to the men they marked, then were free of it. No Feral marked in the future will be affected."

"Are you saying what I think you're saying?" Lyon asked.

"That we may need to kill the ones that have been marked? Allow the animal spirits to mark the ones they should have in the first place? Yes."

Faith felt the blood drain from her face.

Olivia surged to her feet. "Ewan . . . Polaris . . . does not deserve to die for this! Maybe he wasn't the one meant to be marked, but I'll bet he was in the top three of that polar-bear line. He's a good man, every bit as strong physically and morally as any man here.

I've known him for centuries. There's no evil in him. *None.*"

Lyon nodded. "Polaris is a good man and a good fighter. But he tried to kill Hawke." He held up his hand, forestalling Olivia's argument. "We're all but certain he's under the influence of magic, but that doesn't make him any less dangerous. If he can be cured of the darkness, perhaps he'll make a fine Feral Warrior. The same can't be said of all of them."

Good heavens, that was an understatement. They had no idea. She was going to make a terrible Feral Warrior. She barely knew how to kill draden!

As Olivia resumed her seat, Wulfe leaned back. "So why were they marked? Polaris is a good guy, the sabertooth clearly isn't. Eigle got himself killed in his first fight. I understand that the Mage magic probably kept the animal spirits from marking the ones they wanted, but who did they mark?"

Lyon looked to Kougar.

Kougar pursed his mouth thoughtfully. "I'm inclined to believe they were marked at random. Some may make good Feral Warriors . . . or would have if they hadn't been infected . . . like Polaris. Others are the dregs of the race. But most are probably decent men who should never have been chosen."

Or women, Faith thought. Decent men or women.

"The Shaman should take a look at the three we've captured," Kougar said.

Lyon nodded. "I agree. If we're right, Fox will be free of the magic, and we can let him out of the prison. The other two will remain locked up until we can find a cure. If any other new Ferals arrive, they'll join them in the prison. In the meantime, I'll enlist the aid of the enclave here in digging into the backgrounds of everyone who's been recently marked. I want to know who these men are."

"Does it matter?" Kougar's question hung in the air.

Lyon tilted his head. "You think it shouldn't?"

"If we want to maximize our chances of defeating Inir and his army, we need the strongest Ferals. Period. If, goddess forbid, Inir succeeds in freeing the Daemons without us, and I'm no longer certain he won't, then we absolutely must have the strongest. The ones marked are the wrong men."

Faith's stomach cramped. Kougar thought they should all be killed. Even if they were cured. Her pulse began to pound, instinct yelling at her to run. Fight or flight. *Deep breaths.* She struggled to get control. They didn't know she'd been marked. Yet.

Lyon cleared his throat, and all eyes turned to him. "We need to find a cure for the infection. If we succeed, we'll decide where to go from there. If we don't, then we'll have no choice." They would kill them. His expression grew hard. "I don't need to tell you that this discussion goes no further than this room. The new Ferals absolutely cannot know their fates lie in the balance."

"Where are they?" Vhyper asked.

Wulfe nodded. "I've been wondering the same. And why did they run? They caught us by surprise. If they'd kept fighting instead of taking off, they could have made certain Jag and Paenther were dead. They might have succeeded in killing one or two more of us, too."

For a moment, all were silent. Faith didn't know the answer any more than they did.

"They're Mage creations," Kougar said slowly. "Possibly even Mage puppets. And the puppet master, Inir, most likely, didn't want his puppets destroyed. The fact that they ran instead of continuing to fight supports the theory that the animal will only infect the first Feral he marks. Inir, or whoever was controlling the new Ferals in that battle, must have feared he'd lose too many. It was better to pull them out of there, regroup, and attack again later."

"Not only were they outmatched," Hawke said beside her. "But the puppet master was losing his hold on some of them. On Grizz, at least. He may have feared more would slip from his grasp. He called them to him to reinforce that control."

"To steal their souls," Tighe muttered.

Hawke nodded. "Possibly."

"We have to find them." Lyon began to pace, the general planning his battle strategy. After several minutes, he started issuing orders. "First, we retake and secure Feral House. Then we interrogate the prisoners with the Shaman's help—learn what we can from them. Tighe, have Skye contact the Mage resistance, let them know we're hunting the new Ferals and they may be heading for a Mage stronghold."

"I'll drive up to Harpers Ferry," Wulfe offered. "To make sure they haven't gone back there."

Lyon nodded. "Once Feral House is secure, and I no longer need you there." His gaze swung to Kougar. "Find a cure." He straightened and addressed them all, his gaze sliding from one man to the next. "But our number one job is to protect our Radiant."

Heartfelt, murmured assent erupted around the table.

"The new Ferals need her radiance as much as we do, now. Their first goal is almost certainly to steal her."

"They're not getting her," Wulfe growled.

"No way in hell," Tighe concurred.

It was clear they all loved her, and Faith could certainly understand why. Kara was the heart of Feral House.

Lyon lifted his hand. "We'll leave for Feral House at dawn." Which gave them about an hour. "Meeting dismissed."

As everyone stood, Faith rose, and Hawke pulled her into his arms, resting his chin on top of her head. In Hawke's arms, she felt safe.

Yet, never had her life been more in danger.

Chapter
Twelve

They piled into two vehicles. Hawke drove his big black SUV with Lyon in front beside him. Faith and Kara climbed into the far back at Kara's suggestion. Skye, Olivia, and Delaney had remained at the enclave—Skye and Olivia at their mates' bedsides and Delaney because of the babe she carried.

As the vehicle started, Kara turned to her, her eyes sympathetic. "I'm sorry, Faith. I'm sorry Maxim wasn't the man you thought he was."

Faith nodded, brushing her palms over her worn jeans, uncertain how to respond. She hadn't even known Maxim, really, except for his dictatorial, jealous ways. And the cruelty in his eyes that last time as he'd told her all the horrible things he'd done. She kept getting flashes of nightmarish pain and wondered if it would all come back to her eventually, if she'd be forced to relive it all again in her mind.

"I'm glad you're staying." Kara glanced in Hawke's direction, a small smile lifting her mouth before she turned back. "Maybe you'll decide to stay permanently. I'd like that."

Faith's chest squeezed. There was nothing she wanted more that to be with Hawke permanently. If only her situation were so simple. If only she could choose to stay because she was starting to fall for one of the Ferals—a good one this time. Because he wanted her to stay. Not because she would die without radiance if she left. But everything was so complicated. And her choices were no longer her own.

She tried to return Kara's smile, but her effort fell short. "I'd like that, too."

When they arrived at Feral House, the men fanned out. Like the previous night, they were prepared for a battle, although Lyon had been in touch with Pink, and she'd assured him she'd seen no sign of the new Ferals. Wulfe pulled off his clothes, shifted into his wolf, and began sniffing, probably searching for their scent. After a complete circle of the house, he knelt behind one of the cars and shifted back, then rose and dressed again.

"None of them have been here in the past six hours."

Lyon nodded. "Good. Wulfe and Vhyper, replace the broken windows. The rest of you, come with me."

Hawke came over to where she stood with Kara, his gaze soft and concerned, as it always was. As if he walked on eggshells around her. As Lyon took Kara's hand, Hawke wrapped his arm around Faith's shoulders, and, together, they followed.

"Are you okay?" he asked quietly.

"I'm fine, and you can quit asking me that." She

smiled, taking the sting out of her words. "I'm stronger than I look."

But though a hint of approval flashed in his gaze, the worry didn't leave his eyes. "When I saw you a couple of days ago, after not seeing you for days, I knew something was wrong. Very wrong. That's why I came to you that night. But you denied it. And I know now I was right."

"I didn't know what he was doing to me. I didn't remember."

Hawke nodded. "Understood. But my gut still tells me something's wrong, something that you're not telling me. Something that scares you."

Faith looked away, trying to hide the telltale flush she felt rise to her cheeks. How could he possibly see her so clearly?

"I'm not keeping anything from you, Hawke," she fabricated. "Not intentionally. I think the fear may be coming from my subconscious. Things he did to me that I haven't yet remembered." It was time to change the subject before he pressed, and she wound up telling him things she wasn't ready to share. "Who is he?" she whispered, nodding toward the Shaman, who walked a distance ahead of them. He looked like a young teenager.

She felt Hawke's gaze on her but kept her own straight ahead, not wanting to see the knowing look in his eyes. Not wanting him to read the secrets in her own.

"The Shaman is very old, somewhere between six and ten thousand years. I doubt even he knows."

Faith's eyes widened, her jaw dropping.

"He was attacked by Mage magic when he was a teen and never physically aged again, but he acquired a rare ability to sense that magic in others. His gift isn't foolproof, but he's good. And he's very, very kind. He's been good enough to stay in the area since this latest Mage war began. We have need of him more often than we care for, believe me."

If the Shaman could detect magic in others, could he detect the dark magic in her? She shivered, but if Hawke noticed, he didn't comment.

As they entered the house, Wulfe called out, "Pink! Xavier! We're back." To Vhyper he said, "I'll check on them, then meet you in the storeroom." Vhyper opened the door to the basement, started down, and they all followed.

"Why didn't we take Pink and Xavier with us to the enclave?" Faith asked quietly.

"They were safe here, and we can't risk anyone's seeing either of them. The human police are still searching for Xavier. And Pink . . ." He shrugged, as if that said it all. And it did. With her human-shaped face covered in pink feathers and her flamingo legs, there would be no passing Pink off as anything other than nonhuman.

They reached the prisons to find the grizzly and fox prowling their cages as impatiently as any caged beasts. But the lynx merely lay on the floor watching them. As the group approached, Grizz and Fox shifted into men in twin sprays of colored lights, Fox fully dressed, Grizz startlingly naked. Despite the size of him, there wasn't an ounce of fat anywhere. Which was more than she really needed to know.

Fox stared at them, looking thoroughly annoyed. But Grizz growled, grabbed the bars, and shook them as if he were trying to yank them out of the floor. "Let me out of here!" he roared.

Lynks closed his cat eyes, ignoring them.

Lyon and Tighe exchanged a look that said they weren't sure how to go about this. If they meant for the Shaman to go into one of those cages, Faith didn't want to be anywhere near when they opened the doors. Certainly not Grizz's, anyway.

"The Shaman is here to examine you," Lyon said, his voice loud enough to be heard over the bear shifter's fury. "If you've been infected with Mage magic, as we suspect, he has the ability to sense it. We need to know what's happened in order to help you."

To Faith's surprise—to everyone's she suspected—Grizz thrust his hand through the bars, palm up, as if asking for that help.

Lyon stepped forward without hesitation and grasped Grizz's wrist. The big Feral growled but didn't fight him. The Shaman took a step forward, hesitated, then continued forth, laying both hands on Grizz's exposed forearm. He jerked his hands back, then cautiously touched the big man's arm with one hand only. For several seconds, he stood rooted, his eyelids drifting closed. Finally, he stepped away, turning to Lyon. "He's badly infected, though I can't say for certain it's Mage magic. It could be Daemon or a combination."

"Is the animal spirit infected?" Lyon asked.

"I don't know. It's impossible to tell."

Fox stuck his hand out in the same way Grizz had, his jaw set in a hard line. "My turn."

Lyon released Grizz and repeated the move on Fox. The Shaman touched the fox shifter's arm, then motioned him closer to the bars and reached into the cage, pressing his hand to Fox's forehead. The Feral watched the Shaman warily but allowed the touch.

"Nothing." The Shaman pulled away, turning to Lyon. "Completely clean. No darkness or magic whatsoever."

Fox folded his arms, his jaw hard, his stance shouting, *I told you so.*

Lyon opened the door of the cage himself, then held out his arm. "No hard feelings? After what happened last night, I couldn't take a chance."

Fox stared at him for several seconds, letting Lyon's arm hang before he finally, slowly unfolded his own and grasped Lyon's forearm as Lyon grasped his.

"How are Jag and Paenther?" Fox asked.

Lyon nodded as if pleased with the question. "Stable and healing. They'll make it." Lyon turned to the third Feral. "Shift, Lynks."

The cat lifted his lids, blinking at the Chief of the Ferals lazily. Ignoring the command.

Lyon glanced at Fox. "Vhyper tells me you managed to shift your form to the size of a small horse last night. Far larger than your predecessor."

Fox shrugged, his mood still darkly angry.

"Maybe you'd like to demonstrate that to Lynks. You can do it in his cage if you'd like."

Tighe chuckled. "You can show him your teeth up close and personal."

Fox glanced at Tighe, a dangerous smile spreading across his mouth. "Bloody right."

In a quick spray of sparkling lights, Lynks shifted, then rose, fully clothed, to stare at them sullenly. He didn't look well. He looked, Faith thought, as if he'd suffered and wasn't a man used to suffering.

"Put your hand through the bars," Lyon snapped. Lynks did so slowly, and Lyon grabbed his wrist as he had the others.

The Shaman's examination went much as it had with Grizz. "Thick, dark magic. The same as the other." He released the Feral, and Lyon did the same. "It appears that the nine are clean, but the seventeen have most definitely been infected, as you believed."

Faith's stomach knotted. She wondered what would happen if she held out her hand to the Shaman, too. Would he declare her infected? She swallowed hard, watching Grizz once more shake his cage like a wild beast.

"Maybe not all the nine." Hawke released her and stepped toward the Shaman, holding out his hand as the caged Ferals had done. "Check me, Shaman."

Lyon tilted his chin in question.

"I was in that spirit trap," Hawke replied in answer to Lyon's unspoken question. "As was my hawk."

The Shaman took Hawke's wrist as he had the others. With a frown, he lifted his hand to the top of Hawke's head. "I sense no infection, but . . ." His frown deepened. "There is deep trauma within your bond with your animal, warrior."

"I know. We're working on it."

The Shaman nodded.

Lyon's brows lowered with concern. "But you don't sense that it's being caused by magic?"

"No, but I'm not sure I'd detect any magic within the spirit, only the man. If you find a cure, Hawke and Tighe should partake of it, too, just to be sure."

Lyon glanced at the two caged Ferals. "Can their magic be cleared in the usual way?"

"If it's Mage, I would assume so," the Shaman replied. "If it's Daemon, perhaps not."

Faith glanced up at Hawke as he stepped back to join her. "What's the usual way?"

Hawke lifted an eyebrow, his eyes beginning to gleam. "Sex."

Her eyes narrowed. "No, it's not."

"It is. It's during the moment of sexual release that the mind and body are the most open. With the mind opened, the body is able to expel simple magic. Most Therians know that."

"I was a little young when I was last around Therians."

"I'm not risking a woman with Grizz," Lyon said. "He's too violent."

Without warning, the huge shifter reached between his legs, grabbed his long, flaccid member, and began pumping himself.

Faith gasped, covering her mouth with her hand as her gaze slammed into Kara's. As one, they burst into shocked laughter. And just as quickly turned back to the prison. There was something incredibly . . . *intriguing* . . . about watching a man like that get himself off. Grizz clearly wanted to be rid of that magic. Immediately.

"I'll ask Ariana to send one of her maidens for Lynks." Kougar's calm tone made it sound as if this kind of thing happened all the time at Feral House. "It's unlikely he'll be able to hurt her even if he tries."

"I would never demand a woman—" Lyon began, but Kougar cut him off.

"The legends are true, Roar. Many Ilinas are highly sexual creatures who crave sex with corporeal males. Not all, of course. Ariana will send one who is."

Moments later, a woman appeared out of thin air, a

petite dark-haired beauty in a diaphanous long green gown, her loose hair falling nearly to her waist.

"How . . . ?" Faith began.

"Kougar can communicate with Ariana over any distance," Hawke said. "It comes in handy."

"Phylicia." Kougar nodded.

The woman smiled, a seductive look on her face as her gaze tripped from male to male with eager excitement, landing on Fox. "This one? He's beautiful."

"No." Lyon motioned toward the prisons, toward Lynks, but Phylicia caught sight of Grizz, who was still pumping himself, and stuck fast.

"Warrior," she purred. Suddenly, she was no longer standing outside the cages. She was in with Grizz, pulling up her gown.

"He isn't the one, Phylicia," Kougar said evenly.

"Oh, I think he is. The perfect one." A second later, her legs were wrapped around Grizz's waist, her back against the stone wall as he thrust inside her.

As one, Faith and Kara whirled away, covering their faces.

"I'll never get used to this," Kara muttered, stepping beside her.

Faith's body was growing hotter with each slap of flesh against flesh, with each moan of pleasure. In her mind, it wasn't Grizz and the Ilina but Hawke. And her. And she wanted that, wanted him, with every tight breath she drew into her lungs.

"He's dangerous, Phylicia," Kougar said behind them. "Be aware."

"He's . . . *magnificent*," she replied.

Faith glanced over her shoulder, peeking at Hawke, wondering if he was as aroused . . . Her breath caught as their gazes collided, his scorching hot. He hadn't been looking at the rutting couple. He'd been watching her. In his eyes, she saw the promise of pleasure every bit as intense as that they were witnessing. And soon.

Phylicia screamed her release. Grizz roared with his own. A moment later, Phylicia stood once more outside the cage, her gown falling around her calves, her face flushed and damp, her smile radiant.

"*Ah*, that was good. Who's next? Who was it you'd meant me to take?"

"Me!" Lynks was standing, his hands curled around the bars of his cage.

Lyon shook his head. "Wait a moment, if you will, Phylicia. Shaman?"

Once more, Grizz thrust his hand through the bars of the cage. Once more, the Shaman examined him. "No change. The infection held fast."

With an angry growl, Grizz tore his arm from the Shaman's grasp and whirled away.

"We'll find a cure for the magic," Lyon told him. "But until we do, you'll both have to remain here. I'm sorry." He turned to the Shaman. "Has the Ilina been infected?"

A moment later, the Ilina's hand in his, the Shaman shook his head. "She's fine."

Lyon gave her a nod. "Thank you, Phylicia. We need nothing more from you."

The Ilina smiled. "Call me anytime." And she was gone.

"Hey!" Lynks cried.

"Jack off," Grizz snarled.

"I'll not endanger any female unnecessarily." Lyon

reached for Kara's hand and started down the passage that led out of the prisons.

Hawke took Faith's hand, and they followed.

"That was . . ." She didn't have words.

"Moving?"

"Yes," she replied huskily. She glanced up at him. Their gazes collided, heat leaping between them. Desperately, she wanted to be in his arms, in his bed, yet she didn't dare let him make love to her. Certainly not in daylight. Unless he was the kind of guy who went at the deed without any additional exploration, he was too likely to see her feral marks. Or feel them. No, she couldn't let him make love to her, no matter how badly she wanted him to.

She turned away, heart pounding, and struggled to change the subject. "Why is Fox different?" she asked as they passed through the gym. "And what are *the nine*? I'm confused."

Hawke's thumb stroked the back of her hand, a faint tremor in his own that told her how badly he wanted her. "After the seventeen warriors and their animal spirits were lost in the spirit trap six hundred years ago, there were nine Feral Warriors left. The nine. One of them, the previous fox shifter, died a few months ago."

Faith nodded. "So his is the animal who marked Fox, not one of the seventeen from the trap. Which is why there's no dark magic attached to him."

"Correct. The nine are magic-free and are the men chosen by our animals—presumably the strongest of our lines. Those marked by the seventeen lost animal spirits appear to be infected. According to what you were told, and what we've seen, they're not the ones meant to be marked. Not the strongest of their lines."

She nodded. "Fox was the one who confused me since he's a new Feral yet not like the others."

"We'll be taking shifts guarding the house and sleeping," Lyon said, when they reached the main floor. "Tighe and Hawke, you two take the first sleep shift." He glanced at Hawke knowingly. "Make sure there's sleep involved? I need you on your game."

Hawke nodded, his gaze sliding to Faith. At the heat that leaped into his eyes, her pulse stuttered. As they started up the stairs, she started to pull back, but Tighe was right behind them. Maybe, once they got to Hawke's room, she'd tell him she wasn't tired. No, those would be the words he'd want to hear. She could tell him she was too tired. Or she had a headache. And how lame was that?

They reached his bedroom door, and he ushered her inside. She'd seen it earlier right after she'd gone Feral, but this time she actually looked around. Bookshelves lined two full walls, shelves filled with every manner of intriguing thing—books, skeletons of small animals, gadgets of every size and shape. The walls were deep tan, the bedspread a dark blue, and on the wall above the bed hung a dozen antique swords and daggers. The only thing she'd noticed last night was the framed letter from Robert E. Lee hanging on the wall above his desk, a letter urging the strong men of Feral House to join the Confederate cause.

Hawke closed the door behind her. Before she could think of the right excuse, she was in his arms, and he was kissing her. Sensation exploded, thought fled in the heat of the fire that flared between them. He tasted of sin and power and safety. And she wanted him with a hot, shuddering desperation that nearly obliterated everything else.

He pressed her back against the door, hands covering, kneading her breasts, and she lifted to his touch, thrusting her fingers into his short, soft hair, arching against the thick ridge pressed against her belly. Moisture dampened her panties, a moan of pure need escaping her throat. In a distant part of her mind, she was aware that if she meant to keep her pants on, this wasn't the way to do it.

His lips moved over hers frantically, his tongue sweeping against hers, hard and desperate. Long fingers dove beneath the hem of her shirt, caressing her bare flesh, pushing aside the lace of her bra to stroke her bare breasts. He thrust his jeans-clad erection against her, and she moaned again as the fire flared higher, hotter.

Sanity fled. She tugged at the T-shirt tucked into his jeans, pulling it out of his waistband, burrowing her hands beneath to slide her palms against the warm flesh covering granite-hard muscle.

Hawke pulled back, yanked his shirt over his head, sending his masculine scent wrapping itself around her, revealing that gorgeous chest to her hungry eyes. She reached for him, sliding her hands over those rock-hard abs and up to flick his nipples lightly with her thumbs. His groan made her smile, and she looked up to meet his gaze.

Her breath caught at the blazing heat and infinite tenderness that filled his eyes. Her chest began to ache with a pressure nearly too great to contain. And the fear that when he knew the truth, he wouldn't look at her this way again.

He reached behind her, fingering her bra, and she knew she'd already let things go too far.

"No, Hawke."

His hands stilled as he watched her, his eyes tightening with disappointment. A disappointment quickly masked by soft regret. He dropped his hands, cupping her waist instead, his need clear in the tension of his fingers.

"I'm sorry, Smiley. I know you're not ready."

She stroked his face, his handsome, dear, *beloved* face and forced the lie between her lips. "No. I'm not." In truth, she'd never been more ready, her body hot, wet, throbbing with need of him.

He leaned forward, placing a soft kiss on her nose. "I shouldn't have fallen on you like that. Not after all you've been through."

She laughed, the sound strangled. "I . . . understand. After watching Grizz and the Ilina . . ."

His eyes deepened until she thought she'd drown in their dark, steaming depths. "I've been on fire for you since the first time you smiled at me. It's not Grizz and the Ilina. It's you, in my room, no longer tied to another man, that sent me over the edge." He pulled in a deep, shuddering breath and lifted a hand to tenderly brush the hair back from her face. "Every time I touch you, I go a little crazy." His smile was gentle and endearing. "Ironic, isn't it? You make me lose control even as you help me keep it."

A lump that threatened to choke her formed in her throat. He was such a good man, and she was a bad, bad person for lying to him like this. For not telling him, for not telling any of them that they had another new Feral hiding in their midst, another who was likely infected.

Eventually, she'd have to, of course. And when she did, she feared Hawke would never look at her the same way again.

Hawke tried to sleep, but it was impossible, not because he was on the floor—in the right frame of mind he could sleep anywhere—but because his body still burned despite the cold shower. And because Faith lay in the bed a few feet away, tossing and turning, not sleeping any better than he was. But mostly because his instincts kept yelling at him that something was still wrong. That he'd rescued her from Maxim, but she wasn't safe.

He'd given her one of his T-shirts to wear, and he watched as one bare leg slid out from beneath the sheet, curling back over it. Moments later it disappeared beneath the sheet again as Faith rolled over, bunching up the pillow, then flattening it again.

Finally, she sat up, pulling her knees tight against her chest and dropping her forehead in a pose that rang of such misery it made his heart ache. She was like a kid with a secret, he realized. An awful, guilty secret. Barely able to contain it, yet terrified of letting it out. He'd spent two decades tutoring Therian kids before he was marked. He trusted his own instincts. Especially where Faith was concerned.

"You'll sleep better if you get it off your chest," he said quietly.

Her head jerked up, the gaze she turned on him wide-eyed, but she quickly masked her surprise. "What do you mean?"

"You're holding something inside that's become so big it's about to swallow you. You can't even lie still long enough to fall asleep."

Dismay and something else crossed her features. "I'm keeping you awake." She swung her feet over the side. "I'll go somewhere else."

As she stood on the floor, he sat up. "I'd rather you confide in me. You can trust me, you know."

She met his gaze with a pain in her eyes that tore at him, her body coiled tight as a spring. He'd hoped he'd been wrong about the secret, but it was all too clear he'd been right. And he suddenly didn't want to know.

For long moments, she sat there as if frozen with indecision. Then she took the few steps to where he sat on the rug. Never had he seen such a forlorn look in anyone's eyes. Without saying a word, she sat cross-legged in front of him, giving him a heart-stopping glimpse of creamy thigh and pink panty. As he watched, pulse tripping, she lifted one leg, pulling her knee to her shoulder, swinging her foot to the side, giving him a perfect view of the pink silk that covered her enticements. His hand shook to reach for her, to reach beneath that silk and slide his fingers into her waiting heat.

But a quick glance upward revealed a face on the edge of tears, and he knew there was nothing sexual about what she was offering.

"Faith?" He shook his head, not understanding.

"Look, Hawke. Look."

He glanced back down, finally noticing the way her fingers kept stroking the same spot on the thigh just beyond the elastic. Marks. Four . . .

His heart stopped beating. A faint roar started deep in his brain and escalated until his head felt as if it would explode from the noise.

"Feral marks." Though the words came from his

mouth, he barely heard them through the pounding in his head. "You've been marked."

She pulled her knees together, gathering herself close in a protective move. "Yes. I'm one of them. I think it's why I was drawn to Maxim."

He read her lips, but only one word leaped out. *Yes.*

Marked to be a Feral Warrior. Marked wrong. Kougar's words rang in his head. *If we want to maximize our chances of defeating Inir and his army, we need the strongest Ferals. Period. The ones marked are the wrong men.*

Wrong *people.*

They were going to want to destroy her. To make way . . .

The fury leaped inside him, the red haze rising.

How do you unmark a Feral Warrior? Death. Only by death.

Barely aware of his movements, he leaped to his feet as the fury battled to rise, needing to fight. To destroy. He could barely see, barely breathe.

A small sound, a sound that cut through him like a well-honed blade, had him turning back. Through the red haze he saw her. Faith. Sitting where he'd left her, tears running unchecked down her cheeks.

In those eyes he saw no fear, only a misery as deep as the sea. Even as he watched, she rose, pressing her fist against her mouth, and walked toward the door as if she'd leave him. As if she thought his anger was directed at her.

The fury roaring in his ears quieted, the tide of it rolling out as his hawk cried in anguish.

As she reached for the door, he took a step toward her. "Smiley."

She hesitated, looking back at him over her shoulder even as she leaned into the door, tipping her head against it. A sob caught in her throat, then another, and before he could reach her, she was doubled over and sliding to the floor.

He strode to her and swept her up, cradling her against his chest as he moved to the reading chair by the window and settled her on his lap. "Faith," he said softly, brushing her hair off her damp cheek, stroking her head. "Don't cry, sweetheart. Don't cry."

She wrapped her arms around his neck and clung to him, burying her face against the curve of his throat, and his heart began to beat again. He pulled her tight against him, stroking her back, her hair, bleeding with her pain, and his own, as she sobbed.

"It shouldn't have been me," she whispered on a hiccup when the worst of the storm was spent. "I'm the last one who should have ever been marked."

He stroked her back, murmured against her hair. "Not the last, never the last. Maybe it should have been you. Maybe you were the one the animal spirit wanted."

She pulled back, looking at him with disbelief. "You don't believe that."

No, he didn't, but he hated her own certainty. This strong, independent, giving woman who'd spent decades helping street kids, pretending to be little more than a street kid herself in order to win their trust.

Pretending . . .

He shook his head, brushing his cheek against her hair as understanding hit him. Not pretending.

He'd seen glimpses of the lack of self-worth that lay beneath that sunny exterior of hers. The deep vein of hurt. She'd hinted that her enclave had left her behind when she was a kid. He had a bad feeling she'd become a street kid herself that day. A throwaway.

And in some ways, he suspected, she still saw herself as one.

"Why didn't you tell me?"

She looked away as another fat tear rolled down her cheek.

He brushed away the tear with his thumb. "You were afraid of what I'd do, weren't you? Not that I'd hurt you. As close as I was to losing it, there was no real fear in your eyes. You were afraid I'd reject you."

The sobs caught her all over again and she turned and pressed her face to his shoulder and he knew he was right.

"Shh, sweetheart. I'll never turn away from you. Never. We'll get through this, and we'll do it together, you and I."

How, he couldn't begin to guess. The decks were so badly stacked against them, their entire lives had turned into one big goat fuck. But she was in his arms. And she'd finally opened up to him, completely this time.

He gathered her tight against him, breathing her in, loving her. He'd won the first battle, the most important. Faith was his.

Now he just had to find a way to keep them both alive.

Chapter
Thirteen

Faith snuggled against Hawke's warm, hard chest, her arms tight around his neck as she pressed her cheek to his lightly stubbled jaw. As he held her on his lap by the window in his bedchamber, her chest swelled with gratitude and tenderness, almost too much to bear. From the moment she'd arrived at Feral House, he'd been her anchor, her true north, the one who would stand beside her no matter what. She knew that as clearly as she knew the sun would set and rise again tomorrow. How had she lived over a century without him?

Why had she found him now, so late? Too late.

But she had him now, didn't she? She had him tonight. With the release of tension a good cry had afforded her, her body had gone soft against his. The turmoil in her mind easing, she began to notice other things. The woodsy smell of his neck. The softness of his hair where it curled slightly at the ends. The iron strength of the arms that held her with such gentleness. And the thick ridge against her hip.

Her body heated as if the warmth in her heart overflowed, running through her veins and catching fire. With a tender kiss to his cheek, she pulled back to where she could see his face. He peered at her, his dark eyes aching and warm as a summer day. His hand rose, his thumb stroking her cheek.

She leaned forward, kissing him again, earning a kiss in return, but a restrained kiss, as if he were waiting. Or letting her take the lead. Pulling back, she met his gaze. "Make love to me."

His thumb stilled. His chest froze as if he'd stopped breathing. "You're not ready."

"I wasn't ready for you to find my feral marks."

Understanding dawned, and just like that, the predatory creature who'd nearly devoured her was back. "So you put me through cold-shower hell just to keep your secret?" The growl in his voice was belied by the relief shining in his eyes.

She grimaced. "Pretty much."

His expression grew more serious. "You've still been through hell. Even more than I realized. Are you sure . . . ?"

Faith slid her hands behind his neck, twining her fingers. "My whole life has been . . . I don't know. Not a mistake, but . . . not exactly as I might have planned. Only one thing has ever been truly right. More than I'd ever hoped for. You." She pulled her hands forward to stroke his cheeks. "I don't know what the future is going to bring, Hawke. For either of us. But we have this. We have now. And I want you. And I think you want me, too."

"You have no idea."

She reached down, sliding her hand over the thick, hard ridge in his pants, pleased when he sucked in a tight breath, when his eyes turned liquid with promise. "I have some idea," she murmured, then grinned at him cheekily.

He threw back his head and laughed, then swept her up, strode to the bed, and tossed her into the middle of the mattress, following her down.

As his body covered hers, his gaze pinned her, burrowing inside her, intense and passionate. "You're mine." The words were a growl. A vow that he sealed with a searing kiss, his mouth fusing with hers, at once gentle and rough, barely civilized. His hands tilted her head, his tongue swept into her mouth, a claiming that sang with victory inside her soul.

His kiss drugged. Her hands roamed over his bare shoulders, her breath turning more and more shallow with each stroke of his heated flesh.

His own hands moved, one cupping her head and the other sliding down her back to the hem of the T-shirt, then under and back up again, his palm caressing her back, making her skin flush even as she shivered with his touch. While his tongue stroked hers, and her lips, and the insides of her mouth, his hand moved lower, his fingers sliding into the waistband of her panties and lower still to grasp her rump.

She moaned, the sound little more than a rumble in her throat, but it seemed to inflame him.

His mouth tore away from hers, his hands grasped the T-shirt she wore, pulling it over her head. And then he was looming over her, his features a hard mask of passion and gentleness as his gaze met hers, then slowly swept down to her breasts. He reached for her, his long fingers grasping one small breast, kneading it gently, then plucking at the tight bud of her nipple, playing with it as if he'd never seen anything so intriguing.

She grinned, caught between laughter and a tenderness that misted her eyes.

A smile tugged at his mouth. "What's so funny?"

Heavens, I love you. "You. You're looking at it like you've never seen one before."

"I've never seen anything so beautiful in my life." Utter honesty laced his words, and he smiled at her with laughter and joy and devilish intent as he dipped his head and took her breast firmly into his mouth, sucking, flicking her nipple with his tongue.

She arched into his touch, groaning with pleasure, her fingers digging into his soft hair, holding him close.

His hand splayed across her abdomen, then slid to her side, skimming her hip. As he suckled her breast, he grasped her thigh and tugged it gently away from its mate. His hand slid between her legs, his fingers sliding against the silk covering her sensitive places.

"Hawke." She gasped, her hips rocking up to meet his hand.

He released her breast, looking down at her with a thoroughly pleased look on his face before he moved with a quick, animal-like grace, settling between her knees. With one quick move, he had her panties down her legs and on the floor. Then he was parting her thighs, staring between them with a hunger in his eyes that might have terrified her coming from a different shape-shifter. But this man? Her Hawke? No, never.

She shivered with anticipation, dropping her knees, opening wider for him, making him smile with a feral anticipation. Dipping down, he stroked her with his tongue, nearly elevating her off the bed from the exquisite pleasure. His hands slid under her hips, and he raised her, feasted on her with a relish that had her writhing and moaning and laughing from the sheer joy of it.

He lifted his face, his mouth damp and smiling. "Are you ticklish down here?"

"No." She giggled, unable to stop. "It feels amazing."

But instead of resuming his carnal kisses, he pulled her up until she was sitting. "I want to watch you as you come."

She eyed him with hot anticipation as he lay on his back beside her, then grabbed her around the waist. "Come here."

"Where?" She laughed as he picked her up, and grabbed for the headboard to keep herself from pitching forward as he positioned her knees on either side of his face.

"Here," he said silkily as he pulled her hips down.

Looking straight down, her gaze met his, locked on his, as his mouth resumed its feasting. Pleasure shot through her, doubled by the hot pull of his gaze as his tongue licked her, his lips sucking on her clitoris. She cried out with the building storm, her fingers digging into the cherry headboard until she wondered if she'd leave nail marks.

She tried to buck with the pressure building inside her, but his hands held her firmly against his mouth, her body an instrument he alone could play.

"Hawke, don't stop. Don't stop." She was lifting, cresting . . . The orgasm crashed over her with an intensity she could hardly credit, flinging her apart so violently, so thoroughly, she wasn't sure she ever wanted to be put back together again. As she came, his caress changed, his tongue's movement turning into a soft tap against her sensitive clit as the orgasm went on and on until she was out of breath and in danger of hyperventilating. The most wonderful, the most glorious . . .

He kissed her lightly between the legs as she floated down, whole again, if not quite the woman she was before. She lifted one leg, and he ducked out from beneath her, flipping their positions until she was the one on her back and he was looming over her.

"Good?" he asked, watching her with blazing, hungry eyes, wiping his mouth on the back of his hand in a move that resembled a big cat more than a sharp-eyed raptor. A cat that had every intention of devouring her, in every way.

She smiled. "Perfect."

He leaned forward and kissed her neck. "I'm glad." He kissed her jaw. "But we're just getting started."

"Hawke. I want you inside me."

He kissed her mouth, thoroughly, sweeping his tongue inside. "No," he said, pulling back.

"*No?*"

He laughed. "Yes. Just not yet." He gripped her hips and rolled her onto her stomach.

"You're kind of bossy." His finger slid between her legs and into her wetness, deep inside. She gasped, her gasp continuing until her lungs were full to bursting. "Oh," she said on a massive exhale. "I like bossy."

"I thought you might."

Faith pressed her cheek to the bed, smiling with joy as she felt Hawke's mouth on her shoulder, then lower.

When his mouth brushed the curve of her waist, she squirmed with a giggle.

"Ticklish there," he murmured, then continued his thorough exploration of her body with his mouth, nipping her butt cheek, then brushing his lips across the back of her thigh where her feral marks were.

She tensed. He stilled, his fingers lightly stroking the marks. Then his kisses resumed, brushing the crease behind her knee, while a single finger slid between her legs, making her gasp, stroking away the terrible heaviness of those awful marks.

As his hands slowly slid up her thighs, his long fingers curving halfway around them, she wondered how much more of this she could take.

"Hawke. Come inside me."

"Not yet. Aren't you enjoying this?"

"Yes, but you . . ."

His hands slipped back down to grip her calves. "Bend your knees."

When she complied, he pushed her knees beneath her, his hand sliding up and down her spine, keeping her down. She felt as if her rump were practically waving in the air.

"What are you doing?" she gasped, then knew when his finger slid deep inside her again.

"I'm loving you," he said simply, and she wondered if it could be true. Could he feel for her as deeply as she felt for him? Was it possible?

With his finger, he found a place deep inside her that had her writhing and gasping, rocking against him over and over and over with the most exquisite pleasure.

"Hawke. *Hawke.*"

Barely aware, she found herself on her back again, Hawke rising over her, shucking his pants. His body was strong, beautiful. His arousal huge and gloriously curved.

He watched her, his face tight with barely leashed control. "I can't wait."

She opened her arms and her thighs. "Come to me, my hawk. Come inside me. Now."

Bracing himself on his arms, he held her gaze as he slid slowly into her, stretching her with his thickness, filling her as she'd never been filled, joining with her as if she were meant for him and him alone.

When he'd filled her completely, he slowly pulled out, then pushed in again, faster this time, his face strained, his arms quivering. But still he watched her, still he held her in that tender gaze. Her hands hooked around his neck, her legs around his waist as his body thrust harder and harder, a driving, wild inferno that would no longer be contained, pumping, joining them, over and over as she met him thrust for thrust, forcing him deeper, joining with him more completely, and still it wasn't enough. Faster they mated, harder, until they were slick with sweat, their breaths shattered.

"Hawke." His name was a whisper on her tongue, a jewel of perfection she would give to him and at the same time keep for herself. *I love you.* The words she wasn't ready to say filled her head, her heart, until she thought she would burst from the force of them. From the force of the love she felt for him.

She smiled, and he grinned at her, laughing as he drove into her.

Her body began to rise, shooting fast and hard toward a powerful explosion that had her crying out with the wonder of it, her body clenching and shattering in an orgasm a hundred times more powerful than the one before. Because Hawke was in her, with her. As she screamed, he roared, and it was the most perfect moment she'd ever known.

Slowly, Hawke leaned down and captured her mouth as he drove into her again. And again. And once more, this time slow and full. Complete.

On a shuddering breath, he collapsed and rolled, keeping her tight against him until she lay on top of him, her forehead against his chin.

"That was . . ." She gasped for breath. "The most fun . . . I've had in years."

He chuckled, the sound beneath her ear a deep, lovely rumble. "I agree. I don't think I've ever laughed that close to coming before. It almost sent me over the edge."

She lifted up, looking into his face. "You held on nicely."

"Did I?" He grinned at her.

That pressure built up in her chest again until she thought it would burst, or spill down her cheeks in the form of tears. Heavens, she loved this man. She kissed his chin, then tucked her head against him again.

His hand slipped into her hair, holding her head against his pounding heart. "Do you want a shower before we get some sleep?"

She shuddered, the move involuntary. "No. I don't want to move." She didn't want to be parted from him.

"Me either." He kissed her forehead tenderly. "Sleep, Smiley."

In so many ways, her world was crashing down around her. But here, in this bed, in this man's arms, she was safe. For now.

"I love you, Hawke." The words came out unbidden, a cry straight from her heart.

His arms tightened around her. "I love you, too, Faith. You're mine."

She grinned, soft and swift, kissing his chest. But the joyous rush ebbed all too quickly. She shouldn't have told him how she felt. It wasn't fair to him. Not when he might be forced to stand aside as they cleared the way for her animal to mark another. But that was a worry for another day, another hour.

She did as he asked, and slept.

Hawke held Faith as she slept, his heart filled with equal parts delight and fear. He adored her, this darling, darling woman whose grin bloomed inside him, making him laugh even in the throes of primal passion. *She loves me.* But he was terrified of what it meant for her that she'd been marked by an infected animal spirit.

It wasn't that there had never been female Feral Warriors. He knew there had been. The animal marked the strongest, and that didn't always mean physically. The strongest morally, emotionally, mentally.

Faith was all those things.

Goddess, in some ways she was one of the strongest people he knew. She'd stood there while they'd discussed the possible need to destroy all new Ferals, yet she'd shown him her own marks, knowing what that might mean for her.

And the draden. His heart clutched all over again at how she'd stayed to help him fight Lynks and Polaris, knowing the draden would come. She might not have fully comprehended the magnitude of such an attack this close to Feral House, but she'd fought draden before. She knew they'd kill her, yet she'd stayed anyway.

Her own life might have gotten off to a rocky start, but she'd turned abandonment into a life's work, doing good on a level he'd rarely seen among Therians. What if she really was the one meant to be marked? Her heart was certainly big enough. And physical strength wasn't everything. Besides, the physical strength would come with the animal that had chosen her. Perhaps she'd never be able to take on a Mage in her human form, but as a bear or large cat or one of the other animals that had yet to appear, she could be formidable indeed.

He stroked her head as it lay on his chest. What if she really was meant to be one of the Feral Warriors? To live at Feral House. With him.

A thrill of excitement tripped his pulse, then quickly died.

Of course, any future with Faith depended upon his animal and him healing this rift in their bond, surviving this breach. Perhaps once the Shaman came up with a cure for the darkness, the cure would help him, too. A future with Faith also depended upon his convincing the others that she was meant for this role, that her marking wasn't a mistake.

His arms tightened around her as love roared through him. Hardest of all would be convincing Faith herself.

Hawke held Faith's hand as they descended the stairs midafternoon. She'd slept the sleep of the dead for hours, and he'd held her, dozing some, worrying more. When she'd awoken, he'd told her his belief that her marking was no accident. As he'd suspected, she didn't believe him, but he'd gotten a very sweet kiss for saying it. A kiss that had quickly heated to full-blown passion. He'd made love to her thoroughly, then carried her into the shower and made love to her again. He couldn't get enough of her body or that smile of hers, which bloomed every time he pleased her, or that darling, infectious giggle, filling him with a pleasure of the heart that rivaled the pleasure of the body, a joy of boundless proportions that made him want to throw his head back and laugh.

Every time with her was more incredible than the last. Making love to Faith was so different from sex with anyone else that he began to feel as if he'd never really done it before. As if his eyes had been opened for the first time to what lovemaking truly meant.

Just as he was fighting to hold on to his animal and stay alive.

As they reached the foyer, she looked up at him, worry in her eyes. He squeezed her hand, dreading the meeting to come. They had to tell Lyon that she'd been marked, and they both knew it.

The smell of roast beef and the rumble of voices told him where to find the others. As he suspected, they were gathered around the dining table, the wall of windows behind them fully repaired. Hawke seated Faith two chairs down from Kougar and took the seat between, grabbing a couple of plates.

"Can I serve you?" he asked her.

She met his gaze. "I'm not hungry." Her hands twisted nervously in her lap, matching, he suspected, the knots twisting her stomach.

"I'll just give you a little. You need your strength."

"I need a lot more than I can get from food."

"You already have a lot more than you recognize." He put a couple of slabs of warm roast beef on her plate and added two freshly baked rolls, then filled his own plate to overflowing.

As he ate, his brothers' conversation flowed around him, talk that ranged from adding defenses around Feral House to the need to track down the new Ferals.

"First, we have to find a way to cure them of this infection." Tighe reached for the roast-beef platter.

The Shaman looked up from his nearly empty plate. "I would like to speak with your mate, Kougar. I have an idea, but I'll need her help."

Kougar nodded. "I'll ask her."

Hawke caught Lyon's gaze. "Where's Kara?"

"Still sleeping."

Tighe cut his chief a sly look. "Something you're not telling us, Roar? Is my son going to have a playmate?"

Lyon shook his head. "She's not pregnant. Just tired." He frowned. "She hasn't been feeling right since the Renascence. Since Maxim's, apparently. Too many new Ferals pulling energy from her."

"It may be the darkness," the Shaman murmured.

The Chief of the Feral's gaze snapped to the much smaller man. "What do you mean?"

"Darkness is always hungry for power, for energy. If the new Ferals hadn't been infected, I doubt they'd be draining her like this. Perhaps with most of the infected Ferals now gone, she'll recover soon."

Lyon nodded. "I hope you're right."

Hawke set down his fork. He didn't see any easy way to lead up to what he needed to say, so he didn't try. "Faith has been marked."

All eyes swiveled his way, his brothers' expressions a mix of shock and confusion.

"Marked?" Tighe asked.

"To be a Feral Warrior."

Lyon set down his fork, his brows lowered, his gaze pinning Faith. "When?"

Tension ripped through Hawke's body.

"I don't know," Faith said beside him, her voice clear and sure despite the fear she had to be feeling.

Hawke didn't turn to watch her. He wasn't taking his eyes off his brothers. Or his chief.

"I didn't have any idea. Not until last night." Her voice wavered only slightly before evening out again. "I told you I escaped Maxim before he could cloud my mind. What I didn't tell you is that I went feral. It shocked us both, giving me a chance to get away before he could stop me. I looked for the feral marks this morning and found them on the back of my thigh." Her calm evaporated in a trembling draw of breath, and a whispered, "I didn't know."

Tighe groaned.

Vhyper shook his head. "You couldn't be the Wicked Witch of the West. You have to be all Tinker Bell cute and sunny."

Lyon continued to watch her with that piercing gaze of his, seeing all, revealing nothing of his thoughts, though Hawke suspected them clearly enough. "Maxim . . . You were his intended mate."

"I barely knew him. I met him the day before we arrived here and felt an instant connection with him. A pull. I thought . . ." She went silent, and he glanced at her, seeing her cheeks begin to color. "I thought it was a mating pull. He was kind to me then. But he was a monster, and I believe now that the pull I felt was due to the infection."

"Shaman?"

At Lyon's prompt, the Shaman stood. Hawke rose with him, moving behind Faith, his hands on her shoulders, his gaze meeting every one of his brothers' in turn. A silent warning that each of them acknowledged with a nod or a look of dismay. If they'd had any question as to how he felt about her, they did no longer.

Mine. He didn't have to say the word. They all heard it loud and clear.

The Shaman approached slowly with his usual calm demeanor and held out his hand to Faith.

With only a brief hesitation, she placed her own in his. The Shaman covered her hand and closed his eyes. Then he reached for her, one hand traveling unerringly to rest on the top of her head.

"She's infected, but not like the others. The infection is dormant in her, like an unpopped kernel of corn. It's there, deep inside her. But it's not yet affecting her."

"Which is why she didn't rise up against us," Lyon murmured.

"Like *that* would have ended well," Faith muttered.

A quick smile flickered in Tighe's and Vhyper's expressions.

"You should also note," Hawke said quietly, "that she told me about the feral marks. She showed me, despite being privy to the entire conversation yesterday."

Tighe grimaced, and Hawke knew he was thinking about just what they'd discussed—the possible need to eliminate all the new Ferals.

Kougar's frown told him he was thinking the same. He plucked at his small beard. "Why isn't the darkness affecting her? Because she's female and lacking the testosterone? Or because she hasn't been brought into her animal?"

"I don't know," the Shaman replied. "I suppose you'll find out as soon as you bring her into her animal."

Lyon met Hawke's gaze, nodding toward the hallway. "A word?"

Hawke's grip on Faith's shoulders tightened. On a primitive level, he didn't want to leave her unprotected. But he'd made his feelings clear. None of them would hurt her. Yet. The one calling those shots was Lyon. It was his chief he had to convince to leave her alive.

As Hawke walked away to talk to Lyon in private, Faith looked around the dining table at the remaining Feral Warriors, now staring at her with varying degrees of speculation, sympathy, and wariness. Thanks to Mage interference, she was one of them. For now.

"Well, this is awkward," she muttered, wishing she were anywhere but there. She picked up her fork and absently pushed a bite of meat around.

"You really went feral on that saber-toothed bastard?" Wulfe asked, a hint of awe in his voice.

Faith looked up, her expression rueful as she nodded.

Tighe snorted. "I wish I'd seen the look on his face."

"Trust me, it wasn't any more comical than the look on my own."

"You should have seen Croc and me last week when we first went feral." Fox frowned. "He was a new recruit to my unit of the Therian Guard. An idiot, if you ask me, which I can finally admit. I belted him because he had it coming. He went feral, then laughed, thinking he was the new fox shifter—the entire race had been waiting for him to show up. Then he took a swipe at me with those claws, ripping off half my face.

I was more angry at the fact that one such as he had been chosen to be a Feral Warrior than the pain he'd inflicted. So I returned the favor. I'm not sure which of us was more surprised when I drew claws, too. I remember staring at my hand, his blood still clinging to those claws and thinking, for just a moment, that I'd turned into a monster."

Tighe nodded. "I know the feeling. I was married to a human who didn't know I was immortal. I knew almost nothing about the Feral Warriors. So when I went feral that first time . . ." He scrubbed his face. "She thought I was a demon. I was half-afraid she was right. I lost her because of that. Lost my daughter. I was not one of the ones celebrating being marked, trust me."

Wulfe's hand squeezed Tighe's shoulder.

Their stories, freely offered, were a gift Faith cherished. A welcome of sorts. Or at least an assurance that they didn't outright hate her. Yet.

"Can you call on the fangs and claws anytime you want?" she asked.

"Some can," Tighe said. "For most, it's tied to emotion. I would have said testosterone . . ."

She put down her fork. "I was furious."

"That works, too."

"So in a fight, in order to go feral, I have to get mad?"

A couple of them exchanged glances. Most looked away, uncomfortably, as if they didn't think it likely she'd ever be in a fight. Not for long, at least.

Kougar was the only one who held her gaze, studying her. "Female shifters tend to go feral with temper or adrenaline. Anger or fear. And you'll likely feel both in battle. But I've known females who could draw claws or fangs whenever they chose. They were actually far more controlled than the males. And sometimes more effective. But that kind of control comes with experience."

"How many female shifters have you known?" Fox asked.

"Shifters? Hundreds. In my youth, all Therians shifted. But there have been few female Ferals. Six, not including Pink. Faith is the seventh."

Seven in five thousand years.

Female Ferals were rare. But she was no rarity. And the uncomfortable silence at the table said they all knew it. This female Feral Warrior was a mistake.

Chapter Fourteen

Hawke followed Lyon into the hallway, then stopped where he could still see Faith. He'd gone as far as he intended to go.

Lyon glanced back at him, a flicker of frustration on his face before he gave in and backtracked to him. "She has to be locked up in the prison with the others. All new Ferals do."

"The infection is dormant in her. We won't bring her into her animal."

"She's heard the discussions, Hawke. She knows we may have to clear the way for new Ferals to be marked, for the *right* Ferals to be marked. She'll run."

"No, she won't. She won't try to escape this."

Lyon clasped him on the shoulder, genuine sympathy in his eyes. "I'm sorry. I know you care for her."

"I love her, Roar. But more than that, I *know* her. She would never endanger others to save herself. Sacrifice is her life."

"You can't know that."

"She's spent nearly a century on the streets helping human runaways. Yeah. I can."

Lyon's jaw clenched and unclenched in rhythmic bursts. The Chief of the Ferals never made rash decisions. Ever. Which was one of the reasons that, to a man, they'd lay down their lives for him.

"Kara thinks Faith is your mate."

Hawke nodded. "I would ask her to be if things were different. If I were whole . . ."

Lyon sighed. "Why can't any of you fall for normal Therian women?"

Hawke smiled. "Like you did?" Kara, the Radiant who'd been raised human and hadn't even known that immortals existed, had hardly been that.

"Touché."

Pain tore through Hawke's head, one of the lightning bolts he was becoming all too used to, closely followed by his hawk's vicious retaliation. When it was over, when he was able to breathe again, he found Lyon watching him with quiet worry in his eyes.

"You're not getting better." Lyon's statement held no lilt of question.

"No. Not yet. I'm not convinced my hawk isn't infected. He's been fighting me since we got out of that spirit trap."

"But you're holding it together."

"Yes. With Faith's help."

Lyon rubbed his hand over his mouth and sighed. "I don't want her out of your sight."

Hawke nodded, relieved and grateful. "My feelings exactly."

Lyon's hand on his shoulder tightened. "I hope this works out, Wings, I really do."

"Me, too." He'd calculate the odds on that happening, but the answer would be far too depressing.

Faith's head swiveled toward the doorway, her gaze snapping to Hawke's face as he and Lyon returned to the dining room. The small, calm smile of reassurance he gave her had the worst of the awful tension leaching from her body.

"My orders are to not let you out of my sight," he said quietly as he took his seat beside her again.

"No prison?"

"No prison."

A sigh escaped her lips as she looked at Lyon. "Thank you."

Lyon nodded, his expression reserved, but not unkind. "We believe the infection in you is dormant, Faith, but if we find it's not . . ."

"If it's not, you'll do what you must to stop me." She glanced down at her plate. "I know. I agree."

Hawke nudged her with his elbow. "Eat. After lunch, we're going to start your training."

She looked at him in disbelief. "What training?"

"Knives, weight lifting."

Her eyes widened, an expression mirrored by several other faces around the table. "Hawke . . ."

But he cut her off. "At the very least, you have to learn to defend yourself against another draden attack. Strength isn't built overnight. Neither are fighting skills. They take time and a lot of practice."

He was acting as if she'd been marked on purpose.

As if she had a future as a Feral Warrior when they all knew that wasn't true.

He gripped her chin and gently forced her to look at him, to meet his steely gaze. "We don't know for certain that your being marked was an accident." His gaze lifted, and he met his brothers' eyes around the table. "It's time we all considered that. But we need you trained, and we're going to start today." His voice brooked no argument.

It wasn't that she was against learning how to fight draden or doing a little weight lifting, but . . . "There's evil inside me," she whispered, as if everyone in the room couldn't hear her. The knowledge cut like a blade.

Hawke's eyes softened even as his expression remained implacable. "There's an infection inside of you. And we're going to find a cure for it. You're not evil." He leaned forward and kissed her gently on the mouth. In front of everyone. As if he wanted them to see.

"You make it sound so simple," she grumbled.

He smiled at her, a smile of pure male confidence. "It is."

As Hawke released her and returned to his meal, she forced herself to take a bite of roast beef. If only she possessed a dash of Hawke's certainty, of his confidence in her abilities to pull this off, to be of some use to them.

She swallowed the bite, uncertain her knotted stomach would accept it, then took a deep breath. She'd never been a coward. Never. If they needed her to be able to fight, then she'd learn to fight. If this job was for life, and apparently it was, then she would be the best Feral Warrior she could possibly be, sparing herself nothing. If she didn't last long, so be it. But she'd go down battling their enemy, protecting their backs.

And to do that, she had to learn how to wield some weapons.

The first thing she could do was force herself to eat.

Ten minutes later, the meal over, Lyon rose. "The second shift needs to sleep. Kougar, you're in charge."

Hawke held out Faith's chair for her, and she rose along with everyone else.

Tighe came over to her, his eyes kind, and extended his hand. Too far. As if he intended to share with her one of the full forearm greetings the Ferals reserved for one another.

It was one thing to work hard and to do what they wanted, but they all knew it was a lie. That she wasn't supposed to be one of them. She met his gaze, knowing he wasn't mocking her, but feeling that way anyway.

"Tighe . . ."

Though the kindness in his eyes remained, his expression took on a sharpness that was close to reproachful. "Take it, Faith. I don't offer it lightly."

She hesitated, but reached for him. As he grasped her forearm, his hand completely encircling her arm, she barely managed to curl her much smaller hand around the top of his. When he didn't let go, she looked up and found him watching her, his eyes very serious.

"Delaney told me how you refused to get into that car last night as they escaped, how you chose to help Hawke even knowing you were in grave danger. You impressed my wife, and that's no easy feat. You showed heart and courage and a willingness to sacrifice, Faith. Perhaps that was only due to your feelings for Hawke, but my gut tells me otherwise." He clasped her shoulder with his free hand. "My gut, and the fact that you came clean with us about your being marked, even knowing what it might mean for you, tell me you possess a lot of character. A strength that's far more important than any amount of muscle." He released her, his mouth kicking up, flashing a single dimple, though his eyes remained deadly serious. "So, yes, I offer you my respect and welcome. Unless you prove me wrong."

Her heart gave a small, painful thud at the thinly veiled threat at the end of Tighe's surprisingly warm welcome. And for the first time she began to realize the enormity of her situation. She was a Feral Warrior. Once she was brought into her animal, no matter who she'd been before, she would become one of the most powerful creatures on earth. If she used that power for good, to help them, to be one of them, she might find an ally in Tighe. If not, if goddess forbid, the darkness got the best of her, he would be her enemy. Possibly her executioner. They all would.

Except, perhaps, Hawke.

As Tighe stepped back, Wulfe moved forward, offering her his arm as Tighe had, the expression on his badly scarred face closed. When she laid her palm against his massive arm, his dinner-plate-sized hand encircling hers with ease, his expression softened. "Fighting skills can be learned."

She nodded, and he released her.

Fox was next. As he took her arm, he flashed her a smile that had surely slain ten thousand female hearts. "I've been fighting for years," he said, turning serious. "I've trained a lot of warriors, a number of whom came to me without skills. A number of whom were women. I'll teach you everything I know about fighting in human form. But the rest of it, we'll have to learn together."

Vhyper and Kougar stood shoulder to shoulder, watching, arms crossed over their chests. Neither approached her.

"She could be our secret weapon against the Mage," Vhyper said to no one in particular. "We'll send her into battle first, let her slay them with her smile. They'll never notice the rest of us until it's too late."

She couldn't tell if his words teased or taunted, and her cheeks began to warm in a way that wasn't altogether pleasant.

Kougar said nothing, his face expressionless, a gleam in his eyes that sent a shiver down her spine. He glanced pointedly at Hawke, who'd remained beside her, his meaning clear. If she hurt Hawke, Kougar would kill her. There would be no hesitating, no mercy.

To her surprise, Lyon stepped forward, but he didn't offer her his arm as some of the others had. Instead, he took her hand in both of his. "Don't take our caution personally, Faith. We're at war with the Mage—a war that, if we lose, will mean the destruction of the world as we know it."

"And they're trying to turn me into a weapon against you."

He nodded. "Possibly. But last night, you may very well have saved Hawke. You have my gratitude. And I promise you, we'll do everything in our power to free you from this dark magic. The rest is up to you."

She looked at him, uncertain he meant what his words implied, that they would give her a chance to prove herself worthy of being one of them. It was a long shot, of course. Even if they cured her of the infection, she wasn't the one meant to be marked. But if she proved to be a strong warrior, anyway, they might just let her live.

They were willing to give her a chance. Perhaps it was time she gave herself one. She smiled a quick, appreciative smile. "Thank you, Lyon."

He nodded and released her, then turned away.

She felt Hawke's hand on her shoulder. "I need to get some things."

"Where are we doing this, Wings?" Tighe asked.

"Backyard. I want to get her throwing some knives."

Faith gaped at him.

"Backyard it is." Tighe motioned her toward the back door. "It'll be interesting to see what animal you shift into, Faith." He held the door for her, and she stepped out into the warm sunshine as he and Fox followed. "Fighting in your animal is instinctive. But you won't always be in a position to shift. You need to know how to use a knife and swords, how to block attacks, how to attack where you can do the most damage. A year ago, I'd have said most of your opponents would be Mage or draden, but they may well be Ferals now. Or, goddess help us, Daemons."

"How in the hell do you fight a Daemon?" Fox asked.

"We're still figuring that out."

"Some animals are going to be better fighters than others," Faith murmured.

"Always."

"What animals are left? What might I be?" She was starting to wonder, and with the wondering came an excitement she hadn't allowed herself to feel until now.

The back door opened, and Hawke stepped out, igniting a small glow deep in her chest. She always felt better when he was close by. Safer. Stronger.

"Honestly," Tighe said, "I don't know. The seventeen were lost before I was marked. Since I've been a Feral, no one has ever talked about them except as *the seventeen*. Only Kougar and Lyon were around at the time. They're the only ones who know."

Hawke joined them. "It's something we never ask about. Even after all these years, the death of seventeen brothers is just too raw. But Kougar has been telling me things lately, stories of the past. I've been able to piece together a few things. There were once three birds—the hawk, the eagle, and the falcon. And one of my father's best friends was a horse." Hawke handed her the hilt of a knife. "Time to get to work."

For half the afternoon, the three men worked with her, showing her how to wield two knives at once, how to attack a Mage's hands first so he couldn't enchant her with his touch, how to protect her own head and heart. And how to throw a knife so that it landed stuck in a tree . . . or an opponent's eye . . . tip first. At least, theoretically. Mastering it would take years of practice. At one point, each held a two-by-four, urging her to pretend the ends were draden, ordering her to stab at them until the sweat was rolling into her eyes, and her muscles felt like jelly.

They nearly drove her to her knees. And to tears.

"Stop," Tighe said.

She was finding that Hawke was the hardest taskmaster of the three, which was unexpected. Then again, he cared the most that she learn to fight.

"Close your eyes, Faith," Tighe said.

"You've got . . . to be kidding." She was sucking in air through her nose, trying to keep from hyperventilating.

"Trust me. Just close them. You're relying too heavily on your vision. Your other senses haven't yet improved as they will when you come into your animal, but they're still stronger than you realize. Listen to the sound of the board, to the brush of fabric as we move our arms, feel the breeze from the boards. Sense them around you."

She could hardly even hold the knives any longer. But she did as Tighe suggested and closed her eyes. And immediately felt the end of one board bump into her arm and another nudge her hip. She stabbed wildly, hitting nothing.

With frustration bordering on desperation, she opened her eyes. "I can't do this."

"Aye, you can, Faith," Fox said, his voice soft and encouraging.

She swung her gaze to the golden one and glared at him.

His eyes smiled, but his expression remained serious. "Some of the finest fighters we have in the Therian Guard are females. They're quick and light and nimble. The most important thing in winning a battle, even hand-to-hand, isn't strength. It's confidence. The belief that you'll win. Seeing that certainty in your eyes strikes a blow into the heart of your opponent every time. He wonders what you know, what you can do, that he isn't ready for. It fecks with his mind. But to show that kind of confidence, you must believe in yourself. Completely. That's why practicing like this is so important. In the Guard, we train four to five hours a day. Every day."

She groaned.

Tighe tossed his two-by-four aside and came over to her, curving his arm around her shoulders. "Don't get discouraged. It doesn't happen overnight. You did fine today."

"Tighe's right," Fox said. "In my experience, a new

recruit's initial strength and skill has almost no correlation to her ultimate fighting abilities."

Faith gave him a hard, exhausted look. "You're just trying to make me feel better."

"Not at all. Within three days of beginning training, I can almost always tell who will end up at the top of the class. And it has nothing to do with his or her skills. What matters is how hard they're willing to work. How bad they want it. If you put everything you have into what you're trying to accomplish—no matter who you are or where you start—you can move mountains. And you did that today, Faith. You put everything into it. I'm proud of you."

She gave him an exhausted smile. "Thank you."

Tighe stepped beside Fox. "As I said earlier, a lot of us weren't happy about being chosen to be Feral Warriors. Not all of us wanted this job. We got it anyway, for whatever reason. And we've given everything we have to be the best damn Feral Warriors we can be. That's what we're asking of you, Faith. Simply to be the best Feral *you* can be. And cut us some slack when you turn into some big monster of a beast, will you? Remember that we're your friends." He grinned at her, and she laughed.

Fox and Tighe turned away, Tighe clasping Fox's shoulder as they headed back into the house.

Faith looked up at Hawke and found him watching her with a look of pride in his eyes that lifted her spirits more than Tighe's and Fox's words combined. "You did great," he said softly.

She rolled her eyes. "I did terribly. I couldn't kill a balloon if you held it still for me."

He chuckled, and she stepped forward and curled

her arms around his waist, pressing her cheek against his chest. His chin brushed her hair. "Fox is right," he said. "More than anything, you need to start believing, Faith. Believe that you were meant to be marked. That you can do this. Even if you turn into a mouse."

She jerked back, peering up into his face. "A *mouse?*"

He chuckled, setting butterflies to flight in her chest. "That one's a joke. I think." His hands framed her face, and he watched her with so much tenderness in his eyes, she thought she might melt beneath it. "Do you have any idea how much I love you?"

Her heart sang at his words, tears pricking her eyes. "I think I do. Maybe almost as much as I love you. But I almost wish you wouldn't. Your loving me scares me, Hawke. What if I turn into the enemy?"

He stroked her hair. "You're not going to turn into the enemy. And I couldn't stop loving you if I tried. There's so much good in you, Smiley. You're strong, you're giving, you're sweet. Your smile lights me up inside like a dozen suns, and your kiss turns me to putty. You're worth every risk. Any risk."

She was stunned by his words, humbled. And deeply moved. The love she felt for him swelled until she thought it would consume her.

He kissed her, his fingers sliding into her hair, his lips lingering, brushing over hers, the touch sparking an instant fire inside her. He groaned, sliding his tongue into her mouth, one hand gliding down her back to press her hips tight against him. Kissing her temple, he murmured, "You're going to be a valuable member of the Feral team, Faith. If it's the last thing I do, I'm going to see to that. You'll have a purpose here. A home. No matter what happens."

She pulled back to stare up into his face. "What do you mean, 'no matter what happens'?"

A shadow passed over his features, his eyes troubled. "Nothing." He tried to kiss her, to end the discussion, but she turned her cheek, avoiding him.

"Tell me what you meant, Hawke."

He sighed and shrugged. "Nothing. I just . . . I don't know what the spirit trap did to me. I know it damaged me. And the damage is getting worse."

"You're supposed to be getting better. You're immortal."

"I know." A look of resignation crossed his face.

"No, Hawke. You can't tell me I'm going to succeed against all odds, yet give up yourself. While you're finding a cure for me, how about finding one for what's happening to you, too?"

His mouth tightened. "We've tried everything."

"Then try something else," she snapped, then covered her mouth, ashamed of herself. Her anger crumbled beneath the caress of gentle eyes. "I just found you. I don't want to lose you." Her voice cracked on the last.

He wrapped his arms around her, holding her close within the shadows of the trees. The scent of flowers and new grass, of spring's rich promise, felt wrong somehow, in direct counterpoint to their talk of death and loss.

"Even if the worst happens, you won't be alone this time, Smiley."

"I haven't been *that* alone."

"No?" He peered down at her. "Have you lived with an enclave since you lost your own? Have you ever lived with anyone other than the occasional street kid who needed a place to sleep for a while?"

She shrugged. "I'm fine that way."

"No. You're not. I can see the loneliness in your eyes." He stroked her hair. "Why didn't you go with your enclave that day when the warning came that your village was about to be attacked?"

"It was a long time ago, Hawke."

"I want to know what happened. It's part of who you are."

She pulled away, turning to look out over the woods, reluctant to go back there, to that time, to that day, even though . . . so little had actually happened. When he pulled her back against him, she relaxed, looking up at the canopy above, and told him.

"We were living in Belgium early in the First World War. One of the Therians in our enclave was particularly gifted at clouding the minds of humans and getting the information he wanted from them. He'd been out scouting and came upon a German who told him that they were planning an imminent attack on the human village where we lived. The Therian raced back to warn the enclave. My best friend, a human, lived in that town. It was her father who used to call me Smiley. He'd shown me more patience and kindness than anyone in my enclave, and I'd often pretended he was my real father. I begged our leader to give me an hour so that I could warn them, but he said no. I went anyway."

"They didn't wait." Hawke's tone as his chin settled on her crown was heavy with understanding.

"No. On some level, I think I'd known they wouldn't. In my youth, I said good riddance, but . . ." She shook her head. The horrors of the attack and the days that followed were something that she would never forget.

"Were you able to save your friends?"

"No. As much as they cared for me, they didn't believe I could know such a thing. They didn't leave in time."

"I'm sorry." Hawke slid his arm across her upper chest, pulling her firmly against him, anchoring her back in the here and now. "Your leader should be staked and left for the draden for leaving a fifteen-year-old child behind."

She curled her fingers lightly around his forearm as she tilted her head forward and pressed a kiss to his bare skin. "He did what he had to do to ensure the safety of the enclave."

"He could have left someone to wait for you."

"That wasn't his way. He was a rigid man, cold and unbending. They all were."

"You had parents among them?"

"Technically. My mother had little to do with me. And she neither knew nor cared which of the males was my father."

"Others raised you."

"Others fed me, clothed me. I raised myself." She shrugged. "I'd intended to leave them as soon as I was of age, anyway. Circumstances left me on my own a few years early, is all."

"Ten years." He groaned. "It shouldn't have happened, Faith. You were their responsibility."

"They were cold people, Hawke. They cared for no one and nothing but themselves. I didn't understand that at the time. It took years."

"But you care. About others."

"Yes. Humans aren't so different from us. Their bodies are fragile and don't last long, but the hearts and minds and souls that inhabit them are the same as ours. To believe we're better than them is a mistake. We're stronger, yes. But we should use that strength to help them. Not use them to help ourselves."

His chin brushed the top of her head. "I agree."

Her tension drained away with the certainty he understood. She heard it in the tone of his voice and sank back against him. "It was humans who helped me and protected me during those attacks on my village. The same humans I watched die all around me. When it was over, only a few of us had survived, and we banded together. A handful of kids who'd lost everything and everyone. The others weren't Therian, they weren't immortal, but it didn't matter. We became a family, scavenging for food and warmth. We survived.

"I soon realized that there were always kids who were lost and alone, not just during wartime. Runaways. Throwaways. Orphans with no one to protect them. Kids who needed me. After a while, they died or grew up and moved away. Soon, I found myself moving every year or two to another country, another city, and starting over again, finding new kids who needed help. The moving was easy enough since I was born with a gift for language."

"Did you ever find your people?"

She blinked, opened her mouth to tell him she hadn't been looking for them, then shut it again. Of course she had. Not actively, perhaps, but every time she moved, a secret part of her had hoped she'd find them.

"No." It didn't matter, yet even she could hear the sadness in that word.

She felt the quiet sympathy in the brush of his chin and the gentle squeeze of his arms.

"I'm sorry, Faith."

"I'm not. It's a good life, a worthwhile life." She swallowed. "It's where I belong."

He stiffened, releasing her, turning her to face him. "That's where you're wrong." His eyes blazed with soft intensity. "It's not where you belong. Those selfish idiots that gave birth to you and raised you should be strung up by their heels for what they did to you. Not only leaving you behind but making you believe that you weren't worth their time. That you weren't worth anyone's. It's not true." She tried to look away, but he wouldn't let her. "It's not true, Faith. You're worth more than every one of them combined. You're worthy of being chosen a Feral Warrior, one of the greatest honors any Therian can be given." He gripped her face gently in his hands. "I wish you believed that."

"I can't. Because I know I was marked in error."

"No. You don't. At this point, we don't know anything for sure. Except that you're strong and fine and good." He kissed her. "And beautiful." He kissed her again. "And sexy."

She laughed. "Now, *that's* important."

He smiled, his eyes growing heavy-lidded and sexy as hell. "It's a bonus. For me. Only for me." He kissed her again, this time for keeps, pulling her into his arms, sweeping his tongue into her mouth. That quickly, passion ignited, the kiss turning hot and desperate.

"We need to do this indoors," he whispered against her temple. "I need to be inside you."

Damp heat flooded her body, and she nodded, turning willingly as he tucked her against his side and started back to the house. Love welled up inside her, overflowing, drenching her heart with warmth and beauty. She wished there was something she could do to help him recover from whatever the spirit trap had done to him. At the very least, she'd do as he wanted—learn to fight, work to be the best Feral Warrior she could be. And when her time came, she'd do her best to die a hero's death.

Despite Tighe's and Fox's kindness and encouragement, she knew that Hawke was the only one who truly believed she was meant to be one of them. And only because he loved her and couldn't stand the thought of the alternative. For both their sakes, he was fooling himself, trying to make her into something she could never be.

She ached to think what it would do to him when he realized he was wrong. Just as she trembled with fear that he was right about his own damage within the spirit trap. All her life, she'd waited for him, this kind, gentle, beautiful warrior. But their time together appeared destined to be all too short.

Chapter Fifteen

Hawke pulled Faith into the library, then closed the double doors and pulled her into his arms, brushing her hair aside to kiss her neck. Even after the training he'd put her through, she smelled like ripe, sweet raspberries.

"I need to be inside you."

"Here?" she asked on a laugh, a disbelieving lilt to her voice.

"I'm on duty." He unfastened her jeans.

She snorted. "Duty for what?" Then gasped as he slid his hand down into her panties.

He pushed his fingers through her curls and down into heat and wetness. "Goddess, you're ready for me."

"Always." The word trembled on a sigh.

With shaking hands, he released her and knelt before her to pull off her shoes. Then with quick, desperate movements, he shoved her jeans and panties down her legs and onto the floor, baring her slender calves and creamy thighs and all the lush beauty between to his starving eyes. He pulled off his shirt, then shucked his own pants while she stripped off her shirt and bra.

His hands shook, his body quaking and throbbing with incendiary heat as she turned to him, a smile on her lips, passion in her eyes. He lifted her, and she wrapped those lovely legs around his waist. Positioning himself against her damp, swollen opening, he pushed inside. His eyes closed at the exquisite feel of her tight little sheath, slick with arousal, hot and throbbing. And at the feel of her arms around his neck, the sweet torture of her taut nipples teasing his chest, the softness of her lips against his earlobe, and her hot gasps and moans, all driving him up fast and hard. She was fire in his arms, his light in the darkness, and he loved her beyond measure.

Capturing her mouth, he kissed her, sweeping his tongue inside as his body drove into hers, melding with hers, making them one.

Lightning bolted through his head, and he groaned. He knew what followed. But even prepared, the pain of those raking, vicious talons had him rearing back, his mind going white with shock, his body rigid with agony.

"Hawke?" Faith asked softly, worriedly.

As the pain slowly dimmed, as the hawk's angry cries faded away, he felt Faith's soft hand stroke his hair with a featherlight touch, over and over, easing him back.

He swallowed, looking at her. "Bad timing."

"Are you okay?"

A smile tipped the edge of his mouth. "That's my line." With a sigh, he nodded, though it was a lie. The hawk was trying to destroy the connection between them. The animal spirit had been damaged in that spirit trap. Or maybe it was Hawke who'd been damaged. Either way, the bird spirit was trying to gain his freedom, a freedom that Hawke would not survive.

The pain had been one hell of a distraction, but his body still throbbed, demanding release. He pulled partly out of Faith, then pushed himself deep inside her again, the intense pleasure shoving away the last of the lingering shock.

Faith moaned, the sexy sound combined with the scent of lovemaking sending his senses tumbling all over again.

"Can you finish?" she asked softly.

"All too soon. There's nowhere I'd rather be than inside you. And I'm not coming until you fly for me."

She smiled. "Let's fly together, my hawk."

He captured her mouth once more, driving into her hard and fast until they were both breathless and panting, until she cried out with release, squeezing him in hard, rhythmic spasms. He followed her into oblivion, pumping his seed inside her, loving her with his body, his mind, his soul.

For long minutes, he held her wrapped around him, her body melting into his, soft and warm. When he thought he could move again, he pulled out of her, set her on her feet, and kissed her, then grabbed his jeans and dressed.

Life was so unpredictable. For decades, little had changed. He'd spent his life fighting draden, studying whatever subject intrigued him, taking the occasional lover or two. For the most part, he'd lived a calm, predictable immortal life until a few months ago when they'd realized that the Mage were trying to free the Daemons. Ever since, he'd felt as if things were spiraling out of control, but never more than the past few weeks, the past few days. Now he found himself in the center of a vortex, the love of his life in his arms, and death stalking him, trying to rip him from his animal. Heaven and hell snaring him at once.

He finished dressing, watching as Faith tied her shoes and rose to stand before him, her eyes once more sparkling, her mouth swollen from his kisses and lifted in a smile of love and feminine satisfaction. "You are so beautiful," he murmured, brushing the hair back from her beloved face. Then he took her hand and opened the door before he was tempted to strip off her clothes all over again.

Together, they went in search of Kougar and found him standing in the doorway of the media room, talking with Fox. As Hawke approached, Faith at his side, the distinct scent of pine caught his nose. A second later, two wraithlike females appeared in the hallway, then quickly took corporeal form. Ariana, Kougar's mate, and the ever-scowling Melisande.

Faith's hand tightened in his and he squeezed hers gently. The Ilinas definitely took some getting used to. As Kougar went to his mate, Fox stepped over to join Hawke and Faith.

"Amazing that they still exist, isn't it?" Fox asked quietly. "She's a fine thing, the blonde."

Hawke glanced at the fox shifter, seeing a predatory look in his eyes that had him shaking his head. "That's Melisande. Apparently, she tried to kill Lyon a couple of weeks ago."

"And he let her live?"

"That was my reaction the first time I heard. It was something of a misunderstanding, and they've called a truce. Of sorts. But the woman apparently has a chip on her shoulder the size of the South Pole when it comes to Ferals. That one's trouble with a capital T."

"Chips can be knocked off."

Faith snorted beside him. "So can heads."

Fox chuckled low. "She hasn't met the right Feral yet, is all."

Hawke shook his head, but he smiled. "You'd have more luck taming a tornado."

Kougar pulled away from his mate and turned to them. "Fox, Faith, I'd like you to meet Ariana, Queen of the Ilinas and my mate. And her second, Melisande."

As expected, Melisande scowled, but Ariana strode forward dressed in jeans and low boots, looking and acting entirely too human for a queen whose castle sat, literally, in the clouds. Then again, she'd spent the last millennium unable to turn to mist, living as a human. When Kougar had found her again, she'd been working as a maternity nurse in a hospital in downtown Baltimore.

"Hi, Hawke. How are you doing?"

Other than the fact that my bird has turned against me and the woman I'm in love with has just been marked to be one of the guardians of the race without a single skill to keep her alive in battle?

"I'm fine, thank you, Ariana. And you?"

She smiled radiantly and glanced at Kougar. "I've never been better. I'm glad you're back with the living. And the conscious."

"I have you to thank for that."

"I'm glad I was able to help."

Hawke put his hand on Faith's shoulder. "This is Faith."

Ariana shook Faith's hand, then turned to Fox. "You're one of the new Ferals?"

Fox nodded. "I am. Faith and I both are."

Ariana's brows shot up, the smile she turned on Faith delighted and genuine. "About time. If you'll excuse me?" She turned back to Kougar. "Where's the Shaman? I understand we have work to do."

As she strode back to where she'd left her mate and her second, Fox fell into step beside her, stopping before the blonde. "Melisande, is it?" he asked, the Irish lilt in his voice suddenly more pronounced. "A beautiful name for a beautiful woman."

Melisande stared at him as if he'd lost his mind, but a hint of color rose in her cheeks. Interesting.

Fox held out his hand to her. "I'm Fox, Melisande. It's a pleasure to meet you."

Melisande's eyes narrowed, her mouth tilting up in a mockery of a smile. "That's what you think."

"Mel," Ariana said, her tone part plea, part warning. But from what little he'd seen of Melisande, and what he'd been told, the blond Ilina was a law unto herself.

To prove the point, she appeared to fling something at Fox, probably the bolt of energy that he'd heard could drive even a Feral to his knees in pain. But the sound that escaped Fox's throat wasn't a sound of pain. More like pure, unadulterated rapture, like a man in the throes of orgasm. His back arched, his head falling back, his mouth opening wide. And when he recovered enough to close his mouth and stare at Melisande, the grin on his face was that of a hunter who'd just sighted the prey he'd been searching for, for a long, long time.

Melisande's jaw dropped in horror. In an instant, she turned to mist and disappeared.

Ariana and Kougar both stared at Fox, who started laughing like a man who'd just discovered the secrets of the universe.

"What did you do to her?" Kougar asked, genuine amazement creeping into his tone.

Fox shook his head, golden hair brushing his shoulders. "I've no bloody idea."

"Watch your step," Ariana warned kindly. "Melisande is a good person, but she has a violent and justified hatred of Therians. While she's obligated to honor my alliance with the Ferals, she's unpredictable. She won't try to kill you. But that's about all I can guarantee. And if you hurt her, even that's off the table."

"Point taken." But the roguish look on Fox's smiling face made Hawke suspect Melisande was the one who'd better watch her back. And maybe even her heart.

"Hi, Ariana." Kara descended the stairs, looking tired.

Hawke took Faith's hand, thinking this was a good time to make a hasty exit. He'd been avoiding Kara for days now, not wanting Lyon to realize just how bad things were getting. But as he turned to go, Lyon stopped him.

"Hawke, you haven't had radiance in a couple of days."

"I'm fine, Roar."

"Radiance, Wings. Now."

Hell. Though maybe it would be okay this time. Maybe he really was getting better. There was one way to find out. He gave Faith a quick kiss, then released her and joined Kara and Lyon. Fox and Kougar stepped forward, and each of them grabbed one of Kara's arms or ankles. Hawke curled his hand around Kara's wrist, holding his breath. *It'll be fine.* He prayed it was true.

As Kara went radiant, lighting up like the sun, radiance zapped him, and he arched back, contorting like a man electrocuted. Faith and Kara cried out in unison, Kara's light going out as someone yanked his hand away from her.

"Dammit!" Lyon grabbed him when swayed. "Why didn't you tell me?"

Hawke didn't answer. His jaw felt welded shut.

"Let me see your feral marks," his chief demanded even as he turned him and yanked his shirt up his back, exposing his right shoulder. "They're fading."

Hawke's heart sank as the last hope that he and his hawk would ultimately heal died. As his jaw slowly released, he turned to face Lyon. The grief in his friend's eyes punched him hard. Lyon had known him since the day he was born. He'd helped raise him. They all had.

But when Faith came to him, wrapping her arms around him, it was the tears and grief in her eyes that slew him. Who would protect her when he was gone? Who would champion her?

Who would love her as she deserved and needed to be loved?

He'd known he was getting worse, known that if he and his hawk didn't reconnect, he'd eventually die. But until that moment, he hadn't felt it deep in his gut. Now he did. His fading feral marks were proof.

His immortal life was nearing its end.

"We have a plan," Ariana announced several hours later.

The nine were gathered around the war room's huge

conference table along with their wives. And Faith. Hawke glanced at her, seated beside him. Her face was flushed, her hair damp and curling slightly at her temples, her scent the delicate musk of clean sweat, making him think of slick, hot bodies rolling in the sheets . . . or clinging to one another in the library. But the workout he'd been putting her through for the past few hours hadn't been sexual. He'd designated himself her personal trainer and had been running her through the house, ordering her to drop and do push-ups, sit-ups, whatever he could think of, until she was glaring at him as if she were about to start throwing knives again. This time at him.

Which was okay. He wanted her strong and ready when the time came to prove her worth to Lyon and the others. Even if she hadn't been the one meant to be marked, he suspected the Ferals would ultimately accept into their permanent ranks any of the new Ferals who could prove themselves to be genuine assets. And Hawke was determined that Faith would do that. It was the one thing he wanted before his time was up. To leave her safe.

"The Shaman remembered an ancient ritual performed long ago by one of my Ilina predecessors. Since I possess most of the memories of the Ilina queens who came before me, I've been searching for the right one. We think I've found it, but it's going to take a special magic—a magic that can only be accessed in the Cave of the Mystics."

The Shaman was grinning. "That cave was lost millennia ago. At least to those of us who can't turn to mist. Ariana assures me that she and her maidens can take us there."

"Ilina travel? I'd rather regrow my legs again," Jag muttered. He and Paenther had gotten back about an hour ago, good as new.

"What about your cock?" Vhyper asked.

"No." The word sounded strangled. "Not that. I'd take misting back and forth all day before I'd go through that again."

"Where is this cave?" Lyon asked.

"African Sahara." The Shaman folded his hands on the table in front of him. "The cave and its power are as old as time. If we can access it, I believe we can cure the new Ferals of this dark magic."

Lyon nodded. "Good."

Vhyper grunted, tugging on his earring. "Do we want to cure them all? Sabertooth sounds like he was a nasty piece of work long before he was marked." Hawke was no longer the only one who refused to give Maxim the respect of his Feral name. No one referred to him as Catt anymore.

"A valid question." Lyon paced. "The Georgetown enclave is working on digging up information on the men who were marked. They've already sent me what they've found on Lynks and Grizz. Lynks has been a member of his French enclave for twenty-two years, mostly in the capacity of cook. He's well enough liked and puts a lot of time into the local human community, working with children. Grizz is a little more problematic. He's portrayed as a loner with a reputation for causing trouble, which comes as no real surprise."

"Hey." Jag shrugged. "Someone has to cause the trouble. This place is going to get dull with me all happy and shit."

Fox snorted. "You just got chomped in half by a gator

fighting beside a saber-toothed cat. If this is dull, I'd hate to see exciting."

Lyon cleared his voice. "Unfortunately, the kind of trouble Grizz causes isn't the verbal kind. He leads with his fists."

"Who are his targets? Humans or immortals?" Tighe asked.

"Both." That kind of force from an immortal tended to be deadly against humans.

"He may have a good reason," Kara said.

Lyon nodded. "I agree. But he's not just a man anymore. In addition to being a Feral, he's a dangerous grizzly when he chooses to be. That could work to our advantage or to our detriment. Even clear of the infection, I don't know if he can be trusted to protect our backs. I don't know if he can be trusted with our women." He rubbed his hand across his mouth, his tone and body language as undecided as Hawke had ever seen them. "I'm putting this up for a vote. We either cure him, welcome him into our ranks, and trust him until proved wrong. Or we kill him. Tonight. And let the grizzly spirit mark another."

Silence fell over the room. To Hawke's knowledge, such a vote had never been taken, certainly not in recent centuries. But never before had they had reason to doubt that the right Therian had been marked to be a Feral.

His gut soured at the realization it could be Faith's life voted on next.

Wulfe was the first to speak. "I think we should give him a chance. He could have killed half of us out there when the new Ferals turned on us, and he didn't. He fought it, Roar. He let us cut off all four of his legs. *Let.*

Us. Despite his anger-management issues, there's honor in him. And strength of every kind."

"I agree," Fox said. "I spent the night in your prison listening to Lynks scream with pain as he regrew his legs. Grizz never made a sound but for a constant low growl until, through that mind speak, he asked me who'd died, who was injured. He didn't seem to care when I told him Eigle was gone. But when I told him Jag and Paenther might not make it, he howled with a fury that I thought would bring the ceiling crashing down on us."

"I don't have anything against giving a guy a chance," Tighe said quietly, "But neither of you have wives. Or a child on the way."

"Tighe's right. Those of us without mates . . ." Wulfe's gaze turned and met Hawke's. "Or women here we care about . . . shouldn't vote. I won't be responsible if something happens. It has to be on your heads, not ours."

Hawke reached for Faith's hand, twining her fingers with his. She looked up at him, her pensive expression softening, a small smile lifting her lips, lifting his heart.

"Six votes, then," Lyon murmured.

"Five," Kougar said. "Ariana's at no risk." She'd be able to mist away from any danger. "But I suggest a closed ballot. If you agree, I'll collect the votes."

Hawke nodded, as did the mated males. He felt odd voting as one of them, and yet in this he was. Absolutely. If Grizz turned on any woman in this house, in either form, he could easily kill her. Any Feral could, himself included, which was why he'd tried to keep away from them until Faith's presence had miraculously helped him keep control instead of losing it. But he had another concern. That Faith's fate not come to a similar vote.

And there was no way to guess which would help her more. If he voted to give Grizz a chance and the grizzly killed one of them, the others would probably vote all the new Ferals marked by *the seventeen* destroyed. But if Grizz turned out to be a good Feral, Faith's chances of being given a similar chance increased.

In the end, all he could do was vote his gut. And his gut said they needed Grizz.

Kougar shifted into his cat and leaped onto the table, pacing back and forth.

Hawke? As long as one of them was in animal form, they could speak telepathically, to all or one. *Give him a chance or clear the way for another?*

Hawke didn't hesitate. *Give him a chance.*

Less than a minute later, Kougar leaped to the floor and shifted back into a man. "Grizz stays."

Lyon nodded, his expression revealing neither relief nor regret, making it impossible to guess which way he'd voted. And Kougar would never tell.

Hopefully, they'd made the right decision in sparing Grizz's life. He wouldn't get a second chance if he blew this one. But by then, one of them would be dead, or badly injured. And Faith's death warrant all but signed.

A short while later, the group gathered in the large foyer of Feral House. It had been decided that most of the mated males and their mates would remain behind to guard Feral House. One of the Ilinas would stay with them, ready to call in the mist cavalry if the new Ferals attacked again. Kougar would lead the rest of the Ferals and Faith to the Cave of the Mystics. And once the ritual was in place, and the Ferals had recovered from the intense motion sickness Ilina travel apparently triggered, the Ilinas would fetch Grizz and Lynks and bring them to the cave as well. Then, hopefully, all three new Ferals, Faith included, would be cured of the darkness once and for all.

Hawke, too, if he was lucky. And Tighe, if he needed it. Though the Shaman sensed no darkness within either man, Hawke still wondered if the hawk spirit had been infected. What the ritual would do to him in his present state was anyone's guess, but no one had come up with a better option.

Hawke glanced at Faith, standing beside him. "Are you ready for this?"

She gave him a bright little smile that sparkled inside him, a smile with a teasing sharpness. "Are you asking about the Ilina travel or the exorcism?"

He grinned. "Just another fun evening in Feral House."

The Ilina team arrived on a pine-scented breeze, eight petite women appearing first as mist before quickly turning corporeal. All but Ariana, their queen, were dressed in tunics and tights, knives hanging from the belts at their waists—the uniforms of the Ilina mist warriors. Ariana wore jeans, boots, and an olive green tank top that made her look more like an attractive bounty hunter than an immortal queen.

"Melisande." Fox smiled at the blonde standing to Ariana's left. That Feral was on the hunt for a blade between his ribs.

Melisande scowled but ignored him, color blooming lightly in her cheeks.

Lyon stepped back, motioning to Ariana to indicate those of his group that needed transport. Hawke pulled Faith close and kissed her gently. "I'll see you on the other side." As they pulled apart, two Ilinas turned to mist and stepped into them. Hawke's world flipped, tumbling him through space in a film of energy that made him feel like he was crawling out of his flesh. His head and stomach went into a violent spin.

The sensation ended as quickly as it had begun, and he fell to his knees, vomiting, unable to do anything else. Around him, he heard others doing the same. Goddess, that was a ride he'd happily never repeat. As the spinning ended, and his stomach slowly settled, he rose to his feet, helping Faith to hers, then looked around at the small cave, little bigger than the dining room at Feral House. It had already been lit by the light of a dozen small fires in large clay pots. The shadows flickered and danced on the walls—solid walls on every side. There was no way out, no escape, except the way they'd come in. By Ilina.

"Gather around the circle, everyone." Ariana turned to her maidens. "Retrieve the two Ferals from the prisons." When the Ilinas had disappeared, she directed her attention back to the Ferals. "Grizz and Lynks will be unbound. The moment they appear, we'll begin the ritual. At first they'll be suffering and likely immobilized from the travel. After that, they'll try to escape what's happening to them. Or, more accurately, the darkness in them will fight not to be exorcised. They must remain within the fire circle. It's up to you to see that that happens. The ritual itself will not harm you." She glanced at Hawke. "It may even help you."

Kougar met Hawke's gaze. "Accompany Faith into the circle when it's time."

As Hawke nodded, something cold crawled over his skin. No, not over. Under. Inside.

"What the fuck?" Vhyper muttered.

Hawke met his gaze. "It's not just me?" His hawk, already furious with him, set up a chorus of cries loud enough to be four birds, not one.

"Hell, no."

"My animal is going ballistic," Wulfe growled.

Fox rubbed at his arms. "Mine, too."

"Hold it together," Kougar ordered.

"It won't hurt you," the Shaman assured them. "It's the ancient magic." Easy for the Shaman to say. He might have been a shifter once, but he'd long ago lost that ability.

Hawke gripped his head against the agony of talons lancing his brain with every beat of his heart. He smelled Faith's sweetness a moment before he felt her arms go around him, felt her press against his side. She didn't ask what was the matter, didn't make any demands at all, just tried to absorb some of his misery. Love for her welled up inside him. His arms went around her, and he held her close, eased by the simple, precious feel of her in his arms.

Through the screeching in his head, he heard the intonations of ritual, the Shaman's and Ariana's voices rising together as if in ancient song. Moments later, the two new Ferals appeared, each in the mistlike clutches of four Ilina maidens. Four to transport a single unwilling Feral. The women released their charges and zipped away to hover, mistlike, behind the outer circle.

As Grizz and Lynks fell to their knees, retching, Ariana motioned Hawke forward. Biting down on the dreadful pain, Hawke walked hand in hand with Faith into the fire ring. As they stepped between two of the flaming pots, Faith screamed, her hand jerking upward, her arm bending . . . *breaking*. He released her, horrified, then grabbed her again, sweeping her into his arms as her legs bent at odd angles beneath her, her back contorting.

"*What's happening?*" he roared.

"She must remain within the fire circle, warrior," the Shaman said. "It's the only way."

"Hawke, lay her down." Ariana's tone was soft with sympathy. "She'll feel less pain if she's on the ground without the weight of gravity tugging at already-broken bones."

Another cracked with a sickening snap. *Goddess*.

He did as directed, setting Faith carefully on the dirt floor of the cave, though it was all he could do to release her when she was in so much pain. As his hands slid away from her, she met his gaze, her own shiny with tears and dark with misery.

"*Smiley*."

"I can do this, Hawke. Let me do this."

Without warning, Grizz reared up out of his crouch with a roar, shifting into his grizzly in a spray of colored lights. Hawke whirled, placing himself firmly between Faith and the dangerous, furious bear. But Grizz lunged at the Shaman instead, his mouth opening as if he meant to tear the much smaller man's head off. Wulfe leaped at him, shifting into his wolf in midair, slamming into the huge animal, his lips pulled back in a snarl. Though Wulfe's attack barely changed the bear's trajectory, it was enough. Fox shifted more slowly, his reflexes still coming on board, growing until he was larger even than Wulfe, then he was on the bear, too, snarling, biting.

His skin still crawling with cold, Hawke pulled his

knives, ready to defend Faith if any of them drew close. Behind him he heard another terrible snap of bone and she screamed. His hawk joined her, filling his head with its cries. At the edges of his vision, the red haze began to creep.

Hold it together, hold it together. He'd be no use to her if he lost it, now. No use to anyone.

Lynks, still in man form, made a run for the circle, trying to escape, but Vhyper and Kougar were ready for him and easily tackled him to the ground. A few yards away, the two large canines and the bear fought as if to the death, fur and blood flying.

Faith screamed again and again as her body twisted and contorted until Hawke was about to yell from the pain her suffering was causing him. Vhyper and Kougar dragged Lynks back into the circle as the Shaman and Ariana continued to chant, as the Ilinas floated, wraith-like, watching it all.

"It is done," Ariana said at last, her voice barely audible over the roars and screams. The chanting ceased.

The chaos ended as quickly as it had begun. Across the fire ring, the grizzly collapsed, the wolf and giant fox leaping back. Lynks, too, seemed to have lost his fight.

Hawke whirled to find Faith lying bent, her body twisted at horrible angles. Unconscious or . . .

His heart roared as he fell to his knees beside her, reaching for her neck, searching for her pulse. There! Strong and steady against his finger. *Thank the goddess.* Her body jerked suddenly, then began to unbend as if whatever dark power had gripped her had finally let go. As he watched, she untwisted until she lay in her normal shape, the bones snapping back into place, healing almost as quickly as they'd fractured.

Kougar finally broke the silence that had descended over the cave. "Get us home, Ariana."

Never ones to hesitate, the Ilinas swept forward, and Hawke once more found himself in that spinning nothingness. The next thing he knew, he was puking his guts out in the yard behind Feral House, the awful coldness finally gone.

The moment he could raise his head, he searched for Faith, finding her a short distance away, still unconscious. He pushed himself to his feet and went to her as the other Ferals slowly rose to surround Lynks and Grizz, who were lying on the grass as still as Faith. Hawke knelt beside her, grasping her cold hand, eyeing the others, ready to lend his sword if needed.

Grizz was the first to move. With a bear-sized groan, he rolled onto his back and pressed his hands against his head. "What the fuck happened?"

"How do you feel?" Kougar asked.

"Like my head's been put through a meat grinder." He sat up, started to rise, until he saw the drawn knives, then sat back down, hands in the air. "Mind telling me what's going on?"

Kougar motioned to the Shaman. "We think we may have exorcised the darkness. The Shaman can tell by touching you. Don't move."

Grizz lowered his hands to his knees but otherwise remained still as the Shaman touched the top of his dark head and nodded.

"Clear. Not a shadow left."

Lyon strode toward them from the house. "Does this mean the animal spirit is clear as well?"

The Shaman nodded. "Yes. No darkness survived the power we drew in that cave. I'm certain of it."

Hawke heard the words, hope rising and falling in the same instant. Because he felt no different. No better. Like nothing had changed.

As Lynks began to stir, the Shaman touched him, too. Lynks stiffened, and the Shaman pulled back. "He is clear also." He turned to Hawke. "How do you feel?"

Hawke pulled off his T-shirt and looked over his shoulder at the feral marks that were nearly gone. He sighed. "What about Faith?" He pulled the shirt back over his head as the Shaman knelt beside her.

"She suffered the most," the ancient man murmured, touching her head. Hawke had to fight back the possessive growl that tried to rise in his throat. The Shaman frowned, pressing his hand to her forehead, then her cheek, the frown puckering his forehead. "The ritual didn't work for her. She's still infected." He met Hawke's gaze with regret. "I'm sorry."

Ariana and Kougar moved to join them as the Shaman rose to his feet.

"Why didn't it work?" Hawke demanded, but he was afraid he knew the answer.

The Shaman shook his head. "The darkness in its dormant state cannot be vanquished. You must release it. Bring her into her animal first."

Lyon joined them, his expression drawn. "I don't like exposing Kara to another infected Renascence. She still hasn't recovered from the last."

But the woman in question was crossing the yard and heard. Kara slid her arm around Lyon's waist, and he tucked her in close as she looked at Faith. "I'm fine, Lyon."

He lifted her chin, studying her with worried eyes. "No, you're not."

"I'm good enough. Faith needs to be brought into her

animal, and without me, you can't do it. It's my job."

Still, the Chief of the Ferals hesitated, clearly torn between his personal need to keep his mate safe and the greater need to see this newest Feral cleared of the magic infecting her.

He sighed heavily. "Then we'll do it tonight, just before dawn." Pulling Kara against his side, he turned to his men. "Meanwhile, we need to get a lead on the other new Ferals."

"I'll head out to Harpers Ferry," Wulfe offered.

Lyon nodded. "I've already sent Jag and Olivia scouring areas nearby. Delaney is hooked into the FBI's network, looking for reports of strange, large animals."

As the others moved toward the back door of Feral House, Hawke brushed Faith's blue-tipped locks back from her still-unconscious face. The thought of her having to go through that again tore something loose inside of him. But there was no choice, was there? She had to be cured.

"Are you bringing her in, Hawke?" Kougar called, halfway to the patio.

Hawke shook his head, and Kougar lifted his hand in acknowledgment and joined the others. Alone, Hawke tipped his face to the spring sunshine filtering through the leaves, enjoying the feel of the breeze on his face. He needed time out here beneath the trees to think. It had been so long since he'd been able to take to the skies and revel in the freedom. And now it looked like he might never feel that joy again. But he hated even more that Faith hadn't been cured.

Beneath the brush of his hand, she began to stir. Her eyes blinked open, her gaze moving to his. "Did it work?" she asked softly.

"For the others, yes. For you, no."

She sat up slowly, eyeing him with a bleakness that cut him to the core, a hopelessness that told him she expected them to clear the way for her replacement.

He reached for her, stroking her hair. "We're not giving up on you, Smiley. The Shaman believes they can't cure the darkness while it's dormant. We have to bring you into your animal first."

Relief lit her features, then dissolved into an expression that made her look as if she'd bitten into a lemon. "You mean I have to go through that again?"

"It shouldn't be as bad the next time. Neither of the others suffered like you did." He sat on the grass beside her and took her hand in his. "We'll bring you into your animal just before dawn tomorrow morning."

Her eyes slowly turned huge as another thought seemed to occur to her. "I'm going to turn evil."

"Not evil, just . . . infected."

Her hand squeezed his fiercely. "Don't let me hurt anyone, Hawke. Promise me. I couldn't the way I am now, but if I turn into something with big teeth . . ."

"I won't let you hurt anyone."

He hoped he could hang on to his animal long enough to fulfill that promise.

Chapter Sixteen

Wulfe parked his truck behind a deserted warehouse outside Frederick, Maryland, then climbed out, shoved his keys deep in his jeans pocket, and stripped, tossing his clothes into the bed of the oversized pickup. Kneeling beside the truck, hidden from prying eyes, he shifted into his wolf. He'd made a brief foray in and around Harpers Ferry before driving the twenty miles to Frederick. Though he'd tried to convince himself . . . and Lyon . . . otherwise, this trip had little to do with hunting the new Ferals. It was a long shot that they'd have come back here, and he'd seen no evidence of it.

No, this trip was about Natalie and his need to check on her for Xavier.

Okay, not for Xavier. Not *just* for Xavier. The truth was he needed to know that she was all right. He needed to see her for himself even though she wouldn't remember him. He'd taken care to clear her memories of that horrific day—the deaths of her friends at the hands of three wraith Daemons, the Earth opening in front of the stake upon which she'd been tied. The opening had been a wormhole into the spirit trap, and Hawke and Tighe had gone down, as had a couple of her dead friends.

But Natalie had survived, along with her brother, Xavier, and another girl. The Ferals had been able to clear Natalie's and the other girl's memories, but Xavier was blind, and memories were cleared through the eyes. He lived at Feral House, now, helping Pink in the kitchen.

And Natalie was back home with no recollection of where she'd been for a week or where her brother had gone. All she knew was that three of her friends had died horrific deaths. She knew that only because their bodies had been spit out again by the spirit trap, and the Ferals had left them for the humans to find.

In his wolf's form, he trotted into the woods separating him from Natalie's house, having mapped out the coordinates before he left home.

At least she wasn't alone. Natalie was engaged to be married. Wulfe had returned her to her world, leaving her in Harpers Ferry and watching from the shadows as her fiancé swept her into his arms.

He couldn't get the damned image out of his head. It was best for her, he knew that. She had no place in his world. She was human. And he was a widower, as the humans would put it. A mated male with a dead mate, which equated to *damaged*, in his world. Mating bonds were real among Therians, not verbal or legal promises, as in the human world. And a severed mating bond damaged the survivor, one way or another. He didn't have it in him to connect that way with a woman again. And he'd never want to, especially with a human who would only die on him, too. No, he wasn't looking for anything from Natalie, he just needed to know she was okay. In the short time he'd spent with her in the prison below Feral House, she'd touched him in a way he couldn't quite explain.

Some twenty minutes later, he picked up her scent, sending a thrill of recognition through his man's mind. She'd walked these woods in the past couple of days. Alone.

He followed her scent straight to the house he knew was hers—a small two-story Colonial with pale yellow siding and a wooden deck attached to the back. And now what was he going to do? He couldn't trot up to the door and start barking. In his wolf's form, he was huge—far bigger than any normal wolf. In past centuries, he'd terrified humans in his animal form. Today, with wolves so rare, most humans assumed he was merely a big dog. Many weren't quite terrified, though most gave him a wide berth. Which generally suited him just fine.

Today, he wished he could downsize into an innocuous pup and call for Natalie's attention. Though he'd stolen her memories of him, he couldn't risk her seeing his man's face. Nor did he want her to. She might not have been afraid of the scarred mess after that trio of hideous Daemons, but she didn't remember those, now, either. Compared to most humans, he was a monster. And, thanks to his inability to keep his clothes when he shifted, a big, naked one, at that. No, it was far better to stay in his animal. To stay hidden in the woods and hope he caught a glimpse of her. It was already close to sunset. If she didn't pull blinds or curtains over her windows at night, he might succeed. If she did, he was out of luck. Or if she went to her fiancé's place instead of her own.

The thought sat like hot coals in his gut.

He settled into the underbrush about twenty feet from the back of her deck to wait, wondering if he should just leave and forget about trying to see her. If he really needed to know that she was okay, all he had to do was have Delaney or one of the other women give her a call, pretending to be a reporter. Goddess knew the press had been all over her after her miraculous escape from death. But just as he'd about convinced himself to turn around and head home, he heard the sound of a car stop in front of the house. His pulse leaped, his ears twitching, his nose seeking her scent. He heard a door open and close. A moment later, something moved in her house. Natalie? He leaped up, catching a glimpse of blond hair, wondering when he'd last been this excited about something . . . *anything*. And all he wanted was to catch a glimpse of her. He'd turned into a sad-ass peeping Tom.

There! She'd stepped into the kitchen, wearing a trim light green shirt with buttons down the front, her hair loose around her shoulders. He could see her clearly now, pulling a wineglass down from one of the cupboards. The lights shining down from the ceiling cast her face into shadow. Were those bruises beneath her eyes real or just cast there by the lighting?

He watched, fascinated, as she opened a bottle of red wine, poured herself a glass, and lifted it to her lips. Pleasure coursed through him, and he was suddenly glad he'd made the trip. Seeing her like this settled him, easing a tension he hadn't realized he'd been feeling.

She recorked the bottle and turned away from the

window. He sank to the ground, his chin on his paws. It was enough, he told himself. He should go home now and tell Xavier that he'd seen her. That his sister was fine.

A movement caught his eye at the back door. His ears lifted and he pushed himself up. Was she . . . ? Yes! Natalie opened the glass sliding door and stepped out onto her deck. It was all he could do to keep his big wolf's body planted on the soft earth and not bounding forward.

A sigh blew through his man's mind, snuffling out his wolf's mouth with a small, pleased whimper.

She was . . . *beautiful.* In the setting sun, her hair looked like spun gold, her features calm, as always. *Perfect.* She stood erect, her limbs long and lovely, her body curvy in all the right places.

As he watched, she took a sip of the red wine, then lifted her free hand to brush away something on one cheek. Then the other.

Tears.

He whined with misery, his emotions always leaking out when he was in his animal.

Natalie froze, her gaze jerking toward him. Her eyes widened, and he knew he'd been caught. Shit. He was going to scare her to death. Should he turn and run? Yeah, he should. But, goddess, he couldn't leave her like this. Not with tears in her eyes.

He rolled onto his back, scratching his back in the underbrush which, by the way, felt damn good as he put on the Happy Dog act. Then he rolled onto his stomach and laid his head on his paws watching her, hoping she wasn't scared. Then hoping she was because what was he thinking? He was a wolf! He knew he'd never hurt her, but she didn't know that.

The smart thing for her to do would be to back slowly into the house and close the door. And, goddess, he didn't want her to do that.

Another whine escaped him.

Natalie's expression softened as she took a step forward, and another, then sat on the top step leading off the deck into the grass. "You're beautiful, do you know that? Are you really a wolf, or just a very big dog? I should probably be afraid of you, shouldn't I?"

Damn right, she should.

Instead, he made his tail wag, the one thing it never did on its own, and was rewarded by a calm Natalie smile. Goddess, he'd missed those.

She held out her hand and made kissing noises toward him, and it was all he could do not to roll over with glee.

He started toward her slowly, reminding himself to keep wagging his tail, to open his mouth and let his tongue loll out in that dopey way that made dogs look like they were smiling. His gaze remained fixed on Natalie, watching Natalie, mesmerized by Natalie.

She watched him without fear, with a mix of delight and curiosity. "You are gorgeous, do you know that?"

Ha. She wouldn't say that if she saw the scarred mess that was his man's face. Actually, she'd seen his man's face. She hadn't called him beautiful, but she hadn't run away screaming, and that was something. A huge something.

He closed the distance between them, his heart jackhammering against his ribs. Up close, she was even more beautiful, her skin flawless and creamy, her mouth soft with that smile that had kept him company in his dreams. But her eyes still glistened with unshed tears, her lower lashes spiked and damp, and he wished with everything inside him he could give Xavier back to her. If only the Ferals could find a way to steal the kid's memories of them and all he'd seen, and send him home.

Natalie reached for Wulfe slowly. The moment her hand slid into his fur, his body shuddered with pure pleasure.

Desperately, he wanted to shift into man form and tell her the truth, that Xavier was fine. But he'd frighten her shitless if he tried it. Naked, scarred. *Shifting*. Yeah, humans didn't take well to that stuff. He'd tell her the truth, then just have to wipe it out of her mind again.

No, there was nothing he could do. His being here wasn't helping her at all.

And all he'd managed to do for himself was to see her misery firsthand. To know there was nothing he could do to help her.

And to realize how much he wished that she could, in some way, be part of his life.

An hour before sunrise, as soon as the draden were gone for the day, the Ferals, Kara, and Faith made their way through the woods near Feral House, coming out on the rocks high above the rugged Potomac River. Faith clung to Hawke's hand as they stepped down to the wide goddess stone. A light drizzle had been falling most of the night, and she was already soaked and cold, though the shivers that hit her with periodic frequency might be more a result of the nerves that were tying her into knots. She was terrified of what would happen when the shifting triggered the darkness inside her. Would she turn on the other Ferals and try to kill them?

Would she try to escape? Would she lose her clothes when she shifted and end up standing before them all, stark naked?

Kougar had promised her they'd thought of every angle and would be placing a spell that would keep her from getting away, no matter what. The nakedness, Hawke had assured her, would be something she'd get used to if it happened. Which was of little help that morning.

Kara and Lyon led the way, Kara in a flowing red ritual gown topped by a hooded, waterproof raincoat. Faith wore jeans, a fleece hoodie, and a black sports bra Olivia had loaned her. Apparently, the ritual to bring her into her animal required her to cut herself across the chest. Upper chest. Still, a shirt of any kind was going to be ruined. And she just wasn't willing to go topless like the men did. Not yet. Maybe not ever. Unless she really couldn't keep her clothes on when she shifted, in which case she'd get so used to being naked around them, she'd stop thinking about it. Eventually. Maybe.

Goddess, she hoped that didn't happen.

Okay, that just wasn't the main thing she needed to be worrying about.

As if hearing her thoughts, Hawke stopped her and turned her to face him. Raindrops glistened on his nose, but love flared in his eyes as he pressed his warm hand to her cheeks. "I love you," he said softly. No words of reassurance, no promises that everything would be fine. They both knew what was likely to happen.

"I love you, too."

Kougar called up the mystic circle and set the warding that would force them all to remain within the circle until it was dismantled. The men, bare-chested, their golden armbands sparkling with raindrops, began to form a wide circle around Kara. Hawke motioned Faith to join them, and she did, tossing her hoodie onto the damp rock behind her and standing between Hawke and Tighe. Kougar began chanting, leading the ritual, but the others soon joined in. All but the other new Ferals. She was glad she wasn't the only one standing uncomfortably mute.

Across the circle, Kougar pulled a knife, slashed a long line across his chest, then pressed his free hand against the bleeding wound before handing the knife to Lyon.

Faith's gut cramped. She knew she was immortal, of course she knew that. Any flesh wound would heal within a matter of seconds. Ten, twenty at most. She knew that. But it didn't mean the cut wasn't going to hurt like hell.

Warrior after warrior slashed his chest—Paenther, Jag, Wulfe, Fox—curling their fists around their own blood. Tighe cut himself, then handed the knife to her, hilt first. Faith took it, clasping shaking fingers around the wooden handle, her gaze flicking up to Tighe's. He nodded, his gaze a little sympathetic but mostly demanding. *Do it,* his eyes said. And she must.

"If you cut quickly, it'll be over before you feel it," Hawke whispered from her other side.

With a single, jerky nod, she took a deep breath, turned the knife toward her chest, squeezed her eyes closed, and cut fast from the edge of one shoulder blade to her sports bra on the other side.

Scorching pain tore across her chest.

"Good girl," Tighe murmured.

"A little deep," Hawke muttered, "but you'll heal."

"I haven't exactly practiced this."

"Silence," Kougar intoned, a hint of laughter in his voice. "Bloody your hand, Faith, or you'll have to cut yourself again."

"Oh." She pressed her hand against the wound, wincing more at the thought of what she was doing than the actual pain. Already, the wound was healing, the pain receding to nothing. Three cheers for immortality. Hawke curled his hand into a fist around his own now-bloody palm, and she mimicked his action.

When the knife had gone all the way around the circle, Kougar shoved his fist into the air. The others followed, Faith a beat late. She felt like a complete and total fraud.

Kara shrugged off her raincoat, raised her hands, and went radiant.

"Stay here," Hawke told her. Then he and the others gathered around Kara, each touching her bare skin. Faith stood apart for what felt like twenty minutes, but was probably less than one, the drizzle soaking her clothes and hair, making her shiver with cold as she kept her fist clenched tight around the damp blood.

Finally, Kougar released Kara and turned to Faith. One by one, the others followed, circling tight around her, towering over her, their combined body heat chasing away the chill. "Lift your fist," Kougar told her.

As she did, Lyon opened his bloody hand and grasped her fist with it. Kougar pressed his hand atop Lyon's, Hawke's atop Kougar's, each following suit until she felt as if she were holding an eleven-scoop ice-cream cone.

Kougar began to chant, switching to English as the others joined in. "Spirits rise and join. Empower the beasts beneath this moon. Goddess, reveal your warrior!"

Thunder rumbled, an unnatural sound. The sound of violent magic. Faith began to tremble. Beneath her bare feet, the rock started to quake almost as badly as her hands. She felt the anticipation of the men pressing around her, felt their anticipation feed her own. Her breath turned shallow, excitement lifting her pulse.

And suddenly energy powered through her, a blast of ecstasy that had her gasping, and then not gasping because she no longer had a mouth. Not a human mouth.

She fell to the ground. No, not fell. Her feet were on the stone, her body upright among a forest of denim and leather-clad trees, her wings tucked tight against . . . *her wings*. Not trees. *Legs*.

High above her, Kougar's voice rang out. "Henceforth, you will be known among us as Falkyn."

A falcon. Before the incredible transition sank into her woman's brain, another blast crashed through her mind, a driving, pounding need.

Escape! Escape!

The frantic drive tore through her falcon's breast. She tried to fly, tried to break free of the forest of legs, but hands snatched at her.

"Faith, easy!"

"Falkyn. Cease!"

But the desperate need to escape overrode every thought, every instinct until her mind was pounding, screeching. Blank.

"Faith!" Hawke tried to reach her through the terror that had engulfed her. Or the fury. He was all too afraid it was the dark magic driving her frantic attempt at freedom.

The small peregrine falcon broke free of the hands trying to grasp her and lifted into flight, whapping Vhyper in the face with her wing as she rose, only to slam into the mystic barrier Kougar had erected around the goddess stone. The barrier knocked her back, but she remained airborne and dove for the other side only to fall back a second time, harder, plummeting to the rock.

Hawke reached for her, his heart in his throat. Goddess, she had to be all right.

Her wings began to flutter, and he grabbed her, carefully pinning her wings to her body. "Shift back, Faith. Shift back."

Instead, she struggled, shrieking her anger, and tried to bite him. Inside, his hawk screeched in answer. But her nearness in this form did nothing to calm his bird. He felt the hawk's fury rising with Faith's agitation. The red haze began rushing into his vision.

Pushing to his feet, he shoved the falcon at Tighe. "Take her! Before I hurt her."

Tighe had barely grabbed the small, struggling bird of prey when Hawke went feral, his claws and fangs erupting. Wulfe and Paenther grabbed him by the upper arms, their touch helping him struggle for control and not join Faith in a wild flight into the dome above.

"Shift, Falkyn," Lyon demanded. "We'll not release you until you do. You'll never be free until you shift back into human form."

Sparkling lights flickered. Faith reappeared practically in Tighe's arms, once more in her jeans and sports bra. So she *was* one of the ones who could retain her clothes when she shifted. As the tiger shifter pulled back, Kougar and Lyon grabbed Faith's arms and slapped the waiting Mage cuffs around her wrists, black metal bands that would keep her from shifting but wouldn't hamper her movements since they weren't attached to one another. Still, she wouldn't be able to remove them without the counterspell.

High around one upper arm curled a delicate gold Feral armband with the head of a falcon. In many ways, a feminine version of Hawke's own.

She growled low in her throat, easily jerking free of Kougar's and Lyon's holds. Their shocked expressions might have been comical under other circumstances. She was strong all of a sudden, and she fought them, swinging a fist that nearly caught Kougar in the eye. Lyon grabbed her from behind, not underestimating her strength a second time.

Paenther squeezed Hawke's shoulder. "They're not hurting her."

"I know that." But he was shaking with the instinctive need to protect her, the growls coming low and fast.

Bastards.

Hawke heard the word in his head clear as day. Faith's voice. And he could tell by the looks on the others' faces, the startled exchanged glances, that he wasn't the only one.

"Did she really just talk to us telepathically?" Paenther asked. "*In human form?*"

"Shit," Jag muttered.

"A handy trick in battle," Tighe said. "Once we get her back on our side."

Lyon looked to Kougar. "Let's get this shield down and get her back to that cave in the Sahara. Get her cured."

"Agreed."

The sight of Faith fighting off another man was sending him into a tailspin. "*She's mine.*" The words tore between his fangs, barely human.

Paenther stepped in front of him, blocking his view of Lyon holding a struggling Faith. "You must get control, Wings." Paenther's hands gripped Hawke's shoulders hard, but his voice remained even. "Ease down, my friend. Lyon's not hurting her, you know that. We're going to take her to the cave and save her. But she's going to need you with her. You must get control."

Mine! Even as the wildness inside him struggled to break free, to claim the woman he adored, Hawke fought to push back the red haze, to hold on.

"Ease down, Hawke. Come on, my friend." Paenther's calm voice helped pull him back, little by little, until finally he was able to retract his claws and fangs.

Hawke released a hard breath as Paenther let go of him. "Thank you."

Paenther nodded and stepped back, letting Hawke pass.

Hawke strode straight to Lyon. "I've got her."

"I'm not sure that's a good idea."

"Neither am I. But watching you struggle with her is going to make me lose it. It has to be me."

Lyon hesitated, then shoved the struggling woman into Hawke's arms, and she fought him as hard as she had Lyon, her strength easily three times what it had been before. Not equal to his, but not that much less. She'd be able to take most Therian males like this. Most Mage.

She arched into him, trying to twist her body out of his grasp, low growls and hisses coming from her throat. When she glared up at him, her eyes were flat.

The eyes of a stranger. Something inside him roared with pain.

"Let me go." A deadly fury laced her words.

"Do you know me?" he demanded, holding her fast.

Her lip curled, then softened as recognition flared in the brown depths of her eyes. For an instant, his Faith was back, then gone again just as quickly. "Yes, I know you. You have to let me go."

"Why? Where will you go?"

"Away. I must get away. I must go to him."

To him? "To who?"

She fought him, her hip grinding against his groin, damn near setting him on fire. "Maxim. I belong to him."

And that quickly, she doused the flame with ice water.

"You belong to me."

She snarled, her claws and fangs erupting. Hawke felt his own leap out, a dark growl escaping between his lips.

"Easy, buddy," Tighe's voice came from behind him. "Ease down, Wings."

He was fighting for control, riding a knife's edge. "You said you know me. Who am I, Faith? *Who am I to you?*"

A strange look crossed her face, a look he'd never seen before. Dark, predatory. "You're the man I want to fuck."

The word shot straight to his groin, hardening his already-inflamed body. But his heart clenched in denial. This wasn't his Faith. The screeching inside his head intensified as if the hawk spirit were as frustrated as he was.

"It's time to go." Kougar entered his line of vision. "Ariana and company are on their way."

A moment later, the Ilinas arrived, Ariana and two others Hawke didn't recognize appearing out of thin air in front of them. Ariana nodded to him. "Release her, Hawke. We have her."

The animal inside his head let out a screech of anger, his and the hawk's emotions in complete accord. *No. Mine!* But he fought both his own possessive instincts and the animal spirit's demands and let her go.

The moment he released her, the Ilinas turned to mist, and moved in. A second later, they were gone, Faith along with them.

Another Ilina snatched up Hawke in her mist before he even registered what she looked like, then the spinning began—his body, his head, his stomach. And ended abruptly with a slam of power that felt as if his bones had been pulverized.

Suddenly, he was falling through hot air, landing with a thud in a sea of hot, golden sand. The Sahara? Thuds sounded all around him, the shouts of men, the cries of women in pain. And the sound of swords and animals. *Chaos.*

The sickness roared through him as it had the last two times he'd traveled by Ilina, but he fought it back, pushed to his feet, and whirled, taking in the horrific sight in the middle of the sun-scorched desert. Mage sentinels lunged at downed Ferals and Ilinas, alike.

They'd flown into an ambush.

*Chapter
Seventeen*

Hawke pulled his blades against a rushing Mage, searching frantically for Faith through the chaotic battle scene playing out all around him as he squinted against the blinding sun gleaming off the golden sand now streaked with blood and body parts. He dispatched the Mage's sword hand with ease, then pushed into the melee, desperate to find her. If the Mage caught Faith, if they used the counterspell to free her from the wrist-bands, she'd fly off, and he might never find her again. The thought sent a reeling panic pounding through his chest.

Finally, he spotted her battling two Mage a short dis-tance away though the pair appeared to be trying to grab her, not hurt her—neither had pulled weapons. For a moment, he could only stare. Faith was fight-ing them brilliantly, using not only her newly acquired strength, but also the moves they'd shown her, fighting with a speed and agility that spoke of years . . . decades . . . of training.

He pushed toward her. Around him, the other Ferals had shifted into their animals and were tearing at the Mage. Ilinas littered the ground, fully corporeal, dazed, rising, fighting. What in the hell had happened? The Ilinas had gotten them to the Sahara, but clearly not into the cave.

Another Mage joined the fight against Faith. Why? Why try to catch her instead of kill her?

But he knew. She, like Maxim and the other new Ferals, was under the spell of Mage magic. And they wanted her alive, a weapon to use against the uninfected Ferals. Rage barreled through him, the hawk's anger melding with his own, hot and wild.

A Mage lunged at Hawke, but he parried the blow with ease. He was bigger than the Mage, stronger, more skilled, and infinitely more furious. In a single swing, he lopped off this sentinel's hand as he had the one before and continued to make his way to Faith. Another Mage lunged at him, sword swinging, and met the same fate as his predecessors. He'd kill them all, and happily, if not for the fact that Mother Nature tended to rebel when too many of her Mage died at once. As the sands began to rise in a sudden wind, he knew some of them *had* died. And Mother Nature was starting to get pissed.

Two more came at him from opposite directions, and he battled them back, striking one's hand from his arm and thrusting his blade deep through the other's heart, likely killing him. Some sane corner of his mind knew he was losing it. The berserker was beginning to surface. The berserker always came first, followed by the shift that would send him flying off in his bird to goddess-knew-where. Deeper into the Sahara? He had to reach Faith before that happened!

Faith continued to fight, her strength superior to her opponents', one-on-one, but there were three of them. Why was she fighting them if she was being controlled by Mage magic?

Hawke reached the first of the men, running a blade through his soulless heart. The wind whipped harder, sending the sand flaying his face, his arms, destroying visibility. Faith tripped the other and began to run, her tread surprisingly light on the shifting sands. He lopped off the head of her second attacker, spilling blood into the sand, and took off after her, struggling to run. He'd never catch her!

The Earth began to quake under his feet, Mother Nature thoroughly angry, now. The sand began to swirl dangerously fast.

The red haze pulsed into his vision, turning the sand to blood. Fury consumed him, the hawk jerking away the last of his control. He was losing it!

Through the roar of the blasting sand and the yelling, he heard Kougar shout, "Get us out of here!"

Once more he tumbled through nothingness, then found himself on his knees in the predawn gray of the backyard of Feral House, retching his guts out.

"Faith?" Hawke called when he was able.

"She's here." Kougar's voice.

Lightning bolted through his head, a fiery pain that radiated to all corners of his skull followed, as always, by the hawk's cry. Talons tore into his brain with a ferocity that, if real, would have left his brain leaking out his ears as a bloody pulp. *The agony . . .*

He couldn't breathe, couldn't think as his mind went momentarily blank but for the white-hot pain. Tearing, ripping, bleeding, *misery*. He forgot to count, couldn't think, could only survive.

"Easy, buddy." Kougar gripped his shoulder. "What's happening?"

Finally, finally, the talons eased off, the searing pain slowly receding until he could think again. Until he could breathe. "Nothing."

"Right." Kougar didn't believe him.

Hawke struggled to his feet, searching for Faith. Between the motion sickness and his bird's attack, he felt beaten and bruised, but he hadn't shifted. A hell of a way to stop an unintended shift, but he wasn't complaining.

Around the yard, others rose unsteadily, Faith in the middle of them. But even as he found her, she leaped to her feet and took off running, faster than any human . . . or immortal, for that matter . . . should be able to run.

"We'll get her," a soft Ilina voice murmured, and, moments later, Faith was once more on her knees, retching beside him.

Lyon joined him. "We have no choice but to lock her up."

"*No.*"

"Give me another option."

Hawke wished he had one. At least a good one. "Handcuff her to me. She won't go anywhere."

"And if you shift?"

They'd both be gone. No cuffs would hold him in his animal. And he couldn't use the Mage wristbands they now had on Faith. They'd tried that when they first realized his problem, but he'd gone berserk, crazed with a fury that wasn't his. It had taken three of his brothers to take him down.

If he shifted, Faith would run. He knew that, now. And his control was too precarious at the moment. In truth, someone else needed to be guarding her. His animal screeched in fury at the thought of others manhandling her as she fought them. Or defending themselves from her, for that matter.

Faith started to rise, and Hawke grabbed her by the upper arms before she could get away from him again, igniting a storm of kicking feet and slashing claws. He turned her away from him, then bear-hugged her, pinning her arms against her sides so she couldn't continue the attack.

This wasn't going to work. "All right," he told Lyon. "She stays in the prison until we cure her." He turned to Kougar. "What in the hell happened out there?"

"The Mage erected some kind of barrier around the cave, or maybe that entire portion of the Sahara. The moment the Ilinas hit the barrier, they turned corporeal. We all fell out of the sky, right into a Mage ambush. Fortunately, the Ilinas recovered quickly and were able to get us back out of there before we suffered any casualties." He lifted an eyebrow. "The same can't be said for the Mage."

Hawke didn't feel an ounce of remorse for his part in that. "They were trying to capture Faith."

"How did the Mage know about the cave?" Lyon demanded. "How did they know you were on your way there?"

Kougar stroked his beard. "I'm wondering if the infection might be acting as some kind of tracking system for the new Ferals."

Lyon looked at Faith. "Then the sooner we get her cured, the better."

Kougar nodded. "Ariana and the Shaman are working on a way to bypass or destroy the Mage barrier. Meanwhile . . ." He turned to Hawke. "I'll help you get her downstairs."

It took both of them to drag a fighting, kicking Faith down the long stairs and through the basement to the prisons without hurting her.

"She's strong," Kougar murmured, righting himself from one of Faith's leg swipes that nearly knocked him off balance. "Not unexpected—we all get stronger with the animal. But Vhyper's right. She really could be a secret weapon. No enemy is going to expect strength like this from a 125-pound female. Of any race."

They reached the prisons and shoved her into one of the cells, slamming the door closed before she could whirl on them and try to fight her way out.

Feral and snarling, her claws clicking against the steel bars, she growled, shaking the bars. "Let me go!"

Hawke hated seeing her like this, locked up. Crazed. And yet . . . there was something . . . *arousing* . . . about the unadulterated wildness in her.

"Where, Faith?" Hawke asked quietly. "Where do you want to go?"

"To Maxim! I belong to him."

"Maxim hurt you!"

"Let me go!"

"He hurt you, Faith. You have to remember. What did he do to you? Did he rape you? Did he cut you? Did he use those fangs . . ."

Something flared in her eyes. Pain.

Ah, goddess. "He hurt you with those saber teeth, didn't he?"

A violent tremble went through her. "The shower." The words were a growl. "He bit me, impaled me in the shower so the blood would wash away. So no one would know."

His knees nearly gave way beneath him as the image blasted his mind. Sweet Faith enduring such torture in horrible silence. He'd known the bastard was hurting her. He'd known!

But Sweet Faith wasn't here anymore. Not now. The feral woman in the cage watched him, eyes once more blazing as she rattled the cage. "Let me go!"

Kkkeeeeer! His animal was furious, his rage melding with the man's. Hawke raked fingers into his hair, his teeth grinding as he fought to control the fury. He'd die before he ever let that madman near her again.

"Hawke." Kougar's hand landed on his shoulder, but he barely felt it.

Wisps of red haze began curling around the edges of his vision. He hated this. Hated that she struggled to return to the bastard who'd hurt her, caught in the grip of Mage magic. Daemon magic. And he, who loved her beyond measure, couldn't touch her, couldn't hold her because of the bars that separated them.

"Put me in there with her." His bird let out a cry of agreement.

Kougar watched him thoughtfully. "That's not a good idea, Hawke. If you shift into your bird, she could kill you. We have to believe Maxim's ordered her to do just that."

"Do it. My animal wants it. *I* want it."

"Hawke . . ."

He went feral, turning on his friend, holding back . . . barely . . . from clawing him. "*Do it.*"

Again, Kougar studied him for several seconds before slowly stepping forward to unlock Faith's cell. Hawke followed. The moment Kougar unlocked the door, Faith lunged for the opening, but Hawke was ready for that. He met her, colliding with her as he pushed her back into the cell, away from the door that clanged shut behind him.

Fangs and claws drawn, she attacked him as any of his brothers would in a good feral wrestling match— slashing claws down his cheek, across his chest, ripping at the flesh of his shoulder with her fangs until blood splattered her face and hair, the drops of red turning her blue-tipped locks purple. She was a wild woman, untamed. *Magnificent.* The animal inside him welcomed the fight, urged him to join her in the wildness, to revel in it as he'd done in the days before the spirit trap had made battle of any kind a dangerous business. But this wasn't one of his Feral brothers looking for a fight. It was Faith. His sweet Smiley.

The man recoiled at the thought of hurting her. But the man was losing control, red haze growing at the edges of his vision. He pushed it back, suddenly afraid that he'd made a mistake in joining her in here. A growl ripped from his throat as the wildness overpowered him, and he turned on her. Aware, but in little control, he drew claws on her and ripped her clothes from her body, then tore off his own. The wildness screamed for a battle of a different kind.

Not like this! Not like this! His man's brain railed at

what he feared he was about to do even as the last of his control slipped away.

Faith grunted as Hawke body-slammed her back against the wall. She slashed out with her claws, raking new furrows in his cheek to replace the ones that had already healed.

Blood. Hurt him.

No!

Thoughts tried to break through the thick fog that had become her mind. She was acting on instinct, fighting that instinct. Driven by forces not her own.

He threw her to the ground, though she barely felt the collision, then he stood over her, poised for one brilliant moment like a barbarian of old, his body sculpted with muscle, his shoulders broad, his cock hard and thick, protruding like a weapon. His arms hung away from his body as if ready to attack, his chest rising and falling with quick breaths, his eyes burning with battle and lust.

Her body burst into flame in answer, damp heat pooling between her thighs. She wanted battle. *This* battle.

Her legs parted, offering him what they both wanted, and he fell on her, taking her in a single hard thrust that shot her straight into orgasm. Claws out, she raked at his back, and he roared and bit her shoulder with his fangs. Pain exploded, and she reveled in it as he drove into her, pounding her with his body, burying himself over and over.

Not enough.

She reached down and grabbed his buttocks, thrusting herself against him, driving him deeper.

Darkness, haze, pain, lust.

Ecstasy.

Over and over and over again, she came, the orgasms crashing over her, the violence that was driving her finding an outlet in this most ancient of battles.

She felt him shudder his release. From a distance, she felt him pull away.

No! More. More blood. More sex. More!

She sat up and struck out, but he caught her wrist in an iron grip. Then her other.

In her head, a bird began to cry out as if in pain. A soft female voice broke through the violent fog. *He's breaking.*

"*What have I done?*" Hawke knelt between her knees, holding her as she struggled, horror in his eyes as his gaze tore over her. "*What have I done to you?*"

The falcon cried out in her head, slicing away the fog, pulling her into the light. The violence that had consumed her lost its grip, and, slowly, Faith came back to herself. Taking deep, unsteady breaths, she found herself caught fast in Hawke's hold. She stared at the blood streaking his face, shoulder, and chest. *My God, did I do this to him?*

Through the bird's cries, knowledge flowed into her head. Hawke's damaged connection with his animal was shattering. They were going to lose him here, now, if she didn't pull him back.

The violent need to hurt him barreled through her, then receded, pushed back by the will of the falcon. *Ally. Partner.* The thoughts sank into her head.

Save Hawke. This hawk. Need him.

Ours.

Pushing past that alien need for violence, Faith

reached for him, pressing her palms to his face. "Hawke." A distant bird's cry filled her mind. Not the falcon's. The hawk's?

Hawke's gaze was unfocused, his eyes filled with a pain the darkness reveled in, a pain that sliced her heart to shreds. At the push of the falcon, she slid her hands higher, pressing her palms to his temples. The screeching exploded until she gasped from the sound of it. As she held the man, the falcon flew into that maelstrom and, through sheer force of will, began to calm it.

Faith kissed Hawke's cheek gently. "Look at me."

Glazed eyes lifted, confusion and relief warring with the horror. "Faith. You're back." He pulled her into his arms. "I hurt you. *Goddess,* I hurt you."

"No." She kept her palms pressed against his temples. The falcon needed her to, though how she knew that, she wasn't sure. "I wanted it rough. I needed it rough, and you gave it to me. We were both caught up in that storm. You didn't hurt me."

He tipped his forehead to hers, a shudder going through his body. "I'm glad." His hand slid up her side and back down again. "What are you doing?"

"Trying to help you. Hawke, I'm fighting the darkness, but it could win again at any moment. It's pounding in my head, the drive, the demand to escape. To hurt you! But the falcon is helping me. You need my help. Your connection with the hawk is shattering. He's furious."

"Tell me something I don't know. He blames me for getting us caught in that spirit trap."

"That's not it. That's not the problem."

He pulled back, his gaze narrowing even as he brushed

the hair back from her face with shaking hands. "What do you mean?"

"The falcon is talking with the hawk. She's relaying the gist of the conversation to me."

The look he gave her would have been comical if the situation hadn't been so dire.

She shrugged. "What can I say? I have a gift for language."

"*Falcon speak?*"

"I don't know, and it doesn't matter! All I know is the spirit trap frayed the connection between you, you're making it worse, and he's frantic."

"*I'm* making it worse? He's the one who keeps stealing control! How am I the one making it worse?"

"You're not working with him, you're doing nothing to heal the connection."

He stared at her, as if not quite believing, yet trying to. "Tell me how."

"You have to give up control to him." She persisted despite Hawke's scowl. "You have to become one with him."

"You think I haven't tried? He takes over, and I lose hours at a time. *Thirty-seven*, last time."

Faith stroked his hair back from his face before once more pressing her hand to his temple. "You've never given up control to him, Hawke. He snatches it, but you've never truly given it."

The scowl returned. "You don't know what you're asking."

"I'm asking you to do what you have to in order to survive." She gripped his face, leaning forward until she felt as if she were pouring her will into his eyes. "You're going to die if you don't. And soon. The connection is nearly broken." Emotion ripped through the wall of will and darkness, rushing her with anguish and pain. She caressed his cheek. "I don't want you to die."

His jaw clenched beneath her fingers. "If I give in to him—"

"No. Not *give in*. That's just it. You must freely, willingly, *completely* hand him control."

He stared at her. "I can't."

The darkness began to sweep over her again. She felt it rushing back in and snatched her hands from his face. "Hawke!"

He must have realized what was happening because the next thing she knew, she was on her stomach, his warm body lying along the length of her, his hands pinning hers above her head.

"Don't leave me, Hawke. Don't leave me."

"I won't, Smiley. I won't."

But he didn't understand. And she couldn't help him any more. Terror ripped through her at the thought that she'd try to fight him again, that she'd drive him past the brink.

"Don't die," she whispered brokenly as the dark magic swept her away.

"We have to get her cured."

Hawke turned his head from where he lay atop Faith's back, both of them stark naked, as she fought and bucked beneath him, struggling to get free of his hold. Kougar stood just outside the cell door.

"Have you been standing there the whole time?" The thought of another Feral watching him make love to a woman didn't bother him. Hell, if he ever got the chance to take Faith as his mate, they'd all watch. It was part of the mating ceremony. But the thought that Kougar had witnessed him attacking her made him sick with shame. *"Why didn't you stop me?"*

"First, I haven't been standing here the whole time—I shifted and curled up on the floor in the corner. But I heard clearly enough—rough sex and two very willing participants. If you'd been harming her, I'd have stopped you."

Hawke would have liked to get up, but Faith was still thrashing, facedown, lost once more to the darkness that demanded his blood. She couldn't draw it like this, which helped him hold on to his own control. Besides, he was just possessive enough not to like the idea of Kougar seeing the full extent of Faith's beauty, though with her being Feral now, they'd all see her nude, eventually. It was just a matter of time.

He heard the heavy tread of footsteps. Company. He let his forehead fall to the back of Faith's head and almost got a broken nose when she reared back.

"Still both human, I see," Lyon drawled.

"It's been an eyeful," Kougar replied.

Hawke glared at him. "You said you hadn't watched."

Kougar shrugged. "I lied." He turned to their chief. "Any word on the cave?"

"They're not making any progress. Like so many things now, the magic the Mage used seems to have threads of Daemon magic woven into it. We may never break through."

Hawke growled, tired of lying on the floor while the discussion went on high above his head. He pushed to his feet, dragging a struggling Faith with him. She kicked out, catching him hard in the shin. He pressed her face-first against the wall where he could still see his brothers. "She has to be cured."

"Ariana believes the exorcism can be performed in any mystic circle, now that they know how it works." Lyon opened his mouth to continue, then closed it with a frown and a shake of his head.

Hawke read him all too easily. "There was an enormous *but* at the end of that sentence, Roar. Quit trying to spare me."

Lyon met his gaze, his own somber. "They aren't sure. And if it doesn't work, they're worried they may make the situation worse. They may make the magic's hold on her stronger. They want to give it more time. A day or two."

Hawke growled.

"No," Kougar said. "It has to be done now. Hawke's connection is nearly gone, and Faith's situation is driving the nails into his coffin. Separating them isn't the answer. We've got to get her cured."

Lyon's gaze met Hawke's, a deep well of feeling in his eyes. "Then we do it now."

An hour later, they were gathered in the mystic circle behind Feral House. Dawn had broken, though the sun had yet to rise. The earth smelled damp and new.

Hawke stood within the fire circle, with Faith locked in his arms, still struggling. Unlike the goddess stone, this spot didn't possess strong enough mystic energies to create a barrier through which she couldn't pass. If he let her go, she'd escape, and they'd never get her cured. At least they were dressed, more or less. He'd escaped the prison cell long enough to pull on a pair of clean sweatpants and T-shirt from the gym, then returned with several more shirts, afraid he'd have trouble getting one on Faith. He had. She'd shredded two, but the third hung to midthigh, covering the important parts. It was the best he could do with her still literally fighting him tooth and nail.

As Ariana and the Shaman chanted, the magic rose, sliding over him, different from the cold, creeping sensation of the cave's magic. This was more of a pressure that came and went, like snakes wrapping themselves around his limbs and torso and moving on.

Within his arms, Faith cried out, arching back as if in terrible pain.

"Hold on, Smiley. Hold on. Let them free you."

She thrashed in his arms, then cried out again, over and over, each cry more brutal than the last, flaying him. But unlike last time, her body didn't bend in impossible angles, breaking bones. If that started happening, he was going to lose it, there was no doubt in his mind. Simply watching her in pain was bad enough. Deep inside, the hawk's distress melded with Hawke's own silent roar. It was all he could do not to carry her away, to free her from the pain. But he wasn't that lost, not yet. Her only freedom came through exorcising the infection.

Faith screamed, gripping her head, no longer trying to fight him. He held her now, keeping her upright as her body sagged against his. The deepest, most primitive part of him began to roar in earnest, hating this. They were hurting her! The red haze began to swirl. Faith screamed again, and the haze rushed in faster, thicker. He was losing it. He had to help her.

His claws erupted.

He was going to hurt her! Releasing her, he stumbled

back, watching her sink to the ground. Strong hands gripped his shoulders.

"Easy, buddy," Tighe's voice. "Ease down."

"It's done." Ariana's voice barely cut through the screaming in his head.

Too late. The fury roared up, crashing over him, and he was fighting, claws raking flesh, fangs sinking into blood.

The exquisite sensation of shifting rushed over him. Sparkling lights consumed him.

Despair swallowed him whole.

And he knew no more.

Chapter Eighteen

Faith pushed herself to her feet, panting, drenched with sweat, her mind a wreck. Confused. She blinked at the fires in a ring of pots beneath the trees, illuminating the woods brightening with dawn. Feral House with its glowing windows stood a short distance away. Around her, Ferals stood, tense, groaning, while behind her she heard the sound of growling, of battle. Hawke. Even without looking, she knew.

She whirled just as he began to sparkle, watching with horror as he disappeared in a flash of colored lights, the great red-tailed hawk he'd become screeching and lifting into the air.

"No! Hawke!" And it all came rushing back, the darkness, the way she'd fought him. The pain as the magic was driven out of her. "Hawke!" But all she could do was watch as he disappeared over the house.

Follow him! The falcon spirit's will exploded in her mind. *Quickly!*

Faith ran to Lyon. "I have to go after him. I can help him." She thrust out her wrists and the bands that bound her to human form. "Free me!"

Lyon eyed her with uncertainty, a wariness melded with desperation.

"Lyon, I'm cured. It worked. Free me so I can help him!"

Decision slashed through his eyes, his sharp gaze cutting across the circle. "Shaman!"

As she turned, the Shaman rushed to her, his youthful-looking hands grasping the bands as he closed his eyes and murmured. Seconds later, the bands fell away from her wrists. In her head, the falcon's desperation pounded at her. *Go!*

Yes, but . . . she didn't know how. *Show me how.*

The bird's will lifted her, rushing through her with a power and certainty unlike anything she'd ever known. Incredible pleasure swept through her, the sparkling lights barely taking hold before she was airborne, racing into the sky.

The voices of the Ferals trailed behind her.

"Shit, she's fast!"

"Can we trust her?"

"Do we have a choice?"

"Pray she can bring him back to us."

The land fell away. The wind sliding through her feathers, an intoxicating rush she might have enjoyed if Hawke were beside her instead of lost. How was she supposed to find him? Movement caught her attention. Smaller birds. Amazing how well she could see them through her bird's far keener vision. She searched for the hawk . . . wait . . . was that him?

The falcon's affirmation bloomed in her mind. Faith

wasn't about to question how she knew. She picked up speed, uncertain if it was her doing or the bird spirit's, and she didn't care. She was smaller than the hawk. What if she couldn't catch him?

The hawk is in no hurry. We'll catch him.

The falcon's certainty calmed her. And, as predicted, she was soon close enough to see the markings on the magnificent bird, the way the wind fluttered in his feathers as he soared.

Hawke!

The bird gave no sign that he knew she was there. If not for the falcon's certainty, Faith might be afraid she followed a real hawk instead of the shifter she loved. She tried again to reach him.

Please let him go, hawk spirit. Please don't take him from me.

But the great bird continued on his path, following the wide, snaking river west toward the mountains.

In her mind, she heard the cries of her falcon, a musical language she understood as she understood all language. Words directed at the hawk spirit. Faith began to smile as the falcon praised the beauty and greatness of the bird, his strength, his honor, his compassion.

Laying it on thick.

All males need to be praised.

If falcons could laugh, Faith would have laughed, though the situation was still dire. Deep in her mind, she felt the animal spirit's smile.

The falcon continued her feminine plea. *He is needed, great hawk, by my Feral, whom I fought hard to claim. You know this. You feel it, too.*

Gratitude welled up inside Faith with startling force

as she realized the falcon fought to save Hawke. But the rest? Had the falcon really fought to claim her? The idea floated, tantalizing and fragile. Impossible.

Not impossible at all, the falcon said. *You were the one I've been waiting for.*

Chills rippled across Faith's mind. *I thought I was marked by accident.*

You most certainly were not.

Faith listened in wonder. If she'd been wearing flesh instead of feathers, she'd have been covered in goose bumps. The animal spirit had chosen her . . . *her* . . . to be a Feral Warrior. Impossible. *Incredible.*

We shall be magnificent together. But you need the hawk Feral, if the hawk spirit will free him. If they can mend the broken bond between them.

They continued to fly, Faith following Hawke as the falcon spirit talked to the hawk spirit, alternately praising him and cajoling, her tone turning increasingly frustrated.

The hawk spirit is badly offended and violently stubborn.

It wasn't working.

No. I'm sorry.

Faith felt the panic bubbling up, the fear that the hawk spirit would never relent, would never release the man. And with it anger, pure and bright. In the language of the birds, she spoke directly to the hawk spirit, without the falcon's diplomacy. *I know you're angry at him, but there's more at stake here than your pride and your frustration. He's a good man. You know that, or you'd never have marked him in the first place. And he's needed. The world is in danger. The Daemons threaten again. If Hawke has wronged you, it was un-intentional. I've told him what he has to do, that he has to trust you. Give him time!*

She sensed no reply but a fine mist of anger. But her own anger was spent, desperation taking its place.

Hawk spirit, I beg of you, give him another chance. Please. I need him. Emotion welled up inside her so thick, so strong, she thought it would choke her. If falcons could cry, she'd have had teardrops rolling down her feathered cheeks. *I love him.*

Deep in her mind, she heard a shriek of fury. No not fury. Frustration. The hawk's. As if a part of him wanted to relent.

The falcon continued her plea to the stubborn bird. *They are meant for one another, these two shape-shifters. They are meant for greatness. Through us. With us. I beg you to give him one more chance. For me. I have missed you.*

Silence reigned for long moments. Then all at once, the angry emotion that had been battering Faith from the hawk spirit fell away, to be replaced by a rush of love. Hawke's love. It worked!

Faith? Hawke's voice clear, deep, and beloved rang in her head.

The falcon's satisfaction fell through her mind like a warm, cleansing rain.

I'm here, Hawke. Right behind you.

You're cured of the dark magic!

Yes. The ritual worked for me this time.

The hawk dipped and circled her and suddenly he was flying at her side. *How is this happening? I'm flying again!*

In her mind, Faith smiled. *The falcon spirit talked the hawk spirit into giving you another chance.*

She talked . . . ? Thank the goddess. You have no idea how much I needed to be able to fly again. What do you think of it? Of flying?

She heard the joy in his tone, and the terrible pressure binding her chest eased. *I've been so focused on reaching you, I haven't been paying much attention.*

Feel, Faith! It's glorious up here. The others think their animals are better because they're bigger and can rip a Mage to shreds. But if they could feel what it's like up here, they'd mourn their grounded fate. They have no idea what they're missing.

Little by little, the awful tension that had been riding her for so long slid away as she allowed herself time to simply feel the wind rushing through her feathers, the sun warm on her back. A smile bloomed brilliantly in her mind. It was, just as he said, glorious.

She dipped, spiraling through the air, zooming down, then back up with a rush and a mental shriek of joy.

You're a natural, he told her. *It took me weeks of practice to be able to roll like that.*

The falcon's doing all the work.

She took over? His tone was suddenly sharp. Unhappy.

No. It's not like that. I thought about flying free, and she executed it.

Just like that.

Yes.

He didn't reply.

Isn't that how it is with the hawk?

No. The word was thoughtful, but the silence that followed was too full, too complete. *Ahhh!*

The sudden sound of Hawke's pain filled her mind. Fear ratcheted her bird's pulse. *What's the matter?*

The damned hawk's . . . trying to rake out my brain . . . with his talons. Goddess!

The falcon's thoughts bloomed in Faith's head. *The hawk tries to hold on to him as the connection between them splinters. The hawk does not wish to lose this Feral—he is, as you said, a good man, by far the best of his line—but the Feral refuses . . . has always refused . . . to trust him, to become one with him. The spirit trap may have torn the connection between them, but it is their fighting that is destroying the bond.*

Their fighting?

Yes. The hawk yanks away control, but the moment he returns it, the Feral wrenches it back. Only by the Feral's giving up control freely to the spirit, and joining with him completely, will they be able to heal this terrible rift and save your Feral's life. He must do it soon, or he will die. The connection is almost gone. I fear another battle between them, and it will sever for good.

Faith's heart stuttered. *Hawke?*

I need to land, Smiley. I need to shift. I don't trust this damned bird not to take over again. This way. He dipped into a nosedive that was gorgeous to behold. She followed, trusting the falcon, exhilarated by the drop that should be terrifying but was nothing but thrilling joy.

Hawke landed first, on the top of a forested cliff not far from the river, away from people. Slowly, the lights began to sparkle over him. She dropped down into the underbrush beside him, shifting as she did. She turned to him, breathless with the euphoria of her first flight. He stared at her, his body tense, but his eyes overflowing with relief, with warmth, with love.

"You're really cured," he murmured, then pulled

her into his arms, covering her mouth in a hot, tender kiss, one hand sliding into her hair, the other slipping around her waist, tangling in her oversized T-shirt as he tightened his hold on her.

His lips left hers, trailing along her cheek, her cheekbone, her temple, holding her as if she were the most precious thing in the world. She kissed his chest where his shirt hung open. Vaguely, she remembered ripping it when he tried to dress her in the prison cell. Pulling back, he framed her face with his long fingers, looking down at her with eyes filled with tenderness.

"I love you," she whispered.

A smile slowly spread over his face. "I love you, too."

She gripped his waist. "Hawke, your animal . . ." They had to discuss the disconnect before it was too late.

His finger pressed against her lips, silencing her. "Shh. I want to see . . ." He lifted her arm, pushing back the too-long sleeve to reveal the delicate golden armband around her arm. The head of the falcon was barely raised and wouldn't cause her trouble beneath her shirts.

His fingers slid over the surface. "I never realized it would be so small, so fine. It's perfect for you." He looked up, a terrible tenderness in his eyes. A sadness, as if he knew exactly how close he was to dying.

"*Hawke.*"

His knuckles brushed her cheek. "Let me see you shift. Then we'll talk, I promise. Fly for me." His words were pained, as if flying this time had made him remember how desperately he'd missed it. As if he thought he'd never do it again.

Swallowing hard, she nodded and stepped back. With a bare thought of what she wanted to do, she shifted in a rush of unbelievable pleasure and shot into the air with a silent cry of joy. The trees flew past so quickly, she could barely see the branches, let alone the leaves, yet she sensed them perfectly as she zipped past, zooming around the tree trunks, filled with a breathless joy.

She thought of standing in front of Hawke and, a second later, did just that, shifting as she landed.

He stared at her, his mouth half-open.

Her brows drew down, suddenly worried. "What's the matter?"

"My father used to be able to do that." His voice sounded stunned. "I thought . . . I thought it had taken him centuries of practice."

"What did I do?"

He shook his head. "You flew through the trees without hitting a thing. Shifted as you landed, in the blink of an eye." Grasping her arms, he leaned toward her, his expression lighting with wonder. "How did you do that?"

She shrugged. "I thought about flying through the trees and returning to you, and that's what I did."

"No." His grip on her arms tightened. "No, you did so much more."

"The falcon did the rest."

Hawke stilled, his eyes narrowing. "You said that before. That the falcon takes over."

"She doesn't take over, not at all. I think of what I want to do, and she executes the moves. We're a team." Deep in her mind, she felt the falcon's approval.

But only confusion lit Hawke's face. Releasing her, he turned away, then swung back around. "My father could do that. The hawk is capable of it."

"It's what he wants." Even without the falcon's

coaching, she suddenly understood. "He wants to work with you as a team. In perfect unison. In perfect trust. Instead, you push him away. Or you did, until the spirit trap caused the break in your connection, allowing the hawk to fight you for control. Why, Hawke? Why do you push him away?"

"I don't."

She cocked her head. "But you don't fully trust him."

"I'm a man first, not an animal. It's the man's brain that must make the decisions. Otherwise . . ." He shook his head. "People get hurt."

She closed the distance between them and pressed her hands against his chest. "What people? What happened?" she asked softly, because it was clear something had. "Why is your relationship with your animal so different from mine?"

Slowly, he turned away again, standing in profile, staring down the hill as if suddenly fascinated by the rocks and dead leaves littering the sloping forest floor.

"When you first shifted, what was it like between you, Hawke?"

He shrugged. "It was always like this."

"He didn't show you how to fly? He didn't take you?"

"Never." His brows pulled together as he glanced at her. "He tried, I think. Those early days were a fog. Not good."

He kept pulling away, but she refused to let him escape this. Or her. She stepped closer and ran her hand over his broad, tightly muscled back. "Why not?"

"I . . ." He shook his head and looked away.

She kissed his shoulder. "Tell me."

"Faith . . . this isn't the time."

"It is the time. You don't want to talk about what

happened, which tells me it's important. I'm not going to let it go. Not with so much at stake."

The stubborn set to his jaw slowly softened, his mouth forming a rueful twist.

"Tell me what happened."

He turned to her fully and sighed. "You're relentless." But his mouth tipped up in a half smile.

"Only because I love you so very much."

His eyes softened even more as he pulled her into his arms and rested his chin lightly on her head.

"I didn't want to be marked." He groaned. "That's not exactly true." Pulling back, he grabbed her face between his hands and kissed her, a quick soft peck. "I'll tell you, but . . . I need to pace."

As he turned and did just that, Faith perched herself on a small rocky shelf and waited.

"My father was killed by a human mortar shell during the Civil War. I think I told you that."

"You did."

"I was living in Finland at the time, tutoring the only child in a small enclave. Aren. His father was Therian, but his mother was human, and Aren was mortal. I'd been with them five years when I discovered the feral marks on the back of my shoulder one morning. I immediately knew one of the nine must have died. I'd grown up in Feral House. All nine had had a hand in raising me. I was devastated at the thought of any of their deaths, but the fact that I'd been marked made me fear that the one who'd died was my father. We shared the hawk DNA, of course.

"It was a couple of weeks before Lyon's letter reached me. I was alone in the library of the enclave's house when I read it." He frowned. "I wasn't prepared. Not only had my father died, as I'd feared, but so had my mother. Three days after my father died, she was killed by draden. Accidentally, Lyon said, but I knew better."

Bitterness twisted his mouth, a bitterness he'd lived with for over 140 years. "I loved my mother, but she never had half of Kara's strength. She couldn't bear the suffering from the severed mating bond, so she took her own life. Or let the draden take it."

Faith shuddered at the thought of dying beneath those razor-sharp mouths, though she'd all but done that, hadn't she? If Hawke hadn't been there.

"I was furious. It was bad enough I'd lost one parent, but two . . . and the second intentionally . . ." He pressed the heels of his hands against his eyes, then dropped them, his expression bleak. "Aren ran into the room while I was reading that letter. Eight years old. I'd known him since he was a toddler and loved him like a son."

Her breath caught.

"Newly marked Ferals tend to be short on control, and mine had been shattered. He ran right for me, as he always did. But I didn't grab him around the waist and sweep him high like I usually did. I lashed out at him with my claws, unthinking. It was the first time I went feral."

"Oh, God, Hawke." Her scalp crawled with horror.

"I didn't kill him, thank the goddess. I caught him across his face and shoulder, but he nearly bled out before we got the bleeding stopped. It was close." He visibly shuddered. "So close. And he lived the rest of his life with the scars I gave him that day." The bleakness in his voice raked at her heart. "As soon as I was certain Aren would live, I left for Feral House."

"And you never forgave the animal spirit for what you did to Aren."

He stilled, then turned to her slowly, his eyes narrowed as if he'd never considered that. "I understood just how dangerous a Feral could be. I knew what could happen if I lost control. I never lost it again. Not until recently. Not until the spirit trap."

"You never lost control because you held it so tightly. You never trusted the animal spirit because you were afraid of that wildness inside of you. That wildness that made you harm Aren."

He frowned. "I suppose."

"You need that wildness."

"No."

"Yes. You do. That's what makes me so fast when I'm in my falcon." She went to him, pressing her hands against his chest, making him look at her. "Even if you embrace that wildness, you aren't going to be a danger to anyone you don't mean to be. Not now. You're the kindest man I've ever known."

He covered her hands with his, his expression telling her he wasn't sure he believed what she was saying, but he was listening.

"You have an innate gentleness, a goodness, that goes all the way to your core, Hawke. I can't imagine what it must have done to you to have accidentally harmed a child like that. A boy you loved."

He flinched and started to look away, but she lifted her hand and stopped him, forcing him to look at her.

"What you have inside you right now is a battle between that gentleness and the wildness. It's not you against the bird, do you realize that? It's a battle between the two halves of yourself. You've kept the wildness so carefully controlled that you never even realized the war has been raging since the day you were marked. Not until the spirit trap wrenched away your ability to control it. Before that happened, the hawk spirit suffered from your denial of the wildness, but you didn't realize it. You do now. And you're both suffering. Only by embracing both halves of yourself will you heal." She stroked his cheek. "You won't lose your humanity, Hawke. What happened to Aren was a simple matter of your both being in the wrong place at the wrong time. And your being a very-newly-marked Feral."

He was quiet for long seconds, his gaze grazing her face, his thoughts awhirl in his eyes.

Finally, he made a frustrated sound. "I understand what you're saying in theory, Smiley, but I have no idea how to do it short of shifting. And all I know is that if I shift, I won't come back."

She didn't know what to say to that. Because she didn't have an answer. And neither, unfortunately, did the falcon. The females might understand the problem, but it was up to the males to figure out how to fix it. Either they'd find their way, or they wouldn't. But if they didn't . . . and soon . . . she'd lose the man she loved forever. And the thought of it was killing her.

Hawke pulled away from Faith, burning with frustration. He knew that what she said was true, that his breach with the hawk spirit had reached critical stage. But he didn't know how to fix it! He and his bird had been one for nearly a century and a half. He thought things had been fine between them. *What did the damn bird want?* Trust, Faith said. And how was he supposed to trust a creature who would steal him away for thirty-seven hours?

What if he gave himself up to the bird, and the bird took off and never came back? He'd be useless to the other Ferals, nothing more than a wild hawk until he flew too far from the radiance for too long and died. It would be far better for all involved if the connection severed, if he cleared the way for another to be marked. A bird shifter who, like Faith, might have a way with his bird as he himself had never had.

Goddess, he'd never known it could be like that—darting and shifting with breakneck speed and perfect precision. He was good, but it had taken years of practice. And he'd never been able to do what he'd just watched Faith do. When she'd first taken off and zipped into the trees, he'd been terrified she was going to crash. He'd thought she'd kill herself. How could she possibly have darted faster than he could? Yet she had. Far faster than any normal falcon.

He heard Faith move behind him, felt her arms circle his waist, her cheek press against his back.

"I don't want to lose you."

Her words tore at his heart, and he turned and pulled her into his arms. All these years he'd waited for the one who would make his life complete. And now he'd found her. Too late. He rested his chin on the top of her precious head and grieved for all he would miss—Faith's smiles, her laughter, her body swelling with his child. The fire in her eyes as she trained as a warrior and fought at his side. The glow that would shine from within her as she realized her true strength, her true worth.

"Any shifter who can fly like you can will be an asset

to the Ferals." He kissed her hair and arched back a little so that he could see her face. "You're going to have a place with them, Smiley. They're going to need you."

She looked up at him, pain darkening her eyes. "You're giving up."

He released a frustrated sigh. "I don't know how to do what the hawk wants me to do. You tell me to trust him, yet he digs his talons into my head trying to claw my brains out."

"He's trying to hold on to you, not hurt you."

"You can't know that."

For a moment she was silent, her eyes unfocusing as if she listened to a noise he couldn't hear, as if she were listening to the voice of the falcon.

"The connection has been splintering. That's the pain you feel. He yells at you to help him, to do something, and he clings to you to keep the splintering from getting worse."

Hawke stared at her in stunned silence. And felt the truth of her words wash through him. That initial, light-ninglike pain he always felt was the connection fraying. The hawk's cries were of anger, as he'd suspected. But maybe not for the reason he'd believed. If what Faith said was true, he was mad that Hawke did nothing to fix the damage. And he'd been trying to do it himself.

Slowly, the band that had been squeezing his chest began to loosen, that feeling of betrayal. He'd thought the hawk had turned against him. He'd thought he'd been trying to punish him. Instead, he'd been trying to save him.

"The falcon says that the only way for you to re-connect with your animal spirit is to give up control. Become one mind, one will. But you must do it soon,

Hawke. Your connection to him is nearly gone. One more tug-of-war between you, and it'll snap." She looked up at him, her eyes dark with misery. "If that happens, why can't he just mark you again?"

"It doesn't work that way. There is no re-marking."

Pain lanced her eyes. "Hawke." She stilled again. "The falcon says she wishes she could help you, but this is something you have to do on your own."

He lifted a brow. "She?"

"Her voice is female."

He stared at her. "You're really *speaking* to your animal spirit."

"Not in words, not exactly. Certainly not in English or any human language. But she communicates with me in perfect thoughts. And she hears mine in return."

"That's incredible."

An intoxicating gleam entered her eyes, the gleam of certain confidence, as a smile of self-assurance lifted her lovely mouth. "She chose me. She told me that she fought hard to claim me, that we'd be magnificent together."

Part of him wanted to discount her claim as fiction— never had he known a Feral whose spirit animal spoke to him. But he felt the truth of her words, knew them in his heart. The tiny pinch of jealousy washed away in the gratitude that rushed through him for the falcon spirit.

"You weren't chosen by mistake." Though he'd told her that over and over and tried to believe it himself, *wanted* to believe it, the evidence had been overwhelming otherwise. But having watched her zip through the trees and shift as she landed, he no longer had any doubt.

Faith stood before him in the oversized blue T-shirt

he'd put on her in the prisons, her legs and feet bare, her blue-tipped hair uncombed. On the surface, he'd never seen her look more like a street kid, but one look at her strong stance, at her certain face, at the confidence shining from her eyes, and he knew the waif was gone. A Feral Warrior stood in her place.

He kissed her. "You are magnificent," he murmured against her lips as his hand slid down her back, over her buttocks, to the hem of the T-shirt. Having put it on her, he knew precisely what she wore underneath. Absolutely nothing. If his life was almost over, there was only one thing more he wanted. To make love to this woman he loved more than life.

Tears glistened in her eyes as if they'd shared the thought. "Love me," she said softly.

"I do. I will."

He kissed her, savoring the sweet taste of her mouth and the feel of her soft lips against his. His hand slid beneath the hem of the T-shirt, finding the bare silken flesh beneath. Fire pounded through his blood, turning him hard and ready as he caressed her, digging gently into the soft flesh. She moaned and pressed against him, rocking her hips into his, brushing his already-swelling erection. He hissed in a breath, lifting one of her sweet thighs against his hip and settling himself into the vee of her body.

"Tell me I didn't hurt you before. Or that you don't remember."

"You didn't hurt me. I remember it as a whirlwind of wild pleasure. Intense. Incredible. But . . ."

"It'll be gentle this time."

"Yes."

He kissed her slowly, tenderly, taking his time, brushing her lips with his, sliding his tongue between them to stroke the crease. She opened for him, but he took his time coming inside, wanting to savor every moment, every sweet taste of her. He slid his tongue across one soft lip, then the other before melding his mouth with hers and sliding his tongue deep inside. She melted against him, a moan escaping her throat, and his heart and mind overflowed with love.

Pulling back, he stripped off his shirt and enjoyed the sight of her watching him, admiration lighting her eyes.

"You are so beautiful," she murmured. She met his gaze with a wicked, darling grin and reached for him, sliding her fingers over his pecs and up to his shoulders, then down his arms, exploring, a sensual look of pleasure on her face even as that small smile remained. "I can't believe you're mine."

He reached for her hair, tugging a thick lock between his fingers, sliding down to the blue end. "I've waited for you all my life."

Tears turned her eyes to smoky diamonds. He kissed her again, lifting her T-shirt, pulling it up her body and releasing her mouth just long enough to yank it over her head. And then her small perfect breasts were pressing against his chest, her flesh warm against his, need rushing through his body.

Her fingers closed around the waistband of his sweatpants, and she tugged, releasing his heated flesh to the morning air. He shucked the pants, then gathered them and both their shirts, and laid them out on the bracken and underbrush.

"You're making a nest?" Laughter filled her voice.

"I was thinking a bed." His expression softened with the weight of his love. "A bed fit for a princess."

Her smile was the most beautiful he'd ever seen as she knelt beside him, her knees on the clothes. "Your sharing it with me will make it so."

They came together on their knees, kissing, touching. He swept her up and laid her down, her quick laugh a gift he would never get enough of. And then she smiled up at him, her head tilted precisely toward him as if she were a light-starved flower and he the sun.

He lay beside her, propping his head on one hand, his other covering her breast as his gaze skimmed her face, her sweet, smiling mouth. He ached from the beauty of her and the love that welled in her eyes. A love that filled him to overflowing.

With his finger and thumb, he plucked at her taut nipple and she gasped, then grinned.

"You like that."

"I like everything you do."

He chuckled. "Do you?" He tested the theory, rolling her nipple between finger and thumb, watching her expression, watching the way her chest lifted to his touch, hearing the small catch in her breath. He'd studied every conceivable subject since he was old enough to read— art, science, philosophy, history—and never found anything that intrigued him half as much as watching Faith react to his touch.

He slid his hand from her breast, down her rib cage, and over her abdomen, circling one finger slowly around her navel as she watched him as keenly as he watched her. Her quicksilver smile bloomed, and his followed. He'd never been particularly quick to smile, always more thoughtful than emotional, but Faith's smile was utterly irresistible.

Moving slowly, he slid his finger across the top of the

curly dark hair that protected her most precious gifts. Her chest trembled, her breath quickening in anticipation. But as he slid his hand to the side and down one firm thigh instead, her breath expelled, a small letdown . . . until his hand rose up her inner thigh.

"You're a tease," she murmured.

"No. I'm learning what pleases you."

She grinned at him, laughing at him. "Uh-hmm. I can tell you what pleases me most."

"I believe I can guess."

"Can you? Why don't we see if you're right."

His smile broadened, but his hand trembled with barely controlled passion as he slid his fingers once more up her thigh, and kept going. Never taking his gaze from her face, he stroked her soft dampness with his finger and was rewarded with the exquisite sight of her sucking in her breath, arching her back, her beautiful eyelids dropping as her face became a mask of passionate pleasure.

Again, he stroked her, then slid his finger around the hard pearl at the top, flicking it lightly, watching as she gasped. He drank in the sight of her as his ministrations sent her into a rocking frenzy of rising passion. The fire in his own body rose until he thought it would burn him alive, his cock hard and distended and throbbing, but he couldn't take his gaze off her. She was glorious to watch.

Her dark lashes drifted up. "Don't send me there alone."

"No?"

She reached for him. "Please come with me?" The smile on her faced matched that in her eyes as her fingers gripped his shoulders and tugged with surprising strength.

He couldn't deny her. He wouldn't survive this torture much longer anyway. Settling himself between her legs, he braced himself over her, grasping her gaze and holding it as he positioned the tip of his cock at her wet opening and slid home. It was all he could do not to close his eyes and throw his head back, but the look on her face was too fascinatingly beautiful to miss. Her eyes widened, her mouth opening, gasping, grinning as he pushed himself all the way in, joining them completely.

Deep inside, he felt a tiny flare of electricity and a warm, throbbing tug. In his mind, he saw it, the first bright promise of a mating bond. His heart clutched, then calmed with the certain knowledge that they weren't truly mated, that she wouldn't suffer when he died unless they completed the bond in the mating ritual of fire, blood, and sex.

He pulled out and slid into her again, slowly, her body gripping him tight and pulling him deeper as her hips thrust up to meet his. Her restless hands slid over his shoulders and arms, clutching, caressing. Her gasps grew faster and harder, turning to moans and small, hot little cries as he slid out and thrust into her again and again and again.

Her gaze slid away, her eyes closing, her head tilting back in the throes of passion.

"Look at me, Faith."

Dark lashes lifted heavily, and she met his gaze and grinned at him, a womanly smile that nearly drove him to release on the spot. Her eyes focused on him, clung to him, and he felt himself falling deep into those sparkling depths. Love flared up inside him ten times stronger than before, stealing his breath, squeezing his heart in a tender vise.

Her small cries turned frantic; and then she was coming, her expression pure bliss, her cries turning to gasps and moans, her gaze fixed on his, love blazing in her eyes.

And he came and came and came, pouring his seed and his heart and his soul into her.

His body thoroughly emptied, his heart full to overflowing, he sank down onto her, bracing the bulk of his weight on his forearms even as he dropped his forehead lightly against hers, his eyes closed at last. When he could move, he lifted up to look down at her and met her exhausted smile.

"That was perfect," she murmured.

"I agree." He stroked her hair back from her face. "You're perfect." Taking her with him, he rolled onto his back, cradling her against his chest, his cock still buried deep inside her. "I never want to leave you."

Goddess. He cupped her precious head in his hand and kissed her hair. *I will do anything . . . anything . . . if only you can help me repair this break with my hawk. And stay with this woman who has my heart.*

But the goddess couldn't help him. This he had to do himself.

And he didn't know the way.

Faith lay with her cheek against Hawke's damp chest, listening to his heart hammering beneath her ear as quickly as her own beat in her chest. Being with him, making love with him, was every bit as thrilling as her first flight. Breathtaking, mind-shattering. Perfect.

She kissed his chest, feeling her eyes burn with unshed tears as the awful fear that she was going to lose him pressed down on her.

He kissed her one more time. "Get up, Smiley. Let's go home."

She lifted off him, letting him slide out of her, then stood while he rose and handed her the T-shirt. They dressed, then Hawke pulled out his cell phone and started pressing buttons.

"It's me. We'll meet you by the gas station." When she lifted a brow, he mouthed, "GPS." A moment later, he frowned. "What else is new?"

Shoving his phone in his pocket, he met her gaze with a sigh. "According to Lyon, there's trouble. *Again*."

Chapter
Nineteen

"Hawke, Falkyn," Wulfe said, as Hawke handed Faith into the cab of the wolf shifter's pickup. "I'm glad to see that you both . . . made it back into your skins. I assume Falkyn's cured?"

Hawke nodded. "Right as rain. What's the trouble?"

"Lyon hasn't said. We're meeting in the war room as soon as we get back."

When they were on the road, Faith leaned forward. "Am I really going to be called Falkyn all the time, now?"

Hawke glanced back at her. "I'll call you whatever you'd like in private. You'll always be Faith to me." A smile gentled his eyes. "Or Smiley. But yes, your Feral name is Falkyn, now."

She didn't want to offend, but . . . "Why?"

"Tradition," Wulfe said.

Hawke nodded. "I was just talking to Kougar about

the names a few days ago. He says it goes back to the time of the Sacrifice, when most Therians lost the power of their animals and the ability to shift. Realizing that only one of each animal would be able to shift at a time, many tried to kill the shifters, hoping to take that power for themselves. Those first Ferals banded together for their own safety. But they were each from a different clan. They didn't know one another, but battle positions needed to be assigned by animal. The wolf was the tracker, the birds acted as recon. Rather than try to remember the names of each of his men, the first chief called them by their animals for simplicity's sake, and it stuck. It was easier for all of them to remember and to assimilate one another's strengths. Later, as each new Feral was marked, giving him or her a new name—a warrior name—became a symbolic rebirth. Since some of those early newly marked Ferals had been part of the bands that had tried to hunt down the original Ferals, that rebirth was particularly important. It acted as a forgiveness by the originals for past acts against them.

"For millennia, the names have been chosen by Kougar. He says he sees the name in his mind as the Feral shifts, and he says it, and, if requested, spells it for the new Feral the way he saw it."

She liked the name Falkyn, actually. And the idea of being someone new felt right. Faith, she was beginning to realize, had never really believed in herself. Part of her had always felt that if she'd been a better daughter, her mother might have loved her, and her enclave wouldn't have left without her. But Hawke had changed all that. As had the falcon spirit when she'd informed Faith her being marked had been no accident. Falkyn was a Feral Warrior. A woman who believed herself worthy, as Faith never had.

But it was Faith with whom Hawke had fallen in love. Faith who'd fallen in love with him.

"Are you ready to be Falkyn?" Hawke asked her softly.

"Yes. Faith was my past. Falkyn is my future."

He smiled. "Faith is your heart, Smiley. Your sweetness to Falkyn's strength. Don't lose her. As you told me that I must find a way to integrate the two halves of myself, you must do the same. To me, in private, you'll always be Faith." His smile died, his eyes tightening.

Always might be a very short time.

Kougar and Jag were crossing the foyer when Wulfe, Hawke, and Faith walked through the front door a short while later.

"War room," Kougar said. "We have trouble."

Hawke nodded. "So I heard, though I'd love to go *one day* without hearing those words."

Faith looked at him. "I need clothes."

Hawke rather liked the look of the T-shirt . . . and nothing else . . . but he caught Jag noticing just how little she had on and nodded. "Hurry."

An impish grin bloomed on her face a second before she disappeared in a spray of sparkling lights and . . . was gone. Out of the corner of his eye, he caught the movement of the speeding falcon shooting over the second-floor banister.

"What the fuck?" Jag gaped. "She disappeared!"

Hawke found himself grinning with pride at the disbelief on his brothers' faces. "No. She's just incredibly quick."

They were still standing there in stunned disbelief when the small falcon dive-bombed them twenty seconds later. As she shifted back to her human form beside him, Kougar and Jag drew claws.

Hawke shoved her behind him. "Stand down! Faith . . . *Falkyn* . . . take it easy in the house, at least until they get used to your newfound speed."

She peeked at them from around his shoulder. "Sorry." Hearing the laughter in her voice, he glanced at her. She was grinning like a pixie.

Jag laughed out loud. "Do you realize all the ways we can use that kind of speed? Hot damn."

Kougar just shook his head, but there was a smile tugging at his mouth.

"War room!" Lyon's roar echoed through the house.

As the five headed down the hall, Hawke glanced at Faith. The smile she offered him was so full of delight and pride and love, it was all he could do not to snatch her up and kiss her right there. He brushed his hand down her back, over the soft cotton sweater she'd donned along with a pair of jeans. He'd never known a woman to dress so fast. Then again, no other woman was his Falkyn.

As they reached the war room, Kara was just entering. She beamed and threw her arms around Faith. "You're back."

Faith laughed, then sobered. "Did bringing me into my animal exhaust you again?"

"No. Not at all. I feel great."

"I'm so glad." Faith's words rang with heartfelt relief.

They entered the room to find the others waiting. When they'd taken their seats, Lyon stopped pacing and turned to face them.

"The Shaman called. There's a witch in the Mage

Resistance, as they're calling themselves now, who has the ability to sense Daemon energy in the Earth's energy layer. It's been all but nonexistent until the past months. It spiked while the wraith Daemons were on their rampage, then dipped again. For the past two weeks, there's been some sort of strange activity. Now, suddenly, it's spiked again."

"They've freed more Daemons?" Paenther asked.

"She doesn't think so, no. She says it feels more like a power source. As if someone's funneling energy into the blade that imprisons the Daemons, feeding them directly."

"Empowering Satanan," Kougar murmured.

Lyon nodded. "That power source has been pinpointed to a spot in a forest near Warsaw."

"Maxim?" Faith breathed.

"The satellite image reveals a fortress. A castle. And there's more." Lyon's gaze turned to Faith, an ache in his eyes that had Hawke immediately on edge. "I would spare you this if I could." The Chief of the Ferals shook his head and lifted a remote. "I can't."

The one flat screen that remained in the room flared to life. Lyon tapped a few buttons on the laptop open on the table in front of him, and a video image filled the screen. The missing new Ferals stood in what appeared to be some kind of ancient castle. Or dungeon. Polaris, Lepard, Croc, Whit, and Maxim. Oddly, they were all dressed in white turtlenecks and dark pants, now. Only Maxim wore a sport coat.

"Are they really in Poland?" Hawke demanded.

Lyon paused the video image. "It would seem so. Delaney used her sources to confirm that a small private jet left Dulles Airport the night they attacked us, and security surveillance reveals these five climbing on board. Maxim undoubtedly clouded human minds to get them off the ground that quickly and in the middle of the night. As for whether or not we can be certain they are in Poland." Lyon shrugged. "Decide for yourself." He pressed the remote, and once more the video rolled.

Maxim stepped forward with a tight, sadistic smile that had Hawke's hands balling into fists. "Hello, Faith. It's time for you to come to me, now. You belong to me, and we both know it." He smiled, but his smile was cold. Cruel. "You *will* come." He stepped back to reveal two girls, teenagers, their clothes torn, their faces badly bruised, the ropes binding their hands looped around large hooks hanging from the ceiling.

Beside him, Faith gasped. Hawke reached for her hand. "You know them."

"Yes. Paulina and Maria."

Maxim stepped back in front of the camera. "You can save them, Faith. Trade yourself for them. Have the Ilinas bring you here, to my castle." He rattled off what sounded like some kind of address in Polish. "In six hours, I'll begin cutting off their fingers and toes, one by one. If they don't bleed to death first, I'll then begin cutting off their arms a few inches at a time."

Faith had turned white as a polar bear's fur. Hawke gripped the back of her neck, ready to yank back her chair and shove her head between her knees if she started to faint. "Breathe, sweetheart. Breathe."

"Six hours," Maxim snapped. "I know you're a bird shifter now. Come to me through the southernmost chimney. It's the only part of the castle not warded against Ilinas. Or Ferals."

Lyon lifted the remote, and the screen went black.

"The address he gave is near Warsaw, the exact location of the power source that's feeding the Daemons. How the Mage are using the new Ferals in that power feed, I don't know. But it seems likely they are."

"How much of that six hours has passed?" Hawke demanded.

"The e-mail arrived half an hour ago."

Tighe frowned. "He knows we have Ilina travel."

"How in the fuck does he know she's a bird shifter?" Jag demanded.

Hawke met Lyon's gaze. "That's a damned good question."

Lyon nodded. "Any guesses?"

Kougar plucked at his beard. "The new Ferals were connected to one another through the infection carried by their animal spirits. A magic that allowed the Mage to control them. It's probable that they all felt her come into her animal. And could somehow feel that animal take flight."

"A connection severed when we cured her of the infection," Lyon said.

Kougar nodded. "We believe."

Lyon eyed Kougar sharply. "You think there's a chance that connection isn't fully severed?"

"Maxim wouldn't have sent us this invitation if he didn't have some sort of trap planned. There's no way to know what form it might take."

"We're fucked," Jag muttered.

Kougar shrugged. "That's never stopped us before."

Lyon frowned, then sighed. "Paenther will lead the team to Poland accompanied by Kougar, Hawke, Wulfe, Vhyper, Fox, and Falkyn."

"No." Hawke squeezed her hand. "She's not going."

"Hawke . . ." Lyon began

Faith turned on Hawke, a warrior's fire in her eyes. "I have to go! He's going to kill them."

"Smiley . . . he's going to kill them anyway." She flinched, and he despised hurting her, but the words had to be said.

Silence descended on the war room. Faith pulled her hand from his and faced Lyon. "If Maxim is right about the warding, I'm the only one who can get into that castle. I'm the only one who stands a chance of stopping him, of stopping whatever he's doing to feed Satanan."

The thought of her going into that castle alone turned Hawke's blood to ice. "Faith, you heard the discussion. *It's a trap.*"

She gaped at him. "So we're just going to hole up in Feral House while Maxim empowers the Daemons?" Her frustration left on a sigh, her gaze softening as she reached for him, touching his arm. "You've said all along that you thought I had it in me to be a Feral Warrior. That my marking wasn't an accident."

He knew where this was going, and he didn't like it, not one bit. "Yes, but . . ."

"It turns out you were right. I wasn't an accident. And now I'm the only one who can breach that castle. Don't tell me you wouldn't go if you could, even knowing it's a trap. Even if I weren't involved. You'd go because it's your job, because it needs to be done, because Maxim needs to be stopped. This time it's *my* job. *My* mission." She looked to Lyon, her eyebrows lifting.

His traitorous chief dipped his head in acknowledgment.

Hawke ground his teeth. "I can't bear for him to touch you again. To *hurt* you again."

Her eyes softened. "I know. Just as I can't bear the thought of anything happening to you."

He knew he was beaten. He turned to Lyon. "I'm going, too."

"Do you think that's a good idea?"

"It doesn't matter. If she goes, I go."

Lyon nodded, but his gaze was on Faith. "Can you still speak to us telepathically when you're not in your animal?"

Like this, you mean? Faith's voice rang in his head, clear as day, and he could tell by the expressions on the others' faces that they'd heard her, too.

"Good," Lyon said. "Practice to make certain you can target your thoughts to only those you want receiving them. Maxim doesn't need to know you have that trick. And hold back on the speed. Keep that ability to yourself as long as possible, too. He won't be expecting it. Once you're in the castle, you can relay what he says and find a way to get us in there. I want a solid hour of physical training out of you before you go."

Faith stiffened. "Paulina and Maria are in trouble. I need to go now."

"You need to be ready first. You showed some marked improvement in your fighting skills while you were under the thrall of darkness, but we need to see what you can do now. You must be able to defend yourself once you're in the castle because Kougar's right. You'll undoubtedly be flying into some kind of trap. Tighe, will you do the training?"

"Absolutely."

"I'll help, again," Fox said.

Jag snorted. "I'm not missing this show. Just wait 'til you see what she can do, Foxy."

Fox cut Jag an amused look. "Looking forward to it, Jaggy."

Jag hooted.

"I'm going to Warsaw, too. I owe that bastard." Grizz's voice rumbled over the table. "Lepard's fighting it."

Lyon's eyes narrowed. "Fighting what?"

"The darkness. Look at the start of the video, at the eyes of the new Ferals."

Lifting the remote, Lyon did a fast rewind to the beginning, showing all five new Ferals standing. Hawke watched Lepard's eyes and saw what Grizz had seen— the struggle in the snow-leopard shifter's eyes. A struggle absent in the eyes of the other three.

Lyon hit PAUSE before Maxim started speaking, his gaze returning to Grizz. "Explain."

Grizz's big hand flexed and released on the table, over and over as he seemed to gather his thoughts. "When I first came into my animal, the darkness blindsided me, sweeping me under. I don't remember much. Every now and then, I think I broke through, aware that something was wrong, then I'd be pulled under again. Then the order to attack you blazed in my mind, and I found myself doing it. Following it blindly, unable to stop. I fought it. And lost."

"You didn't lose, boyo," Fox murmured. "Not completely, or you'd have bitten off my head instead of my rump."

Grizz gave a brief nod. "I fought it. I think Lepard is, too."

Olivia, seated at Jag's side, made a sound of distress. "Why isn't Polaris? He's a good man."

"This kind of infection will affect each one differently," Kougar said calmly. "Some will be pulled deeper than others. It has little to do with strength or will. A few may be able to fight it, but none will be free of the darkness until they're cured."

Wulfe grunted. "So, what you're saying is that although Lepard may be fighting the darkness, it's not going to do us much good."

"Correct."

Lyon turned to Lynks. "Do you feel the need to go, too?"

"Not at all. I'll stay here."

Lyon nodded, his gaze fanning out to encompass the room. "Be ready to leave in an hour."

Hawke rose to his feet, his gut grinding. A hundred things could go wrong. A thousand. If only he could breach that castle instead of Faith, but to do that he had to be able to shift. And he was afraid he knew what would happen if he tried. Game over.

He wanted to deny her this, to keep her safe and protected. But she was right. She had it in her to be a fine warrior. The strength, the courage, and now the confidence. It was time for her to seize her destiny.

Even if it killed him to watch her go into that castle alone.

An hour later, Faith stood deep in the shadowed woods with the other Ferals, staring at the huge centuries-old castle in the clearing ahead. Maxim's castle. The shiver that went through her had little to do with the cool drizzle falling in the spring woods and everything to do with the evil she knew she'd soon be facing. Alone.

Both the Ilinas and the Ferals had tried to breach the castle, but as Maxim had warned, it was fully warded against them. Only through the chimney flue might she gain access.

Hawke stood beside her, his hand on her shoulder, lending her strength and courage. But the thing that terrified her most was that even if she managed to get out of that castle alive, he might not be here when she returned. Though she'd fought his protectiveness, knowing she had to go, she knew the thought of her battling Maxim alone was tearing Hawke apart. And might, literally, end up rending what was left of his connection with his animal.

She turned to him, now.

He met her gaze, his eyes dark wells of worry. "I wish I could go for you." He curled his arm around her shoulders until she was tight against him.

"I wish you could come *with* me." She tried to smile, but it was a sorry effort. "I wish . . ." But there was no use in saying the words. They both knew, both felt the desperate need for him to renew his bond with his animal. But Hawke was the only one who could do it, and he didn't know how. Faith slid her arms around his waist and looked up at him. "It's going to be okay. I'm going to fly in there and open the back door and let the rest of you in. We'll battle them together." That was the plan, at least—for her to find a bolt-hole, or some other kind of back door, and wrench it open before the new Ferals could stop her.

He kissed her forehead. But when he pulled back, his eyes were sad and deeply worried. Since they'd found no kind of trap upon arriving outside the castle, they felt certain it lay within. Faith prayed that her newfound strength and speed would allow her to thwart Maxim's plans. Because not going wasn't an option. Not when Maxim was empowering the Daemons. Not when Paulina's and Maria's lives hung in the balance.

She could do this. She had to do this.

"Ready, Falkyn?" Paenther asked quietly.

Hawke pressed a kiss to her temple, strengthening her with his love. When he released her, the look in his eyes was more than love. Pride shone there, too. Pride in her.

"Kick. His. Ass."

She laughed softly, tears filming her eyes. "We'll do it together."

"Deal."

Finally, she turned to face Paenther, Kougar, and the others, her heart thudding in her chest. "Wish me luck." She threw them a small smile and shifted in that glorious rush of energy, shooting into the air. It was an incredible feeling—the shifting, the flying with such speed and accuracy. She felt powerful, invincible.

For a bright moment, she wondered if she might not be able to pull this off as cleanly and easily as she'd quipped to Hawke.

Keeping her eye on the south chimney, she flew up, high over the castle to avoid the warding, then down again. As she neared the flue, she slowed, testing for heat that might indicate fire, or any kind of warding that might knock her back. At the top of the chimney, she landed on bird's feet, tucking her falcon wings against her body as she sent her senses outward, letting the falcon spirit assess the situation. If there was a trap waiting for her, neither of them could sense it.

Her mind trembled at the thought of facing Maxim again. And bled from the memory of the girls' bruised and terrified faces as they hung from those ropes. It was time to go.

Taking a deep, mental breath, Faith dove into the flue, the falcon's keen senses guiding her down, far lower than she'd expected to go, deep below the ground. This wasn't good. The first thing she'd have to do was find her way back upstairs if she wanted any hope of locating a door for the others.

Finally, she emerged from the flue, darting over the scene she recognized too well from the video, a scene that scored her heart. The girls still dangled from the curved, stone ceiling of a firelit dungeon. In a circle around them stood the five new Ferals, including Maxim.

Spying the stairs, she headed for them . . . and crashed, suddenly and brutally, falling out of the air, shifting as she fell. With a spine-jarring thud, she landed on bare stone in her human form.

She fought to shift back, but nothing happened. She tried to scramble to her feet and couldn't . . . couldn't move! *Dammit*. She'd known he'd try something, but she'd hoped to at least be able to fight. Suddenly, she was rising slowly, pushing herself up calmly. *Are you doing this?* she cried to the falcon spirit.

I am not. Can you shift?

No. I can do nothing!

He seems to be in control, now. The vile one.

"Faith!" Maria cried. The hope in the girl's face tore at Faith's heart. The certainty—now so misguided—that help had finally arrived.

She was standing now, facing the others, facing the man who lived in her nightmares. Dressed in his usual attire, his hair slicked back, Maxim watched her, a cold smile on his face.

"I'm glad you finally joined us, Faith. You're just in time."

Pure fear trickled down her spine. She was trapped, unable to perform the mission she'd come for, and the others needed to know it. *I'm in the dungeon, but I've been caught in some kind of magic,* she said, speaking to them alone as she'd practiced. *He's controlling my movements. The stairs were warded. I doubt there's any way in or out except the chimney flue.*

Faith. Hawke's voice caressed her mind, the word aching with frustration. And regret. He couldn't help her. No one could help her.

We hear you, Kougar replied. *Grizz, too, was briefly controlled, but only within the vicinity of the castle. Ariana and her maidens misted him out of here. She says he's fine again.*

Grizz must have attacked them. *Is everyone all right?*

Well enough, Kougar replied.

Her gaze swung to the other four new Ferals. As she began moving with a will not her own, walking across the bare, ancient stone toward the man she loathed, she studied the other men, one by one, standing at attention like Maxim's personal guard. Polaris, Croc, and Whit watched her with emotionless eyes. But not Lepard. His hair as white as his turtleneck, he was motion contained, a whirl of energy and power battened down by an unnatural force. And in his pale blue eyes, she saw that struggle, just as Grizz had said. Just as she'd seen in the video. But as long as the Mage controlled him, he was of no use to her.

She wondered if perhaps his animal had fought for him as the falcon had her.

His actions will tell us whether he is the one meant

to be marked, the falcon spirit replied. *Or the one the infection sought.*

The one the infection sought?

"Hawke didn't accompany you?" Maxim asked, his words stealing her attention. His loathsome gaze followed her as she approached.

He smiled even as anger flashed in his eyes. "Pity. I was looking forward to ripping off his wings, so to speak. He will die. The next time I see him, he will die."

Fury coiled inside her. And bone-chilling fear.

"How is this happening, Maxim? Why am I controlled? Why are all of us, but you?"

"Because the Mage Elemental, Inir, chose me to be the group mind for the new Feral Warriors, my dear Faith. I control you all, your actions, your will. I'm the one who ordered the new Ferals to rise up against the nine. The Mage infection made my control complete, until several of you were cured of it. Now it seems I control your actions, if not your will, when you're close by. It is enough. For now."

"If the Mage chose you, they're using you, Maxim. They're using you to feed power into the imprisoned Daemons." She didn't expect him to care, but it was worth a try.

"They're using all of us."

"Why would you help them?"

Maxim's smile was slow and terrible. "Utopia. No *laws* protecting the weak. No banishment. Blood spilling when and where I please. And the power, dear Faith, the power."

"You're sick."

Maxim laughed. "So they say. So they've always said. I'm a predator of the purest kind, now. I have found my true calling!" He crooked his finger at her. "Come. You have a part to play."

She continued forward, fighting without success against the steps she was being forced to take.

"Within Inir resides a wisp of Satanan's consciousness," Maxim continued. "*I* am the center of the wheel linking Inir, the new Ferals, and Satanan himself. *I* am the conduit through which your Feral energy will be channeled into the Daemon blade to Satanan, then connected to the wisp of consciousness within Inir. Satanan's full consciousness, his magic, and his knowledge will become Inir's, through me. It has already begun. The connection is formed. But five Ferals are not enough. Six are required to open the connection fully. And now I have you."

As Maxim spoke, he pulled her toward him through will alone. She defied him in the one way she could—relaying everything he said to the Ferals outside the castle. They needed this information, no matter what happened to her. Finally, her feet stopped moving, and she stood before Maxim. With quaking terror, she stared into eyes of true evil.

As he watched her, he went feral, his eyes turning yellow, fangs erupting from his gums, though not the huge saber teeth that would appear with his animal. With a single, brutal swipe, he laid open her cheek with his claws. Pain screamed through her face, blood running down her chin and neck and into her sweater as the wound healed and the fire died.

"Take your place," Maxim said coldly.

Blinking away the tears of pain, Faith turned, carried by feet that no longer answered to her. The girls hung in the middle, Maria whimpering, fear and pleading in her eyes. Paulina had closed her eyes, a hard expression on her face, as if she knew all too well that no one ever got rescued. Only the tears silently tracking down her young cheeks betrayed her terror. Faith's heart broke at her utter inability to help them.

Beneath the girls, carved into the stone itself, lay a wide pentagram. On a low stone pedestal directly in front of Maxim sat a bleached skull painted with crude red and gray stripes, what looked like blood and ash brushed on with nothing but fingertips. Maxim passed his hand over the skull, murmuring words too low for even her sharp Feral hearing. What was he doing? A pressure began to build in her ears, making them pop. The hair began to stand up on her skin. *What was he doing?*

A strange rattling noise began, and she realized that the skull had begun to shake of its own accord. Faith's breath caught, her pulse tripping with real fear as the feel of magic rose in the room, pressing in on her from every direction. The skull began to glow, subtly at first, a hint of light which grew, changing colors—blue, green, yellow. With a sudden, horrific scream of air, the skull burst into flame—an unnatural, magical fire. Shock blasted her body like a jolt of electricity, igniting inside her a low, dark burn.

Her gaze flew to Lepard's and she saw in his eyes the same horror she felt. And she knew, given the chance, he would fight Maxim, too. She spoke to him telepathically, telling him of the dark magic the animal spirits had been infected with, and of the cure.

The skull is the key, Lepard told her. *It empowers him and increases his control over us. So long as he lives, none of us will ever be entirely free of him.*

If we can destroy the skull?

You'll weaken his power and perhaps, since you've been cured of the Mage infection, you'll no longer be under his control at all. The darkness still has the rest of us. I fight it, but . . .

It's powerful. I know.

You're really a Feral Warrior? His voice held only surprise and curiosity.

I am. Pride flowed warmly through her, joined by a brush of approval against her mind—her falcon's.

"Only one thing more is needed to fully open this conduit." Maxim's gaze rose to hers. "Blood. Human blood."

Maria gasped.

Faith's stomach spasmed. She was going to be ill.

Maxim lifted a knife, his gaze still fastened on her. "You'll do the honors, Faith. You'll cut out their hearts."

Maria began to scream and kick. "No, Faith! No, no, no!"

Faith's scalp turned hot, then cold. Her body began to shake with the force of her will as she fought the compulsion to step forward, to cross the circle, and to take the knife. As she fought to keep Maxim from killing the girls she'd come to care for so deeply.

As she lost.

Chapter Twenty

Faith's voice rang in Hawke's head, the horror in her words turning his blood to ice. *He's going to make me kill the girls. He's going to make me kill them!*

Hawke knew her, knew what this would do to her. Goddess, he'd suffered for nearly a century and a half from merely harming Aren. He had to reach her. The minute Faith finished carving up the girls, Maxim would turn that knife on her, Hawke had no doubt. Maybe not to kill her. She'd only wish he had. Even if she managed to survive this, killing the girls would destroy some essential part of her.

He had to get into that castle!

If only he could shift, he could fly in to help her. *Dammit.* If only he could have been the Feral the hawk wanted him to be. Faith was right.

I blamed you, he told the hawk. *I'm sorry for that. I failed you. In so many ways, I've failed us both.*

The hawk's cry in his head had a strange quality to it. A cry without anger. Almost of . . . understanding. Forgiveness? His heart began to pound.

What would happen if he handed over control right now? Now, when the falcon was nearby, when the hawk might be ready to forgive him. Would the hawk take off again, leaving the others behind? Did he know Hawke would die if he did? Did he understand that Faith would likely die, too?

Goddess. What if he did understand? What if he could be trusted in this desperate hour?

Hawke's breaths were beginning to come fast and shallow, sweat dampening his brow. There was only one way to find out, wasn't there?

Faith needs us, buddy. I'm asking you, I'm begging you, to take me to Faith now. I'm her only hope. We're her only hope.

Goddess, what was he doing? "Take me to her" meant shifting. And what if it didn't work?

Shit, what difference did it make? What did he have to lose? His connection to the animal was all but gone.

His hands began to shake. Could he really throw his lot in with the bird? With the wildness? The memory of the day he'd attacked Aren was still too fresh. It still cut too deep. But as Faith had said, he wasn't that newly turned Feral anymore, and hadn't been for a long, long time.

And this might be Faith's only chance.

Hawke turned to Kougar. "I'm shifting. I'm going in after her."

The other Feral stared at him.

Hawke swallowed hard and lifted a hand. "I can't

get in there through my will alone. It's up to the hawk spirit."

"And if he takes off with you as he has in the past?"

Hawke shrugged. "I've been told that one more struggle for control with him, and our connection will snap. It's only a matter of time, Kougar. I don't have anything left to lose by trying."

Kougar stared at him long and hard, then extended his arm, his free hand clasping his shoulder. "I beg of you, spirit of the hawk, bring him back to us. He's the best of us, and you'll never mark a better man. We need him, both you and us."

"If this fails . . ." Hawke began.

"If we can get Falkyn out of there, I'll watch over her."

"She was no accident. The falcon chose her."

"I suspected as much."

Hawke released Kougar's arm and stepped back, his pulse erratic as he risked everything. He would either fly again. Or die.

He closed his eyes, took a deep breath, and focused on Faith. Just Faith. Nothing else mattered but reaching her. Nothing. Slowly, he released the breath, willing the tension over what he was about to do to slide away. *Okay, buddy, it's up to you. Our lives are in your hands, now.*

He started to pull on the energy to shift, but it barreled through him so fast, it was a moment before the euphoria caught up with him. He was already flying!

Goddess, it worked! He was conscious, flying, aiming for the chimney Faith had flown into. For the first time, he didn't feel like he was flying alone, and it was just as Faith had described. The animal spirit wasn't exactly in control, yet neither was the man. They both knew where they had to go—into that castle after Faith. But it was the bird who powered the flight. Hawke had always been able to fly in his bird, but this was something altogether new. It felt as if the hawk spirit had brought along booster rockets!

As one—one creature, one mind—they shot down the flue, intent only on saving Faith.

And the falcon.

Huh. The bird hadn't spoken to him, yet he felt the hawk spirit's need to claim the other bird spirit as fiercely as his own to claim his mate. And Faith was, without a doubt, his mate.

They erupted into the room he'd seen in the video, what could only be called a dungeon, the walls dark stone, stained with centuries of smoke. And blood. In the center of the open room hung the two girls above a large pentagram carved into the stone floor. *A Daemon's sacrificial pentagram,* he relayed to his men outside.

One of the girls screamed as Faith lifted a knife in front of her and aimed it at her breast. Muscles straining, her mouth granite hard, tears streamed down Faith's beloved face, cutting out his heart and honing his determination to stop this.

Around the women stood the other new Ferals—Lepard, Polaris, Croc, and Whit, like soldiers at attention. Or puppets on steel wires. At the head of the circle stood Maxim, his expression one of hungry glee.

Without conscious thought or direction, Hawke swooped toward Faith, desperate to keep her from killing the girl. Just as her blade pierced the girl's chest, he reached her, shifting into his human form on the fly, grabbing the knife from her hand.

Maxim yelled with anger.

Hawke! Faith's voice sang in his head even as she whirled toward him, claws and fangs erupting, weapons he knew would be used against him. *You did it! You shifted.*

I just needed the right motivation.

Her sweet laughter rang in his head for one bright moment, a glimmer of light peeking out of the darkness. *Destroy the painted skull, and you might free me. But the only way to stop this ritual is to kill Maxim.*

He'd gladly do both, though that would surely be easier said than done. Sliding one of his own knives into his free hand, he turned to find the five male Ferals stalking him with blades gleaming in the flickering torchlight.

The smile on Maxim's face told him this confrontation was exactly what he'd been waiting for. And Hawke was raring for the fight. For the first time since he fell into that spirit trap, he felt whole again. Hell, more than whole. Strong, powerful, *right,* as he'd never been. Like a rubber band snapping into place, he'd become one with his animal at last. The bird made a low cry of agreement, his anger completely gone.

Hawke turned, keeping each of the warriors in sight. He was a skilled fighter, but no one . . . *no one* . . . could take on six Feral Warriors bent on his death and come out alive. And he had no doubt his death was Maxim's goal. That saber-toothed bastard appeared to be the one pulling all the strings. Adrenaline pulsed in his blood, his senses flying out in every direction. The first thing he had to do was move the fight away from the girls.

He lunged for Maxim, but Polaris, still firmly under the thrall of the dark magic, blocked him with a massive stroke of his blade. Hawke parried the blow, then whirled as Croc came at him from behind, then Whit. With both hands he fought them, his speed double what it had been before, yet the blades came too fast. Maxim shifted into his saber-toothed cat, eyes gleaming. Whit, the white tiger, did the same. Could he possibly fight off so many animals at once before they tore him to shreds?

Hawke. Faith's voice was a cry of despair. *Get out of here!*

No.

It's too late. The magic has been activated. The blood . . .

His gaze snapped to the girl hanging over the now-glowing pentagram, and to the blood dripping from her bare feet from a wound he hadn't been quite soon enough to prevent. But he wasn't giving up, dammit, not when he'd come this far. And he wasn't about to leave without Faith.

Her plea that he shift and escape gave him an idea. The hawk cried his satisfaction and just like that, thought became reality. In the blink of an eye, he shifted back into his bird, dodging the striking blades and snapping teeth as easily as Faith had flown through the tree limbs. *Incredible* what he and the hawk could do together.

Careful not to transmit his destination until the last moment, he weaved his way through the attacking Ferals until they were shouting with fury and confusion, unable to keep him in their sights. Finally, he flew for the skull and shifted back into human form as he landed. Before Maxim could react, Hawke grabbed the macabre, glowing thing and slammed it to the ground, crushing it beneath the heel of his boot.

The evil glow flickered out.

The saber-toothed cat gave a furious roar and leaped at him, those fangs gleaming in the torchlight.

Hawke, it worked! Faith's voice rang in his head. *I'm free.*

As he dove out of the big cat's way, slicing his blade deep into the cat's shoulder, power crawled over Hawke's skin. Out of the corner of his eye, he watched the symbol on the floor flare with an unnatural greenish glow. He might have destroyed the skull, but he hadn't destroyed the ritual itself. Maxim had to die.

Hawke smiled. It would be his pleasure.

The other four Ferals circled around him. Destroying the skull hadn't freed the rest of them. Only Faith. She'd been cured of the infection. They hadn't. Maxim apparently still had them under his control.

Let's get him, Hawke! Faith's battle cry rang in his head.

He looked for her beyond the circling Ferals, finding her, awed by the warrior's fire in her eyes. Thought pictures appeared in his head—the two of them flying together, attacking Maxim together.

His hawk cried his approval, but the man didn't like it, not at all. It was too dangerous. The slightest mistake, and she'd be dead.

Suddenly, Lepard, Croc, and Polaris turned on Faith in perfect synchronicity. No, not perfect. Lepard was off, a beat behind. As if he struggled against the compulsion.

Before Hawke could warn her, she was gone, shifting and flying high out of her would-be attackers' reaches in the blink of an eye.

Let me go alone, he told her. *Fly back up through the flue. Get out of here.*

Not a chance. Her voice rang hard as steel. *We're a team, now. The four of us. Two Ferals, two animal spirits. One for all and all for one.*

Faith . . .

I thought you'd learned your lesson with the hawk, she said testily.

I refuse to lose you.

You're not going to lose me! You'll be right there with me. Give in to the wildness, Hawke, and trust that we can do this. Because we can!

Where in the hell had she gotten all this confidence? She was asking the impossible!

The Ferals turned back toward him, slowly lifting their blades.

Deep in his mind, he felt the hawk's stillness, his waiting.

This was the final test, he realized, of his trust in the wildness that had claimed him, that had marked him. He'd spent a century and a half holding back that part of him.

He'd given in to it to reach Faith. But that didn't mean he could just abandon . . .

Hawke, I love you. Faith's sweet voice caressed his mind. *Give in. For me. For us. Please?*

The shudder started in his head and traveled all the way down his body, goose bumps rising on his arms. She wanted him to give in. To the wildness. To the hawk. To seize what his father had once had with this animal spirit. The strength, the speed. Goddess, *yes.* And suddenly it wasn't hard at all. For love of Faith he could do anything.

As the polar bear lunged, Hawke shouted into the castle's dungeon, "One for all and all for one!"

Kkkeeeeer! In his head, his hawk made a sound that could only be called a war cry. And then he was shifting, flying up to where the falcon circled. Below, all five Ferals had shifted and now paced, watching their prey with hungry eyes—the huge crocodile, saber-toothed cat, snow leopard, white tiger, polar bear. The sight of such animal majesty? *Magnificent.* The fact that they wanted him dead? *Like hell.* Adrenaline rushed through his veins, clearing his mind, even as the thought of Faith getting anywhere near them filled him with dread.

A sense of confidence pressed at his mind, the hawk's reassurance. His belief they could do this.

I think this is the hardest thing I've ever done, buddy. But I trust you to help me keep her safe. I trust you.

Ready? Faith asked.

Hell. *Ready.*

As one, they zipped down, dive-bombing the saber-tooth. But as they drew close, the white tiger leaped, nearly snatching the falcon out of the air. Tail feathers fluttered free as she darted away.

Faith!

I'm okay. He could almost hear her falcon's heart pounding.

He couldn't do this. If she'd been a second slower, she'd have been tiger food. *New plan. With the skull destroyed, the warding's probably down. We'll open the gates for the other Ferals. We'll take on Maxim then.*

But even as the words flew from his mind to hers, the pentagram flared brighter. Magic, thick and crawling, began to shake the walls of the dungeon.

We're out of time, Faith cried. *The magic is trying to capture me, to use me to feed the Daemons. It's now, Hawke. Now or never.*

Shit. *All right, we have to draw Maxim away. Pretend to be injured and head for the opposite wall.*

Without hesitation, the beautiful little falcon spiraled down as if she were indeed injured, flying in a disjointed manner to the precise spot he'd eyed, well away from the animals.

Land and shift, he told her. Three seconds later, she was on the stone floor, a woman once more, falling to her knees, her head bent as if in agony. Good girl. He followed her, landing and shifting into human form more effortlessly than he'd ever been able to. Awe and gratitude filled his heart and mind, and he embraced the hawk spirit with both, receiving a warm rush of appreciation and pride in return.

Three of the animals started toward them, but as Hawke had counted on, Maxim held them back. He thought Hawke and Faith were beaten, and he wanted to deliver the killing blow.

Hawke stood as if guarding his injured mate as the sabertooth stalked them. "You're not going to touch her, Maxim," he snarled. The walls shook with the force of the terrible, rising magic, making his skin crawl and his stomach clench. "She's mine! My woman. My mate."

The great cat roared his fury, as Hawke had counted on, and leaped.

Now! Hawke shouted silently. As one, he and Faith shifted into their birds and flew at the sabertooth, the falcon aiming for the back of the cat's head, the hawk for his soft underside.

As she reached the great cat, Faith shifted back to human form, straddling his back and plunging her knife deep into his skull in one fluid, graceful move. Hawke zipped between the cat's legs, shifted, and plunged his blade deep into its chest. Maxim thrashed, releasing a horrible roar of anger and pain. Blood poured over Hawke, but he finished what he'd started, digging out the bastard's black heart.

The cat collapsed on top of him. The feel of magic vanished, the glow from the pentagram winking out.

Hawke pushed aside the heavy carcass and rose, battle ready, prepared to finish the fight or take on the other animals. But all were gone except for Lepard. A man once more, the snow-leopard shifter was on his knees across the dungeon, and appeared to be struggling.

"Did you see where they went?" Hawke asked Faith, who was already running for the girls. The pair, still hanging over the pentagram, were both crying openly now.

"No. But I've let the others know what happened."

As Hawke approached Lepard, the man looked up at him with a ferocity that had Hawke pulling his knives. Until he heard his snarled words.

"*Stop . . . me. Tie . . . me.*"

Glancing around, he spied an extra coil of rope against a nearby wall and grabbed it, pushing a barely resisting Lepard to his stomach and tying him hand and foot.

"Where are the others?" Hawke demanded.

"Ran," Lepard managed to get out, his voice guttural, as if he forced the words through a constricted throat. "Called."

"By whom?"

"Don't . . . know."

"Ten bucks says it's Inir." He rose, looking down at the big male trussed up like fresh game ready for the barbecue. "Don't go anywhere." He joined Faith as she laid the second of the girls on the floor, far from the bloody pentagram.

The girl stared at Faith with a mix of fascination and wariness. But no fear. "What are you?" she breathed.

Faith smiled. "I'm what I've always been, Paulina. Just someone who wants to help you." She looked up as he approached, her face splattered with blood, her cheeks flushed, her eyes bright with victory and soft with love. And she'd never looked more beautiful to him.

He glanced at the other girl, the one who'd been injured. She was still crying softly as she pressed the torn sleeve of Faith's sweater to her chest.

"How bad is the cut?"

"Not bad at all. I think Maxim must have put some kind of bleeding spell into that pentagram for it to have drawn as much blood from her as it did. I barely nicked her, thanks to you."

He studied the girl's pallor. She hadn't lost much blood overall. She'd be fine. "We have to take their memories. Try it. If you have trouble, I'll help you."

Faith's smile bloomed, confident and sure.

Remembering her unique ability to hear him even when neither of them was in their animals, he added, *You might add a suggestion or two while you're at it. To go home or to seek help or to get off the streets.*

Or to talk to the director of the art school and to dump the pimp boyfriend. Her smile turned wry. "If only I'd had this ability before. Helping kids would have been so much easier."

"But it wouldn't have changed anything. You'd still have been out there with them."

Her expression turned thoughtful. "I suppose you're

right. We all have our journeys to take, and this was mine."

"I have money," he told her. "And everything I have is yours. Get them what they need, starting with tuition for that art school."

Her smile turned beatific, flipping him head over tail in love with her all over again. At the sound of Feral footsteps behind him, he turned to find Kougar and Wulfe racing into the dungeon. Kougar looked at the dead sabertooth with cold-eyed satisfaction.

He joined his friends. "Did you catch the other three when they escaped?"

Kougar shook his head. "We never saw them. They must have gone out through an underground passage. Bolt-holes are common enough in castles like this. Paenther and the others are searching for them."

"I suspect Inir called them."

"I agree. The last thing he wants is us cutting the strings off his puppets." Kougar nodded at Lepard, who lay on his side, still struggling against his bonds. "You caught one."

"Lepard caught himself. He's been fighting the magic, as Grizz suspected. We're just helping him."

On a pine-scented breeze, Ariana appeared before them, first mist, then flesh, a distraught look on her face. Hawke sighed. There was trouble. Again.

"Kara's missing," she announced without preamble.

Her words slammed into him like a fist. Not Kara. His gaze collided with Kougar's.

Wulfe snarled. "Those Mage are going to die."

Hawke shook his head. "How did this happen? Lyon always senses where she is."

"I don't know." Ariana went to Kougar, and he pulled her close. "He knows she's alive, but he can't get a read on her whereabouts. It's as if something is hiding her from him."

"He must be going crazy," Wulfe said.

"He is. Lynks is missing, too."

Kougar's expression turned grim. "Get me back there, Ariana, and send your maidens for the others."

"Hawke," Faith called. "I can't go. Not yet. Paulina says there are other girls in the castle. Maxim left more than a dozen in cages."

Hawke turned to Kougar. "Faith and I will get the girls to safety, then call for a pickup."

"I'll send Brielle to you," Ariana said. "If anything goes wrong, she can call in the troops."

"Good. Thank you." Hawke glanced at what was left of Maxim. "We'll need to get rid of the sabertooth. Can you imagine the humans finding it?"

Wulfe groaned.

"We'll dispose of it in the Crystal Realm," Ariana said. A moment later, she and Kougar were gone.

As Hawke turned to Faith, Wulfe said behind him, "I'll start looking for the caged girls." Hawke nodded and went to join Faith.

"Any luck?" he asked her.

Faith looked up, her eyes bright with unshed tears. "I did it. If this works, they may both wind up in school. I think Maria's going to be a schoolteacher. She loves to learn, just like I do." Both girls lay sleeping, now, their expressions soft and peaceful. The tears began to spill down Faith's cheeks as she stood and turned to him.

He pulled her into his arms, fairly certain he knew where the tears had come from. "You heard about Kara."

She nodded against his chest.

"We think they have Lynks, too."

With a sniffle, she pulled back, meeting his gaze. "Or Lynks took her."

"What do you mean?"

"The falcon told me something. When we were wondering about Lepard, she said that his actions would tell us whether he was the one meant to be marked, or the one . . . the one the infection wanted."

"Ask her what she meant."

Faith's lashes swept down, then up again a moment later, clarity gleaming from her beautiful eyes. "None of the new Ferals was marked by accident. The magic was designed to force the animal spirits to mark the worst of the line, not the best. The one most susceptible to evil."

"It failed with you."

"Yes. The falcon fought hard against it and managed to claim the one she'd wanted. But the saber-toothed cat spirit wasn't as successful. Perhaps neither was the lynx."

Hawke stared at her, taking it all in. "If the falcon spirit is right, and she has been in everything else so far, then there were no mistakes. Each new Feral is either the best or the worst of his line. If Lynks is the latter, then even cured of the magic, he might be working against us."

"That's what I'm afraid of."

"This changes everything. And Kara . . . *Goddess*." What kind of danger was she in?

Faith's eyes turned fierce. "The Feral Warriors will find her, Hawke. *We'll* find her. The bastards who took her don't stand a chance."

Hawke nodded slowly. He had to believe it. Kara was so much more than the Feral Warriors' Radiant, their strength. She was their heart.

But Faith was *his* heart. He kissed her, needing her warmth, and receiving a rush of love that he knew would sustain him through anything, a wholeness far beyond anything he'd ever dreamed possible. For the first time, his heart and body were in perfect accord thanks to the animal inside him and the woman in his arms.

"Together, we can do anything," he murmured against her lips.

"Let me see your shoulder," she said suddenly, pulling out of his arms and lifting his shirt from behind. A moment later, she was beaming at him. "Your feral marks look as good as new."

Whole.

In his mind, he heard the sound of a satisfied bird and felt a wash of the spirit's approval so rich and full, it reminded him of his father's, as if in death, a piece of him had remained behind with the animal spirit who'd claimed them both.

Faith watched him, her eyes brimming with tears. "We made it." She flashed him that darling grin—a grin that no longer held even a touch of uncertainty. No, this was the smile of a confident, powerful woman. A sweet, dangerous little pixie with blue-tipped hair.

"Be my mate, Smiley. Stay with me forever."

His love. His life.

"Forever, my Hawke. I'm yours."

Hawke's heart soared.

At Avon Books, we know your passion for romance—once you finish one of our novels, you find yourself wanting more.

May we tempt you with . . .

- **Excerpts** from our upcoming releases.

- Entertaining **extras**, including authors' personal photo albums and book lists.

- Behind-the-scenes **scoop** on your favorite characters and series.

- **Sweepstakes** for the chance to win free books, romantic getaways, and other fun prizes.

- Writing **tips** from our authors and editors.

- **Blog** with our authors and find out why they love to write romance.

- **Exclusive content** that's not contained within the pages of our novels.

Join us at
www.avonbooks.com

AVON

An Imprint of HarperCollins*Publishers*
www.avonromance.com

Available wherever books are sold or please call 1-800-331-3761 to order.

FTH 0708